Misunderstandings

A Pride and Prejudice Variation

By AnnaMarie Wallace

ANNAMARIE WALLACE

"Misunderstandings"

By AnnaMarie Wallace

Copyright © 2024 Desert Mystery Publishing, LLC

All rights reserved

MISUNDERSTANDINGS

ISBN: 9798334173477

Chapter One

Fall 1811

As the Bennet family crowded into their carriage for the journey to the Meryton assembly, complaining and bickering began in earnest. Lydia insisted that her dress was being wrinkled because Mary was sitting too close. Mary, attempting to be heard over Lydia's voice, cried that she was sitting as close as she possibly could to Kitty without actually being in her lap. Kitty objected to Mary's proximity. Jane and Elizabeth sat with their parents on the opposite bench in silence, ignoring the squabble with a tolerance born of prolonged exposure.

Upon arrival at the assembly hall, the coachman leaped down to open the carriage door. Mr. Bennet exited the coach with alacrity, grateful for the fresh air and space in which to stretch his limbs. The quiet was welcome, though it was not to last, as his wife and daughters soon followed his example, making their way out of the carriage and all but pushing him into the hall.

The noise of the musicians and the assembled dancers were a new affront to Mr. Bennet's already strained senses, and so it was with great relief that the gentleman bowed to his female relatives, wished them a pleasant evening, bade them all behave themselves, and retired to the card room, where cigars, brandy, and – most importantly – quiet were to be had.

Inside the ballroom, though, there was much to please feminine senses. The ladies of the neighbourhood were all wearing their finest attire, as this event had been long anticipated and eagerly awaited. The musicians were beginning the music for a cotillion. Negus had already been set up on the side table, accompanied by light biscuits. Everything, in short, was in place for the delight of the assembled guests.

Lydia and Kitty immediately vanished into the throng to find their usual partners. Mary sidled over to the nearest wall, where she could find a chair and sit peacefully, while reading the book she had secreted in her reticule. Jane and Elizabeth paused in the doorway for a moment, enjoying the anticipation of the dance.

"Go in, girls!" Mrs. Bennet insisted. "We are blocking the entry."

So admonished, the two eldest Bennet girls moved to the right of the entry. Sir William, who acted as a self-appointed Master of Ceremonies for events such as this one, approached them, accompanied by his daughter, Charlotte. "Mrs. Bennet, Miss Bennet, Miss Elizabeth, I understand our new neighbours are soon to join us," he said, with a bow. Charlotte moved to stand beside Elizabeth. The two had been dear friends for many years, despite a disparity in ages; Charlotte was twenty-seven and Elizabeth was twenty.

"Mr. Bingley; is that not his name?" Mrs. Bennet was being ingenuous, as nothing had been spoken of in the neighbourhood save that selfsame gentleman for the past week. She was quite well aware of his name.

"It is, indeed, Mrs. Bennet. Mr. Bennet has met him, has he not?" Sir William inquired.

"Oh! Yes, I believe I did hear something about that," she said, evasively. "Though Mr. Bennet had little to say of the meeting. What do you know of him, Sir William?"

Jane and Elizabeth stepped a little closer, so as to hear what Sir William might say. Mrs. Bennet was quite right; Mr. Bennet had indeed gone to meet Mr. Bingley, and had returned home with little to report other than the fact that their new neighbour had worn a blue coat. Such a dearth of information had proven frustrating for his wife and five daughters, who wanted to know his age, his hair colour, eye colour, height, preferences for foods, favorite dance – at the very least!

Sir William was able to satisfy the Bennet ladies in a few of these particulars, supplying Mr. Bingley's hair colour (reddish blonde), eye colour (blue), and height (a little taller than Sir William). Further details would have to wait until such time as they might meet the gentleman himself.

Just then, all eyes turned to the front of the hall, where three gentlemen and two ladies stood framed in the entryway. "Ah! And there he is!" cried Sir William.

Hastening to the doorway with his daughter, Charlotte, in tow, Sir William bowed deeply and his daughter curtsied elegantly to assembly's new guests.

"Mr. Bingley! How good of you to join us!" Sir William said, enthusiastically. "Will you not introduce me to your companions, sir?"

Mr. Bingley murmured his assent, and proceeded to introduce his younger sister, Miss Bingley; his older sister, Mrs. Hurst, and her husband, Mr. Hurst; and his great friend, Mr. Darcy. Sir William then took it upon himself to introduce Netherfield's new residents around the assembly hall, beginning with the Bennet family, who were standing nearby. It escaped no one that Mr. Bingley's eyes had widened upon beholding Jane Bennet

Once the circuit of the hall was complete and Sir William could find no one else to introduce, Mr. Bingley excused himself and made his way back to Jane. He requested her hand for the next dance; she curtsied, eyes downcast, murmuring that it would be her pleasure, and when the music began he led her onto the dance floor.

Charlotte Lucas sidled over to Elizabeth. "There is evidently nothing wrong with Mr. Bingley's eyesight; he saw immediately that your sister is by far the prettiest lady in the room."

Elizabeth replied, "We may add that to the small list of things we know about our new neighbour: excellent eyesight."

"What think you of the other newcomers to the neighbourhood, Eliza?"

Elizabeth simply shook her head. "I have no information with which to form an opinion, other than the fact that the two ladies do not know how to dress for a country assembly. I have never before seen five feathers stuck into a turban at an assembly!"

Charlotte raised her eyebrows. "Oh? I think we know more than that; based on their manners during my father's introductions, I think we can also say that they believe themselves far superior to those to whom they were introduced."

"I cannot disagree, Charlotte. And what think you of Mr. Darcy?"

"Oh! He does have quite an air about him, does he not?"

"Indeed; but I note that he has not yet asked anyone to dance."

"And Mr. Hurst?"

"I confess that I have paid little attention to that gentleman; evidently, Mama's teachings have found fertile soil, as married men are of no interest to me."

"She would be delighted to know that, Eliza; you should inform her at your earliest opportunity!" The two girls laughed together.

At that moment, Miss Bingley and Mr. Darcy walked past them. Miss Bingley held Mr. Darcy's arm tightly; he seemed to be trying to pull away from her grasp, but she would not release him. So it was that when he directed her attention to something on her left, and she turned her head rather too quickly to see, that the very tip of the longest feather in her turban flailed about and jabbed Mr. Darcy in the eye. He cried out, averted turned his face, and attempted to step away from the offending plumage, but Miss Bingley remained in possession of his arm, albeit for the briefest of moments, yet sufficient to upset Mr. Darcy's balance when she released that arm in surprise. He staggered back, flailing wildly, tripped over someone behind him, and in his effort to right himself brought them both crashing to the floor.

Even as Mr. Darcy fell, however – despite his closed eye, the confusion of arms and legs, the surrounding shouts of alarm – he was aware that the unfortunate person with whom he was entangled was smaller than he, of delicate stature, and liable to be hurt by his greater weight. Twisting as he fell to pull the other close, Mr. Darcy absorbed the impact of the fall with his right arm, and thereby found himself lying partially atop a young lady, one to whom he had but minutes ago been introduced.

The room was filled with a horrified silence. The young woman beneath him stated firmly, "Get *off* me, sir. At once.!" And then, it seemed, everyone at the assembly, spoke at once.

And Miss Bingley cried, "Oh, Mr. Darcy!"

And Charlotte Lucas said, "Eliza! Are you injured?"

The musicians stopped. The entire congregation of people soon stood in an accusatory circle around the fallen girl and Mr. Darcy. There were many horrified gasps, and then the shocked murmuring began.

"Compromise!"

"She tripped him deliberately!"

"No, he tripped her!"

"Why is he still on top of her!"

"Elizabeth Bennet! Who would have thought this of her!"

"What was that man's name again?"

"Where is Mr. Bennet?"

Mr. Bingley was immediately at Mr. Darcy's side, helping him to rise. Charlotte and Jane ran to Elizabeth, who was having difficulty getting up.

"Lizzy, are you hurt?" Jane asked, extremely distressed.

"My ribs!" her sister gasped.

Mrs. Bennet now arrived on the scene. "Mr. Darcy! What were you about, sir?" she gasped in horror.

"It was an accident! The feather! I tripped! I did not touch her!" Mr. Darcy was equally horrified.

"Did not touch her!? Heavens, sir, I beg to differ!" Mrs. Bennet exclaimed. "You were on top of my daughter!"

Mr. Darcy was ashen-faced. He had never *seen* such an event, had never *imagined* such an event, and certainly had never expected that he would be *involved* in such an event! He saw immediately that there was no way to explain that Miss Bingley's feather had caused this catastrophe, that there was nothing he could say or do that would reverse the events of the past sixty seconds, and that he would now be required to marry an unknown country girl or lose his honour entirely.

As if conjured by his thoughts, an older gentleman now appeared. "Mr. Darcy, is it?" he said, quite calmly.

Mr. Darcy could only nod; speech was impossible.

"I am Mr. Bennet, this young lady's father. I expect to see you in my study tomorrow morning at Longbourn to discuss tonight's events and its consequences."

Mr. Darcy bowed his assent without a word. He turned to his friend and managed to say, through gritted teeth, "Bingley. I need to leave. *Now*."

Chapter Two

The entire Netherfield party was soon in the carriage, returning to Netherfield Park. Miss Bingley was openly weeping. "Oh, Mr. Darcy! I am so sorry! This is entirely my fault!"

Though he knew full well that Miss Bingley was begging for reassurance that it was *not* her fault, Mr. Darcy could not bring himself to oblige her. It was, of course, very much her fault. Had not been for her feather, her ridiculous headdress that topped an even more ridiculous gown, he would not now be in the worst situation of his life. He laughed to himself, bitterly. He was on the brink of being forced to marry a complete stranger. And not *just* a complete stranger. It was far worse, as a complete stranger in London might have at least been possessed of a dowry and society connections, but a stranger who was a simple country girl! He could not even recall what she looked like. And he would have to marry her? Unbelievable!

The carriage arrived at Netherfield in twenty minutes. Mr. Darcy had not uttered a single word since requesting an immediate return to Netherfield.

"Mr. Darcy!" Miss Bingley said again. "Surely there is a way around this; surely you need not marry her!"

"Caroline," her brother said, warningly.

"No, Charles! He cannot!"

"This is your doing, Caroline. You and your absurd feathers!" her brother exclaimed, angrily.

"He should say that he is already betrothed. Surely if he is betrothed, he cannot be forced to marry another!"

Mr. Darcy finally spoke. "And I imagine that you believe I should say I am betrothed to you, Miss Bingley? Is that your plan?"

She blushed deeply.

"Miss Bingley," Darcy said, heavily. "Truthfully, I considered that path; but that leaves the young lady compromised with no hope of recovery. Of all of us, she is the least to blame."

"I do not doubt that she did this on purpose?"

"Did what on purpose, Miss Bingley? Loosened a feather in your headdress, directed it toward my eye, pushed me so that I would trip over your slipper, and manage to get herself under me as I fell? I find it unlikely."

Miss Bingley could think of nothing to say to this.

"I shall present myself to her father tomorrow and do what honour requires of me."

"Is there truly no other way, Darcy?" Mr. Bingley enquired.

Mr. Darcy shrugged. "I do not know of one, no. I can only hope that the girl is at least tolerable."

Chapter Three

The Bennets returned to Longbourn as soon as all the Bennet girls could be located. This took some time. Elizabeth had to be helped up from the floor, quite carefully, as she was in a good deal of pain. Mary was easily found sitting with the older ladies, but Jane had to be sent to find Kitty and Lydia; this required some considerable searching, as they were flirting with two of the younger Lucas boys behind some draperies.

Mary was grateful to have a reason to go home early, but the two younger girls set up a howl of outrage. The news that their older sister had taken a bad fall did little to mute their displeasure, but the look on their father's face told them that they had best comply immediately.

The ride back to Longbourn was fraught with difficulty. If it had been overly crowded in the carriage on the way to the assembly, it was all but impossible now, as Elizabeth could not be made comfortable. Kitty was forced to sit on Lydia's lap, which did not improve their tempers.

Mr. Bennet was finally forced to intervene. "Kitty! Lydia! Your sister is badly hurt; can you not think of her comfort!?"

There was silence in the carriage. "I am sorry, Lizzy," Kitty whispered, finally. "I am being thoughtless."

Elizabeth could only gasp out, "Thank you, Kitty."

Upon their arrival at Longbourn, Elizabeth was helped upstairs to the room she shared with Jane. Lucy, the maid shared by all the Bennet ladies, removed Elizabeth's dress and helped her put on a nightshift.

Mr. Jones had been sent for by Mrs. Hill immediately upon the arrival of the carriage. He came promptly; upon being told what had befallen Elizabeth, he examined her carefully, with Mrs. Bennet and Jane in attendance.

"Her ribs are badly bruised, but they do not appear to be broken, Mrs. Bennet," was his diagnosis. "Unfortunately, there is nothing to do but allow them to heal. I can give her some laudanum to numb the pain; a few drops in her tea will help to ease her discomfort."

"How long?" Elizabeth managed to ask.

"Four to six weeks, Miss Elizabeth. And you must rest, so as not to cause yourself further injury."

Elizabeth shook her head, violently. "Four to six weeks?!"

Mr. Jones nodded, emphatically. "Yes, I am afraid so. I know this will be difficult for you, Miss Elizabeth, as active as you are, but there is nothing for it."

She bowed her head in acknowledgement. Mr. Jones left, and Jane held her sister, gently, while she wept.

Shortly thereafter, Mr. Bennet made his way up to her room. "Papa," Elizabeth whispered. "Papa, it was not my fault! He knocked me down and fell on top of me!"

"I know, daughter," he said, pain in his eyes.

Jane put in, "I saw the whole thing, Papa. Lizzy did nothing wrong."

"I believe you, Jane, Lizzy, but it will not matter."

"Surely he will not come tomorrow, Papa. He is a wealthy man; he will have no interest in marrying an unknown country girl," Elizabeth insisted.

"You may well be right; and in that case, your reputation will be ruined, as well as that of your sisters. Would you destroy their chances?"

"But everyone saw what happened!"

"Lizzy, you are not a child. You know it will not matter." Her father was sympathetic, but firm.

"I can go to the Gardiners. No one in London will know what happened."

Mr. Bennet hesitated. Elizabeth was his favourite daughter. Of all the girls, this was the one he least wished to lose, the one in whom he had the greatest delight. And to lose her like this, as the result of a stupid accident at an assembly! Unbelievable. But his duty as a father, as a father to the other girls as well as to this one, was clear. "Lizzy, if he offers, you must marry him. Surely you see that. But, dearest child, let us wait and see what tomorrow brings. For now, you must rest and recover." He kissed her on the forehead and left.

Elizabeth could only shake her head in disbelief. "Jane, I beg you to tell me that I am dreaming. I will wake up shortly and it will be the morning of the assembly, and I will steer well clear of clumsy gentlemen!"

Jane stroked her sister's hair to try to bring her comfort, but could think of nothing helpful to say.

Chapter Four

Breakfast the next morning was a somber affair at both Netherfield and Longbourn. At Netherfield, Miss Bingley again attempted to convince Mr. Darcy of the benefit to be gained by claiming a betrothal with herself, until her brother bade her be silent.

After breaking his fast, Mr. Darcy enquired of the Netherfield housekeeper as to where Longbourn would be found, and he was given directions. As he turned to leave, the housekeeper stopped him. He looked at her in surprise, clearly not expecting to be detained by a servant.

She blushed a little, looking uncomfortable at her own boldness, but she evidently intended to be heard. "Mr. Darcy, I heard what happened last night."

"I imagine the news has made its way through the grapevine quickly," he retorted, unhappy at being so accosted. "That is no surprise; it is the same in any country neighborhood."

"Mr. Darcy, you have no interest in my opinion, but I will tell you that Miss Elizabeth is a good girl, well-liked by everyone. She is not a fortune-hunter, and I will warrant that she wants to marry you no more than you want to marry her."

"I doubt that," he said, bitterly. And with that, he turned on his heel and left.

***

At Longbourn, Elizabeth had not been willing to come downstairs to break her fast; she had requested and received a breakfast tray in her room. Her mother had entered Elizabeth's room on the heels of said breakfast tray, intent on making certain that her daughter was prepared to accept the marriage offer that she was certain was about to ride up to her front door.

"I will not marry him, Mama," Elizabeth said. "So you may as well save your breath."

"You will, Lizzy," her mother replied, quite firmly. "Or your sisters are ruined."

Elizabeth shook her head. "I do not believe that, Mama."

"You do not *want* to believe it, Lizzy. But let me ask you this: if Lydia had been playing about with one of her young lads and had been found pinned beneath him, what would you say?"

"I would say that she should marry him, but that she had brought it entirely upon herself."

"What if she had not brought it upon herself, but it was an accident? And all the neighbours were gossiping about the Bennet girls?"

Elizabeth burst out, "But everyone knows that I did nothing! Everyone saw what happened – he fell on me!"

"What if Jane wanted to marry someone but could not because her sister's reputation was in question?"

Elizabeth fell silent. Then she turned her head away.

***

Mr. Darcy waited for his horse to be saddled; following the housekeeper's directions, he soon found himself in front of what must be Longbourn. His practiced eye showed him an old manor house, well-kept, but not overly large or fine. He estimated the likely income of the estate to be two thousand pounds a year, perhaps two thousand five hundred, but certainly no more. Netherfield was far larger and more elegant. And, of course, neither could be compared to Pemberley.

Giving his horse to a stable lad, he knocked on the front door. It was opened promptly by an aged butler; he began to give his name, but the butler said, "Mr. Darcy, is it?"

He agreed that this was indeed his name, and that he wished to speak with Mr. Bennet. He was led into the house; the interior of which was in keeping with the front view of the manor house – old and clean, but not fashionable or elegant. He gave a little laugh, but it was not a happy sound. For this to be the home of his future in-laws! He, Fitzwilliam Darcy, the nephew of an earl, owner of an enormous estate in Derbyshire, one of the *ton's* most sought-after bachelors, to be reduced to this! For the hundredth time since the previous night, he silently cursed Miss Bingley, her feathers, and the Meryton assembly room. From there, he moved on to cursing feathers of all kinds, headdresses of all kinds, and assembly rooms all over England.

The aged retainer escorted him to a library, in which Mr. Bennet was seated behind a large mahogany desk. "Close the door, Mr. Hill," was Mr. Bennet's instruction. The butler bowed, and left, closing the door behind him.

Mr. Bennet rose, and bowed politely; Mr. Darcy returned it. Mr. Bennet indicated a seat and waved Mr. Darcy toward it.

Mr. Darcy glanced around the room. Books! It was nothing to Pemberley's library, but there were several rare and quite valuable tomes. He made some conversation about the books, to which Mr. Bennet made no response, other than a raised eyebrow.

Realising that there was nothing to be gained by delay, Mr. Darrcy said, "I am here at your behest, Mr. Bennet."

"And I assume you know what I wish to discuss?"

"I imagine that I do."

"And?"

"And I will do what honour requires of me, Mr. Bennet," Mr. Darcy replied, coldly.

"But you are not happy about it, I collect?"

"Would you be happy, in my place?"

"I suppose not; though I must say that you do not know what a treasure you are getting, Mr. Darcy."

"Spoken like a loving father," Mr. Darcy said, caustically.

"I am, I confess, but Elizabeth is special. I have five daughters, Mr. Darcy, so you may understand that I know what I am about when I say that I know something of young girls. You may take me at my word: Elizabeth truly is unique."

Mr. Darcy shook his head. "It does not matter; you may rest assured that I will do what I must."

There was a minute's silence. Mr. Bennet finally said, "She has almost no dowry; her mother brought four thousand pounds into the marriage, and Elizabeth will have her share of that once her mother has passed away."

Mr. Darcy did not reply, but this thoughts were acrid. He had turned up his nose at ladies with dowries of thirty thousand pounds and more, and now he was to be bound to an unknown lady with virtually no dowry at all. It was absurd.

"You have not asked after her, Mr. Darcy." Mr. Bennet's voice was reproving.

"Asked after her? What do you mean?"

"She was injured last night."

He tried to look interested and failed. "How?" he managed to say.

"Her ribs are bruised. She is in a good deal of pain."

"I am sorry to hear of it." Mr. Darcy answered as politeness required.

"She must rest for at least four weeks, the apothecary says."

Mr. Darch saw a ray of hope in the gloom. "So she cannot wed immediately."

"No. And I do not want an unseemly show of haste in any case. I expect you to request her hand in marriage, have marriage articles drawn up, and return to wed her."

"Anything else?" Mr. Darcy asked. The sarcasm in his voice could not be missed.

Mr. Bennet shook his head and leaned forward. "Look here, Mr. Darcy. What happened was a terrible accident. It was not her fault and it was not your fault, but I need not tell you that we must abide by society's rules. We must make the best of a bad situation."

Mr. Darcy said, "I do not disagree with you, but I cannot help but feel that the advantage is all on your daughter's side."

"And why is that? Because you are wealthy and we are not? Is that truly what you think?" Mr. Bennet shook his head. "You have a lot to learn, Mr. Darcy. And I suspect Elizabeth will have her hands full in teaching you."

Mr. Dary could not reply.

"Will you wait here for a few minutes, sir? I think Elizabeth will want to speak with you."

Chapter Five

Elizabeth had been looking out the window, wishing she could walk outside and enjoy the perfect weather. October was a delightful month, she had always felt, being on the cusp of fall and winter. It was cold, yes, and there was a snap in the air betokening the winter to come, but there was not yet snow and ice. One could happily walk in only a pelisse and half boots, and possibly not even need gloves! But could she do that now? Could she walk out in this lovely weather? No! Instead, she was stuck inside for days and days, and whose fault was that? Certainly not mine, she thought, bitterly. Maybe that haughty woman with the feathers, now *there* was a likely scapegoat. Or that man – Mr. Darcy, was it? – who evidently could not be bothered to look where he was going.

Her position at the window revealed Mr. Darcy arriving at Longbourn. She watched him toss his mount's reins to John, the stable boy, and march into the house. She almost smiled, as he looked as if he was marching off to his own execution.

She wished he had not come; she wished he had chosen to ride away, quite fast, rather than marry an unknown country girl. The fact that he *had* come meant that she would very likely have to marry him.

Jane came into the room and sat beside her. "He is here, you know."

Elizabeth nodded. "I saw him arrive."

"He has a fine horse," Jane said, trying to sound cheerful.

Elizabeth answered, still looking out the window, "Jane, having a fine mount means nothing other than the fact that he is wealthy, and of that I was already aware." She turned to face her sister. "Jane, I cannot marry a stranger. Surely, surely Papa will not make me do so."

"Lizzy, there is no choice. You must know that."

"Must I know that? Why must I?"

"You know the rules as well as I."

"I did not break any rules!"

"You did not, but rules were nonetheless broken," Jane said, softly.

"Reframing the situation in such a way does not change the fact that I will be forced into a marriage, as if I had deliberately done something wrong."

Mr. Bennet had appeared in the doorway in time to hear this last sentence. "Lizzy, I do not think you are interpreting the matter correctly. Rules such as these are designed to protect the young lady; you, in this instance."

"But I am being punished, not protected!"

"You do not know that; I believe him to be a man of honour."

"And you are willing to bet my entire future on a ten-minute conversation?"

"Lizzy, my dearest child, I beg you to believe that if I thought the man to be a monster, I would send you to the Gardiners immediately."

Elizabeth considered that. "Might I be permitted to meet him?" she said, finally.

"I anticipated that request; he is awaiting you in my study."

Elizabeth closed her eyes for a moment, and rose, albeit with some difficulty. "I will come down directly, Papa."

Her father left the room. Jane helped her sister take off her night rail.

"What do you want to wear, Lizzy?" Jane asked, gently, standing in front of Elizabeth's closet.

"The oldest, ugliest thing that I own," Elizabeth said promptly.

Jane shook her head. "Try again."

Her sister sighed. 'Very well; the blue dress, I suppose."

Jane found the dress indicated and helped her sister into it. "Let me put your hair up, Lizzy. You can hardly want to meet your husband for the first time with your hair in plaits."

"Something simple will do. There is no need for us to try to impress him, is there?" Elizabeth asked.

Jane turned her sister around to face her. "Lizzy, you are being selfish, and it is not like you."

"Selfish! How?"

"Do you not think he is as upset as you are? Like you, he did nothing wrong. And like you, he is being punished by the rules of society. Do you think he is pleased to marry someone he does not know? Especially as he is a wealthy man; he doubtless had his choice of ladies to wed. He may have even had his eye on someone, and now he cannot act on his inclination."

Elizabeth was silent, biting her lips.

"And he is a man of honour, as Papa says, because he could have gotten on that fine horse this morning and ridden away. Instead, he is here, ready to do what honour demands. Can you not give him at least a chance?"

Elizabeth sighed, deeply. "I suppose you are right, Jane. Very well; I will try to behave myself."

Jane pinned up Elizabeth's hair, and the two girls went downstairs together. They moved slowly, as Elizabeth was still in a good deal of pain.

***

Mr. Darcy stood as the girls entered Mr. Bennet's study. He recognized the blonde girl as the young lady Mr. Bingley had asked to dance immediately after their introduction. It was the other girl, the dark-haired one, who had been knocked to the ground. He glanced at her; she was not ugly, but she was certainly not the beauty that her golden-haired sister was. Brown hair, brown eyes, and a scattering of freckles on her nose.

"Miss Elizabeth, I believe?" he asked, bowing to her. His voice sounded cold even to his own ears.

"Mr. Darcy," she returned, equally coldly, dipping the briefest of curtsies.

There was a minute's silence. "I must apologise, Miss Elizabeth, for knocking you down last night. I assure you that my actions were not deliberate."

"I rather assumed that you were not in the habit of knocking young ladies to the floor, Mr. Darcy."

"Indeed, I am not; then again, I am not in the habit of having to evade feathers flying out of a lady's headdress."

"Perhaps you should, in the future, get into the habit of avoiding young ladies who wear such outlandish headdresses."

His lips quirked. "I promise you that I shall."

Another silence.

Mr. Bennet cleared his throat. "Mr. Darcy, I believe there is something you wish to say to my daughter?"

Mr. Darcy hesitated, knowing that once he spoke the words, there would be no going back. You are a fool, he chastised himself; there is already no going back. "Miss Elizabeth, will you do me the honour of giving me your hand in marriage?" He berated himself for his wooden tone, as he saw tears gathering in the young lady's eyes.

"Lizzy?" Mr. Bennet prompted her.

"Are you unwilling, Miss Elizabeth?" Mr. Darcy enquired.

"Unwilling! Yes, of course! How else should I be?" Elizabeth erupted. "I do not know you, sir."

"And I do not know you, madam," he returned, angrily. "But I am willing to do what must be done in order to ensure your reputation. I ask that you do me the same favour."

She looked at him, scorn in her eyes. "The same favour? Do you mean to tell me that you worry for your reputation? I am certain that your friends would all congratulate you on having gotten out of a mess with so little trouble to yourself."

"Such men are no friends of mine, I assure you," he replied, biting off each word.

"Do you truly mean to tell me that you fear for your reputation?" She sounded more puzzled than angry now.

"Miss Elizabeth, I have a very sweet, very shy young sister. Do you think I would relish having her learn that I had knocked a young lady down to the ground, fallen on top of her, however inadvertently, and then rode away without a second thought? What would she think of me? And what would I think of myself? Whatever you believe of me, please believe that I am a man who values his honour."

Elizabeth sat for a minute, silently. Then she said, "May I ask you a few questions, sir?"

"Of course."

"Where do you live?"

He replied, "I have an estate in Derbyshire, called Pemberley, as well as a townhome in London."

"And where do you spend most of your time?"

"I prefer the country to the city; I spend two or three months out of the year in London, and the rest of the time I am at Pemberley."

"Does your very shy, very young sister live with you?"

"She does."

"Have you been married before?"

"No."

"Is there a lady who may be discomfited by your unexpected marriage?"

It took him a moment to understand her. "Ah. No, there is no lady with whom I have a relationship or understanding of any sort."

Turning to her father, she pleaded, "And there is no way out, Papa? Truly?"

"Truly, my dear. You know that I would not let you leave me were it not necessary." There was a deep sadness in his voice; it was evident that the man loved this daughter deeply.

Elizabeth took a deep breath and immediately winced; her hand flew to her rib cage.

"I apologise, Miss Elizabeth. I should have asked how you are feeling today," Mr. Darcy said, quietly.

"I am in pain, Mr. Darcy, but I am told that I will live to dance another day," she said.

She has a sense of humour, at least, Mr. Darcy thought. That was something.

She continued. "Very well; I accept your proposal, sir. But I would prefer not to wed immediately. I assume you would want to travel to Derbyshire following the wedding, and I do not think I could tolerate a carriage ride of such a duration at this time."

He bowed his head in acknowledgement. "Quite right. Let us plan to marry in four weeks' time, here in your parish. This will allow you the opportunity to heal, and allow me time to have the marriage articles prepared. Would the eighteenth of November suit?"

Elizabeth nodded, looking away.

Mr. Bennet said, "I will have the banns called beginning this Sunday."

Elizabeth and Jane rose; Mr. Darcy rose and bowed as they left the room.

Mr. Bennet eyed Mr. Darcy, knowingly. "You are surprised that she did not jump at the chance to marry you, once she knew you had an estate and a townhome, are you not?"

"I am," Mr. Darcy confessed.

"You are doubtless beleaguered by young ladies eager to ensnare you," Mr. Bennet went on.

"You are correct."

"My Lizzy is not like other young ladies, Mr. Darcy. Your wealth will mean little to her. She will value your character, not your purse."

Mr. Darcy bowed to his host, stating that he would leave immediately, as he needed to go to London to have his solicitors prepare the marriage articles, and proceed to Derbyshire to have his home made ready to receive his bride. Promising to return no later than two days before the wedding, he took his leave.

But as he mounted his horse, he thought back over their brief conversation. The chit truly had not wanted to marry him! He was baffled.

Chapter Six

Mrs. Bennet had very much wanted to be part of the discussion with Mr. Darcy in the study, but her husband had refused to allow it. Mr. Bennet was certain that his wife could not be trusted to restrain her delight at the prospect of her second daughter marrying a man of wealth. Mr. Bennet felt strongly that the marriage must take place, despite his daughter's reservations, and he feared that even the most honourable of gentlemen might have second thoughts if forced to listen to Mrs. Bennet's raptures.

As a result, Mrs. Bennet had been forced to wait in the drawing room until Mr. Darcy had departed. She had been trying to fix her attention on her sewing, but with limited success. Did Mr. Bennet understand the importance of this marriage? It was not only a matter of saving Elizabeth's reputation, though that was important; this was also a matter of the family's security. Most specifically, of her own security, once Mr. Bennet had passed on.

When she heard the front door close, she jumped to her feet and hurried to Mr. Bennet's study. "He is gone, Mr. Bennet?"

"He is, Mrs. Bennet."

"And?"

"They will marry."

She clapped her hands together, child-like in her excitement. "When?"

"November eighteenth. He will go to London to have the marriage articles written, then to his estate to prepare it for his bride's arrival."

"His estate!"

"Yes, Mrs. Bennet. It appears that your prayers have been efficacious, as he is quite wealthy."

Her husband's tone of voice alerted her to the fact that he was not as overjoyed by this occurrence as she. "Do you not approve, Mr. Bennet?"

"Of a man being made to marry Lizzy, simply because a feather tickled his nose? You can hardly expect me to be pleased, Mrs. Bennet."

"I can tell you that the feather did a good deal more than tickle his nose; it was thrust directly into his eye."

"Nonetheless…"

"But he is at least willing to marry her; is that not a reason for joy?"

"I suppose it is, Mrs. Bennet, though she deserves far better than an unwilling bridegroom."

With that, they both fell silent, each with their own musings; Mr. Bennet to lament the event and Mrs. Bennet to mark this day in her mind as the happiest day of her entire life.

***

Upstairs, Elizabeth sat silently, tears running down her cheeks, as her older sister held her gently, mindful of her ribs.

Hoping to at least make Elizabeth smile, Jane said, "At least he is handsome. Do you not think so?"

Elizabeth wrinkled her nose. "Is he, do you think? Handsome?"

"Oh, indeed. I prefer blonde-haired men to those who are darker, but I cannot deny that your Mr. Darcy is quite good-looking."

"He is not 'my' Mr. Darcy. I suppose he is good-looking; but I hardly think that to be a good foundation for a marriage."

"Did he not say that he prefers living on his estate, to living in the city?"

"Yes."

"And if he has a house in town as well as an estate, it follows that he is wealthy enough to support a wife and children."

"Very well; these are important attributes," Elizabeth agreed, rather sulkily.

"And you will write me as you discover more of his fine attributes, as you doubtless shall."

"Jane, you are an incurable optimist. What will I do, without you to cheer me?"

"I will write every day, and every word shall be cheerful and gay, until you are tired of seeing my handwriting."

Elizabeth assured her sister that this could never happen, but then fell silent, marking this day in her mind as the worst day of her entire life.

Chapter Seven

Returning to Netherfield, Mr. Darcy could hear the Bingleys and the Hursts speaking as he made his way to the drawing room.

Miss Bingley was saying, "I cannot understand why he does not claim to be engaged; I would be a far worthier mistress of Pemberley than this simple country girl."

To which Mr. Bingley replied, "And *I* cannot understand why it is that *you* do not understand, Caroline. Darcy is an honourable man; he will not abandon the young lady who was compromised as a result of your ridiculous headdress."

Miss Bingley replied hotly, "But he was always meant to marry me!"

Mrs. Hurst murmured something that he could not quite make out.

Thinking it best to interrupt before he was forced to hear more of this distasteful conversation, Mr. Darcy walked into the room.

Miss Bingley said, quickly, "I had hoped to see you at breakfast, Mr. Darcy."

He shook his head, soberly. "When something unpleasant must be done, it is best done quickly."

"So you are engaged, then?" Mr. Bingley asked.

"I am."

Miss Bingley made an odd choking sound and ran from the room. Mrs. Hurst hesitated, and followed her younger sister, though at a more sedate pace.

"I am sorry to have caused your sister distress, Bingley, but I have always done my best to avoid giving her any expectations," Mr. Darcy said.

The gentleman so addressed sighed. "This is not your doing, Darcy. Caroline had hopes, if not precisely expectations. She will likely to continue to have hopes right up until the day you speak your vows. Which will be when, by the by?"

"November eighteenth. Might I ask you to stand up with me, Bingley?"

"I would be honoured, Darcy. Will the wedding take place here in Meryton?"

"I certainly cannot marry her in London, with the *ton* watching her every move and marveling at my bad luck," Mr. Darcy said, coolly. "So yes, here in Meryton."

"Darcy, she is not a bad-looking girl, at least," his friend said, hoping to comfort him.

Mr. Darcy thought back over his interview with his prospective bride. "But she is no beauty, either. I suppose it does not matter, as long as she can produce an heir."

"Her mother birthed five children; that must be viewed as a good sign."

Mr. Darcy's eyebrows rose. "Five? Truly?"

Mr. Bingley looked at him in amusement. "You know nothing of the family, Darcy?"

"I prefer to know as little as possible. Bingley, I need to send a message to Mrs. Holmes, to let her know that I will be in town tomorrow, and a message to Mr. Grey, to arrange for an appointment to draw up marriage articles."

Mr. Bingley nodded. "I will call for a footman."

Chapter Eight

The next morning saw Mr. Darcy in his carriage, bound for London. He planned to meet with his solicitor, Mr. Grey, to discuss marriage articles, and then make his way to Pemberley to discuss the situation with his young sister, Georgiana. Georgiana was shy and ill at ease even with people she knew well. He could not simply arrive at Pemberley and present a stranger as his wife.

Elizabeth would have to make allowances for Georgiana's shyness. But it boded well, he thought, that she had four sisters – four! – as this meant she would have had considerable experience in dealing with young girls. That was one good thing about her. It might be the only good thing.

When he arrived at his town house in Grosvenor Square, Mr. Alfred and Mrs. Holmes greeted him at the door.

"Will you want a bath, sir?" Mrs. Holmes enquired. "And luncheon?"

"A light repast is all I require at this time, thank you, Mrs. Holmes. I will take it in my study. Then I will be on my way to see Mr. Grey." He hesitated. These two long-time servants deserved to know what was afoot. "I am to be married; marriage articles must be drawn up."

"Congratulations, Mr. Darcy." Mrs. Holmes spoke first; Mr. Alfred echoed her words. They both sounded surprised. Of course, they would have known if he had been courting someone of importance.

"The mistress' rooms will need refreshing, sir," Mrs. Holmes said.

"I do not know when she will be here in London, Mrs. Holmes, so we need not concern ourselves with that quite yet. We will be married in Meryton, in her home parish, and then we will go directly to Pemberley."

"Very good, sir," Mrs. Holmes said, curtseying.

He made his way to his study. There was no correspondence to demand his attention, as everything had been forwarded to Netherfield. Instead, he simply sat and brooded on the unfortunate events of the past few days. What had possessed him to go to that blasted assembly anyway? He should have remained at Netherfield, even if that meant spending the evening in the company of Caroline Bingley.

A light tap on the door alerted him to the arrival of the food he had requested.

"Please put the tray down, Mrs. Holmes. I thank you." The housekeeper curtsied and left without a word.

***

Thirty minutes later, the food had been consumed, and Mr. Darcy was on his way to his solicitor.

"Mr. Darcy, it is good to see you looking well, sir," Mr. Gray said, offering his hand.

"Thank you, Mr. Grey. I appreciate you making time to see me on such short notice."

"Of course, of course."

In truth, Mr. Darcy had expected – and would have tolerated – nothing less. Mr. Grey's father had served as the solicitor for Mr. Darcy's father, and the Darcys were likely the most important of the firm's clients. Being ready to serve the Darcys at a moment's notice was expected.

"I am about to be married, Mr. Grey."

The solicitor looked even more surprised than the housekeeper and butler. "Indeed! I had no idea that you were – well, congratulations!"

"You are quite right to be surprised; I was not courting anyone."

The solicitor remained silent, though his eyebrows were arched inquisitively.

Mr. Darcy did not feel that he owed the man any explanation of the circumstances that had resulted in this hasty union; Grey was there to serve him, not to have his curiosity sated. "I will be married on November the eighteenth, and will take my wife directly to Pemberley. I need the marriage articles drawn up immediately."

"I understand that you are in a hurry, Mr. Darcy, but there is quite a bit to discuss, sir. Her pin money, her dowry, her jointure, dowries for daughters – there are any number of details that we must consider."

Mr. Darcy shrugged. "Use the marriage articles that were drawn up for my father upon the occasion of his marriage to my mother. I do not care to spend any more time on it than I must."

The solicitor looked unhappy, but he bowed and said, "Very well, sir. I will have three copies ready for you in two days' time."

Mr. Darcy bowed politely and left. Standing by his carriage, with the coachman waiting for instructions, Mr. Darcy thought he may as well get the worst of this over and done. No, he was wrong; the worst of it would be teaching this country girl how to be a proper mistress of Pemberley. No, indeed; the worst would be tolerating her conversation over meals. No, hold. The worst would be if she and Georgiana took a dislike to one another. He groaned, silently. There were so many 'worsts' that he could not being to count them!

But informing his aunt and uncle, the Earl and Countess of Matlock, of his impending nuptials must certainly be on that list of 'worsts'. As he had told Bingley, when something unpleasant must be done, it is best done quickly. He would pay the Matlocks a visit now.

***

Upon being announced at Matlock House, he was surprised to find his favorite cousin, Colonel Richard Fitzwilliam, second son of the Earl and Countess, in residence as well.

His aunt bestowed a kiss on his cheek, saying, "Fitzwilliam! What an unexpected pleasure this is. I had not known you were in Town."

Colonel Fitzwilliam slapped him on the back. "Darcy! I thought you rusticating in – what was it? Merryville?"

"Meryton. Yes, with Bingley. What are you doing here, Richard? How are we to be kept safe from the French if the army lets its officers run about in London?"

"On leave, old man. But again – what brings you here?"

His aunt chimed in as well. "You look glum, nephew; what troubles you?" she asked, motioning him to sit.

His Aunt Elaine had always been a good friend. She was, of course, his favourite aunt, as the only other aunt he had was Aunt Catherine. Aunt Cat was certainly no competition to be anybody's favourite anything. Ha! Well, that was one good thing to come out of all this; he would no longer have to tolerate Aunt Cat's absurd assertion that he was betrothed to her daughter, Anne.

"I *am* glum, Aunt Elaine. You have the right of it."

"Georgiana is well, I trust?" Colonel Fitzwilliam said, quickly, anxiously. He served as a guardian to Georgiana, along with Mr. Darcy.

"Oh, yes, quite well. We are all quite well."

"But there is something wrong. Has your favourite horse gone lame?" Colonel Fitzwilliam asked.

"Oh, if only it were something as simple as that!"

"If you do not tell us immediately, I shall pour my tea over your head," the Countess threatened.

"It would be a waste of good tea, Aunt. Very well; I am to be married."

She gasped. "Married!? And by the look on your face, I take it that you are less than pleased with the situation?"

"Less than pleased? Yes, that is quite right. She is a country girl of no fortune and barely tolerable looks."

"Did you compromise her, Darcy?" Colonel Fitzwilliam said, directly.

"Richard!" his mother chastised.

"What else am I to surmise?" Colonel Fitzwilliam asked, shrugging. "He shows up here, even more out of sorts than usual, and tells us he is to be married. We would have known if he had been courting someone."

"There was a compromise, but it was entirely accidental."

"Tell us what happened; perhaps I may be of assistance," his aunt said.

"I was in Meryton, a small country village in Hertfordshire, at my friend Bingley's request. He is leasing an estate there, called

Netherfield, to see if the country life suits him. If it does, he will purchase an estate in accordance with his father's wishes."

"Bingley? He is the one with the terrible younger sister, is that right?" his aunt asked.

Colonel Fitzwilliam added, "She is indeed terrible; but she has no interest in a poor soldier, so I am safe from her."

"Happily, I am not wedding his sister. In any case, there was an assembly, and I attended it only because the alternative would have been to remain at Netherfield. The sister you just spoke of would have insisted on remaining there with me, and that was more than I could bear. Though I see now that it would have been the better alternative. In any case, at the assembly, Miss Bingley was wearing a turban, adorned with feathers. At the worst possible moment, one of the feathers came loose and hit me in the eye. I tried to step back, to avoid being further injured by the feather, not knowing that there was a young woman immediately behind me."

"So you stepped back and she fell?" Colonel Fitzwilliam demanded

"She fell, and I fell on top of her." With that Mr. Darcy groaned, and put his face in his hands.

"Oh, my." His aunt covered her mouth with her hand.

"Indeed. And it was witnessed by the hundred or so people present."

"Is it possible that the young lady did this deliberately?" his aunt asked.

"I can hardly think that she could take credit for making a feather come loose."

"No, but she might have seen her opportunity and made the most of it."

Mr. Darcy said, "Aunt, I think that impossible, particularly as she does not want to marry me."

"Now *that* is impossible," the Countess declared.

"Not so; I told her of my estate and my townhome in London, and she was completely unimpressed."

The Countess sat for a long minute in thought. "That is actually rather heartening, Fitzwilliam. Whatever else she may be, she is not a fortune hunter. Well, then, I am evidently about to have a new niece. What is her name?"

"Elizabeth. Elizabeth Bennet."

"I have never heard of her."

"I did not expect that you would have. The family is completely unknown and unimportant."

"You should bring her to Town immediately, Fitzwilliam, so as to quash any rumours that result from this unexpected union."

"No, I do not plan on bringing her to Town."

"That is a mistake, nephew." The Countess' tone was firm.

"I do not think I can trust her behaviour to be acceptable to the *ton*. I will take her to Pemberley. If she cannot be made into a suitable wife, as I fear will likely be the case, she must remain in the country."

"The *ton* will be disappointed not to meet your wife, Fitzwilliam; you know that," his aunt warned him.

"Then the *ton* might have to live with disappointment."

"They will assume the worst if they do not meet her."

At that moment, the Earl came in. "I thought I heard your voice, Darcy." He strode toward his nephew, who turned and met him with an outstretched hand. "All is well?"

His wife spoke. "Fitzwilliam is to be married, Henry."

The Earl's brow knit. "I had not heard that you were courting anyone, Darcy."

The story had to be told again. The Earl was visibly upset. "You should have offered them money, Darcy; surely there was no need to actually marry the chit!"

Mr. Darcy shook his head. "Can you imagine that my father would have approved of such an action?"

"I suppose not, but your father was rather a high stickler, Darcy, if you will forgive me for saying so."

"I prefer to be a high stickler as well, Uncle. I would have been asking the man to sell his daughter's honour! She is a gentlewoman; her father owns an estate. And you would have me ask him to sell her reputation, for what, five thousand pounds? Ten thousand? The amount does not even matter; the concept itself is abhorrent to me."

"I am glad to learn that she is of gentle birth; but you may nonetheless be saddled with an impossible wife, all because of a feather."

"I know it, Uncle. But she is young; it may be that she can be taught."

"For your sake and Georgiana's, I sincerely hope so," the Earl said, sounding unconvinced.

"Fitzwilliam, if this Elizabeth Bennet is vulgar, you must send Georgiana here to live with me," the Countess insisted. "Georgiana is full young; she cannot be exposed to such a person."

Colonel Fitzwilliam agreed, adamantly. He took his role as Georgiana's co-guardian quite seriously.

"I shall do so; I assure you that my sister will not suffer as a result of my misfortune," Mr. Darcy promised.

"When will this unfortunate union take place?" the Earl demanded.

"On the eighteenth of November; I have Grey working on the marriage articles now and they will be ready in two days' time. Once I have them in hand, I will go to Pemberley to prepare Georgiana."

"Do you wish us to attend the wedding?" the Earl asked.

"I beg that you do not, Uncle; I cannot think you would enjoy the proceedings or the company."

"I will come with you to Meryton," Colonel Fitzwilliam announced.

"Are you certain you wish to, Richard? It will not be a pleasant event, I fear."

"Nonetheless, I will accompany you," Colonel Fitzwilliam insisted. "It is a difficult situation, and I suspect you would be glad to have some family support."

Mr. Darcy nodded. "Indeed, I would be glad, as I find myself becoming morose."

His cousin eyed him, knowingly. "Morose is rather the usual state for you, Darcy."

Mr. Darcy just shrugged.

"Will you stay to dinner, nephew?" his aunt asked.

"Yes, I thank you. I did not relish going home and sitting with no company but my own gloomy thoughts," Mr. Darcy confessed. "Let us speak of happier things. How long are you free, Richard?"

"I have accumulated a month's leave; I will be glad to spend a good part of it with you and Georgiana."

"From here, I go to Pemberley and then back to Meryton."

"Excellent," his cousin said. "I will accompany you to Pemberley and then to your wedding. I am eager to see Georgiana, as well as to meet your new bride."

"You are likely more eager than I," Mr. Darcy said, heavily. "Any news from Aunt Cat?" And the rest of the evening was spent in pleasant conversation. Mr. Darcy's upcoming marriage was not spoken of again, though it must be foremost in everyone's minds.

***

Later that evening, after Mr. Darcy had left, the Countess asked her son, "Why did you elect to accompany Fitzwilliam? I had thought to have you to myself for the entire month!"

Her son said, thoughtfully, "I have a few reasons, Mother. First, while Darcy is never light-hearted, he is now unusually distraught, and I do think he can use some family support. Second, I have a feeling that it is not as dreadful a situation as he fears. I would like to have the opportunity to judge it for myself."

"I expect you to report back to me, of course."

"Of course, Mother," he replied, smiling at her fondly.

Chapter Nine

Mr. Darcy was in the habit of purchasing small gifts and trinkets for Georgiana whenever he returned to Pemberley from London. He did not want to disappoint her, particularly as he was bringing her bad news, so he made it a point to buy some new music sheets, a fine cashmere shawl, and a pretty hair clip.

He returned to his solicitor, where the marriage articles awaited him. Mr. Darcy then made ready to journey to Pemberley, sending a message to Matlock House telling Colonel Fitzwilliam to be ready at dawn.

Pemberley was a three-day carriage journey from London. Mr. Darcy's first stop was to pick up Colonel Fitzwilliam at Matlock House. Colonel Fitzwilliam, seasoned soldier that he was, was up and ready, belongings packed in a single small trunk.

"Is she at least pretty?" Colonel Fitzwilliam asked, as the carriage bore them away.

Mr. Darcy shrugged.

"A trim figure?" his cousin pressed him.

Mr. Darcy shrugged again.

"Do you know nothing whatsoever about her?"

"She has brown hair and brown eyes…" he trailed off and added, "And I believe she is rather short."

"So you have never taken a good look at the young woman who is to be your wife?" Colonel Fitzwilliam sounded disbelieving.

"Leave it, Richard, will you?" Mr. Darcy snapped.

***

Mr. Darcy and Colonel Fitzwilliam stopped at the inns Mr. Darcy usually favored when traveling between London and Pemberley, rising at dawn to start out again. Mr. Darcy tried not to think about his future, but it was difficult; his thoughts returned, again and again, to the night of the assembly. He saw the events unfolding before him: the feather coming loose, the feather in its unerring arc toward his face, himself stepping backward and raising his arm as it touched his eye – ah, he had forgotten that. Yes, he has raised his arm to shield his face; what need had he to also step back? No need at all; it had simply been a reflex.

The girl was not complicit; of that he was certain. Despite his aunt's suspicions, she could not possibly have anticipated that Miss Bingley's feather would come loose, that it would hit him in the eye, that he would step backward. He could absolve her of that, at least. Nor was she a fortune hunter; her protests at being made to marry him proved that. And she had a sense of humour, he now recalled. Brown hair, brown eyes, freckles, short, not a fortune hunter, has a sense of humour: that was the complete list of things he knew about his future wife. It was not much.

MISUNDERSTANDINGS

***

They arrived at Pemberley in the afternoon of the third day. Georgiana came running out to meet them. "Brother! Cousin!" she exclaimed, and she hurled herself into Mr. Darcy's arms.

Stepping out of her brother's embrace, she then ran full-tilt at Colonel Fitzwilliam, who lifted her into the air, laughing.

It was not quite the behaviour of a well-brought-up young lady of fashion, Mr. Darcy thought wryly, but he was grateful for her affection.

"Is everything all right, Brother?" she asked, her brow creasing in concern at his somber expression.

"Let us go inside," he said.

Mr. Darcy had sent a message ahead, letting Mrs. Reynolds know that he and Colonel Fitzwilliam were coming, so Colonel Fitzwilliam's usual room was ready for him. Both gentlemen excused themselves to go upstairs to wash up a bit. Soon the three of them were in the family drawing room.

Once the maid bearing trays of tea and small sandwiches had departed, Georgiana immediately said, "I know something is not right, Brother; please tell me!" The siblings were close; though Mr. Darcy was usually of a sober disposition, Georgiana knew that something had occurred to make her brother more somber than usual.

"You do not want your gifts from London first?" Mr. Darcy asked.

"Well, I want them, of course, but first – what is it you are afraid to tell me? Is someone hurt?!"

"No, sweetling, I promise you. Everyone is well. It is something else entirely."

"Well, it cannot be that bad, then. Go on, Brother."

Mr. Darcy took a deep breath. "I am to be married."

There was a moment of silence. Then she gasped, "A sister! I will have a sister! Oh, I am so happy! What is her name? But wait – I did not even know you were courting someone! Why was it a secret?"

Colonel Fitzwilliam chuckled. "Well, at least someone is happy about it!"

He had not expected his sister's first reaction to be one of joy. Perhaps telling Georgiana would not be as dire an ordeal as he had feared. "No, I was not courting anyone. You are right to be surprised."

And he told the story again. As he spoke, he wondered how many more times he would be forced to recount how he had knocked a young lady to the floor and fallen on top of her, bruising her ribs, and forcing the two of them to marry.

Georgiana listened in growing horror. "But – but – is she forcing you to marry her?"

"No; in fact, she is completely opposed to the marriage, but her father is compelling her. He is right to do so, Georgiana; you can see that she had been utterly compromised. It might not have been so dreadful if she had simply fallen to the floor, but I was actually on top of her. You can imagine how that appeared to those who were watching."

She thought for a minute. "So you do not know her at all?" she asked, finally.

"No; I did not even know her name at the time of the event."

"And what is her name?"

"Elizabeth."

"That is a nice name."

"I suppose it is; does it matter?"

"No, I imagine it does not, but I am trying to look for what good I can find."

"Here is another good thing. She is not a fortune hunter. Even after she was made to understand that I am a man of property, she was nonetheless opposed to the marriage."

"I can think of another good thing," Georgiana said, a smile beginning on her face.

"Yes?"

"She is not Miss Bingley."

"No, she is not, and that truly is a very good thing," Mr. Darcy agreed, a slight smile creasing his face. "So you see it might have been worse."

"When is the wedding?"

"The eighteenth of November. I plan to arrive two days earlier, so that her father and I may review the marriage articles."

"That will also give this Elizabeth comfort."

"Indeed? How?"

"She will know that you plan to marry her; she will not find herself waiting at the church, hoping that you arrive."

"Or hoping that I do not arrive, perhaps."

"She does not know you as I do; if she did, she would be eager to wed you. I am coming to the wedding, of course."

"No, Georgiana." His voice was stern.

"No? Why not?"

"She may not be a suitable companion for you."

"Brother, you expect her to travel all the way back to Pemberley in a carriage, accompanied only by two men, two strangers? I cannot think any young lady would be comfortable in such a situation. But if her new sister were to be there as well, she would be far easier. Would she not?"

"I do not know. I suspect it will be an uncomfortable journey no matter what. Richard, what do you think?"

"I think she is right; Georgiana's company would do a good deal to ease the tension of those travel days."

Mr. Darcy sighed. "Very well; Georgiana, you may accompany us."

MISUNDERSTANDINGS

"Oh, good! A sister!! And now I would like my presents, Brother!"

***

Once Georgiana had finished gushing over her gifts, Mr. Darcy asked Mrs. Reynolds to speak with him in his study.

"Mrs. Reynolds, I am to be married," he said, coming directly to the point.

"Oh! I did not know you were courting, Mr. Darcy."

It was almost funny, how everyone said the same thing. "I was not, Mrs. Reynolds. The situation was rather unexpected."

"Unexpected?" Her voice rose.

"No, no, Mrs. Reynolds. It was nothing that anyone did to cause this; it was an accident. But the result of it is that I am to be married on the eighteenth of November; we will return to Pemberley directly."

"Is it Miss Bin – no, it is none of my business, I am sure."

"It is *not* Miss Bingley, Mrs. Reynolds; please reassure the servants."

"Oh! Well, Mr. Darcy, I did not intend to –"

"No, I am certain you did not. In any case, her name is Elizabeth Bennet. She is a gentleman's daughter, though her father's estate is quite small. I know not if she is capable of being a true mistress of Pemberly. I hope we may continue to rely on you, as we have for so many years, to oversee household matters until we determine what Miss Bennet is capable of." His tone was grim, more so than usual.

Mrs. Reynolds did not know whether to be delighted or sorry. Was she to congratulate the Master on his upcoming nuptials? Or console him for being forced, as he evidently had been, into marriage? In the end, she simply curtsied and left.

***

Mr. Darcy agreed with Georgiana that it was cause for rejoicing that his bride was not Miss Bingley. But he could not deny that Miss Bingley was attractive and had a dowry, whereas Elizabeth Bennet was not well-dowered nor well-connected. Was she pretty? He closed his eyes and tried to bring her image into his mind, but he failed. Brown hair, brown eyes, and petite was all he could recall. And freckles. And, evidently, a sense of humour.

He opened his eyes and sighed. How had everything gone so wrong? All this because of a loose feather?

Chapter Ten

Winter 1811

Longbourn was abuzz with excitement. Elizabeth was to marry in a few weeks' time! There was so much to arrange! What would she wear? What would be served at the wedding breakfast?

But not everyone was so excited about the upcoming event. Elizabeth, for one, was entirely silent when her preferences were canvassed. When asked what she wished to wear for her wedding, she shrugged. When asked if she wished to carry a bouquet of white flowers or just greenery, she said that she did not care. When asked what she wished to have served at the wedding breakfast, she had not replied and had turned away. She had no interest at all in what must be the most important day of her entire life.

Mrs. Bennet was happy. Oh, she complained about Elizabeth's recalcitrance, as her daughter's disinterest meant that all the decisions were left to her Mama to make, but no one was fooled by her grumbling. It was no secret that Mrs. Bennet preferred to make decisions herself, as that way they would be the *right* decisions.

Lydia, on the other hand, was unhappy. It had long been her goal to be the first of the Bennet sisters to be married. As it was unlikely that she would find a husband in the next few weeks, she would fail in this ambition. It was so unfair! Why could that man not have fallen on top of her? She would not be as sulky as Lizzy if she were to be the first to marry, and to a rich man, at that!

Mr. Bennet was also unhappy. He was about to lose his best-loved child, and through no fault of his own. A stupid accident, caused by a straying feather and a clumsy man, would deprive him of her company forever. He had always known that Elizabeth would marry and leave him, but he had anticipated that this was at least a few years' off, possibly more. He was certain that her marriage was necessary, of course, but he was not pleased about it.

Jane, too, was unhappy. She loved her sister dearly, and knew that the idea of marrying in such a manner was utterly abhorrent to her. The two sisters had long spoken of their hope of marrying for love; marrying under circumstances such as these would be distasteful to either of them. Jane did her best to cheer Elizabeth, speaking of long visits and an ongoing correspondence, but Elizabeth seemed intent on being despondent.

Mary was happy. It was right and proper for a marriage to take place after so dreadful a compromise. A man falling right on top of a woman! That was sinful in the extreme; a marriage certainly had to take place. The one fly in the ointment, in her opinion, was the long wait. Four weeks! They should have been married immediately.

MISUNDERSTANDINGS

Kitty was neither happy nor unhappy. She was simply confused. She had always (secretly) thought that Lydia's desire to be the first to wed was impossible, and she could not understand why Lydia would even want to be the first. She was happy at being proven right in this regard. But Lydia was unhappy, so Kitty could not be truly happy herself. It was all so perplexing, and Kitty only knew that she would be glad when it was all over.

***

Charlotte Lucas came to visit, sitting beside Elizabeth in her bedroom. She counseled her friend to get over her temper and make the best of it. She began with, "It might have been much worse, Eliza."

"I know that, Charlotte; it might have been Mr. Fielding instead of Mr. Darcy." Mr. Fielding was a seventy-year-old widower who still attended the assemblies.

"As long as you can find humour in the situation, all is not lost," Charlotte said, hoping to bring a smile to her dear friend's face.

"I find humour in it because otherwise I would put on my coat and my boots and begin to walk, and not stop walking until I found myself at the edge of the world, and I then would jump, " Elizabeth said, bleakly.

"Eliza! Stop this at once!" Charlotte was suddenly and unexpectedly furious. "Do you know what I would give to be in your shoes? Do you know how badly, how *very* badly, I wish it had been *me* that Mr. Darcy had fallen on? I would be dancing for joy right now! And here you are, acting like a spoiled child. Poor you, poor Eliza, who must marry a wealthy man, a handsome man, an honourable man. Honestly, if you do not stop your childish behaviour this minute, I will slap you, Eliza, I swear that I will!"

Elizabeth stared at her friend, startled speechless. She took Charlotte's hand, and said, "Dearest Charlotte, I never thought – I did not think –"

"No, you did not! But you *must* think, Eliza, you must stop these childish tantrums and grow up. Do you want to be twenty-seven years old and unmarried, as I am? Do you want to still be living at Longbourn when your unknown cousin comes in and takes possession of it? Is that what you want from life?"

Elizabeth considered Charlotte's words. While Jane could be counted on for soothing commiseration, Charlotte was always ready with good and practical advice.

"You are right, Charlotte, of course. I will stop acting like a spoiled child, as you quite accurately said, and I will make the best of what fortune has given me."

"You should at least take an active interest in your wedding. This is, after all, a day you will remember for the rest of your life," Charlotte suggested.

"I agree. I will start this very minute, Charlotte." With that, Elizabeth got up and marched into the parlour, where Jane sat with Mrs. Bennet. "Jane, will you stand up with me?"

"Of course, Lizzy!" Jane replied readily, though she was astonished at this sudden about-turn from her sister.

Turning to her mother, she said, "Mama, I would like to be married in my green dress. And I will carry white flowers. As for the wedding breakfast menu, I believe I may safely leave that to you and Cook. Is there anything else that requires a decision from me?"

Her mother and sister stared at her in amazement.

"No? Very well. I shall be in my room, composing a letter to Aunt and Uncle Gardiner. I think they should be invited to my wedding, and I do not know that anyone has written them."

And she swept out of the drawing room and made her way up to her bedroom, careful of her ribs, to tell Charlotte that her wise counsel had been heeded.

Chapter Eleven

Elizabeth received a response from her Aunt Gardiner in three days' time.

Dear Lizzy,

I am shocked beyond words! You are to be married? Because a gentleman fell on you? I am tempted to say that surely there must have been a way around this, but even as I write, I know that there likely was not. If the entire neighbourhood saw the event, wagging tongues will have already turned it into something it most certainly was not.

Your uncle and I will surely be in attendance. Please tell your parents that we will arrive on the sixteenth of November, and we will depart the day after the wedding. I shall leave the children with their nursemaid, as I imagine Longbourn will be hectic enough without the addition of small children.

Is there anything I might bring you from London? A particular bridal gift? You must let me know.

Your surprised but always loving,

Aunt Gardiner

Elizabeth was tempted to write back that the bridal gift she wanted was a ticket to Canada, but she forbore.

"What does your aunt say?" her mother asked, as Elizabeth had read the letter over breakfast.

"She and my uncle will come to Longbourn on the sixteenth of November and will stay until the day after the wedding; the children will remain in London."

"The sixteenth? That is the same day that your Mr. Darcy will return, is it not?'

"Not 'my' Mr. Darcy," she replied. "But yes, the same date."

"You will be glad to have Aunt and Uncle Gardiner at your wedding, I think," Jane ventured.

"I am, of course," Elizabeth replied.

Her tone was rather dull, for which her mother scolded her. "Lizzy, I thought you had decided to make the best of the situation."

"I have, I am. Very well, let me amend that. I am trying. Will that not content you, Mama?"

"I suppose it will have to."

"In any case, Mama, your joy makes up for my lack of it."

Jane replied, softly, "I do not think your Mr. Darcy will see it that way."

Elizabeth automatically answered, "He is not my – oh, never mind!"

Chapter Twelve

As he had promised, Mr. Darcy was back at Netherfield on the sixteenth of November, in the middle of the afternoon, accompanied by both Colonel Fitzwilliam and Georgiana. He had been glad to have their company, as their presence had prevented him from sinking further into melancholy. His valet, Carstairs, and Georgiana's maid, Susie, had come to Netherfield as well, in a second carriage.

Miss Bingley was flustered to see Georgiana and Colonel Fitzwilliam in the entryway with Mr. Darcy. "Georgiana! I had not expected –"

"It is Miss Darcy," Mr. Darcy said, stonily. "I do not believe you have been given permission to use my sister's given name."

"I beg your pardon, Mr. Darcy; I was simply surprised at seeing her, though delighted, of course." Miss Bingley made a fast recovery. "And this is your cousin, Colonel Fitzwilliam, I believe?"

The Colonel bowed and greeted her politely.

Miss Bingley said, "I will have rooms prepared for them immediately. Meanwhile, may I offer refreshments?'

"We would be grateful, Miss Bingley," Georgiana said, quite properly. "It has been a long journey."

"I am rather surprised that you accompanied your brother, Miss Darcy, given the circumstances," Miss Bingley said.

"He is to be married; should I not be by my brother's side, regardless of how the union came to be?"

Miss Bingley thought for a minute, but could not manage to construct a suitable reply. She ushered her company into her drawing room and rang for tea. When the maid brought in the tea tray, she asked that her brother be told of the arrival of the guests.

"Miss Darcy! Darcy! Colonel! It is a pleasure to see you all, though – well, it is a pleasure in any case!" Mr. Bingley said, stepping into the drawing room.

"I know what you were about to say, Bingley, but my sister and my cousin have spent these past weeks telling me that I must make the best of things."

"Quite right, quite right. The family is not so bad, you know, Darcy," Mr. Bingley said, earnestly.

Miss Bingley sniffed loudly. "He has been paying a good deal of attention to the eldest Miss Bennet. Really, Charles, you cannot be serious about her."

"She is an absolute angel, Darcy! I have not seen much of Miss Elizabeth, as her ribs are still giving her some trouble and she is often resting in her room, but Miss Bennet is the most beautiful, the kindest, the gentlest lady of my acquaintance."

"And I say he can do far better than an insignificant country girl with no dowry," Miss Bingley insisted.

Mr. Darcy said, "Miss Bennet is the daughter of a gentleman; she is above your family, socially, Miss Bingley. In fact, she may not be willing to be attached to the son of a tradesman, however wealthy he may be."

"But what are her connections?" Miss Bingley said, insistently. "She has none."

"Well," Mr. Darcy said, mildly. "She is about to be my sister, so there is that."

There was a moment of silence. Mr. Bingley began to laugh, as his sister scowled. "Yes, Caroline, there is that! Is that not enough of a connection for you?"

The housekeeper came in to tell Miss Bingley that the guest rooms were ready and the Darcys' luggage had been brought to their rooms. Mr. Darcy, Colonel Fitzwilliam and Georgiana rose and followed the housekeeper upstairs.

Once Mr. Darcy had allowed Carstairs to help him into fresh clothing, he went next door to see how his sister fared. She, too, had changed her dress and washed her face, with Susie's help.

"She is dreadfully rude," Georgiana whispered to him.

"Miss Bingley? Oh, indeed. As you reminded me, our situation might have been far worse."

"We should go to – what was it, Longbourn? – and greet your Elizabeth."

"She is not 'my' Elizabeth," he said. "But I suppose we must."

Colonel Fitzwilliam appeared in the hall. "We are going to visit your Elizabeth, are we not, Darcy?"

"She is not 'my' Elizabeth," Mr. Darcy found himself repeating. "But we are going to Longbourn, yes."

Mr. Darcy agreed that they were to do that directly. Mr. Darcy offered his arm to Georgiana and the three made their way downstairs.

Miss Bingley was waiting for them at the bottom of the staircase. "I thought perhaps we might play a duet, Miss Darcy," she said, eagerly.

"I thank you, Miss Bingley, but we thought to visit Longbourn now," Georgiana said.

"Oh! No, I hardly think *that* necessary," Miss Bingley replied, quickly.

Mr. Darcy looked at her in surprise. "Really, Miss Bingley? It is not necessary for me to visit my betrothed? You do surprise me. Nonetheless, to Longbourn we shall go. I wondered if your brother might wish to join us; you are welcome, too, of course."

"I am certain Charles has other occupations today, as do I," she said, firmly.

"I am sorry to hear it, but might we not enquire of your brother directly?" Mr. Darcy asked.

At that moment, Mr. Bingley appeared. He had quite obviously changed his clothing in preparation for paying a visit, as he looked quite fine. "I am off to Longbourn to visit Miss Bennet. Will you accompany me, Darcy?"

"We were planning to go there as well, Bingley. My horses are resting; might we use your carriage?"

"Let us all go. Caroline?"

"Your sister has assured me that she has other occupations today," Mr. Darcy said, swiftly. "Let us be on our way."

Neatly done, Brother, Georgiana thought, successfully stifling a laugh. And the five of them were soon in Mr. Bingley's carriage and on their way to Longbourn.

"What think you of your brother's engagement, Miss Darcy?" Mr. Bingley enquired.

"I do not yet know what to think; I will know more once I meet the lady. But I have always longed for a sister, so I am predisposed to be in favour of the match," she replied.

Mr. Bingley looked at her with some concern. "You do know that the situation that necessitated the marriage was not your brother's fault, nor that of Miss Elizabeth?"

"I do understand that, yes. If blame must be apportioned, I suppose it must be assigned to whoever put the feathers in Miss Bingley's turban."

"She blamed her maid for it, as I suppose you might guess."

Colonel Fitzwilliam smothered a laugh.

"Oh, no! What happened to the maid?" Georgiana asked, dismayed.

"Turned out without a reference," Mr. Bingley answered, succinctly.

"Surely you did not let your sister do that, Bingley," Mr. Darcy said, leaning forward in some alarm.

"Of course not; I found the maid and gave her a reference, as well as the full quarter's wages and travel money to get her back to London."

"Good; I am glad to hear of it," Mr. Darcy said, relaxing.

"It was not even the maid's fault. Caroline stuck the silly things in the turban herself, against the maid's advice. Ah, here we are," he announced, as the carriage pulled into a graveled driveway.

Georgiana quickly leaned forward to look out her window. The house was as her brother had described it; solid-looking and clean, but not fashionable or elegant. Not that it mattered; Brother was not marrying the house.

The coachman opened the carriage door; Mr. Darcy exited first and offered a hand to help his young sister out. Mr. Bingley, clearly excited, and in a rush to see his young lady, practically jumped from the carriage. Colonel Fitzwilliam followed him.

The carriage had evidently been spotted coming up the drive, as the front door opened and the old butler Darcy remembered from his earlier visit stepped aside to admit them. "Mr. Darcy, Mr. Bingley, and…" And here he trailed off, waiting for the identity of the newcomers to be revealed so that the visitors might be properly announced.

"Miss Darcy and Colonel Fitzwilliam," Darcy supplied.

"Miss Darcy and Colonel Fitzwilliam," the butler echoed, nodding. He made his way to the parlour, the guests following him.

"Miss Darcy, Mr. Darcy, Colonel Fitzwilliam and Mr. Bingley," he announced.

"Miss Darcy? Colonel Fitzwilliam?" several feminine voices chorused in surprised tones.

As the five guests advanced into the parlour, its inhabitants rose and curtsied. Mr. Darcy was able to identify Mrs. Bennet, Miss Bennet and Miss Elizabeth, but there were two people he did not know.

There was a flurry of introductions; Mr. Darcy learned that the two strangers were Mr. and Mrs. Gardiner, and that Mr. Gardiner was Mrs. Bennet's brother. The Gardiners, he was soon told, lived in London; Mr. Gardiner was a merchant. Wonderful, he thought to himself, not only has she no dowry to speak of and no connections, she also has relatives in trade. Could it get any worse?

Elizabeth was delighted to see that Mr. Darcy had brought along his young sister. The girl was about fifteen years old, blond-haired and dark-eyed. The blonde hair was rather a surprise, as her brother was dark-haired. His cousin, Colonel Fitzwilliam, appeared to be about ten years Mr. Darcy's senior. He was broad-shouldered and muscular, as one might expect from a soldier. He was not as handsome as his cousin, but his face was cheerful and open.

Georgiana immediately went to Elizabeth's side; Jane and Elizabeth were sitting together on a sofa, but Jane moved to a chair so that Georgiana might sit with Elizabeth.

Mrs. Bennet loudly announced her pleasure at seeing them all, and offered refreshments. "It is so good to see you again, Mr. Darcy. I trust that your journey was uneventful? Colonel, what an honour it is to have you with us." Without waiting for a response, she turned to Mr. Bingley. "Oh, Mr. Bingley, you are very welcome. Is he not, Jane?"

Miss Bennet, blushing, murmured that Mr. Bingley was indeed very welcome.

Mrs. Bennet went on to comment on the weather (unusually fine), the neighbours (Mrs. Crawford was ill again, but given the state of her roof it was not to be wondered at), the quality of the meat available at the butcher's (better than usual).

Mr. Darcy moved to sit nearer to Miss Elizabeth and his sister, so as to eavesdrop on their conversation. It was likely to be far more interesting than the goings-on of Meryton, as reported by Mrs. Bennet, and he was anxious to ascertain that Georgiana would not hear anything inappropriate from this unknown country miss.

Elizabeth was saying, "I understood that Mr. Darcy had a younger sister, but had not dared to hope that he had brought her with him. I am glad, very glad, to meet you, Miss Darcy."

"Oh, no, you are to call me Georgiana."

"Very well; and I am Elizabeth, though my family all call me Lizzy."

"I shall try both names and see which suits you best," Georgiana replied.

"Or you might do as my mother does; Lizzy for everyday and Elizabeth for when she is unhappy with me."

"Then it would always be Lizzy and never Elizabeth," Georgiana said, staunchly.

"Well, I see you are the most agreeable of young sisters," Elizabeth said, smiling at her.

"I have always wanted a sister," Georgiana said, with a happy sigh.

"But perhaps not one obtained in quite such a way," Elizabeth said. "I do not expect the Darcy family to be happy at the situation. The Colonel – may I enquire as to how he is connected to your family?"

"Oh! I forgot that you did not know. He is the second son of the Earl and Countess of Matlock. His father, the Earl, was our mother's brother."

"I see; it is good of him to accompany your brother."

Mr. Darcy listened to the exchange in amazement. Georgiana, generally so shy and retiring, conversing in the most animated tones with a complete stranger. And his future bride had made no comment upon discovering that he was the nephew of an earl! He shook his head; it was incomprehensible.

He heard his name. "Mr. Darcy?"

"Yes?" He looked up. It was Elizabeth.

"I believe you and I must exchange at least a few words, sir," she said. "Surely we cannot yet be at odds with one another, as we have scarcely met."

Georgiana giggled. Giggled! Mr. Darcy could not recall the last time his sister had actually giggled. This Miss Elizabeth was already changing his sister's character, and likely not in a positive way. Surely it was not acceptable for a young lady to giggle. Was it?

Mr. Darcy said, sternly, "I apologise for my inattention, Miss Elizabeth; I was reluctant to interrupt your tête-à-tête with my sister."

"That is an acceptable excuse," she said. "I shall allow it this once."

Was she teasing him? No one ever teased him; he was not certain how he was meant to react. His uncertainty must have shown on his face, as Mr. Bingley said, laughing, "It is clear that you have had little prior conversation with Miss Elizabeth, Darcy. She has already befuddled you."

Befuddled? He was never befuddled. Was he? Perhaps it was best to change the subject.

"Are you still in pain, Miss Elizabeth?" That was a safe enough topic of conversation, and indeed, it was incumbent upon him to inquire after his betrothed.

"A little, yes," she admitted.

"I am sorry to hear it," he replied, coolly.

He saw Mrs. Gardiner looking at him rather intently. Did she wish to speak with him? He looked at her. "Mrs. Gardiner?"

"Mr. Darcy, forgive me, but is your estate in Derbyshire?"

"It is," he replied, tersely. Was he about to be begged for some sort of favour? Already? They had just been introduced, and already he was being importuned.

She nodded in satisfaction, "I thought as much; I was born and raised in Lambton, and I knew your parents. Your sister favors her mother quite a bit."

Mr. Darcy's face lit up immediately. "Lambton! That is not five miles from Pemberley! May I inquire as to your maiden name?"

"I was Madeline Harris. My father owned –"

"The bookshop! Of course! I recall that you often helped me find books!"

"You are quite right; what a voracious reader you were! Are you still?"

"Oh, indeed!" And Mr. Darcy soon found himself speaking in the most animated tones with this merchant's wife, glad to be able to give her the latest news from her home town. He found himself delighted with the conversation; it was not a familiar feeling.

Colonel Fitzwilliam sat back, watching the conversations with amusement. Georgiana had said she had always longed for a sister, and this very well may have been true, judging by the animated conversation she was enjoying with Elizabeth Bennet. And despite Mr. Darcy's well-known pride, he was conversing quite animatedly with the wife of a London merchant! It was all quite illuminating; Colonel Fitzwilliam was glad he had decided to accompany his cousin to Meryton.

Georgiana asked Elizabeth. "But where are your other sisters, Elizabeth? You have three others, is that not right?"

"Quite right; Mary, Catherine, though we call her Kitty, and Lydia. I suspect they will be down shortly. Kitty and Lydia do not like to miss any possibility of excitement, and Mary will want to make sure the proprieties are observed."

As if summoned by Elizabeth's words, three young women then came into the room with a good deal of chattering; the gentlemen rose to their feet. Mrs. Bennet introduced them as Miss Mary, Miss Kitty and Miss Lydia.

Miss Lydia spoke to Mr. Darcy immediately. "So you came back! We had a bet on whether or not you would; I said that you would and Kitty said that you would not."

Kitty immediately retorted, "You have that backwards, Lydia. I said he would, and you said he would not."

"No, you are wrong," Lydia said, loudly. "I won the bet. Now you must give me your green ribbon!"

Mr. Darcy glanced at Georgiana, whose mouth had fallen open in shock. He shook his head; these rag-mannered creatures were to be his sisters? Mrs. Bennet began scolding her two youngest daughters, causing the two of them to flounce out of the room.

Elizabeth turned to Georgiana and said, "And do you still wish you had a sister? Because I can assure you that Kitty and Lydia have served to make many a young lady happy to have no female siblings."

Georgiana laughed. "But you and your elder sister must surely counter the example of the younger ones. Oh! I am sorry, Lizzy, I did not intend any criticism."

"I beg you not to apologise; if you do not criticise them, I shall begin to question your judgement, and that would be a poor beginning to our relationship."

Georgiana said, "Then I shall simply say that they are full young, and are likely to grow into better manners."

"You are kind to say so; I wish I could be certain of that, but time will tell."

"Your middle sister is quiet," Georgiana said, softly, indicating Miss Mary, who sat straight-backed in a corner chair, out of earshot.

"She is religious," Elizabeth sighed.

"You say that like it is a bad thing," Georgiana said, surprised.

"Indeed it is, if it prevents a person from reading anything but the Bible and religious texts."

"And is that the case with your sister?"

"It is; and I will freely admit that it is as difficult to have a sensible conversation with her as with my two youngest sisters."

"I had not realised how difficult it could be to have a sister; I think now I must have idealised the relationship," Georgiana said, thoughtfully.

"Ah, but then there is Jane."

"She seems very lady-like," Georgiana ventured, glancing out of the corner of her eye at Miss Bennet, who had her eyes downcast and a blush on her cheeks, as Bingley spoke with her.

"Lady-like! She is, of course, but more importantly, she is kind, generous, gracious, and everything that anyone could possibly want from a sister."

"She is quite dear to you?"

"Well, all my sisters are dear to me, but Jane is dear to me *because* of who she is, rather than *in spite of*."

Georgiana now could not stop from laughing out loud. Mr. Darcy was baffled; how could twenty minutes of conversation have effected so dramatic a change in his sister's behaviour? He was still not certain if this change was salutary or injurious, but he rather suspected the latter.

Mr. Bennet walked in; Mr. Darcy rose to his feet and presented his young sister and his cousin to the master of the house. Mr. Bennet acknowledged the introduction most courteously, saying he was delighted to learn that Elizabeth would be gaining a lovely new sister. He then asked Mr. Darcy to join him in the study.

Mr. Darcy leaned toward Georgiana, asking if she would be comfortable if he left her with Miss Elizabeth, reminding her that Colonel Fitzwilliam was there if she needed anything, to which Georgiana replied, "Oh, we have no need of you at all, Brother. You may leave me with my new sister for as long as you like!"

More befuddled than ever, Mr. Darcy followed Mr. Bennet from the room.

Chapter Thirteen

"I see you have returned," Mr. Bennet said, offering Mr. Darcy a brandy.

Mr. Darcy declined the beverage; he had already determined that Mr. Bennet was possessed of a keen intelligence. Mr. Darcy suspected he would need his wits about him.

"No? You will forgive me if I indulge, I hope?"

Mr. Darcy nodded, and Mr. Bennet poured himself a small glass.

"Did you think I would not return?" Mr. Darcy enquired.

"I thought you would; but my character reading is not always accurate, as Lizzy often reminds me."

"I could not do otherwise and be at peace," Mr. Darcy said.

"And it is for that reason that I am comfortable assigning Lizzy to your care. It also speaks well of you, I think, that you brought your sister with you."

"Indeed?"

"Yes; it shows me that you care for your sister, as she doubtless begged to be invited, and that you had some consideration for

Lizzy, as well. I know Lizzy will be far more comfortable in the long journey back to Derbyshire with a young sister at her side."

"They are getting along quite well already," Mr. Darcy said, nodding.

"I imagine this surprises you," Mr. Bennet said, looking at him sharply.

"Your character reading appears astute enough to me, Mr. Bennet. Or do I call you Papa now?" he asked, with an attempt at humour.

Mr. Bennet stared at Mr. Darcy for a minute before laughing heartily. "Oh, you have a sense of humour! That is delightful. A sense of humour is a requirement for anyone hoping to enter into a serious relationship with Lizzy."

"I am glad to be able to accommodate her," Mr. Darcy said, rather sourly.

"But you should call me Bennet or Thomas, if that appeals to you, as we are shortly to be related." Now serious, Mr. Bennet leaned forward. "You have the marriage articles? I must be certain my daughter is protected."

Nodding, Mr. Darcy reached into his coat pocket and pulled out all three copies. He handed them to Mr. Bennet, who took a copy and began to read. Soon, Mr. Bennet's eyebrows rose, and he looked at Mr. Darcy over his spectacles.

"Is there a difficulty?" Mr. Darcy asked.

"None at all; you are surprisingly generous."

Mr. Darcy thought back; he had told Mr. Grey to simply copy whatever his parents' articles had been. Yes, doubtless his father had been quite generous with his betrothed, as theirs had been a love match. "These are the same articles my father used for his own marriage."

"That explains it. Pin money of two hundred and fifty pounds a quarter. Lizzy will not know what to do with such funds. I suspect the lion's share will be spent on books."

"Is she a reader?" Mr. Darcy was surprised.

"Lizzy? A reader? That is like asking if the sea is wet!"

"I am glad to hear it; but I do not imagine she will need to spend money on books. There are upwards of thirty thousand volumes in the Pemberley library, and new books are added regularly. John Hatchard has standing orders as to what books are to be sent to me."

" Hatchard and I are well-acquainted with one another, though more by post than otherwise. I do not enjoy travel, but your description of your library might tempt me to overcome my scruples."

"I have been admiring some of the books in your room here, Bennet. May I browse your shelves while you peruse the marriage articles?"

Mr. Bennet assented, gladly. He settled back to read the marriage articles carefully. Mr. Darcy was settling thirty thousand pounds on Elizabeth, for her own use if her husband should predecease her. Any daughter born to the couple would be given a similar sum as a dowry. The eldest son would, of course, inherit Pemberley, but any additional sons would be given a choice of the dozen satellite estates owned by Mr. Darcy. The man was clearly far, far wealthier than any of them had imagined. Even Mrs. Bennet, whose imagination was inclined to run wild when it came to her daughter's suitors, could not have imagined such affluence.

His musings were interrupted by Mr. Darcy's gasp. "You have a first edition of the King James Bible!"

Bennet chuckled. "I do, indeed. Evidently, Hatchard prefers my custom to yours, Mr. Darcy, as it was he who found it for me. It cost me a pretty penny, and I can only beg you to not mention this to Mrs. Bennet, who would have preferred that those funds be used to purchase new dresses for the girls."

Mr. Darcy said, "I hope you will bear me in mind in the event that you ever decide to sell this book. I will pay any sum that you name."

"I do not imagine ever selling it, but Elizabeth is to inherit my library, as she is the only one of my daughters who could appreciate such a legacy. One day that Bible will be yours."

"May that day be far off," Mr. Darcy said, automatically. He realised, as he spoke, that he meant it; he found himself liking the older man. "And you are welcome to visit the Pemberley Library at any time, sir."

"I may very well take you up on that offer. I will be no trouble at all; you can move a bed into the library and leave trays outside the door."

Mr. Darcy found himself smiling. It was always a treat to meet a fellow bibliophile. "What think you of the odds of finding a First Folio? But hold; business first. Have you any questions for me?"

"No; you have been more than generous with my daughter, and that has relieved my mind considerably. Tell me, what direction have you given Hatchard with respect to finding rare books?'

The brandy made its way back to Bennet's desk as the two gentlemen settled in for a long discussion of the volumes they each hoped to purchase. Mr. Darcy quite forgot his young sister, cousin and betrothed in the parlour.

Chapter Fourteen

Meanwhile, Georgiana had confessed to Elizabeth that her brother was quite concerned about marrying a young woman of whom he knew nothing whatsoever. "But you must be equally worried," Georgiana said. "I admit that I had not considered how you must be feeling."

"That is quite natural, Georgiana; you know and love your brother, and it is right that his feelings should be your primary concern."

"Will you allow me to attempt to alleviate your worries, Lizzy?"

"I hope that you will," her new sister replied, only half-joking.

"My brother is the very best of men!" Georgiana replied promptly.

"But any sister would say that, would she not?" Elizabeth asked, with a raised eyebrow.

"I suppose she would, yes; but in this particular case, it is the complete truth."

"Also what any loving sister would say," Elizabeth replied. "Georgiana, I beg you not to alarm yourself unduly. He and I will learn about one another; it is likely best to let that process untold at a natural pace."

Elizabeth felt now that the Colonel was being neglected, and so made an effort to include him in their conversation. "Colonel, Georgiana here tells me that her brother is the very best of men; I maintain that any fond sister would say the same. What say you?"

"She is right, but if we are being accurate, it must be admitted that Darcy is also proud and rather stubborn," he replied.

"I have found all men to be stubborn, particularly if they are in a disagreement with a woman; is that not so?"

"You are right, of course." Colonel Fitzwilliam was highly amused. This Elizabeth Bennet had a good deal of spirit; it would be entertaining indeed to watch her cross swords with Darcy.

"Let us amuse ourselves by watching Jane and Mr. Bingley," Elizabeth suggested, with a sly smile.

"You know that Miss Bingley does not approve of the match, do you not?" Georgiana asked.

"She has made that abundantly clear; but if her brother is not strong enough to resist her importuning, then he is not the right man for my sister."

Georgiana recounted the discussion that had taken place at Netherfield earlier, repeating her brother's words about Jane soon being connected to the Darcy family, and was that not a good enough connection?

Elizabeth burst out laughing. "Oh!" she said. "That was well done indeed! I only wish I might have seen Miss Bingley's face. Oh, dear, I am sorry; as an older sister, I am meant to be an example of good manners for you, am I not? And instead, here I am laughing at someone else's discomfort. You will have to learn to ignore me when I am being a bad example, Georgiana."

Georgiana could not imagine ever ignoring her new sister, nor could she now imagine a better sister than the one her brother was about to give her. She could only hope that the two principals would be as delighted with one another as she was with the two of them.

Shortly thereafter, Mr. Darcy and Mr. Bennet walked back into the parlour. Mr. Darcy spoke. "I should have asked this first, I believe; is all in place for the wedding?" He looked at Mrs. Bennet as he spoke, rather than his prospective bride.

Mrs. Bennet sat up straight at being so addressed. "It is, Mr. Darcy; her dress is ready, and the breakfast –"

And here he interrupted her. "What time shall I be at the church?"

"The ceremony will take place at ten o'clock in the morning, Mr. Darcy. As I was saying, the breakfast will then – "

He interrupted her again. "Very well. I believe we have stayed well past the polite duration of a visit, Georgiana. Shall we go? Bingley?"

And with that, the Netherfield party took their leave. In the coach, Georgiana berated her brother. "I do not think you spoke two words to Elizabeth, Brother. Richard spoke with her more than you did."

"We shall have more than enough time to speak, Georgiana; I see no need to hasten the process. Bingley, are you serious about Miss Bennet?"

"I am, indeed," his friend said, immediately.

"Despite the terrible manners of her younger sisters? I confess that I was utterly appalled."

"I agree that their manners need improving, of course; but it is not the sisters I hope to marry, Darcy."

"And despite your sister's opposition?"

"Caroline's opposition is rather a recommendation, do you not think, Darcy?"

"I could never have said so, Bingley," his friend replied, humorously.

"No, for you are far too well-mannered. Miss Darcy, do you not agree that Caroline's disapproval is a recommendation?"

Georgiana reddened. "You cannot expect me to comment, Mr. Bingley."

"No, I suppose not. But I noticed that you and Miss Elizabeth were enjoying one another's company, as I think you spoke to no one else in the room."

"She is absolutely delightful!" was Georgiana's fervent response. "But I noticed, Brother, that you had no interest in the wedding preparations. You cut Mrs. Bennet off rather rudely."

"Did I?" Mr. Darcy asked, absently.

Colonel Fitzwilliam said, "You certainly did. I admit that I was rather shocked at your bad manners."

Mr. Darcy shrugged. "The details of the event hold no interest for me. I will be there on time; that is all that can be expected of me."

Colonel Fitzwilliam went on. "Also, I must suggest that you have your eyes examined the next time you are in London; Miss Elizabeth is a beauty! Not in the same manner as her elder sister, but nonetheless, she is everything lovely."

Mr. Bingley agreed that Miss Elizabeth was a very attractive young lady, with a light and pleasing figure.

Mr. Darcy did not deign to reply; he looked out the window of the carriage, as his sister and cousin exchanged a concerned look.

Chapter Fifteen

At Longbourn, Mr. Bennet called Elizabeth into his study as soon as their guests had departed.

"Did you and Mr. Darcy have a productive discussion, Papa?" Elizabeth asked. "You spent quite a bit of time together."

Mr. Bennet looked at his daughter over his spectacles. "He is far, far wealthier than we had imagined, daughter."

"I care not about such things, Papa, you know that."

"I do know that, but hear me out. He is giving you two hundred and fifty pounds a quarter for pin money!"

Her mouth opened; no sound came out, and she soon closed it. "Very well."

"That is all you can say? Very well?"

"May I ask that you not tell my mother and my sisters of this?"

"That is a reasonable request, as you would be endlessly beleaguered by requests for funds and gifts. But wait, there is more. He is settling thirty thousand pounds on you, in the event that he predeceases you. Your daughters will each have thirty thousand pounds as dowries. Your eldest son will inherit the main estate, but there are more estates for any additional sons to inherit. Have you ever imagined such a thing?" he asked.

"No, I have not," his daughter replied, honestly. "But what of his character, Papa? Is he a good man?"

"He must be, Lizzy. He returned to wed you, did he not? He said that he could not live with himself had he done otherwise. And you note that he brought his sister with him so that you would feel more comfortable on your journey to Pemberley. What man of poor character would have done so?"

"And she is an utterly delightful creature, Papa. I know nothing of the man, and if he does not become more communicative than he was today, I never shall; but his sister is all that I could have hoped for."

"I am glad to hear it. You will miss Jane, of course, but from what you say, your new sister will more than compensate you for the loss of the other three."

"I think so; but Papa, did you see that Mr. Darcy had no interest at all in the wedding preparations? He did not even let Mama speak a full sentence on the subject!"

"I did see that, Lizzy; I am sorry, child. Most men have little interest in such details. I can assure you that he was congenial when speaking with me, and it will doubtless interest you to know that he has a library of thirty thousand volumes."

She shook her head, decisively. "I do not believe that."

"What cause has he to lie about such a thing?"

"I know not; but no one who behaves as he does could possibly own so many books."

Her father laughed at her; after a minute, she began to laugh as well. "Very well; I know one has nothing to do with the other. But I am glad to hear it. Since he very likely will never speak with me, I can spend many profitable hours in his library."

Chapter Sixteen

The next day, Georgiana breakfasted with her brother, her cousin and Mr. Bingley. Miss Bingley and the Hursts kept town hours and so had not yet left their rooms, a situation which suited everyone currently at the breakfast table admirably.

Georgiana began, "We will go to Longbourn again today, will we not?"

Mr. Darcy looked at her in some surprise. "Is there a reason to do so?"

His sister looked equally surprised. "Is there a reason *not* to do so? She is to be your wife, Brother. Should you not spend time with her?"

He looked at her rather sternly. "You are labouring under something of a misapprehension here, Georgiana. This is not a marriage of affection; it is a marriage of necessity. I think she has no more interest in seeing me than I have in seeing her."

Georgiana shook her head. "I do not believe that, but in any case, has she not the right to expect some attention from you?"

He scoffed. "I think not; I am marrying her, and that is all the attention she should hope for."

Mr. Bingley spoke up. "I think Georgiana has the right of it, Darcy. Miss Elizabeth is a fine young woman; she is intelligent and sensible. She will feel your lack of attention keenly, and surely that is not a good beginning to the marriage."

Mr. Darcy shrugged.

Mr. Bingley turned to Georgiana and said, "I plan to visit Longbourn today; would you like to join me?"

"I would indeed!" Georgiana replied, enthusiastically.

Colonel Fitzwilliam added, "I would enjoy a visit as well; I find Miss Elizabeth utterly delightful."

Mr. Bingley nodded. "Very well. It is too early now for a social call; let us plan to leave at one o'clock in the afternoon."

Georgiana and Colonel Fitzwilliam agreed, saying that they would be ready at the appointed time.

Miss Bingley soon joined her guests. Upon learning that her brother, Georgiana, and the Colonel were to go to Longbourn, but that Mr. Darcy would remain at Netherfield, she told the latter that she would be pleased indeed to bear him company while the others were at Longbourn.

Miss Bingley did not notice Mr. Darcy's look of alarm, but Colonel Fitzwilliam did. He was scarcely able to restrain his laughter when Mr. Darcy announced that upon reflection, he had concluded that he did indeed have an obligation to visit with his betrothed that day.

***

At a quarter to one o'clock, Mr. Darcy, Georgiana, Colonel Fitzwilliam and Mr. Bingley made ready to depart. Miss Bingley had evidently had her fill of being left alone at Netherfield, as she now indicated a desire to visit Longbourn.

Her brother scowled at her. "Hear me well, Caroline; if you are insulting in any way to any member of that family, I will put you in the carriage directly and have you returned to Netherfield."

"I cannot imagine what you are on about, Charles; I have never been rude to anyone in my entire life."

Georgiana had to turn away, lest her expression be seen by her hostess.

There was no conversation in the carriage as it trundled the three miles to Longbourn. Upon their arrival, Mr. Darcy exited first, extending a hand to his sister. Before Georgiana could move, Caroline Bingley reached over, grasped Darcy's extended hand and leaned upon it heavily as she stepped down. "I thank you, Mr. Darcy," she fluttered.

Mr. Darcy looked at her in some exasperation, thinking again how fortunate it was that it had not been Miss Bingley pinned beneath him at the assembly, and then helped his sister out.

The five of them soon found themselves in the Bennet parlour. The Gardiners were present, but the younger sisters were absent.

Another young lady was present, one Mr. Darcy had not met. She was introduced to everyone as Miss Lucas; she and Miss Elizabeth were evidently the best of friends.

Colonel Fitzwilliam sat beside Miss Lucas, thinking that she looked sensible. "Miss Lucas, may I ask what you think of your friend's upcoming marriage?"

Miss Lucas looked at him levelly. There was no eye fluttering or giggling or the like; she spoke calmly, saying, "I think her fortunate that Mr. Darcy is doing the honourable thing by marrying her. The situation might have been far, far worse for her."

"But what of my cousin? Is he fortunate as well?"

"He is far more fortunate than he knows, Colonel. Elizabeth Bennet is not only lovely and accomplished, but she is also well-read, witty and highly intelligent. She will make an excellent wife, mother and mistress of the estate. If your cousin had to select one young lady in that room to collapse upon, he could not have selected better."

"That is an enthusiastic recommendation, indeed, Miss Lucas."

"It is not false praise, Colonel; I mean every word of it."

"I am heartened to hear it. Darcy and I are cousins by blood, but we are truly more like brothers. I do like what I see of your friend."

Mrs. Bennet was gratified to find that Miss Bingley, unlike the groom, was deeply interested in her plans for the wedding; but alas, all too soon she discovered that Miss Bingley's interest existed only to find fault.

Upon hearing that the parson was delighted at the opportunity to conduct a marriage ceremony for a young lady he had known since she was born, Miss Bingley said, "Do you mean to say that it will be the parson who will conduct the ceremony, and not his Bishop? For my dear friend, Mrs. Anderson, was married by a Bishop, and she assures me that no less a personage will do for any person of consequence."

Upon hearing that Miss Elizabeth would be married in her favorite day dress, she said, "Do you mean to say that a new dress was not purchased for the event? I should think it a sorry thing indeed, not to have a special dress made for my own wedding."

Upon hearing that the wedding breakfast would consist of two kinds of hot rolls, tongue, ham, eggs, as well as tea, coffee, chocolate and a wedding cake, she said, "It seems a paltry affair, but I suspect it will do well enough for a country wedding."

Mr. Darcy looked at Mr. Bingley expectantly, hoping he would be true to his word and send his sister back to Netherfield. Instead, the man only winced and murmured, "Caroline!"

Miss Bingley ignored her brother. She now launched into a long description of a society wedding she had attended the previous year, ending with, "But I suppose one cannot hope for such elegance here in the country!"

Georgiana was astonished at Miss Bingley's bad manners, and did not want to hear more. She turned to her new sister, asking, "Might I see your dress, Lizzy? Or is it bad luck?"

Elizabeth answered readily, "I think it is only bad luck if your brother sees it, but I am no expert on such superstitions. You are welcome to do so. Charlotte, you have seen it, of course, but do you want to join us?"

"Oh! No, Eliza, I am enjoying my conversation with the Colonel."

Elizabeth and Georgiana excused themselves, and went upstairs. Elizabeth took the dress out of her closet and laid it upon the bed for Georgiana's inspection.

"It is so pretty, Lizzy!"

"I think so as well; I suppose I could have asked for a new dress, as Mama would have been happy to accommodate me, but I thought this was good enough, considering…"

"Considering! Why, Lizzy, you are as bad as my brother!"

"What do you mean?"

"It is as if the two of you think that the wedding is unimportant, unworthy of attention, because of – well, I do not know how to put it, exactly!"

"Because we are being forced to marry, do you mean?"

Georgiana blushed. "I do not know a nice way to say that, Lizzy."

"I imagine there is no nice way, as it is not a nice thing!" Elizabeth spoke hotly.

Georgiana was now quite distressed. "I am sorry, I have upset you." She sounded as if she were in tears.

"Oh, Georgiana, please, please, do not cry. You are not at fault. I *am* upset, I suppose, though I thought I had recovered myself."

"I would not want to have to marry a stranger; I can imagine how that might feel," poor Georgiana offered.

"It has nothing to do with your brother; it is simply the idea of it. I always thought I would marry someone that I cared for, someone I respected, someone I had affection for. But because of a *stupid* feather in someone's *stupid* turban, that cannot happen. Instead, I am marrying the man who fell on top of me. It is unfathomable."

"If it makes you feel any better, Miss Bingley, the owner of the fateful feather, is even more upset than you are, as she hoped to marry my brother herself."

Elizabeth stared at Georgiana, and then began to laugh. She threw her head back, and laughed long and hard, wrapping her arms around her injured ribs. When she finally recovered herself, she said, "Georgiana, of all the things that people have said to me to try to make me feel better about my situation, *that* is the best. I did not know that about Miss Bingley. The fateful feather, indeed, what a wonderful phrase!"

Georgiana was flushed with elation; she had made Lizzy feel better! But she was not yet done. "Lizzy, the point is that this is still your wedding and his wedding. It is an important event for both of you, no matter how it came to be. Do you not see that?"

Elizabeth shook her head. "I do understand your point, Georgiana; but there is an important component missing."

"Affection?"

"Yes; if a couple have affection for one another, they count the days until they can be together. Do you not see that in my case, this wedding means that I will leave my family and friends behind, and journey off with a complete stranger?"

"I do see that, yes; but it is still an important event," the younger girl insisted.

"It is, yes, but one that might be dreaded, rather than anticipated. But, dear Georgiana, I am not dreading it as much as I was, and I have you to thank for that."

"Because I told you that he is a good man?"

"No; because you will be there with me."

Georgiana blushed. "I am so glad, Lizzy. I always wanted a sister, as I told you, but I never imagined she would be as wonderful as you."

"Allow me to return the compliment. When I was told that I had to marry Mr. Darcy, the only thing that gave me comfort was knowing that he had a younger sister who lived with him. I have had sisters all my life, and could not imagine living without them. And you, Georgiana, are a far better sister than I had imagined."

"What did you imagine?"

"Honestly? I was worried that Mr. Darcy's sister would be a bit like Miss Bingley."

"Proud, you mean?"

"Yes; your brother appears to be rather proud, if you will forgive my saying so, and I was concerned that you would be as well."

"I do not think I am," Georgiana said, quite seriously.

"No, indeed; in fact, my father teased me yesterday, saying that while I would miss Jane, having you as a sister would compensate me for the loss of my three younger sisters."

"That is a fine compliment, indeed!" Georgiana blushed in delight.

"Yes, and from a man who does not give them often, let me assure you. Well, back to the dress. It will do, will it not?"

"Yes; will you carry flowers?"

"I thought a bouquet of white flowers."

"Perfect. Who is standing up with you? Oh, Miss Bennet, of course."

"Yes, of course. That has been our plan for the past twenty years."

"You would have me believe that you and she discussed this from the moment of your birth?"

"I see that I must watch my tendency to exaggerate when in your company; very well, then, the past ten years."

"*That* I readily believe."

"Tell me, is it true that there is an enormous library at Pemberley?"

"Oh! It is two stories tall, and every wall is lined with books! There is a huge fireplace, and tables and chairs; it is quite magical, truly. Do you enjoy reading, Lizzy?"

"It is my favorite thing in all the world."

"That is what my brother says as well," Georgiana said, sounding satisfied. "The two of you have that in common, at any rate."

***

Returning to the parlour, Elizabeth had the satisfaction of seeing Jane and Mr. Bingley sitting together on a sofa, their heads together. She herself would be denied the joy of marrying for love, but it looked as if Jane would have her dream realised.

Mr. Darcy was looking out the window; with Georgiana absent and Colonel Fitzwilliam engaged by Miss Lucas, he had no interest in speaking with anyone present. He looked up as his sister entered the room. "Are you ready to leave, Georgiana?"

Elizabeth stared at him in amazement. They were to be marred the next day, and he would not even look at her? Her repressed fury suddenly getting the better of her, she marched up to him and curtsied. "Hello, Mr. Darcy. My name is Elizabeth Bennet. I understand we are to be married tomorrow morning, so I thought I may as well introduce myself."

Mr. Darcy was completely taken aback. He stared at Elizabeth. Then he looked to his sister, hoping for assistance, but Georgiana had begun to laugh.

"No, no, Mr. Darcy; I beg you to attend me," Elizabeth chastised him, sharply. His eyes snapped back to her face. "I plan to wear a green dress; I mention this so that you might recognise me. What will you wear, sir, so that I might recognise you?"

His mind went blank. After a moment, Bingley stood up and spoke, laughter in his voice. "Miss Elizabeth, I believe Mr. Darcy will be dressed in black. What colour will his waistcoat be, Miss Darcy?"

"I imagine he will wear a grey waistcoat; I believe that is the one his valet packed for the occasion," Georgiana replied, promptly.

"There you are, Miss Elizabeth; he will wear a grey waistcoat. And his cravat will be very finely tied, of that you may be certain. It is by these signs that you may recognize your future husband," Mr. Bingley told her.

"Yes, I noticed the skill of his valet when his cravat was all but stuffed into my mouth," Elizabeth said, dryly. "Very well; I will look forward to seeing you, your grey waistcoat and your finely tied cravat in the morning, sir." With that, she curtsied, whirled around and left the room.

There was a moment of stunned silence and then the entire room, with the notable exception of Mr. Darcy, erupted in laughter. Mr. Darcy, once again, felt utterly befuddled.

***

That night, the Bennet family had their evening repast as a family for the last time. Mr. Bennet was seen to wipe a tear from his eye more than once. Mrs. Bennet chattered on about how wealthy her new son was. Mary had much to say on the sanctity of marriage according to the Reverend Fordyce. Kitty and Lydia now understood that their new brother had a house in Town and were begging to be invited to visit. Jane attempted to comfort Elizabeth, squeezing her hand and telling her that all would be well.

***

After dinner, Mrs. Bennet asked Elizabeth to come into her room. "What is it, Mama? I am quite weary."

"I must speak with you, child." She sounded quite determined.

"What about?"

"Things you must know before you are married."

"Oh." Elizabeth had friends in Meryton who had married, and they had all said the same thing: their mother had had "The Talk" with them the night before the wedding. They spoke of their embarrassment, as well as the mother's embarrassment, but all agreed it was important.

Fifteen minutes later, both Elizabeth and her mother were red-faced and relieved it was over. Elizabeth left her mother's room, shaking her head in horror, muttering, "I will never do that, not with him and not with anyone."

She encountered her Aunt Gardiner in the hallway. "I presume you had a particular talk with your mother?" her aunt inquired.

"I did, and I am not anxious to repeat the experience. I beg you to excuse me, Aunt."

"That is what I expected you would say. May I not have five minutes of your time?"

Elizabeth sighed, but saw that her aunt was determined to have her say. They went to Elizabeth's room. "Jane, will you allow us a few minutes of privacy?" Mrs. Gardiner asked.

"Of course!" Jane immediately rose and departed.

"Now I want you to forget everything your mother told you, and listen. Elizabeth, you are an intelligent and sensible woman, and you live on a farm. Surely you had some notion of the basics already, did you not?"

Elizabeth looked at her aunt in astonishment. "No, indeed, for I could not believe that people were required to behave like animals!"

"Let me tell you that when you are engaging in such activities with a man for whom you have affection, it is a completely different experience," Aunt Gardiner told her. "It is an essential part of a successful marriage, for it binds two people together in a way that cannot be achieved in any other manner. I hope and pray that Mr. Darcy gives you ample time to learn to feel affection for him before requiring you to share his bed, but in any case, I tell you that this is something to look forward to, not something to dread."

Elizabeth thought about it. Finally she said, "I find this difficult to credit, Aunt, but I know you would not misadvise me. I will remember your words and try to keep an open mind."

"That is all I ask," her aunt said. "I hope that you will write to me and tell me how you get on."

"I shall, of course."

"One last thing; has he told you anything about Pemberley?"

"His estate? No, not a word. I do know that you are from Derbyshire, Aunt; have you seen Pemberley?"

Her aunt threw her head back and laughed. "Oh, Elizabeth! What a surprise is in store for you!" Still laughing, her aunt hugged her, kissed her forehead, and left.

Elizabeth did not expect to sleep much that night, and that expectation was certainly realised.

Chapter Seventeen

The next morning, Elizabeth was awakened by Jane. Elizabeth looked at her sister blankly for a moment, until realisation sank in. "No," Elizabeth said, firmly, and rolled over.

"Yes," Jane insisted. "Lizzy, it is six o'clock; we must get you ready."

"I have changed my mind," Elizabeth said. Her voice was muffled, as she had now put the pillow over her head.

"I cannot blame you, particularly after his poor behaviour yesterday, but you know there is no choice."

"You go in my place, Jane; as long as you wear a green dress, he will not know the difference."

"I think not; he may not know the difference, but his sister will."

"Oh! Georgiana! Is she not a lovely creature?"

"She is, indeed, and she will be disappointed if you are not at the church on time."

At that moment, Mrs. Bennet threw open the door and walked in. "Lizzy! How is it that you are still abed? Get up at once!" She

MISUNDERSTANDINGS

marched to Elizabeth's bed and threw off the covers. "Up! Up! Up!"

Elizabeth groaned. "I can dress in thirty minutes; there is no need for me to be awakened so early."

"Lizzy, you know you will need to be bathed first, and Lucy must do your hair."

Grumbling, Elizabeth crawled out of her bed slowly. She allowed Jane to lead her to the bath; Lucy had already filled it with warm water. Her hair was washed, dried and brushed out.

"Am I permitted breakfast?" the reluctant bride demanded. "I should eat before I am dressed, should I not?"

"You should, yes; and here is Mrs. Hill with a tray for you." Indeed, the Bennet's long-time housekeeper stood in the doorway, beaming from ear to ear, with a tray in hand.

"I thank you, Mrs. Hill," Elizabeth said. Then she muttered, "I am glad to see that someone is happy today."

Her mother overheard her, and said, "Oh, I am happy as well, Lizzy!"

"One daughter married, four more to go? Is that it?" Elizabeth demanded.

"Yes, that is it exactly. Jane will not be far behind you; Mr. Bingley is bound to offer for her soon."

Finally, Elizabeth was deemed ready. Mrs. Bennet had decreed that Kitty and Lydia would walk to the church so that Elizabeth's dress would not be crushed in the carriage. Both younger girls had set up a howl, but Mrs. Bennet had stood firm, and so Kitty and Lydia had set off on foot thirty minutes earlier.

***

Elizabeth arrived at the church at precisely ten o'clock. Her mother and younger sisters were already inside; she remained outside with Jane and her father. Jane would enter the church first and walk to the altar; then Elizabeth would enter the church on her father's arm.

Jane hugged her sister, whispered "Lizzy, I love you!" and entered the church.

"Papa," Elizabeth whispered, clutching Mr. Bennet's arm in panic. "Papa, are you certain? There is no other way?"

"I am quite certain, Lizzy," he whispered in return. "But I am now equally certain that you will be happy with him."

A tear slipped down her face. "Papa…oh, Papa! I shall miss you so!"

"My dearest daughter, there are not enough words in the entire world for me to tell you how very, very much I shall miss you!" And with that, he wiped a tear from his eye and walked his favorite daughter into the church.

Chapter Eighteen

Mr. Darcy had also awakened at six o'clock in the morning. His valet had drawn him a bath and had laid out his clothing. Mr. Darcy was dressed and ready by eight o'clock. He went downstairs to Netherfield's breakfast room; Georgiana and Mr. Bingley were already there.

"Good morning, Georgiana, Bingley."

"Good morning, Brother!" Georgiana sang out, joyfully. "I see you are wearing the grey waistcoat, as I predicted!"

Mr. Darcy glanced down at his clothing; he had not thought to notice what Carstairs had laid out for him. He walked to the buffet and began to fill his plate.

"Are you nervous, Darcy?" Mr. Bingley asked.

"Nervous? Why would I be nervous?" Mr. Darcy was puzzled.

"Truly, man, I begin to believe that you have ice water in your veins! I would be too nervous to eat!" Mr. Bingley exclaimed.

"There is nothing to be nervous about; the whole thing will take thirty minutes. We will be forced to mingle with her relatives and friends at the breakfast, and as soon as may be, we will be on our way back to Pemberley. You are packed up, Georgiana, are you not? Richard?"

His sister assured him that her trunks were already strapped onto the servants' carriage and she was ready to depart. Colonel Fitzwilliam scoffed at him; as a soldier, he was always ready to depart.

***

The party from Netherfield was at the church at a quarter to ten. The front row had been reserved for family, so Georgiana was able to sit close to the altar.

Mr. Bingley and Mr. Darcy stood at the altar, waiting. Mr. Darcy noted that the church was quite full; he wondered idly if it was this full for all weddings in the area or if his bride was a particular favourite of the neighbourhood.

Mr. Darcy pulled out his pocket watch every few minutes; where was she? He wanted this to be over with. Mr. Bingley finally whispered, "Darcy, it is not yet ten. Put the watch away."

Finally the church door opened and Jane Bennet walked in. Mr. Bingley's eyes lit up and he took a deep breath. Mr. Darcy thought dourly that Mr. Bingley was doubtless now imagining that Miss Bennet was coming to the altar to marry him. Heavens, Bingley should propose to the chit and get it over with.

As soon as Jane stepped up to the altar, smiling beatifically at Mr. Bingley and Mr. Darcy, the door opened again and Miss Elizabeth walked in on her father's arm. Mr. Darcy noted that she was wearing a green dress. She stepped up to the altar, released her father's arm, and stood beside Mr. Darcy.

"You had no trouble recognising me, I collect?" he whispered.

"None at all; Georgiana's hint about the grey waistcoat was most helpful," she replied, staring straight ahead.

The parson cleared his throat and began.

Chapter Nineteen

Elizabeth retained no memory at all of the wedding service. She could remember walking up the aisle on her father's arm and she could remember walking back down on Mr. Darcy's arm. But everything in between those two events was forever a complete blank.

She was handed in to the Darcy carriage and taken back to Longbourn for the wedding breakfast. As they pulled up to the entryway of her home, her husband – husband! – cleared his throat and said, "I plan for us to leave for Pemberley as soon as possible; please do not delay."

Elizabeth looked at him in surprise. "This is my last opportunity to farewell my friends and family. You expect me to watch the clock as I do so?"

He looked at her sternly. "It is a three-day journey; we must make haste."

Her eyebrows drew down. "If it is a three-day journey, an extra hour or two should not much matter."

They stared at one another for a long minute, neither ready to back down at this first hurdle. It was Georgiana who broke the stalemate, saying, "Brother, I would be happy to help make up the lost time by rising an hour earlier each day that we travel. Elizabeth is certainly entitled to make her farewells to the people she has known her entire life, is she not?"

Unwilling to admit that he had been unreasonable, Mr. Darcy did not reply, turning his head to look out the window. Understanding that this was a tacit consent for Elizabeth to enjoy her wedding breakfast, Georgiana nudged her new sister and nodded at her. Elizabeth nodded back and mouthed the words "Thank you!"

As soon as they entered Longbourn, Elizabeth was swallowed up by the crowd. From what he could hear, Mr. Darcy soon discovered that his wife – wife! – was indeed a favourite in the neighbourhood. Miss Bennet stood beside her as men, women and children all crowded around Elizabeth, wishing her well, begging her to come back and visit as soon as may be, and thanking her for many past kindnesses.

Georgiana was able to make her way to Elizabeth's side and Elizabeth promptly reached out an arm to pull her close. Standing with Miss Bennet on one side and Georgiana on the other, Mr. Darcy admitted, albeit reluctantly, that Elizabeth was already treating Georgiana as a cherished sister. He could *almost* feel grateful to her for that.

"Darcy! There you are!" He turned to find Bingley beside him, grinning from ear to ear. "She is very pretty, Darcy; you must at least see that. Not as pretty as her elder sister, of course, but nonetheless quite attractive."

"I suppose so."

"You suppose so? Good Lord, man, have you even taken a proper look at her?"

He had not, Mr. Darcy confessed to himself. So he turned his head to look at Elizabeth. She was not tall; Georgiana was a full three inches taller. Her hair was brown, an ordinary colour, he thought. Just brown. Her eyes, he knew, were brown. Everything was brown, he thought, in some disgust. But hold; her skin was fair, with that sprinkle of freckles on her nose that he had noted earlier. The freckles spoke of time spent outdoors. Now she threw her head back to laugh, and her entire countenance lit up.

But Mr. Darcy refused to admit to any merits in his bride. "She is tolerable, I suppose."

"Tolerable! I would not be as fastidious as you are for a kingdom, Darcy."

Mr. Darcy scowled at him.

Mr. Darcy had not noticed Miss Bingley at the wedding, but she was now approaching him as he spoke with her brother. She said, dolefully, "Oh, Mr. Darcy, what an unhappy day this is."

He felt, perversely, that he must disagree with her. "Is it, Miss Bingley? Why is that?"

"Caroline," Bingley said, warningly.

Miss Bingley ignored her brother. "You are being forced to wed an insignificant country girl against your will. Is that not a reason for gloom?"

Mr. Bingley said, angrily, "And do we not recall whose fault this is, Caroline?"

Mr. Darcy said, "Oh, no fault need be assigned. As my sister often reminds me, it might have been much worse."

Miss Bingley said, "Oh? And how might it have been worse?"

Mr. Darcy opened his mouth, ready to say that it would have been worse if he had fallen *forward*, onto Miss Bingley, rather than *backward*, onto Miss Elizabeth, but he was too much the gentleman to do so. Instead, he closed his mouth and turned away from her.

Elizabeth found herself standing between her two sisters; Jane, who had been her dearest companion her entire life, and Georgiana, her new sister, the one ray of light in what appeared to be a dark future. Everyone Elizabeth knew was in the room, or so it seemed. The Longs, the Gouldings, the Sampsons, the Butlers – everyone was there, everyone had memories to share and blessings to give.

Charlotte, of course, hugged her and extracted a promise of a most regular correspondence.

Meanwhile, Mr. and Mrs. Gardiner approached Mr. Darcy and asked for a word in private. Mr. Darcy, remembering his pleasant conversation with the lady in the Bennet parlour, managed to control his first instinct to refuse, and instead consented.

Mr. Gardiner began, "Elizabeth is special, Mr. Darcy. You have no notion of it yet, of course, but you could not have been more fortunate."

Mr. Darcy looked at the man, skeptically. "I understand that you are fond of your niece, sir."

"No, no, this is not question of fondness. I ask that you take time to get to know her, to appreciate her special qualities, and not write her off as an unanticipated nuisance."

Mrs. Gardiner now added, "Yes, that is it exactly. You are your parents' son; I know you to be a man of honour. Take time to know her and give her time to know you. Be gentle with her."

Mr. Darcy promised, as solemnly as he felt able, to do as they bid. With that, they released him, and it was with a sigh of relief that he rejoined the party. After what seemed to him to be an eternity, the crowd began to thin out. Georgiana appeared beside him, saying, "Lizzy gave orders to the footmen to have her trunks strapped to the carriage; it will not be long now, Brother. I am certain we did right to let her have this time to make her farewells."

And indeed, not thirty minutes later, Mr. Darcy, Georgiana, Colonel Fitzwilliam and Elizabeth stood in the parlour with the Bennets and the Gardiners. Amid tears, hugs, kisses and repeated demands for letters, they were in their carriage and pulling away from Longbourn, Georgiana and Elizabeth on one bench of the carriage; Mr. Darcy and Colonel Fitzwilliam on the other.

Chapter Twenty

Mr. Darcy now discovered the wisdom of having Georgiana and his cousin with him; if it been just he and Elizabeth in the carriage, the silence would have been oppressive. But the animated – and, he admitted, rather entertaining – conversation between his companions made the journey far more bearable.

Georgiana had, she told Elizabeth, never been to a nicer wedding. Mr. Darcy could not recall that his sister had *ever* attended a wedding, but Elizabeth could not know that.

Colonel Fitzwilliam said that he thought the wedding breakfast sumptuous; Mrs. Bennet was clearly a consummate hostess. Elizabeth allowed that her mother had a reputation as such, and had felt that the first wedding in the family deserved all the attention she might bestow.

"The wedding cake was delicious; I have never tasted better!" Georgiana added.

Elizabeth smiled widely. "I will pass on your compliments in my first letter home; Mama will be delighted, I assure you, and will read your comments aloud to anyone who might be prevailed upon to listen."

"Your sister, Miss Bennet, is beautiful. She must have many admirers," the Colonel commented.

"Truly, Colonel, she is lovely both inside and out; the gentleman who succeeds in winning her heart will be fortunate."

"Mr. Bingley hopes to be that gentleman, I believe," Georgiana said, slyly. "Does she favor his suit?'

"I think she does; but he must do something about that sister of his."

"She is dreadful!"

"She is, yes, and I would not like to see Jane forced to live with her."

"I think it reasonable for a new bride to arrange her household to her liking," Colonel Fitzwilliam added.

"I think so as well, Colonel. We will be kept abreast of events, as Jane is an excellent correspondent."

The Colonel begged Elizabeth to address him as Richard, saying, "We are cousins now, you know."

"And I am Elizabeth, or Lizzy."

"Brother, when will we stop?" Georgiana addressed Mr. Darcy, who had remained silent.

"I thought to drive on until we stop for the evening, so perhaps five hours. If you need a break before, though, there is an inn about two hours from here."

"Yes, please; five hours is far too long."

Mr. Darcy leaned his head out the window to give the coachman directions. Elizabeth threw Georgiana a grateful look. Five hours! She would certainly need to stop before then.

There was silence, as both Georgiana and Colonel Fitzwilliam tried to think of a way to force Mr. Darcy to speak to his new wife.

"Brother, will you not tell Elizabeth about Pemberley?" Mr. Darcy's estate was his favorite subject; if this did not work, there was no hope.

Mr. Darcy turned to his sister; the look on his face told her that he knew what she was about. Elizabeth was not helping matters, Georgiana thought; her new sister had turned away, looking at the scenery.

"You recall that I told you there was a library, do you not, Lizzy?" Georgiana asked.

"I do, yes," Elizabeth said, turning back to Georgiana with a light in her eyes.

"What do you enjoy reading?" Georgiana asked.

"Oh! Almost anything!"

"Really," Mr. Darcy said, caustically. "Animal husbandry?" There; that would teach her to mind her speech.

"Indeed, yes; my father and I have had many discussions as to the best breed of pig for the tenant farms, and we both did a good deal of reading before making a decision."

"And what did you decide?" Mr. Darcy asked, certain that she was making this up out of whole cloth.

"We have been working on crossing our Cumberland pigs with Yorkshire Whites. I think it will be a successful cross," Elizabeth replied.

Mr. Darcy opened his mouth and then closed it again. The Colonel, seeing Mr. Darcy's expression, laughed at him. "You did not believe her, Cousin!"

Elizabeth continued, "Frankly, though, I only read such books in order to converse with my father about the estate, as he has no son with whom to share his endeavors. I prefer classic literature and poetry."

Georgiana asked, "Have you a favorite poet?"

"Oh! Cowper, to be sure. Also Coleridge and Wordsworth. Shakespeare, of course, must be on anyone's list of favourites."

"Do you read novels?" Mr. Darcy asked, finding himself drawn into the conversation, despite himself.

"Oh, yes. I am no literary snob; I will read a gory and terrifying Gothic novel with the greatest pleasure. Are there any such novels in this famed library of yours?"

Mr. Darcy replied, "There are, at Georgiana's insistence, though it must be confessed that my mother enjoyed novels as well."

"I will look forward to reading them." Feeling now that she should offer some conversation in return, she asked after Mr. Darcy's literary preferences.

He answered, perversely, "I do not have a good deal of time to read for pleasure."

Georgiana added, "It is true that Brother works very hard."

Elizabeth nodded, saying, "Papa often says that the estate requires more hours from him than he would like; he would prefer to spend all his time with his books."

Mr. Darcy remained silent, indignation swelling in his breast. How could she compare Longbourn, a tiny, insignificant estate, with Pemberley! Then he remembered that she had not seen Pemberley, nor had it been described to her. Her experience was limited to her family estate. He supposed he should be grateful that she was a gentleman's daughter. What if his fall at the assembly had been broken by a shopkeeper's daughter? He shook his head; it did not bear thinking about.

"Brother?" Georgiana looked at him with concern.

"No; it is nothing."

"Very well. Lizzy, I have never asked – do you play?"

"A little, yes. I am not as diligent as I should be when it comes to practicing. I would almost always prefer to be out of doors."

That explained the freckles, Mr. Darcy thought. He glanced her way. It was only a light sprinkling, as he had noticed before. Caroline Bingley would never have permitted freckles to appear on her face, which should doubtless be viewed as a recommendation for freckles.

"And you, Georgiana? Do you play?"

"Oh! Music is my passion," Georgiana replied, fervently.

"I cannot wait to hear you!"

"Will you play duets with me?"

"I do not think my skill will do the duets any credit, but I am willing to try."

"That would be wonderful!" Georgiana gave a great yawn. "Oh! My apologies. I am rather drowsy; carriage rides always put me right to sleep. Lizzy, may I lean my head on your shoulder?"

"Of course," Elizabeth answered, promptly, smiling fondly at her.

Georgiana closed her eyes, leaned her head on her new sister's shoulder, and was soon asleep.

Chapter Twenty-One

With Georgiana asleep, Colonel Fitzwilliam and Elizabeth conversed in a low tone. Mr. Darcy took out a book and began to read.

Elizabeth looked at his book with interest. Seeing her eyes on the volume, Mr. Darcy asked, "Did you not bring a book?"

"Alas, I cannot read in a carriage; the motion makes me ill."

"That is unfortunate," he replied, his eyes already back on his book.

"Indeed." She returned her attention to Colonel Fitzwilliam, asking about his military career, but soon began to wish rather desperately for the promised stop. She was grateful to hear Mr. Darcy say, "Ah, here we are," as the carriage was drawn to a halt.

Mr. Darcy reached through the window to open the door; he helped Georgiana out first. Then he extended a hand to Elizabeth. She took it. Her grip was firm, her flesh soft and warm. He did not immediately release her hand, as he had expected to do; instead he found himself holding onto it and raising his eyes to hers. There was a brief moment when time stopped. Shaken, he dropped her hand and turned to his sister, feeling disturbed by the encounter. "Come, let us go inside."

Elizabeth was also disturbed by their brief contact. For an instant, she felt a connection to this man, despite his manner toward her and her continued unwillingness to be his wife. She shook it off and followed Mr. Darcy, Colonel Fitzwilliam and Georgiana into the inn.

Some twenty minutes later, refreshed, the journey was resumed. "We will stop for dinner?" Elizabeth asked.

"Yes; in Bedford. Georgiana, Richard, you recall the inn we stayed on there, do you not?'

"The White Stag? Yes; it was comfortable, as inns go," Colonel Fitzwilliam allowed.

"I have never stayed at an inn," Elizabeth confessed.

Her companions turned to her in surprise. Noting their expressions, she explained, "I have never been further from home than London, and of course there is no need to stay at an inn in the course of so brief a journey. Tell me what I might expect."

Georgiana wrinkled her nose. "Noisy, of course; that is always the case. But Brother often journeys to visit his other estates, so he is a proficient traveler. Any place he selects for us will be clean, comfortable, and offer good food."

Mr. Darcy felt compelled to explain. He produced a small black leather book from a compartment in the carriage. "I write down my experiences; if an inn is dirty or the food is unsatisfactory, I make a note of it so that I do not visit it again."

Colonel Fitzwilliam began to chuckle as Elizabeth held out a hand. "May I?"

He passed it to her. She opened it and found, in impeccable handwriting, a list of inns he had stayed at, the date of his visit, the proprietor's name, and a summary of what he had found. She read aloud, "*Soup good, pudding a disappointment. Bed clean but hard.*" She raised her eyes to his and said, "Truly, I do not quite know if I should be impressed or concerned by such attention to detail. But it will evidently operate in our favour."

He took It back from her and flipped through the pages, then handed It back to her. She saw the page before her was titled 'Bedford.' Skimming down the page, she came to '*The White Stag. Food good, beds soft and clean. Proprietor is Josiah Whitlow. Allows reservations in advance.*'

"Darcy has his uses, you must admit, Elizabeth!" the Colonel laughed.

She agreed, and asked, "So you have made a reservation, and Mr. Whitlow is expecting us?"

"Exactly. I have reserved three rooms for the four of us, as well as rooms for the servants; they are likely already there, as they left before we did."

Three rooms for the four of them! Was he expecting to sleep with her that night?! Elizabeth's eyes widened and she forgot to breathe.

Mr. Darcy noticed her odd reaction and, after a moment's thought, arrived at the correct conclusion. Hoping to reassure her on that score, he said, "You do not mind sleeping with Georgiana, I trust?"

"Oh! No! Not at all! Indeed, I almost never sleep alone, as Jane and I have always shared a bed!" She was almost giddy with relief.

Mr. Darcy saw her relief. It was not to be wondered at, he thought, after some consideration. Surely she knew that at some point they would share a bed, though doubtless she hoped the event would not take place at an inn. As he thought further on the matter, he realised that she might know nothing whatever about what would happen between them. He had always assumed that young ladies were told what to expect by their mothers. Would Mrs. Bennet have had this conversation with Elizabeth? Or would she not, as such a talk would doubtless be an unpleasant chore? He rubbed his face with his hand, feeling – what was that word again? Yes – befuddled.

Chapter Twenty-Two

The inn was, as promised, clean and comfortable. Sharing a room was an unexceptionable event for Elizabeth, but a new experience for Georgiana; as a result, she was quite excited. Their trunks were brought up, and both were happy to change into clean dresses for dinner.

As Elizabeth helped Georgiana with her dress, she asked, "Does your maid usually travel with you to help you?"

"Yes; but with you to help me, I have told her to not bother with me. I do not doubt that she is enjoying a rest from my demands."

"I cannot imagine that you are a demanding mistress, Georgiana."

"I try not to be, but – oh! We shall have to get you a maid! Mrs. Reynolds will know who will suit."

"Who is Mrs. Reynolds?"

"The housekeeper at Pemberley. She is more a member of the family than a servant, and has been with us for my entire life. Brother's as well. She was all set to hate you when she had heard there was a compromise, but Brother explained what had happened, and now she hates Miss Bingley instead. Which I think she did before all this, anyway."

Elizabeth began to laugh. "Your brother described you to me as young and shy. Young you are, but shy? Has he another sister somewhere, and it is that sister he was describing?"

Georgiana blushed. "I am talking too much."

"Not at all; I adore it! I am merely curious how it is that he does not appear to know you."

"I *am* shy, truly. I have always been so. But there is something about you, Lizzy, that makes me happy. And evidently when I am happy, I start chattering! I had not known that about myself until now."

"Well, chatter away! So Miss Bingley has been to Pemberley, has she? She must have done so if Mrs. Reynolds hates her."

"Well, Miss Bingley has never really been invited, but she always comes if Mr. Bingley comes. We have not been able to stop her without being rude. Everyone at Pemberley has been very much afraid that Brother would marry her, which would only happen if he was compromised, as he does not care for her. Brother has always been afraid of a compromise; his valet sleeps in his room with him when Miss Bingley is about."

"And now he has been compromised by Miss Bingley's fateful feather. It sounds like something out of a farce, does it not?"

"It does, but I am so, so glad that it is you and not Miss Bingley!" Georgiana's voice was fervent.

Elizabeth could not very well say that she rather wished it *had* been Miss Bingley, so she said nothing. There was a tap on the door, and they heard Mr. Darcy's voice saying that dinner was ready for them.

***

Elizabeth had to admit that Mr. Darcy's little black book had proven useful, as the meal served to them was delicious. Georgiana spoke a good deal about their cook at Pemberley, and what particular delicacies Elizabeth could look forward to. Colonel Fitzwilliam joined in praising the Pemberley cook; Elizabeth tried to respond as was expected, but it was becoming wearying, particularly as Mr. Darcy remained silent throughout the meal.

When dinner was over, the Colonel relaxed over a glass of brandy as Mr. Darcy escorted his sister and Elizabeth back upstairs to their room, bowed at the door, and left them. As the two ladies helped each other prepare for bed, Georgiana was unexpectedly silent. After the candle had been extinguished, she whispered, "Lizzy?"

"Yes?"

"I think you are in pain; I saw you wincing at dinner."

"I am a bit, but there is nothing to be done for it."

After a short pause, Georgiana spoke again. "Lizzy?"

"Yes, Georgiana?"

"Will you not at least make some effort to like my brother?"

Elizabeth was silent for a minute. Finally, she took a deep breath and exhaled loudly. "It is difficult, Georgiana. This is not how I imagined my life unfolding."

"I understand that, of course, but if you remain stubborn and unyielding, and he does the same, what sort of life will that be? Not only for you and for him, but also for me. Three unhappy, silent people at the breakfast table sounds rather dreadful."

"You are right, Georgiana. I shall request a breakfast tray in my room," Elizabeth said, hoping a little humour would lighten the conversation.

"That is not what I – oh, Lizzy, whatever shall we do?"

Elizabeth could not answer; she resolutely rolled over and shut her eyes.

***

Downstairs, Colonel Fitzwilliam berated his cousin. "Good Lord, Darcy, can you not make an effort to speak with her? She is a delightful young woman; have you any idea how lucky you are?"

Mr. Darcy shrugged. "She talks a good deal."

"Yes, we are all talking a good deal to try to compensate for your silence."

"I would just as soon have us all be silent!" Mr. Darcy whipped out.

His cousin stared at him.

"Richard, I was supposed to marry well! An heiress! Someone with a dowry and connections! What use is this simple country girl to me?"

"What *use*?" Colonel Fitzwilliam was incredulous. "Whatever are you talking about? To help you, to share your life, to bear your children, if you are so fortunate!"

Mr. Darcy shook his head and refused to speak another word.

Chapter Twenty-Three

The next morning, Elizabeth breakfasted with Colonel Fitzwilliam and the Darcys, while the servants carried their trunks down to the carriage. Colonel Fitzwilliam and Georgiana made every effort to speak with Elizabeth, but Mr. Darcy's sullen silence cast a pall upon the meal.

It was as Georgiana had feared; the young girl kept casting urgent glances at Elizabeth, silently urging her to 'make an effort,' as she had put it, but Elizabeth refused to meet her gaze.

Finally, Georgiana said, in exasperation, "Will the two of you not speak to one another?"

Her brother looked at her, displeasure clear on his face. Georgiana would generally have quailed before such a look, but today she would not back down. She stared back at him. Finally, he said, "Very well; Elizabeth, I trust you slept well?"

Without looking up, Elizabeth replied, "I did, though I am still in some pain from my ribs."

"I am sorry to hear it." Then silence.

Georgiana said, "Elizabeth, did you want to say anything?"

Both Elizabeth and Mr. Darcy scowled at her. Finally, Elizabeth said, "And you, Mr. Darcy? I hope you slept well?"

He replied, "I did," and turned his attention back to his eggs.

Georgiana thought that they were more alike than they knew, as they were both exceedingly stubborn. Unable to stop herself, she burst out, "Must you two be so obstinate?"

Without looking up, her brother murmured, "Let it be virtuous to be obstinate."

And without looking up, Elizabeth immediately murmured, "*Coriolanus*."

And they both looked up, stared at one another in surprise, coloured, and returned their attention to their plates.

Aha, Georgiana thought, exchanging a delighted glance with the Colonel. That is a beginning.

***

Once they were back in the carriage, Georgiana enquired as to where their next overnight stop would be. "Leicester? As we did on our way to Meryton?" she surmised.

"Yes," her brother replied. "We shall stop for luncheon, of course, and you must let me know, Georgiana, if you have need of any additional stops." He paused. "And Elizabeth, you as well."

Elizabeth inclined her head to show that she had heard him.

Georgiana said, "You are evidently quite familiar with Shakespeare, to be able to identify a quote so quickly, Lizzy."

"I admit to a fondness for *Coriolanus*, despite its almost oppressive length."

"I believe it is the second longest Shakespearean play," Mr. Darcy added, unable to resist a literary conversation.

"I think it is; only *Hamet* is longer," Elizabeth replied. "Though it must be admitted that *Hamlet* holds the reader's attention more readily."

"A ghost is bound to be more appealing than a collection of Roman politicians," Mr. Darcy agreed.

Georgiana was delighted. They were having an actual conversation! She did not want it to end. "Elizabeth, have you a favorite play?" she enquired.

"Oh! It would quite hard to pick a favorite, would it not? But if pressed, I would say *MacBeth* for the tragedies, *Much Ado About Nothing* for the comedies, and *Henry V* for the histories."

Georgiana saw her brother nodding. "Do you agree with her selections, Brother?" she asked.

"In part," he replied. "I would pick *Twelfth Night* over *Much Ado*."

Colonel Fitzwilliam added, "I am surprised not to find *Romeo and Juliet* on anyone's list of favorites. Is that not a popular play?"

"*Romeo and Juliet*! A play that teaches us that doom awaits those who marry against the advice of their elders? I think not." And with that, Elizabeth turned her head away and did not speak again until the carriage stopped for luncheon.

The Colonel and Georgiana rolled their eyes.

***

"Elizabeth, why will you not help this along?" Georgiana asked, when the two ladies withdrew to wash their faces before dining.

"Honestly, Georgiana? I do not know. You are right, of course; he and I must both find a way to make peace with our situation, or everyone around us will be made to feel our unhappiness. Perhaps it is too soon; remember, please, that I have just lost my family. Am I not to be permitted some time to accustom myself to that?"

"You have not lost them, Lizzy, and I do not doubt that when you begin receiving their letters, you will feel comforted. And you have a fine new family, with a lovely, beguiling, adoring little sister!"

Elizabeth could not help herself; she laughed delightedly at Georgiana's description of herself, and was still chuckling when the two ladies joined Mr. Darcy and Colonel Fitzwilliam at the table.

Mr. Darcy looked at his new wife with a raised eyebrow and a frown.

"Mr. Darcy, I apologise if my mirth is untoward; Georgiana has an unexpected streak of mischief in her character." She tried to compose herself, as evidently any signs of good humour were considered bad manners.

"Truly? I have never seen it," he replied, frowning, certain that he should disapprove of such a thing.

"Do not repeat my words, Lizzy; I will be mortified!" Georgiana begged, laughing.

"Well, you shall simply have to be mortified. Georgiana describes herself as lovely, beguiling and adoring!"

"She is all of those things," Colonel Fitzwilliam agreed.

"You are absolutely right," Elizabeth said. "And I am completely enchanted with her!"

Back in the carriage, Georgiana soon fell asleep with her head on her new sister's shoulder. The Colonel felt he had had his fill of trying to keep a conversation going, and so spent the hours watching the scenery. Mr. Darcy had his book out, but as no pages were turned, Elizabeth knew he could not be engrossed in it. She probably should engage him in conversation, but she could not bring herself to do so. Instead, she leaned against the side of the carriage and closed her eyes. She could not sleep, not with so many unhappy thoughts whirling around in her head, but at least pretending to do so meant she would not have to speak with him.

It was full dark when they arrived at his preferred inn at Leicester. This would be their final stop before entering Derbyshire. All four travelers were weary and climbed the stairs to their rooms in silence, until Mr. Darcy said, "I will let you all know when our dinner is ready."

Georgiana nodded, and went into the room she would share with Elizabeth. Elizabeth looked at Georgiana keenly, seeing that the situation was wearing on her. "I think you are taking too much upon yourself, Georgiana."

"What do you mean?"

"I know that traveling is tiring, even when accomplished in a carriage as comfortable as yours, but I believe you are suffering as much from the awkward silences in the carriage as from the rigors of travel."

"You are right," Georgiana said, shortly, not looked at her.

"It is not up to you to repair the situation, Georgiana. The burden falls to your brother and myself."

"And if I saw any willingness from either of you to take on that burden, I would gladly step away from it."

Elizabeth had no ready answer. Finally, she said, "Tomorrow we will arrive at Pemberley; I am certain that life will look quite a bit brighter."

And with that, Georgiana had to be content.

Chapter Twenty-Four

It was early afternoon on the third day when Mr. Darcy looked out the window and said, with much satisfaction, "We are now on Pemberley land."

Elizabeth looked out her own window; she saw a dense forest, but no house. "I do not see the house," she said. "Am I looking out the wrong window?"

Colonel Fitzwilliam chuckled; Mr. Darcy replied, "No; it will take some time before you can see the house."

About fifteen minutes later, Mr. Darcy rapped on the roof of the carriage. The coachman brought the carriage to a stop.

"This is the best view of the house, I think," he said, and he exited the carriage. Mr. Darcy knew he was trying to impress Elizabeth, hoping that she would understand what a 'catch' he was, and how fortunate she had been that he had come back to Meryton to marry her. He was not proud of himself for that, but he could not help himself.

Georgiana said, "Oh! It is, yes! Come, Lizzy, look." And with that, she took her brother's hand and climbed out. Elizabeth followed suit.

Elizabeth had always thought that the phrase 'took my breath away' was sheer hyperbole. Now she knew better, as the vista before her actually caused her to stop breathing for a moment. The house was still some distance off, but she could see that it was enormous, a full six stories tall! And it was not just big; it was perfectly situated on a small rise overlooking a large blue lake. She stood awestruck for a time, not moving, simply staring.

She gradually became aware that Mr. Darcy, Colonel Fitzwilliam and Georgiana were both watching her, evidently waiting for a response. "It is – well, it is rather large, is it not?"

They all laughed. "Yes, it is rather large," Mr. Darcy replied. Perhaps now she would understand why he had been so perturbed at having been forced to marry an unknown country girl of no consequence whatsoever!

Elizabeth *was* impressed by the size of it, but her appreciation was dimmed by her suspicion that Mr. Darcy expected her to be grateful to live in such a fine – well, yes, admittedly *very* fine – house. How little he knew her; she would have been happy in a cottage, if she could have shared it with a man she loved.

Georgiana said, "Come, let us go home."

As the carriage pulled up to the front of the house, Elizabeth was surprised to see a long line of servants standing outside the front door. Mr. Darcy looked equally surprised, as he had not planned to have this particular courtesy paid to his unwanted wife. He looked sternly at Georgiana, who looked back at him with a raised eyebrow and a tiny shrug. Evidently it had been his little sister who had arranged this welcome for Elizabeth, doubtless by speaking with Mrs. Reynolds before they had journeyed south. But now there was nothing to do but to pretend he had orchestrated this show of respect for a new mistress.

Elizabeth's feelings were in an uproar. She had been given no warning that she was to be mistress of such an enormous estate, and she felt now that had she known, she would have refused to say her vows, no matter the consequences. She had never been ambitious; her desires were all for love, for affection, for the warmth of a kindred soul. Properties, servants, what good were these things on a cold winter's night?

Nonetheless, now she was here and here she would evidently stay. She forced her lips into a smile as she was introduced to the butler, the housekeeper, the cook, and on down the line to various maids and footmen. She repeated each name as it was given to her, but she knew it would take many more repetitions before she could confidently identify any of them.

***

Mrs. Reynolds had indeed spoken with Georgiana before they had departed from Meryton; they had agreed that a formal welcome for the new mistress would be most appropriate. It would do the marriage no good if the new Mrs. Darcy was not shown the attention that her position deserved.

Seeing Elizabeth repeat each name, and smile at each servant, Mrs. Reynolds was immediately heartened. This was no fancy, stuck-up madam; no, this was a real woman with a heart. Whether or not she was able to be the mistress that Pemberley needed was another matter entirely, of course, but she would make certain the new Mrs. Darcy was given every opportunity to succeed in her new role.

Chapter Twenty-Five

If Elizabeth had been impressed by the exterior of Pemberley, the interior was absolutely overwhelming. She had never seen such a place; she had never imagined such beauty. She began to have some understanding of why Mr. Darcy might be proud. To live in what was a veritable palace, a breath-takingly lovely palace, would likely make any man proud!

Then she thought of what might be required of the mistress of such a place, and she trembled. She stood motionless in the entryway, looking at a huge drawing room to her right, a long hallway to her left, and two enormous staircases, one to the right and one to the left, curving up, up, up to another floor.

But if she was frozen in place, her traveling companions were not. Mr. Darcy was speaking to the butler, who had been introduced to her as Mr. Baldwin; Georgiana and Colonel Fitzwilliam were talking with the housekeeper, Mrs. Reynolds. Georgiana motioned to Elizabeth to join her.

"Mrs. Darcy," Mrs. Reynolds said, curtseying deeply. "I am very, very glad to meet you. Miss Darcy tells me that you did not bring your own maid. May I suggest that we interview a few likely candidates tomorrow?"

"Yes, of course," a flustered Elizabeth replied. "I shared a maid with my sisters; it did not seem fair to deprive them of Lucy's services by bringing her with me." Elizabeth could not imagine what Lucy would have made of Pemberley; it was likely she would have fainted dead away at her first sight of it.

Mrs. Reynolds said, "I will be ready to meet with you at your convenience, of course, Mrs. Darcy. You will probably want to rest today, but perhaps tomorrow after you break your fast?"

"Yes, that would be most acceptable," Elizabeth replied, hoping that she did not sound as panicked as she felt.

"You will doubtless want to make changes to the mistress' quarters, as they have not been refreshed since we lost Lady Anne," the housekeeper went on. As she spoke, she began walking up the stairs, Georgiana beside her. Elizabeth was confused; was she to go with them? Should she wait for Mr. Darcy?

Georgiana made a small 'come here' motion with her hand; Elizabeth responded immediately, holding onto her skirts with one hand and holding on to the banister with the other. The staircase went on forever, but eventually they reached the second floor.

"Goodness, Georgiana, how many times do you walk up and down these stairs each day?"

"You will get used to it, Lizzy. But it is true that I try to come down in the morning with everything that I think I will need until it is time to change for dinner."

"And, of course, the maids are here to bring up – or down – anything you might need, Mrs. Darcy. There are over a hundred servants, all in all, and they are all here to serve you," Mrs. Reynolds added.

"A hundred! I am certain I did not meet that many when we arrived, though there were a good many."

"No, of course; only those servants who were not occupied with tasks were given the opportunity to meet you upon your arrival. Believe me, everyone wanted to be chosen to stand on those steps when you arrived; it was accounted a great privilege."

Elizabeth was dismayed to realise that every detail of her dress, her hair, her manner of walking, and every other facet of her appearance and behavior would be discussed at great length in the servant's hall that evening. Papa, she thought desperately, please come and rescue me!

Mrs. Reynolds and Georgiana escorted Elizabeth down a long hallway. Mrs. Reynolds stopped in front of a large mahogany door and opened it wide, stepping back and motioning for Elizabeth to enter. The room was huge, with an enormous bed on a raised dais, a fireplace that she could have easily stood up in, two full-length mirrors, a writing desk, a dresser, a well-upholstered chair, and tables on either side of the bed. The bed hangings, paper and carpet were all rose-themed, with gold trim. It was rather too gaudy for Elizabeth's quieter tastes; if she were to be allowed to redecorate it, she would do so immediately.

Mrs. Reynolds opened a door on the far side of the room, saying, "This is the sitting room that you will share with Mr. Darcy."

Share? Share a sitting room? Elizabeth peered into it; she did not see much of the furnishings, as her attention was focused entirely on a door on the other side of the sitting room. "And that is…" She trailed off.

"Yes, Mr. Darcy's room, of course."

"Oh! Of course!" Elizabeth choked out. And she backed up, back into what was to be her own room.

"You will want to wash up and rest before dinner, I am sure, Mrs. Darcy. I will send Anna to help you. If there is anything you need, anything at all, you may rely upon me to supply it." And with a warm smile, the housekeeper curtsied and departed.

"Are you quite well, Lizzy?"

Elizabeth turned quickly. She had quite forgotten her new sister's presence. "In truth, I do not know, Georgiana." She walked to the bed and sat on it. The bed was extraordinarily soft. "If I put my head under this pillow, and wish very, very hard, perhaps I will wake up back home. Oh, no, Georgiana, I am sorry, I did not mean to upset you!"

Elizabeth rose and went to hug Georgiana. "I am a little – well, more than a little – overwhelmed with all this!"

Georgiana whispered, "Lizzy, when all is said and done, it is just a house!"

"No, Georgiana, it is not just a house," Elizabeth said, earnestly. "It is an enormous responsibility."

"Funny," Georgiana whispered.

"What is funny?"

"That is exactly how Brother describes it."

Elizabeth said, "But do you not see that he was brought up to it, trained from an early age, to know the house, the land, the tenants, the finances – everything! I was not so raised. I expected that if I married at all, it would be to a merchant, or an attorney, or possibly even the master of a small estate, something the size of Longbourn. But – but this! No, Georgiana, this is not something I can creditably manage."

"Lizzy, you must only do as much as you feel able to. Do you think anyone expects you to immediately become Pemberley's perfect mistress? Mrs. Reynolds likes you; I can tell. She will teach you everything you need to know."

"She will need a century in which to do so!"

"Lizzy, I think you do not realise that Mrs. Reynolds has been acting as the mistress of Pemberley since my mother died, twelve years ago."

Elizabeth took that in. After a moment, she said, "All by herself?"

"Yes. She took it on and never uttered a word of complaint, because everything she does is a labour of love. If you cannot love my brother or me, perhaps you can find it in your heart to love Pemberley."

"I do love you, Georgiana, despite the brevity of our acquaintance."

"Well, then, do it for me. Do it for Mrs. Reynolds. Do it for the hundreds of people who rely on Pemberley for their livelihoods," Georgiana said, earnestly.

Elizabeth thought for a long minute. Finally, she straightened up, took a deep breath, looked Georgiana in the eye, and said, "Very well; I will do my best."

Chapter Twenty-Six

Anna turned out to be a middle-aged woman with a no-nonsense air about her. She bustled into Elizabeth's room, shooed Georgiana out, and dove into Elizabeth's trunks to find a suitable dress for dinner.

"You will need clothes, Mrs. Darcy," she said, shaking her head over the contents of the trunks. "Mrs. Darcy will require a good many more gowns, as well as warmer apparel. It gets cold here in Derbyshire."

"I do not doubt it, Anna; but surely we can find something suitable for a family dinner."

"Perhaps this green dress..."

"That is my wedding dress, so I think not."

Anna looked at her in amazement. "This? This dress was your wedding dress? Oh, I beg your pardon, Mrs. Darcy, I did not intend –"

Elizabeth replied, rather abruptly, "No matter, Anna, but let us choose something different."

They finally settled on a blue gown that Jane had lovingly embellished with white flowers along the hem and the edges of the sleeves.

Anna quickly took Elizabeth's hair down, brushed it out, and put it up in something far more elaborate. "There! Quite nice, Mrs. Darcy."

Elizabeth thanked Anna, and started out the door. Realising that she had no idea of where she was going, she turned back and asked Anna which way the dining room might be. Anna smiled at her, saying that it would take some time for Mrs. Darcy to know her way around. She called a footman over and directed him to escort Mrs. Darcy to the family drawing room.

Elizabeth said, "Jackson, is that right?"

The footman went red with pleasure that the new mistress had already learnt his name. "Yes, Madam."

Elizabeth made an effort to memorize their route, pausing to count doors, but Jackson assured her that there would be a footman standing outside the drawing room to escort her back to her room when the evening ended.

The family drawing room clearly was intended to accommodate only a small group, as it would not seat more than ten people comfortably. The drawing room Elizabeth had noticed upon her arrival at Pemberley could easily hold thirty guests. However, the furniture in this small drawing room was as elegant as if royalty were to sit there. Mr. Darcy, Colonel Fitzwilliam and Georgiana were waiting for her.

Mr. Darcy and the Colonel rose as she entered.

"I hope I have not kept you waiting," Elizabeth said, politely.

"Not at all," Colonel Fitzwilliam answered immediately.

Mr. Darcy did not respond.

"I like what Anna did with your hair," Georgiana said. "Were you pleased with her?'

"I was, but I think someone closer to my own age…"

"Oh, indeed; Anna will not be a candidate to become your lady's maid. Mrs. Reynolds knows what she is about, I assure you."

Dinner was soon announced. The family dining room was also sized for intimate dining, as no more than ten people could have dined there comfortably. The furniture was dark and substantial; Elizabeth was glad to see that there was a footman stationed behind each chair, as she was not certain she could have managed to pull it out with ease.

She felt very much out of place compared with Mr. Darcy's perfect sartorial elegance and Georgiana's beautiful pink gown. Anna was right; she needed new clothes. Should she ask Mr. Darcy for her pin money? And how did one go about getting new clothing when one was isolated on an enormous estate? The extent of her ignorance about how to live the life that she had been so unceremoniously dropped into was almost paralyzing. But, taking a deep breath, she decided that she would be able to rely on Georgiana and Mrs. Reynolds.

Dinner was sumptuous, with three full courses as well as an elaborate sweet course. "Is this how you dine every night?" she asked Georgiana.

"Oh, no, this is meant to be a welcome dinner for you, Elizabeth," she said.

"I am relieved to hear it. I was concerned that I would have to let out all my dresses!"

Everyone was done eating; why do we not rise? Elizabeth wondered. Finally, Georgiana whispered, "You are the mistress here, Lizzy!"

"Oh! Yes, of course," Elizabeth said, utterly mortified. They had been waiting for her to rise, to signal the end of the meal! She tried to regain some measure of composure by saying, regally, "I think we need not observe the separation of the sexes."

Mr. Darcy's lips twitched; he was doubtless trying not to laugh at her.

In the drawing room, Georgiana asked if Elizabeth might enjoy some music. "Oh, indeed, that would be lovely," Elizabeth said. Not only would the music soothe her troubled soul, but it would preclude the necessity of conversation.

It was soon clear that Georgiana was a superior performer. She played a number of complex pieces without the need for music sheets, and it was evident that her heart was caught up in it.

Mr. Darcy watched Elizabeth as she listened to the music. It was obvious, of course, that she was uncomfortable in her surroundings. It had been almost amusing to watch her realise that she had to get up from the table to signal the end of the meal.

Elizabeth soon felt Mr. Darcy's eyes upon her. She swiveled her head to return his gaze, but he looked away. She wondered if he intended to share her bed that night. How would she know? Would he tell her? Was there some sort of signal of which she was ignorant?

Eventually, Elizabeth felt she could retire without causing offense. Wishing Georgiana and Mr. Darcy a pleasant night, she stepped outside the drawing room to find a footman waiting there. "George, is it?" she asked.

He bowed to her, very correctly. "Yes, Madam; this way." She followed him and found herself back in her own room where Anna was waiting for her. In short order, Elizabeth was made ready for bed. Exhausted by the events of the past days, she fell almost instantly into a deep sleep.

Chapter Twenty-Seven

The next morning, Elizabeth woke in her new bedroom. Her first thought was to wonder if Mr. Darcy had come to her room last night; surely if he had done so, he would have awakened her. She did not like the uncertainty of not knowing when he would claim what her mother referred to as his 'marital rights.' But it was impossible to ask, so she would have to live with that uncertainty.

Uncertainty had become a way of life, she thought. During the past month, she had felt like a leaf tossed about by heavy winds. Elizabeth was not normally a passive individual; the experience of having no control over her life was extremely unpleasant. She would feel better, she thought, if she could make some decisions for herself. She would do so directly.

She sat up, now feeling stronger and more determined. She needed a maid, that much was certain. What had Mrs. Reynolds said? Ah – that there would be interviews after she broke her fast. Very well. But first she would have to dress and find her way to the breakfast room.

Looking about the room, she spied a bell cord. She rose, and pulled it. A few minutes later, a young woman arrived.

Curtseying silently, she began rummaging through Elizabeth's dresses, which had been hung, presumably by Anna, in a large closet.

"What is your name, please?" Elizabeth asked politely.

The young woman promptly turned to face Elizabeth, curtsied again, and said, "I am Carrie, ma'am."

"I did not meet you yesterday, did I? If so, I apologise for forgetting your name."

"No, ma'am; I was busy and so was not given that privilege."

"Well, then, good morning, Carrie. But not the green dress, please; as I explained to Anna last night, that was my wedding dress."

Carrie nodded, saying, "Of course, ma'am," and pulled out a cream-coloured gown. She worked fast, and had Elizabeth ready for breakfast in short order. A footman was again waiting outside her bedroom door, and he led her downstairs to what was evidently the family breakfast room. Elizabeth walked inside and almost walked out again; Mr. Darcy was there, but Colonel Fitzwilliam and Georgiana were not. She would be alone with Mr. Darcy for the first time ever.

Mr. Darcy had already seen her, so it was too late to withdraw. He rose as she entered the room. "Good morning, Elizabeth."

"Good morning, Mr. Darcy." Her tone was frostier than she had intended. Wincing, she decided to try again. "Do you have any breakfast recommendations for me?"

He shook his head. "I do not recall your preferences."

"I am generally an eggs and toast sort of person."

"You might enjoy the muffins," he said.

"Very well." She filled her plate and made her way to the table, where a footman immediately pulled out a chair for her. She wondered how many footmen there were at Pemberley; doubtless, Mrs. Reynolds could tell her.

Mr. Darcy watched her as she nodded her thanks to the footman and unfolded her napkin. She was a dainty eater; he had observed that in their few days together. But was he supposed to make conversation with her over breakfast? He suspected that if he did not do so, the servants would soon be whispering about their relationship. Though they probably already were, he thought, as it would be known to the servants that Mr. and Mrs. Darcy were not sharing a bed.

"What are your plans for today?" he finally asked.

"I had thought to meet with Mrs. Reynolds," Elizabeth replied promptly. "She wants me to interview lady's maids, as I did not bring one."

Mr. Darcy nodded, briefly, before returning to his ham.

To Elizabeth's relief, the Colonel joined them, speaking heartily about how sorry he would be to return to his regiment, as he would miss all this fine food.

"When are you due back, Colonel – uh, Richard?"

"I will return to London tomorrow immediately after breakfast and spend the remainder of my leave with my parents."

There was silence, broken by Georgiana's arrival. "Good morning, Brother! Sister! Oh, is that not fine? I have a brother *and* a sister!"

Her greetings were returned, and then there was silence.

Finally, Georgiana said, through gritted teeth, "If the two of you will not at least make an effort to converse with one another, I will write to Aunt Elaine and beg her to let me live with her!" And with that, she threw her napkin onto her plate and left the room.

Mr. Darcy and Elizabeth stared at one another for a few minutes before returning their attention to their plates.

***

Elizabeth was guided to Mrs. Reynolds by one of the ever-present footmen. She could not like Georgiana's threat over breakfast, but she also could not blame the girl for not wanting to live in a home that was not peaceful. Elizabeth recalled that Georgiana had not grown up with four sisters, and so was unaccustomed to conflict within a family. Indeed, with a much older brother and no one else, she had probably never even been witness to a quarrel.

Mrs. Reynolds was in the housekeeper's room, which was – as Elizabeth had expected –spacious and well-furnished. The housekeeper rose and curtsied as Elizabeth entered.

"How are you finding Pemberley, Mrs. Darcy?"

"Rather confusing!" Elizabeth replied. "I doubt I will ever be able to find my way from one room to another without being led there by a footman."

"I felt much the same when I first went into service here."

"And how long until you did not need the footmen?"

"Six months; I am certain you will do at least as well."

"I hope you are right, as it would be rather embarrassing to have to ask directions after years of marriage."

Mrs. Reynolds offered Elizabeth a cup of tea, which Elizabeth politely declined. "Mrs. Reynolds, before we begin interviewing the maids, I have something of a dilemma."

"Oh?"

"I do not have the sort of clothing that I am evidently expected to have; Anna was quite dismayed."

"She has already spoken with me about it, and I have consulted Mr. Darcy. Mrs. Morris is our local seamstress; while she is not a London modiste, she has made a good number of Miss Darcy's gowns, and that should suffice until Mr. Darcy takes you to London. Mrs. Morris can come here, if you like, or you can go to Lambton to see her."

"How will she be paid?"

"Her bill will be sent to Pemberley, of course; there is no need to concern yourself with that."

"I understand I have pin money for clothing, but I have not yet received it, as we were married only four days ago." Four days! Four days ago she had been plain Miss Elizabeth Bennet! Plain and *happy* Miss Elizabeth Bennet! It was best not to think about that any longer, she told herself, sternly.

"Mr. Darcy will give you your first quarter pin money directly, I do not doubt. He is not a parsimonious man by any means; anyone will tell you of his generosity."

"That is good to hear," Elizabeth responded, politely. "I would prefer that Mrs. Morris come here, to begin with. I will be happy to journey to Lambton once I have appropriate clothing. I do not want to embarrass Mr. Darcy."

Mrs. Reynolds agreed with her reasoning, and promised to set it up directly. The interviews began; Mrs. Reynolds called her candidates in, one by one.

A slight, red-haired young woman was the first. Her name, Mrs. Reynolds said, was Millie. Millie was the daughter of one of the cook's assistants, and was now an upstairs maid, hoping to be promoted to lady's maid. Elizabeth spoke to her, kindly, but could scarcely get a word out of her, as she was evidently overwhelmed at speaking to the new mistress.

The second candidate was Carrie, the young woman who had helped Lizzie dress that morning. Carrie was a parlour maid; like Millie, she was hoping for a promotion. She was more loquacious than Millie, and informed Elizabeth that Miss Darcy allowed her to see her fashion magazines, *La Belle Assemblée* and *The Lady's*

Magazine, as Carrie was interested in keeping up with the latest styles.

The third candidate was Sally. Sally was about the same age as Carrie, and was also a parlour maid. She was a pleasant young woman and well-spoken; but she did not have the same interest in fashion that Carrie had.

Once Sally had left, Mrs. Reynolds said, "Carrie, yes?"

"Yes; I suspect you did not even need me to do the interviews, Mrs. Reynolds," Elizabeth said, smiling.

"I thought it likely that you would want Carrie, but wondered if perhaps you wanted someone quieter."

"No, I like a bit of talk, as it happens. And the fact that she stays abreast of fashion is good. I am not well-versed in such things and will doubtless be grateful for her help."

"I will make the arrangements, Mrs. Darcy. Carrie will be delighted, as will her mother, who has been an upstairs maid here at Pemberley her entire life."

Mrs. Reynolds had been extremely helpful and not the least concerned about Elizabeth's obvious unsuitability; thus, Elizabeth thought it safe to be frank with her. "Mrs. Reynolds, I grew up on an estate, but it was less than a tenth the size of this one. I want to be a good mistress for Pemberley, but I am not sure where to even begin. Will you help me?" Elizabeth's voice was pleading.

"Oh, you poor child, of course! The Master told me there was an accident that resulted in your wedding; you must have been so frightened, going so far from home!"

"He did not tell you what happened?"

"No; it is none of my business, of course."

And Elizabeth found herself telling Mrs. Reynolds about the dance, the feather, the fall, the bruised ribs, her father's insistence on the marriage, her own reluctance, and finally her decision to comply. "Not that I had a good deal of choice in the matter," she ended, hoping she did not sound too bitter.

Mrs. Reynolds listened in silence. Finally, she said, "Mrs. Darcy, I know it does not feel like it now, but I think you and the Master will do well together. He is a kind and generous man; I have known him since he was a small boy and I have never had a cross word from him. He has been somewhat morose, however, since his father's demise. I hope your presence will make him less so."

Elizabeth smiled weakly. "Georgiana has issued an ultimatum: if Mr. Darcy and I do not make an effort to converse with one another, she will write to her Aunt Elaine, whoever she may be, and ask to be removed from Pemberley."

"Aunt Elaine is the Countess of Matlock."

"Oh! Richard's mother?"

"Yes, and the Countess would be here as fast as her carriage could carry her, to take Georgiana back to London with her."

"So there are teeth in Georgiana's threat."

"Indeed there are; but I think she has the right of it. If you will forgive my plain speaking, you and the Master have got your backs up about this whole thing, and neither of you wants to give the relationship the chance it deserves."

Elizabeth sighed. "I suspect you are right, but it goes against the grain to be forced into a marriage."

"I truly hope you can get past that, Mrs. Darcy. It would be a shame for you and Mr. Darcy to find yourselves in an unhappy marriage simply because of Miss Bingley and her feather. Well, enough of that. Let me tell you something of the duties that are within the purview of the mistress of Pemberley."

Mrs. Reynolds spoke about visiting tenants; managing the household finances; approving menus; hiring and training staff; procurement of supplies from local merchants; charitable contributions; updating decorations and furniture; entertaining; providing the servants with clothing; and giving clothing, food and blankets to the estate's dependents. Elizabeth's eyes grew rounder and rounder as she listened.

Finally, Elizabeth said, "They tell me you have been acting as the mistress of Pemberley, but you cannot possibly be doing all this, Mrs. Reynolds. I mean no offense, but no one person can do all of that."

"It is kind of Mr. and Miss Darcy to say so, but no, indeed not. I do what I can, of course, but the estate has needed a mistress desperately since Lady Anne passed on."

"I beg you to advise me as to where to start."

"Visiting tenants, I would say. That is something I have not been able to do, as my presence is required here in the house. It would be good for the tenants to meet you, Mrs. Darcy."

"I always visited my father's tenants, so this would be easy enough for me to take on. Is there a list of tenants, Mrs. Reynolds?"

"Mr. Darcy will have a list," she was assured. "Lady Anne had a room that she used as an office; that is where the household ledgers are kept. That is your office now. May I show it to you?"

"Of course!" Her own office! Good heavens, being mistress of Pemberley was like having a full-time occupation!

She followed Mrs. Reynolds, and was shown into what might have passed for a parlour, where it not for the large desk and floor-to-ceiling bookcases. She stepped up to the bookcases and discovered that they held ledgers; each ledger had a year marked on its spine. She opened one, and was heartened to discover that it was familiar. She had kept Longbourn's household ledgers for years; this was much the same, though on a far, far grander scale.

"Have they been kept up to date?" she asked.

"Yes, by me," Mrs. Reynolds assured her. "I will continue to do so if you wish." Her tone clearly conveyed her hope that the new Mrs. Darcy would take on this task. Elizabeth was happy to assure her that she was capable of dealing with this particular chore, at least.

"I admit that I am glad to hear it, Mrs. Darcy," the redoubtable woman confessed. "If I am honest, this is likely my least favorite task."

Glad to learn that she could be useful in at least this respect, Elizabeth told Mrs. Reynolds that she wished to spend some time reviewing the ledgers so that she might begin to get familiar with the house's expenses. Mrs. Reynolds excused herself, telling Elizabeth to call on her with any questions. Opening the top drawer, Elizabeth found an ample supply of paper, pens and ink.

The amount of money spent in maintaining the household had Elizabeth gasping. The hundreds of pounds spent on candles, flour, sugar and other staples – her head was spinning! But, as she soon saw, the principals of keeping the ledgers balanced were no different from what she had been accustomed to at home.

After two hours, she leaned back and considered what she had learned. She felt she now had some understanding of the household finances, though Mrs. Reynolds' list of tasks that fell to the mistress of the estate was still quite intimidating. Leaning forward again, she quickly wrote down as much as she could recall: tenants, menus, charity. What else? Hiring and training servants – surely this could be left in the hands of Mrs. Reynolds for the female servants and Mr. Baldwin for the male servants. Buying supplies – doubtless Mrs. Reynolds was taking care of this now. Charitable contributions? This was doubtless being done by Mr. Darcy. Redecorating? She hoped to start with her own room.

Later, a footman escorted her back to her room, where she gratefully sank down into the comfortable armchair. But before she felt at all ready to face Mr. Darcy again, it was tea time.

***

Mr. Darcy had spent the morning working his way through a pile of correspondence. He needed to get out onto the estate, talk with tenants, smooth over problems, note what needed repairs. But his father had taught him to do the work he most disliked first, not last, and so he sat at his large mahogany desk when he would have very much preferred to be out, riding the estate. Away from *her*.

Converse with her? What on earth was there to say? He imagined how he might begin. 'Now that you have seen my home, do you recognise how lucky you are? And how unlucky I am?' That would probably not be the most gentlemanly thing to say. Or perhaps, 'Is there the slightest chance that you might speak with Mrs. Reynolds and find something useful to do, now that you are the mistress of one of the largest estates in Derbyshire?' No, probably not that, either.

Richard was not helping matters, he thought. It was all well and good for him to be attentive to Elizabeth, but he was about to leave for London and then his regiment. It was not Richard who had to be married to a stranger.

And why was Georgiana now so lively and so – well, so disruptive? If it had not been for Georgiana, he felt he could have easily lived with this new person in his house, paying little attention to her other than what was required to beget an heir.

But before he felt at all ready to face Elizabeth again, it was tea time. He made his way to the family drawing room. Elizabeth and Georgiana were already present. Elizabeth, mindful of her *faux pas* the previous night, rang the bell for the tea to be brought in.

There was, of course, a silence. Finally Mr. Darcy, aware of Georgiana's ultimatum, managed, "Elizabeth, I trust you are comfortable at Pemberley?"

Elizabeth murmured, "Pemberley is beautiful, of course."

"And your room?" Mr. Darcy continued.

"The bed is wonderfully soft, but the furnishings and paper are not to my taste," Elizabeth confessed.

Mr. Darcy said, "Of course; fashions have changed much in the past decades. You must certainly redecorate it to your wishes." There; was that not the proper response from a husband?

Elizabeth assured him that she was not interested in fashion; she merely preferred a simpler style.

"Have you found a maid? I believe your intention this morning was to conduct interviews," he went on, doggedly, hoping this conversation was satisfying his sister.

"I did; her name is Carrie."

"Oh, yes, the parlour maid."

Elizabeth's brows rose. "I did not think you would know the name of a parlour maid."

Insulted, he replied, "Not know the name of a maid? I can name every single servant in the house, as well as his or her parents. Shall I begin? I think alphabetically would suit. Let me see – Albert is a footman who is on duty here on the ground floor during the day; his father is a coachman and his mother is a dairymaid. Anna is Mrs. Reynolds' maid; I believe she was sent to help you upon your arrival. Her father is a footman who is assigned to the second floor; he helped you find your way downstairs last night. Amelie is a cook's assistant…"

"Stop," Elizabeth said, almost laughing. "I am sorry I doubted you, and I will say that your understanding of those in your employ is most impressive. Is it usual for housekeepers to have maids? I never heard of it."

"It is probably not common practice, but it demonstrates how highly Mrs. Reynolds is regarded here at Pemberley. I think Anna is more an assistant housekeeper than a true ladies' maid, but in any case, she reports directly to Mrs. Reynolds."

"Mrs. Reynolds and I discussed the duties I must take on, and we agreed that I should start by visiting tenants. She suggested that you might have a list of them."

Mr. Darcy was surprised. "Duties? Visit tenants?"

"Is there a difficulty? I visited tenants on my father's estate."

Mr. Darcy hedged, "There are rather more tenants here at Pemberley." He was not certain he trusted her to interact properly with the tenants.

"I gathered as much; nonetheless, it is my duty to get to know them and offer support as needed. I see you are surprised, Mr. Darcy; did you think I would sit in my room and eat chocolates all the day?"

He could not admit that this was exactly what he *had* expected. Instead, he said, "I will have the list ready for you tomorrow. You will need a horse, of course; if you are on foot, it will take you a month to pay these visits."

"I am not a terribly competent horsewomen," she confessed.

Colonel Fitzwilliam walked in and greetings were exchanged. Mr. Darcy continued his conversation with Elizabeth. "But you *can* ride, can you not?"

"I can, but I never feel secure, being that high up on an uncontrollable animal."

"None of the horses in the Pemberley stable are uncontrollable. And you will be accompanied, of course. Will that help?"

"It will, yes."

"I will talk to the stablemaster about finding a mount for you."

***

Later, when she went upstairs to change for dinner, she found Carrie waiting for her. She curtseyed to Elizabeth and said, fervently, "Oh, Mrs. Darcy! Thank you for choosing me! I promise you that you will never regret it."

"I am sure I shall not, Carrie, but you need not curtsey to me."

Carrie looked shocked. "Mrs. Reynolds would have my head, Mrs. Darcy!"

"We need not tell her. At home, I shared Lucy with my four sisters and my mother; if she had curtsied every time she saw one of us, nothing would ever have gotten done."

Carrie laughed. "Very well, Mrs. Darcy. But if Mrs. Reynolds or Mr. Darcy is in the room, I must, of course."

"Of course," Elizabeth replied. "I do not want to get you into trouble with anyone."

***

That evening was much the same as the one before, but this time Elizabeth observed when the others had finished their meal, rising from her chair at the proper time. Back in the family drawing room, Georgiana played the piano, while she, Mr. Darcy and Colonel Fitzwilliam listened in silence.

After they had expressed their appreciation for her playing, Mr. Darcy addressed Elizabeth. "I will accompany you on your visits to tenants tomorrow."

She looked at him, understanding immediately from his tense expression that he did not know if she would comport herself properly. She stared at him. "As you wish."

Again, she waited for some sign that he wished to accompany her upstairs. When it did not come, she excused herself and followed a footman to her room.

In short order, Carrie had Elizabeth changed into a nightdress and into her bed.

Chapter Twenty-Eight

Colonel Fitzwilliam was to return to London on one of Mr. Darcy's horses the following morning. He had been offered one of the Darcy carriages, but declined; horseback would be faster, he said.

The Colonel asked for a few moments with Darcy in private. Once in Mr. Darcy's office, he said, "You can have no doubt as to why I wished to speak with you alone."

"I am certain that you wish to speak about Elizabeth," Mr. Darcy said, flatly. It seemed that Elizabeth was the only subject on everyone's minds just now.

"Quite right. Darcy, she is a lovely, intelligent woman. Anyone with any sense would understand that what she brings to a marriage is worth more than all the money and connections in the world, particularly when her husband has far more than he needs of both. Are you laboring under the belief that my parents will not approve of her?"

Mr. Darcy hedged. "I think they had rather different expectations for my marriage."

"They very likely did, and once they meet Elizabeth, they will understand that you did far better than they might have ever imagined. Do not underestimate her, Darcy. I believe she is more than capable of dealing with the cats of the *ton*."

Mr. Darcy said, woodenly, "I will keep your words in mind."

Colonel Fitzwilliam sighed, knowing that his cousin would do no such thing.

***

Georgiana's farewell to her cousin was tearful. Darcy did not weep, of course, but it did not escape Elizabeth's notice that Darcy, too, was affected by his cousin's departure.

"Stay safe, Richard," Mr. Darcy said, in a somber tone.

Georgiana added, "Come back to us soon!"

Elizabeth thanked him for his kindness to her and told him that she would pray for his safety.

Colonel Fitzwilliam leapt onto his horse and rode away, leaving his cousins to stare after him for several minutes.

Mr. Darcy turned his attention to Elizabeth, saying that he was ready to visit tenants with her immediately. Elizabeth nodded, saying that she would change into a riding habit and be back downstairs directly.

Thirty minutes later, Elizabeth came downstairs, dressed in her riding habit. It was an old garment, stained in places, and faded from many washings. Mr. Darcy looked at it with considerable dismay. "Heavens, Elizabeth! Have you no other riding habit?" His tone was disbelieving.

She blushed, fiercely. "I believe Mrs. Reynolds told you that I needed clothing."

"She did, but I did not suspect the need to be quite so dire!"

"Must I dress well to impress the tenants?"

He wanted to say that Mrs. Darcy was expected to *always* dress in the forefront of fashion, but thought this hardly helpful. "I understand that Mrs. Morris is to come to Pemberley this week; may I suggest that you include several riding habits in your order?" His tone was cold. His wife did not even possess a decent riding habit!

Elizabeth did not speak; she nodded to show that she had heard, and walked out the door, head held high.

Mr. Darcy's favorite stallion, Vulcan, was saddled and ready for a morning gallop; the beast pranced a bit upon seeing his master. Beside Vulcan was a mare that he recognised as the horse Georgiana had ridden before graduating to a more spirited mount. Juno was a gentle creature, trained to a sidesaddle. "Elizabeth, this is Juno."

She nodded, and approached the house carefully, stopping at some distance from the animal.

He realised that Elizabeth was afraid. "Horses can sense fear, Elizabeth," he scolded her.

"And how is that helpful just now?" she burst out.

She had a point, he thought. He walked to Juno and stroked the mare's soft nose. "Give her this," he told Elizabeth. Reaching into his coat pocket, he pulled out an apple. "Like this." Motioning for Elizabeth to come closer, he took her hand, opened it so that the palm was facing up, and placed the apple on it. "Go on," he said, ignoring the little *frisson* that insisted upon racing up his spine at her touch.

Elizabeth offered the apple to the mare; Juno took it, carefully, and crunched it down.

"There; now she knows that you are considerate of her."

Elizabeth looked up at Mr. Darcy. "Thank you," she said. "I did tell you that I was no horsewoman."

"You did; I simply did not realise…"

"That I was not being modest?" She laughed at him.

She had a nice laugh, he thought, surprised to have noticed such a detail. Perhaps she had not laughed before this? "Yes, exactly."

"I am not guilty of false modesty, I assure you."

"I know that now. Are you ready?" he asked.

"As ready as I shall ever be, I suppose," she said, taking a deep breath.

"Elizabeth, if you are as afraid as all that, perhaps we should not go." But if she cannot ride, how can she be a competent mistress of the estate, he wondered.

"I shall be fine, I am certain." Elizabeth was determined; if riding a horse was required of her, then she would ride.

Mr. Darcy led Juno to the mounting block. After a moment, Elizabeth followed him. He stood beside the horse as Elizabeth put her left foot into the stirrup, swung her right foot up over the saddle and around to the other side of the horse, and then moved her right foot to lie beside the left.

"Well done; I know riding side saddle is not easy," he said, glad that she was at least able to get into the saddle.

Elizabeth blew out a breath. "It is not easy at all. I wish ladies were not expected to ride sidesaddle; it seems most unnatural."

"Georgiana says the same thing."

Elizabeth looked over at the stallion, who was now stamping his left front foot impatiently. "What is your horse's name?"

"Vulcan."

"He is most eager."

"He is; I should probably let him have a bit of a gallop, so as to let him blow off some steam."

"Go on, then."

Mr. Darcy nodded at her, then leapt onto Vulcan's back in one smooth motion. Man and horse took off like an arrow. Juno was startled and began to move, but Elizabeth gently pulled on the reins and the horse stopped.

Fifteen minutes later, Mr. Darcy and Vulcan returned. "He will behave now, I think," Mr. Darcy said.

"So – no leaping fences today?"

Mr. Darcy smiled, albeit unwillingly. "No, we will not leap fences. Are you comfortable?"

"Yes." *As comfortable as I am going to get,* she thought.

"Then let us go."

As they rode, Mr. Darcy told her about the families he planned to visit today. The Armstrongs were long-time tenants; third generation, in fact. Mrs. Armstrong had been heavy with child when he had last seen the family, so he assumed there would be a new baby in the home. The Winchesters lived next door to the Armstrongs, and the eldest Armstrong daughter was being courted by the eldest Winchester son. The families favoured the union, though it was not clear where the couple would live if they married.

"Is there not a cottage available for them on the estate?" Elizabeth asked.

"There is not; that is the difficulty."

"So they would have to live with one of their families."

"Yes, and both families are already rather large."

"Perhaps a room may be added to one of the houses?"

"That was my thought as well; I will look at both dwellings today to see where a room might most easily be attached."

They rode in silence, until Mr. Darcy said, "Here we are."

As they drew near, Elizabeth saw two well-kept cottages with thatched roofs, side by side, with enclosed gardens and poultry coops. A small boy had been playing in the yard of the home closest to them; he looked up at the newcomers and ran inside, yelling, "Mama! Mama!"

Mr. Darcy dismounted with ease and held Juno's reins as Elizabeth slid down. Elizabeth looked about her, but saw no place to tie the horses. Mr. Darcy guessed her concern and said, " You need not fear; they are trained not to run off."

Elizabeth thought this unlikely, but held her peace and knotted the reins around the pommel of the saddle.

A middle-aged woman emerged from the house, holding a baby. Curtseying, she said, "Good morning, Mr. Darcy." And she turned to Elizabeth, a question in her eyes.

"I am Mrs. Darcy; good morning, Mrs. Armstrong."

"I had not heard that the master had married!" Mrs. Armstrong said, looking confused.

"You are the first tenant we are visiting," Elizabeth said, knowing that word would get around the estate rapidly. "So it is no surprise that you have not heard the news."

"I wish you both very happy," was the automatic response, as Mrs. Armstrong curtsied hastily.

"I see you have a new baby," Elizabeth continued. "Boy or girl?"

"A fine new son! His name is George, after my own father," Mrs. Armstrong replied.

Elizabeth stepped closer to admire the baby. Little George opened his eyes wide and gurgled at Elizabeth. Charmed, Elizabeth, stroked his cheek with her gloved hand.

"Do you want to hold him?" Mrs. Armstrong asked, seeing Elizabeth's face.

"Oh! May I? Thank you!" Elizabeth was handed baby George; she held him with the ease of long practice. "Mrs. Armstrong, what may we send you? Clothing for the baby? Food? What would be most useful?"

"The master was most generous with the other children, ma'am; we do not need anything more."

"A new baby must have something of his own; perhaps a new blanket?" Elizabeth insisted.

Mrs. Armstrong looked delighted. "That would be appreciated, my lady!"

Elizabeth smiled at her. "I am not a 'my lady', Mrs. Armstrong. I am just Mrs. Darcy."

Mr. Darcy, unwillingly impressed by Elizabeth's easy way with his tenant, now saw Mr. Armstrong coming toward him. "Robert," he said, nodding at the man.

"Mr. Darcy, welcome home. I'd heard that you were away, but not that you had come back with a wife."

"As Mrs. Darcy was explaining, you are her first visit; I suppose we cannot take anyone by surprise after this."

Robert Armstrong chuckled, and allowed that this was probably so.

"Is your Penny still hoping to marry Arnie from next door?"

"She is, if we can think where to put them."

"I thought we might look at both cottages to see where a room or two might be added. They can have the Carter cottage and farm when it is vacant."

The Carters were an elderly couple with no children. Mr. Darcy had found he could not be at peace with asking them to leave, though their farm was lying fallow and the couple relied on Darcy charity for food and drink.

Robert shook his head. "Those two will live into the next century, I do not doubt."

"No, it will not be as long as all that. But in the meantime, we cannot ask the young people to wait to wed; nothing good ever comes of that!" Both men laughed, and went into the house, followed by Elizabeth, still cuddling the baby, and Mrs. Armstrong, who was completely delighted that the new Mrs. Darcy was paying the family so much attention. She was already planning how she would tell the story to her friends.

The men quickly decided that there was no easy way to add on a room that would not compromise the integrity of the entire house. The entire party walked to the neighbouring cottage, the home of the Winchester family, where introductions were again performed. Elizabeth handed the baby back to his mother so that she might properly greet Mrs. Winchester.

This cottage was constructed rather differently from that of the Armstrongs, and it was easy to see where an addition, even a substantial addition, might be easily built. Mr. Darcy promised to have it dealt with directly, and thought it would likely be finished in a month's time. The families were delighted to be able to plan the wedding at last.

As Mr. Darcy and Elizabeth returned to the Armstrong cottage, Elizabeth was glad to see that the horses had indeed simply stayed in place. But she was dismayed to see that there was no mounting block close at hand! How was she to get on the beast? Mr. Darcy immediately understood her predicament, and laced his gloved hands together for her to put her foot onto. Elizabeth flushed, but saw no alternative. Stepping into his hands, she felt herself lifted easily onto Juno's saddle.

"Thank you, Mr. Darcy," she said, not looking at him.

He nodded, not looking at her.

***

They visited two more tenant families before deciding to return to Pemberley.

"How many families are there?" Elizabeth inquired.

"Thirty-six," Mr. Darcy told her.

"Thirty-six! Heavens! How am I ever to visit all of them?"

"A few at a time; no one expects anything more than that."

"I must remember to send a blanket for the Armstrong baby."

"I imagine Mrs. Reynolds has a store of them somewhere."

"Good; I shall ask her."

"I noticed that the Armstrong's store of coal is running low; we do not want the baby to become chilled, so I shall have the steward bring more," he spoke quietly, as if speaking to himself.

"May I ask you something?" Elizabeth said, after a hesitation.

"Of course."

"How is it that Georgiana does not have a governess, nor a companion?"

He rode in silence for a few minutes; Elizabeth began to think she had offended him. Finally, he sighed, and said, "Her governess left us to take care of an ill sister; I had thought, then, to hire a companion for her. I was on the point of offering the post to a Mrs. Smith, but my Aunt Elaine checked her references, and we learnt that they were false."

"That does happen, of course. But you did not then offer the post to someone whose references were genuine?"

"I had planned to, but Bingley invited me to Hertfordshire." His voice was expressionless, but his meaning was clear; with all the fuss and bother of being forced into a marriage, he had not had the chance to hire a companion.

"Perhaps she does not need one, now that I am here?" Elizabeth had intended it to be a statement, but it came out as a question."

"Perhaps not. But I must make it a point to speak French with her, as her accent needs work. And I shall want to hire a piano master as well."

"I am able to speak French with her."

"You speak French?" he asked, doubtfully.

"Bien sûr," she responded, well aware of his disbelief.

"Qui était ton prefesseur?"

"Mon pére!"

Of course; Mr. Bennet would have certainly taught his favorite daughter French.

"Very well; I trust that you will speak French to Georgiana with some regularity."

Mrs. Reynolds greeted Elizabeth upon her return to Pemberley, informing her that Mrs. Morris would be delighted to make clothes for the new bride. She would come the following day with fabric samples and patterns.

***

At dinner that evening, Elizabeth recounted her visits to the estate tenants to Georgiana. "I have sent a blanket and a baby rattle to the Armstrongs; Mrs. Reynolds evidently keeps such things on hand for tenants," Elizabeth told her Georgiana. Turning to Mr. Darcy, she asked, "You did promise me a list of tenants; unless you intend to accompany me on all my visits?"

"I will give you a list and allow you to proceed at your leisure; but you must take a footman with you whenever you leave the house." He looked at her with narrowed eyes, as if daring her to object.

Elizabeth opened her mouth to do exactly that, but recalling that these excursions would be made on horseback and in unfamiliar territory where she might easily lose her way, she felt that this admonition was reasonable. Unwilling to give him the satisfaction of a verbal response, she looked away.

That night, alone in her room, Elizabeth finally put pen to paper to write to Longbourn. She was certain Jane would soon become frantic with worry if a letter was not soon received.

> *Dearest Jane,*
>
> *I am quite well in body, if not in spirit. Mr. Darcy is indeed quite wealthy, as we had suspected. My bedroom is enormous, though rather gaudy. I have my own maid, Carrie, who has finally been persuaded not to curtsey every time she lays eyes on me.*
>
> *Pemberley is enormous. I think I shall never be able to find my way around, but I hope that one day soon I shall at least be able to find the breakfast room without the help of a footman.*
>
> *Georgiana is a lovely, sweet girl, who I am proud to call my sister! Her brother, however, continues to regard me as an unwelcome visitor. I went to visit tenants yesterday, and he accompanied me; I am certain that he simply wished to make*

certain that I was able to do so without embarrassing the Darcy name. As if you and I have not been visiting tenants since I was ten years old!

The estate is huge, so tenant visits must be done on horseback. I was terrified, of course; you know that horses and I generally do not get along. However, the stable master selected a sweet little mare named Juno for me, and it was not as bad as I had feared.

But I did have to wear my grey riding habit, which as you will recall is quite stained and worn. Mr. Darcy felt the need to comment upon it, despite the fact that he had already been told him that I needed new clothing. I was mortified, as you would imagine.

Can he not understand that I am as unhappy as he is; nay, more so, as he did not have to be removed from his home and family?!

I beg that you will tell my parents and sister than I am well, but you need not burden them with my unhappiness.

Your Loving and Discouraged Sister,

Lizzy

Elizabeth read over the letter; she felt better for having written it, but there was no point in worrying Jane. She threw the sheet of paper into the fire and went to bed.

Chapter Twenty-Nine

Colonel Fitzwilliam arrived at his parents' house in two days' time. Horseback was far faster than a carriage, if less comfortable, he thought. Greeted at the door by the family's butler, he took the stairs two at a time to get to his bedroom.

Thirty minutes later, now presentable, he went downstairs to greet his mother. Kissing her on the cheek, he said, "I have much to report, Mother!"

"Is he married?"

"He is."

"And?"

"She is perfect for him."

The Countess looked at her son, surprised. "I understood her to be a simple country miss with no dowry, no connections, and nothing whatever to recommend her."

"She is from the country, yes; and it is true that she has no dowry and no connections, but she has a good deal to recommend her, in my view."

"Such as?"

"She is well-read, highly intelligent, quite lively, pretty, and a good conversationalist."

"Really! Well, that is most heartening. He needs liveliness far more than he needs money and connections," his mother observed. "He has become quite dour."

"My feelings exactly. But there is a problem."

"Oh, I already know what the problem is," the Countess assured him. "Darcy will not unbend enough to recognise her good qualities."

"Precisely."

"Well, I will visit them and see what I can do."

Chapter Thirty

A few weeks after the wedding, Elizabeth had begun to receive mail from her family. Georgiana had been right; correspondence *did* make her feel more connected with those she had left behind, lessening her feelings of loss.

One morning, she received a letter from a person she did not know. Upon opening it, she read:

Elizabeth Bennet:

I cannot refer to you as Mrs. Darcy, as you cannot deserve that title. If I had not read the marriage notice in the paper, I would have said that the report of Fitzwilliam Darcy marrying an insignificant nobody from nowhere in particular was a complete falsehood.

I am assured, however, that the marriage did indeed take place. I do not doubt that you feel quite triumphant; but know that by marrying so far above your station, you have been the means by which my nephew has become estranged from his noble family, as well as the means by which my own daughter has been thrown over by her intended husband.

> *I know not what arts you employed to lure Darcy from his duty to his family, but you will never be recognised by any of us.*
>
> *Lady Catherine de Bourgh*

Mr. Darcy walked into the family drawing room as Elizabeth finished reading the letter. He saw Elizabeth go white, give one great gasp, leap up and head for the staircase.

"Elizabeth!" He stopped her.

"No. Please excuse me, I must –" And she burst into tears.

He took the paper from her shaking hand, and read it quickly.

"Oh, Lord," he muttered. "Elizabeth, sit down."

She shook her head.

"I insist, Elizabeth," he said, sternly. He took her arm and all but forced her back onto a sofa.

"Who is she?" Elizabeth whispered.

"My aunt."

"Richard's mother?"

"Certainly not. A different aunt."

"And is she right?"

"She is not."

"You are not estranged from your family because of me?"

He hesitated. He would likely not spend as much time with his Aunt and Uncle Matlock, as he could not bring Elizabeth there.

But no good could come of explaining that. Finally, he responded, "No."

"And were you engaged to her daughter? You will recall that I asked this exact question before we were wed. I asked if there was a lady who would be discomfited by your sudden marriage!"

"I understood your question to refer to a lady who was expecting a proposal; I assure you that this is not the case here. My aunt has been laboring for years under the delusion that I would someday marry her daughter, but her daughter and I were never betrothed. I am certain that my cousin, Anne, breathed an enormous sigh of relief upon hearing of my marriage."

"You should have warned me!"

"What, that my aunt would be disappointed? She would have been so if I had wed *anyone* other than Anne. And I certainly did not expect such a letter; this is intolerably ill-bred behaviour. Had I seen this letter before you read it, I would have tossed it into the fire."

"And will the rest of your family recognise me? The insignificant and undowered country miss?"

Mr. Darcy did not reply.

"Well?"

"I cannot say; the Earl and Countess of Matlock are my aunt and uncle, as you know, and I do not know what they will do if we go to London."

"If? So your intent is to hide me away here in country for the remainder of my life?"

"You stated a preference for living in the country," he said, evasively.

"I see," she replied, acidly. And he suspected that she did indeed see. Whatever else she might be, he knew that she was not unintelligent.

"Elizabeth, will you join me in my study for a minute?" he asked her, thinking that a distraction from the letter might be in order.

"Of course." She could not imagine what could not be said there in the drawing room, but no matter. She rose, consigned Lady Catherine's letter to the fire, and followed him.

He sat at his enormous mahogany desk, which she noted was covered in well-ordered stacks of bills, correspondence, and other papers, and motioned for her to sit in one of the upholstered armchairs across from him.

"Yes?"

"I would like to give you your first quarter's pin money."

She shook her head.

"Is there a difficulty?" He restrained a sigh; why was everything so difficult? Could she not just hold out her hands for the money, as any young lady would?

"I have no desire for so much money. Perhaps – twenty pounds?"

"Twenty pounds?" he repeated.

"Is that too much? Ten would more than suffice, I assure you."

"Too much? Your pin money is two hundred and fifty pounds a quarter!"

"I am aware of the contents of the marriage articles," she said. "I simply have no need for so much. Normally, I would buy books, but having seen your library, I cannot imagine that I will need to purchase a book for the next few centuries."

He stared at her, baffled. Finally, he opened his desk drawer, drew out some bills and offered them to her. "Here is fifty pounds. I trust you will come to me if you require more."

She stared back at him. Finally, she rose, took the bills, tucked them into her skirt pocket, curtsied and left without another word.

Mr. Darcy had no idea what to make of the entire encounter.

Chapter Thirty-One

It took a few days for Elizabeth to thaw out after the unfortunate incident with Lady Catherine's letter, but she finally put the event in its proper perspective. It was to be expected that there were would be a disappointed mother who had hoped to have Mr. Darcy for her own daughter. Doubtless, there were many more such mothers in London; she could only hope that there were to be no more vitriolic missives in her future.

Mrs. Morris, Lambton's dressmaker, came to Pemberley and received a gratifyingly large order for dresses, riding habits, and more. She was delighted to report to her friends that the new Mrs. Darcy was kind, friendly, and not the slightest bit proud.

Carrie offered a number of suggestions as to Elizabeth's apparel from her perusal of Georgiana's fashion magazines, and was pleased when many of her suggestions were incorporated into Elizabeth's clothing. Mrs. Morris even told Carrie that if she grew tired of being in service, she might become Mrs. Morris' apprentice! Carrie blushed with pleasure, but had replied that for now she was more than content to serve the new Mrs. Darcy.

Once the new clothing had arrived, Elizabeth gave all her previous gowns to Carrie, saying that Carrie should take what she liked and the rest could be given to tenants who had need of clothing. Carrie had remade a number of Elizabeth's old gowns to great effect, as she was a talented needlewoman.

***

Christmas was at hand; Elizabeth had no idea what would be expected of her at this time of year. Mrs. Reynolds would know, though; the woman knew everything when it came to Pemberley.

"May I have a few minutes of your time this morning, Mrs. Reynolds? No, if I am honest, it will likely be more than a few minutes," Elizabeth said.

"Of course, Mrs. Darcy! I am always at your service," the older woman replied with a smile. What a pleasure it was to have a mistress at Pemberley at long last!

"Christmas is but a few weeks away; what are the holiday traditions here at Pemberley?"

Mrs. Reynolds sighed. "Well, when Lady Anne was here, there was an elegant Christmas ball, and all her friends from London would come. Those were merry times, indeed. More recently, though, there has been little in the way of celebration, Mrs. Darcy. The servants will expect their bonuses, of course."

"Of course. And the tenants?"

"I make up boxes and the footmen deliver them, but..." And here Mrs. Reynolds trailed off.

"But what?" Elizabeth asked.

"Many of the tenants recall a time when Lady Anne delivered the boxes herself. You must understand that the tenants appreciate the interest of the master and mistress of the estate."

"Of course they do!" Elizabeth exclaimed. "They know that when times are difficult, they will be forced to rely on the generosity of the estate. Tenants can only feel secure if the master and the mistress are attentive and kind, and thus likely to be of assistance when it is required."

"You understand this quite well; I am glad," Mrs. Reynolds said, warmly.

"So it would be best if I were to deliver the boxes. I will also give the servants their holiday envelopes."

Mrs. Reynolds beamed at her. "I am so glad you are here, Mrs. Darcy."

Elizabeth would have liked to remark that it was too bad that her husband did not feel the same way, but she managed to restrain herself.

"Mrs. Reynolds, one more thing. Do the Darcys exchange gifts?"

"They do not, no."

Elizabeth was relieved. She thought she could think of a suitable gift for Georgiana, but it would have been impossible to buy something for her husband, even with her outrageous amount of pin money.

Chapter Thirty-Two

Over the next months, Elizabeth took on more and more of the responsibilities required of the mistress of Pemberley. She delivered the tenants' Christmas boxes with Georgiana for company, fixing herself in their minds as an attentive and generous mistress. She presented each servant with the customary holiday bonus, making certain to call each person by name. She felt that she soon be able to name all the servants in alphabetical order almost as well as her husband.

She was a little alarmed at how easily she had become accustomed to a life of luxury. It was easy to forget that not all beds were as soft as hers; that not every home had fresh flowers in every room, supplied by the estate's greenhouses; that not every meal was delicious; that not every door was automatically opened by a footman when one approached it. But the lavishness of her life could not make up for the fact that her husband held no affection for her. It was that one, simple, stark fact that made her situation unenviable.

She was ready to admit that he was not a bad man, not by any means. He was kind and thoughtful in his dealings with his sister and his dependents. He was also extraordinarily generous. He had not only given her fifty pounds, but he had insisted that the new clothing and the expense for the redecoration of her room be paid for by the estate, rather than out of Elizabeth's pin money.

Her husband did not actively shrink from her touch. He often helped her up from a low chair or held out his arm to escort her somewhere. She still experienced an odd tingling up her spine whenever he touched her, though he appeared to have no such reaction. And he had never made a single gesture of true affection toward Elizabeth.

Elizabeth had written a number of short, cheerful letters to Jane, Charlotte and Aunt Gardiner. There was no point in worrying anyone, she thought. If she was not entirely happy in her new life, it was no one's concern but her own.

She had two consolations; one, of course, was Georgiana, who continued to be a delightful companion. Elizabeth knew that Georgiana was concerned about the state of her brother's marriage; her threat to move out was likely the only reason that she and her husband had conversations at all! The other consolation was the Pemberley library, which was everything that Georgiana had promised. Elizabeth had never seen so many books in one place; she was not certain she had even known so many books existed.

Elizabeth had, with Mrs. Reynolds assistance, redecorated her room to her own satisfaction. The rose and gold hangings and paper had been replaced with green and cream, calming colours far more to Elizabeth's liking. The overly pink carpet was now in the attic, and a soothing pale green carpet adorned the floor in its stead. Elizabeth had left the furniture in place, thinking that she had already spent enough money in gratifying her own taste; spending more on furniture would be irresponsible.

Mrs. Reynolds had asked if she would not like to redecorate the sitting room shared by Elizabeth and Mr. Darcy as well, but Elizabeth had simply shaken her head. She did not think Mrs. Reynolds needed to know that Elizabeth had yet to even enter the sitting room.

Her husband had never even hinted at wanting to share her bed, so she no longer waited in the drawing room after dinner to see if there was any indication of such a desire. She decided that she must have misunderstood what her mother and her aunt had explained; they had suggested that men were universally eager to have marital relations whenever possible. Either that was not the case, or Mr. Darcy found her quite unattractive.

And it was most unfortunate, as she was beginning to find him more than a little attractive. Not only was he quite handsome, but he was a good man. He was held in high regard by his sister, his servants, and his tenants. Everywhere she went, she heard her husband described as the best master imaginable. She smiled and agreed, as it was quite evidently true.

Elizabeth was aware that the servants knew that theirs was not a true marriage; there was no way to hide the fact that the master and the mistress had not yet shared a bed. She was uncomfortable knowing that the servants were talking about her, but as there was nothing she could do to amend her situation, she resolved to put it from her mind as best she could.

***

Mr. Darcy was also aware that the servants knew the state of his marriage. At first, he had thought his wife rather a plain little thing. But how wrong he had been! She was, in fact, quite an attractive woman. Those shiny mahogany curls, the long lashes framing dark chocolate eyes, the porcelain skin, those few scattered freckles! He thought, more and more, about what it would be like to take her to bed. But he knew she harboured no affection for him, so he would essentially be forcing himself upon her. The thought of such an act was utterly repugnant to him. At some point, of course, they would do what must be done in order to produce an heir. For now, though, he would have to be patient.

He had to admit, as he saw her going about her duties, that she had turned out to be a far, far better mistress for the estate than he had dared to imagine. She occasionally consulted with him about a situation she had discovered with a tenant, asking for help or for an opinion. It was because of her astute observations that he had learnt that the Davis family was in need of assistance, as rats had gotten into their supply of flour and ruined the entire barrel. It was due to Elizabeth's quick action that the doctor had gone to the Browning family's cottage in time to give assistance to their youngest child, who had been dreadfully ill. And it was due to Elizabeth's intervention that the Henderson daughter had married her lover before it became obvious that the girl was with child.

She had organized and delivered the Christmas boxes for the tenants, made certain that the servants had gotten their holiday bonuses, had greenery brought into Pemberley to give it a festive air, and had sung Christmas carols as Georgiana accompanied her on the piano. He had not known that she could sing, but she possessed a lovely alto voice.

He was aware that Georgiana was more delighted than ever with her new sister, and the two of them evidently spent a good deal of time together. Elizabeth's French was impeccable; as a result, Georgiana's French had improved dramatically and her accent was now excellent.

Elizabeth's appreciation of his library had been most gratifying. She had been completely speechless when it had first been shown to her. Upon being assured that she might take whatever volumes she liked, as long as they were returned to their proper shelves, she made good use of it. He had recently become curious as to her literary tastes; he recalled that she had said she would read anything and he found that she had not exaggerated. She read classics, poetry, novels, adventure tales, and even his books on farming techniques.

Everywhere he went, Elizabeth was asked after and praised. He had been surprised at first, but had learned to smile and agree. He was well aware that his situation might have been much, much worse. If that damnable feather *had* to come loose and fly right into his eye, he might have fallen upon any number of young country girls who would have – what was it she had said? Yes; spent the day eating chocolates! He began to feel some measure of contentment with his fate.

He did not think she felt the same, though. She rarely looked him in the eye, even when they were speaking to one another. Once, he had come upon her sitting at a table, with her head buried in her hands. He had backed out without speaking.

He was baffled by that; did she not have everything a woman could possibly desire? A beautiful home, new clothes? An enormous amount of pin money? Even a horse, as Juno had become Elizabeth's, and they were often out together. He had noted that the stable master had taken it upon himself to offer a few riding tips, and her riding had improved. She had ordered three new habits, and he thought the dark blue one particularly attractive with her glossy mahogany – and here he stopped himself. He was already feeling rather uncomfortably frustrated, as he had not gratified his natural male urges in quite some time, and there was no point in making it worse.

He knew that Elizabeth did not shrink from his touch. She was happy to take his hand if he offered to help her up from a low chair; she would take his arm when it was offered. He still experienced an odd tingling up his spine whenever he touched her, though she appeared to have no such reaction. But she had never made a single gesture of true affection toward him.

***

Georgiana watched her brother and his wife with frustration. She suspected that Elizabeth felt something far warmer than indifference for her husband, and she was certain that her brother felt the same. After all, look how they behaved when they were together! In the evenings, after dinner, the three of them sat together in the family drawing room. Elizabeth would pour tea for them, and they would each speak about what they had done that day. Georgiana often saw her brother look over at Elizabeth and quickly look away, so that Elizabeth would not see that he had done so. And Elizabeth would look over at her husband, and quickly look away. What was the matter with these two?

Chapter Thirty-Three

Early spring 1812

One day, Elizabeth came down to breakfast with a letter in her hand and a delighted smile on her face. Mr. Darcy realised, with a bit of a start, that he had rarely seen her wearing such a happy expression.

"Good news?" he inquired, looking up from his newspaper.

"The best!" she answered, cheerily.

"What happened?" Georgiana asked.

"Jane and Mr. Bingley are engaged!"

"Oh, that *is* good news!" Georgiana cried.

"I am not surprised," Mr. Darcy said. "That did seem to be the way the wind was blowing. I am only astonished that it took so long."

"If it had been up to Mr. Bingley, they would have been engaged some time ago, but Jane refused to listen to his proposals until he promised that Miss Bingley would not live with them," Elizabeth reported, with some glee.

Georgiana laughed. "Good for Miss Bennet! No one should have to live with Miss Bingley."

"Georgiana," Mr. Darcy said. "That is not polite."

Elizabeth intervened. "Can our sister not say what she thinks in the privacy of her own family? I know Georgiana would not speak so in front of others."

"Indeed not!" Georgiana said, indignantly.

Mr. Darcy, now feeling rather wrong-footed, shrugged and turned back to his newspaper. But he listened intently as the conversation continued on without him.

"When will they marry?" Georgiana asked.

"In three weeks' time."

"Mr. Bingley will be a good husband," Georgiana said.

"I think he will be, yes. They are lucky; they are very much in love."

There was silence. Georgiana said, "But love may come after marriage, may it not?"

Mr. Darcy found himself awaiting Elizabeth's response, curious as to what she would say to that, but he was to be disappointed. Instead, he heard her say, "Jane hopes we will all attend, and she says Mr. Bingley intends to ask Mr. Darcy to stand up with him."

"Brother?"

He looked up, pretending to not have heard their conversation. "Yes?"

"Evidently Mr. Bingley will ask you to stand up with him; will we go to the wedding?" Georgiana asked.

Elizabeth was not looking at him, but he could tell by her posture that she was listening intently.

"I suppose we must." Aware that he sounded less than pleased with the prospect, he tried to amend his speech by saying, "I know Elizabeth will be glad to see her family."

"Oh, I will, indeed! Thank you, Mr. Darcy." Now she did look at him, her eyes glowing with delight. Her visage was so appealing that he could scarcely look away.

"And I will go as well? Brother?"

Mr. Darcy imagined himself alone in a carriage with Elizabeth for three days there and three days back. The silences would be terrible, he thought. "Of course, Georgiana."

***

Bingley did indeed write to Mr. Darcy asking that his friend stand up with him at his wedding. Bingley's letters were notoriously illegible, but Mr. Darcy was able to determine that Bingley was absolutely delighted to be marrying the woman of his dreams. Mr. Darcy could make out the words "beautiful," "angel," and "lovely," as evidence of Bingley's joy.

How he envied Bingley his bride! No, that was not quite right. Certainly he envied Bingley his ability to *choose* his bride, rather than having a fateful feather choose for him, but he knew that he would not trade Elizabeth for her elder sister. Miss Bennet was beautiful, of that there could not be two opinions, but there was a complacency, a placidity in her expression that he could not admire. Particularly when he compared it with the endless mobility of Elizabeth's features.

He realised that he often knew what Elizabeth was feeling by simply glancing at her face. The joy on her face when reporting that Jane was engaged to Bingley had been unmistakable; he rarely saw that sort of happiness, and thought now that he would like to see that expression more often. He was glad he had agreed to make the journey to Meryton; her eyes had lit up like twin candles when he had done so.

***

Elizabeth was delighted that she would be permitted to attend Jane's wedding! She realised that she had expected Mr. Darcy to refuse to go; after all, it was a long journey, and there was always a great deal to be done around the estate. But he was not a monster, she chastised herself; Bingley was his good friend and he must certainly want to attend his wedding.

Elizabeth went about her estate duties with a light heart. To see her family in three weeks! To see Jane walk up the aisle to her chosen husband! What a joy that would be! She would need to give Jane a wedding gift; but what? Would Mr. Darcy want to help select it, as it would be from the Darcy family?

She decided she would have to ask him. She broached the subject after dinner in the drawing room. "We must bring a wedding gift for Jane and Mr. Bingley. Have you any preferences, Mr. Darcy? Georgiana?"

Mr. Darcy had a ready response. "My mother usually gifted the bride with an elegant tablecloth."

Elizabeth raised her eyes to his face. "Which she doubtless embroidered herself?"

"Of course," was his immediate answer.

Of course she did. Elizabeth was becoming rather weary of hearing about her perfect predecessor. She sighed and confessed, "Jane is far more skilled at embroidery than I; my efforts would be less than impressive to her expert eye."

Georgiana quickly intervened. "Mrs. Morris would be able to create a beautiful tablecloth, would she not, Elizabeth?"

"She would; but you know, Carrie is a skilled needlewoman. I imagine she would enjoy creating a design for Jane. It is a good deal of extra work for her, so I would want to reward her efforts," Elizabeth decided.

"What about you, Brother?"

"Me? What about me?"

"Elizabeth is having an exquisite tablecloth made for her sister; what will you give Mr. Bingley?"

"I had not given it much thought," he confessed.

"A box of expensive, smelly cigars!" Elizabeth suggested, smiling. She was teasing him; he thought now that it was rather enjoyable. No one else had ever teased him in that light-hearted way.

"Or a snuffbox, filled with snuff!" Georgiana added.

Getting into the spirit of the conversation, Elizabeth went on. "A bottle of fine cologne; Jane is fond of roses, and I am certain Mr. Bingley would not mind smelling like roses in order to make her happy!"

Georgiana began to laugh at that and could not stop. Mr. Darcy looked at her and smiled; the smile turned into a grin; the grin turned into a laugh. Elizabeth, looking at him in amazement; she laughed as well, though in astonishment as much as anything else.

"You have a dimple!" she cried out. "On your left cheek; I had no idea!"

Mr. Darcy stopped laughing immediately.

Georgiana whispered, "Oh! You did not know?"

"No; I have never seen him laugh," Elizabeth said. And tears started in her eyes. She knew her husband so little that she had not even known that he had a dimple! Worse, there was evidently so little joy in his life that he had not laughed aloud since their marriage. Had he been allowed to marry a woman for him he felt affection, he might have laughed a good deal. What unhappiness that fateful feather had brought to both of them!

Unable to control her tears, she rose and ran up the stairs to her room without another word.

Georgiana hissed, "Go after her!"

Mr. Darcy was frozen in astonishment. She had not known he had a dimple because he had not laughed since knowing her? How must that have made her feel! He shook his head, unable to understand what he could possibly do to repair the situation.

"Brother?"

He heard his sister's voice, dimly, over the roaring in his ears. He turned his head to look at her.

"Fitzwilliam, you must go after her!" Georgiana rose, went to where he sat and took his hands. "You will lose your chance with her if you are not careful," she said, and there were tears in her eyes. "Please, Brother."

He nodded, and slowly went upstairs, wondering what on earth he was to say. Arriving at her bedroom door, he knocked. He heard a very low "Come in," and he turned the knob and entered.

She was sitting on the bed. She rose as he entered. "I am – I am sorry, Mr. Darcy. I do not know what came over me." Her voice was wooden.

"William."

"What?"

"My name is William."

"Fitzwilliam, I thought it was," she said, quietly.

"Too long; I would like you to call me William."

"Very well." There was a note of hope in her voice.

"I am sorry."

"For?"

"Everything." And finding that he could speak no more, he bowed to her and left her room.

***

He did not go back downstairs. He knew he was being rude to his sister, but he could not face her or anyone else just then. How had things come to this pass? Was he so unapproachable, so stoic, that he had never laughed in his wife's presence?

He went into his own bedroom, and waved Carstairs away. From there, he wandered into the sitting room that he shared with Elizabeth. Except that he had never shared it with her, had he? He noticed now, for the first time, that while she had redecorated her own room, she had not touched their sitting room. Hers was a thrifty soul, he knew; she would not waste a shilling on a room that no one used.

He came now to a decision. He did not love her, of course. He had never loved anyone outside his own family, and he had come to believe that he did not have the capacity to love in the romantic sense of the word.

But she *did* have that capacity, he thought. Elizabeth could easily have loved and been loved by a husband, had he not fallen upon her like the great big oaf that he was. Instead, she was living with him; living well, he reminded himself, living in a mansion, attended by innumerable servants, with an almost limitless supply of funds for gowns and whatever fripperies women prized. But was that enough for her?

It would have to be, he thought, grimly; there was no escape for either of them, this side of the grave. But at least he could be kinder to her, give her more attention, show her his appreciation. That he could do, and that he would do. It be would a beginning.

***

Elizabeth watched her husband leave her room as her tears were drying on her cheeks. He had asked her to call him by his first name! She had thought she would likely be calling him Mr. Darcy until she took her last breath on this earth. "William," she thought. "William. It suits him." She was glad he had not insisted on Fitzwilliam; it was a cumbersome name.

And his apology for 'everything' was a recognition that all was not well between them. It was not much, she thought. It was not a declaration of love. But it was something.

Chapter Thirty-Four

The next morning, Mr. Darcy put his paper down when Elizabeth entered the breakfast room. He recalled his resolution to be more attentive to her, and began, "I noticed the new decoration of your room last night; it is very pretty."

She looked up, quickly. "I thank you, Mr. – William. It was kind of you to let me change your mother's choices."

"Her taste was from an earlier era. If I am honest, I prefer your colours, the green and cream, to the pink and gold."

She nodded, not certain what to say, but he could tell she was pleased.

Emboldened, he went on. "I thought you might like to do something similar with the sitting room that we share."

"I – I had not thought – well, we do not use the sitting room."

"I know that; but we might, someday, might we not? And we would wish for it to be fresh and new."

"I will think on it," she said, clearly feeling all the awkwardness of the conversation.

Feeling that he had done all that he could, William went back to his newspaper.

"William," Elizabeth began.

He looked up, happy that she was using his name.

"Will you give Mr. Bingley a gift? I am simply curious, after our discussion last night."

"Actually, yes, I will. There is a particular French brandy that he is fond of, and it is rather difficult to obtain. I have a case of it in the cellar, and I will gift him a bottle of it."

"I imagine he will be quite appreciative."

"He will, indeed, particularly when I remind him of the time he got so drunk on it that he had to spent the night at Darcy House, unable to get himself home."

They laughed together, and Elizabeth had the pleasure of seeing the dimple pop out.

'He really is quite a handsome man; Jane was right,' she thought.

Georgiana joined them, and a discussion of their upcoming journey began. Elizabeth had spoken with Carrie that morning about a tablecloth for Jane; as predicted, Carrie had been delighted to have been entrusted with such an important task. She had shrugged off the suggestion of extra wages, but Elizabeth was determined to reward her for her efforts.

"I thought of offering Bingley and your sister the use of Sunset House for a wedding trip," Mr. Darcy said.

"Sunset House?" Elizabeth asked.

"It is one of the satellite estates," Georgiana explained. "It is in Brighton, a lovely house right near the ocean. Our parents used it as a romantic getaway, did they not? Brother?"

"They went there on their wedding trip, and thereafter spent the entire month of June there every year," Mr. Darcy agreed.

"I imagine Jane would love it," Elizabeth said. Her tone was cool; she would have loved a wedding trip to the sea. But her husband had never considered taking her there.

Mr. Darcy heard the change in her voice and looked at her, questioningly. She avoided his gaze, and turned her attention to Georgiana.

"Is your music master coming today, Georgiana?" Elizabeth asked. William had found a retired London music master in Lambton and had offered the man enough money to bring him out of retirement once a week for Georgiana's benefit.

"Yes; I have been practicing endlessly to try to satisfy him."

"It is good that he is pushing you; even someone as talented as you must work at it," Mr. Darcy said.

"And your playing! You were always good, but now, Georgiana, when you come out, you will be in demand in every drawing room!" Elizabeth exclaimed.

"Oh, let us not discuss that!" Georgiana sounded dismayed.

"I am sorry, dearest; I know you are dreading it," Elizabeth said.

"But you know that at some point…" Mr. Darcy began.

"No, not now, Brother, please! Let us talk about it when we must, but not before!" his sister exclaimed. The mere thought of being the center of attention was horrifying to Georgiana.

Elizabeth quickly changed the subject back to the upcoming trip. "And will we to go the same inns that we visited on our way up to Derbyshire last year?" The conversation then centered on the forthcoming journey.

***

Elizabeth had written to Jane immediately, telling her that the Darcy family would attend her wedding and asking to be put up at Netherfield, as the idea of William spending any time in the company of her younger sisters and maternal parent was enough to make her tremble. She was well aware that he thought her family ill-bred; sadly, it was hard to argue against that opinion. Jane had written back that Mr. Bingley would be delighted to welcome them to Netherfield.

Carrie had completed the tablecloth; it was absolutely gorgeous. Elizabeth had forced Carrie to accept money for the extra work, which had been accepted only because Elizabeth swore that otherwise she could never feel right about asking Carrie to do anything at all.

Elizabeth knew that her younger sisters would expect gifts from their now wealthy older sister, so she and Georgiana embarked on a shopping trip to Lambton. Georgiana was delighted, of course, as shopping with her brother was not nearly as fun as shopping with another female. Elizabeth had briefly described her sisters to Georgiana, so that the two could decide on gifts together.

"A book for your father, a shawl for your mother, music sheets for Mary, and ribbons for Lydia and Kitty," was Georgiana's opinion.

"I think Lydia and Kitty will expect something rather grander than ribbons, but I agree with your other suggestions."

"Bonnets are rather hard to pack without squashing them, so what else?" Georgiana mused. "Oh! Oh! Combs! There is a shop in Meryton that has the most beautiful decorative combs!"

"That is perfect, Georgiana. And combs are small, so it will not be a problem to pack them; you are so clever!"

Georgiana was right; Mr. Caster's Combs had a selection of ladies' combs and fans that would have rivalled anything in London. Elizabeth was entranced. By the time she was ready to leave, she had purchased combs for Lydia, Kitty, and Mary, as well as one for Mama, and two for herself. She had also purchased a lovely painted fan for her mother, knowing that Mama would have it beside her in the drawing room to show her friends for the next decade. The fan and the comb were far better gifts than a shawl.

At the bookseller's, she was fortunate in finding a volume that she thought Papa did not own: a seventeenth century edition of *Don Quixote*. The bookseller had purchased it for another person, who had not, after all, been able to afford it. "I am surprised that you did not alert my husband to this find," she said.

"The Pemberley Library contains an even older edition, Mrs. Darcy," she was told.

With the purchase of music sheets for Mary, the two ladies completed their shopping, and treated themselves to tea and biscuits as a reward for their labours.

Chapter Thirty-Five

The day of their departure finally arrived; it was still cool, but the skies were clear and the roads dry. The Darcy traveling coach had been readied with hot bricks and blankets, as well as a basket of viands. Carrie, Carstairs and Susie were traveling in a separate carriage.

Elizabeth felt happier than she had since the Day of the Fateful Feather, as she now thought of it. She was going home to see Jane married to the man she loved!

Mr. Darcy saw her joy, and realised that he did not feel joy. On the contrary, he felt rather out of sorts, and he knew why. He had done everything in his power to make her comfortable, but she was incandescent with happiness simply to be returning to Meryton. He simply could not comprehend it. But perhaps this journey, three days in the carriage each way, would provide an opportunity for him to gain a deeper understanding of her mind and heart.

Once they were underway, Mr. Darcy began. "Tell me something about yourself, Elizabeth."

She looked at him in surprise. She glanced at Georgiana, a question in her eyes.

Georgiana looked both surprised and pleased. "Yes, Elizabeth! We know nothing of your life as a young girl in Meryton."

She thought for a minute. Then she said, "When I was a girl, my favorite thing in all the world was climbing trees."

"Really! What did your parents think of that?" Georgiana asked.

"Papa thought it funny; Mama thought it hoydenish. I suppose they were both right."

"When did you stop?" Mr. Darcy inquired.

"When I was thirteen, I fell from a very tall tree and broke my arm. It was quite painful. Papa agreed with Mama that I should stop, and so I did."

"Do you miss it?" Mr. Darcy asked.

"I do, in fact. The world looks different when you are so far above it…" Her voice trailed off.

'I will build her a treehouse,' he thought. And then shook his head; he did not have time for such nonsense.

"Your turn," he heard her say.

"My turn?"

"Yes; tell me something that I do not know about you."

He thought, and grimaced.

"If it is a painful thought, you need not share it," she said, hastily.

He blurted, "I had an older brother."

"I did not know that. What happened to him?" she asked, concerned.

"He lived for only two days; he is buried in the family graveyard."

"I am so sorry! What was his name?"

"Fitzwilliam, like mine."

Elizabeth was confused. "You were given the same name as your deceased brother?"

"It is a family tradition that the heir be given the family name of the mother. My father did not think he could break with that tradition, despite the oddness of giving me a name that had belonged to my brother."

"So if we have a son –" Which was unlikely in the extreme, as things now stood.

"Yes; his name will be Bennet."

"Do you wonder what your life would be like if he had lived?" Elizabeth asked, speaking softly.

"I used to think about it quite a bit; now I realise the futility of it."

"What would you have done? What would be different?" Elizabeth asked. This had to be a difficult conversation for him, she thought.

"I would have been gifted one of the smaller estates, so I would still have been an estate owner."

"And would you have liked that? Being responsible for a small estate?"

"Very much."

"You surprise me; you are so much the Master of Pemberley that I cannot imagine you in a lesser role."

"It would have been a far easier life; I would have had more time to read, to ride, to play chess. In short, more leisure time."

"I can understand your feelings," Elizabeth said. "There is a great deal involved in keeping Pemberley and its dependents safe and well." After a few minutes of silence, she added, "I did not know that you play chess, though I should have guessed it. Perhaps we might have a match one day."

His eyebrows rose. "You play chess?"

She chuckled. "My father taught me."

"So he must have a chess set; I hereby challenge you to a match, Elizabeth."

"And I accept the challenge, Mr. – William." She was still trying to get accustomed to using his name.

Georgiana had listened to the exchange with a smile. Brother and Elizabeth were – finally! – making an effort to get to know one another. It was most promising.

When they stopped for the night, Elizabeth and Georgiana shared a room while William slept alone. She had become accustomed to the idea of William never sharing her bed, but she still found it puzzling. Perhaps she would ask her aunt about it.

***

The next day, as the carriage continued south, Elizabeth felt that William should be given some warning as to her family's expected behaviour. He had seen little of them before they had gone to Derbyshire; in fact, he had not exchanged more than a dozen words with her mother.

"William," she began. "May I tell you something about my family?"

He arched one eyebrow. "I suppose you may as well; we shall be forced to be in company with them, will we not?'

He saw Georgiana frowning at him. What had he said wrong? Oh – *we shall be forced* sounded like it would be an unpleasant interaction. You are better than this, Darcy, he scolded himself. "Elizabeth, I would indeed like to hear about your family." There; that was better.

She had noticed his original statement and quick correction, but chose to let it go. "You have met my father, so you know that he is an intelligent and well-read gentleman. Like you, he was not the first-born son. He had an older brother who lived well into adulthood. My father had decided, quite happily, to spend his life in scholarly pursuits. He had, in fact, been offered a position at Cambridge."

Mr. Darcy grimaced. "And then his brother died."

"Exactly. My father does his best with the estate, but it is very much out of duty, not out of pleasure. Making matters worse, the estate is entailed to male heirs, and my mother did not bear a son."

"So the estate will be lost? I had not known about the entail."

"The estate will go to a distant cousin, whom none of us have ever met. There was a breach in the family, long ago, which has never been healed."

"So your father is tending an estate that will be lost to the family; that is indeed a difficult situation." Mr. Darcy felt his respect for the man triple.

"Now then; imagine how my mother feels!" She looked at him expectantly; evidently he was meant to imagine it.

Mr. Darcy hazarded, "Guilty, perhaps, that she did not bear a son?"

"Yes, though she could hardly be blamed for that. And what else, do you think?"

He considered it. "Concern for her future, perhaps, depending on what she brought into the marriage, how much of it remains, and what has been added to it from the estate's earnings."

"Exactly; she entered the union with four thousand pounds. That amount is intact, but the interest has been used as her pin money. Unfortunately, nothing has ever been added to it, thanks to the expense of keeping five daughters in gowns, gloves and shoes."

"So – four thousand pounds for herself and any unmarried daughters, if her husband predeceases her," Mr. Darcy concluded.

"Yes. She is terrified of being forced into penury."

"You know I would never let that happen, Elizabeth," he said, realising that he had never reassured Elizabeth or her family that he could be relied upon for support.

"I appreciate you saying that, William, and it would mean a great deal to my mother if you were to reassure her yourself. But Jane's marriage to Mr. Bingley will also go a long way toward calming her fears."

"And will you tell me about your sisters?"

"Jane has always been an angel. If she has a fault, it is that she refuses to believe that people are not uniformly good."

"She has met Miss Bingley, has she not?" Mr. Darcy knew that was not gentlemanly, but as Elizabeth had pointed out, he could say such things in the company of his family.

Elizabeth smiled at that. "She has; and her letters were originally full of how she and Miss Bingley just had to get to know each other better in order to appreciate one another. It was only later that she began writing that she knew she could not live with Miss Bingley. I am glad that her eyes opened! Do you know what has become of Miss Bingley? I only know that Jane was promised that Miss Bingley would not live with them."

"I do not know, but I will certainly find out. The next sister is, I believe, Miss Kitty?"

"No; Mary is next."

Mr. Darcy had a faint memory of a mousy girl who was fond of sitting in corners. "Tell me about her."

"Mary is in the unfortunate position of being the middle sister. Jane and I were always the best of friends, as are Kitty and Lydia. But Mary had no one. By the time Jane and I were old enough to understand that Mary felt left out, the damage had been done. She had become religious, reading nothing but her Bible and biblical commentary. She does play the piano, however. Georgiana, you might try making a friend of Mary, if the opportunity presents itself. She is a quiet, well-mannered girl who would do you no harm. If you do not object, William," she added hastily.

William said, "I do not object, no; she seems a harmless young lady."

Georgiana nodded. "I will try, Elizabeth."

"I thank you. Next is Catherine, though we call her Kitty. She is, unfortunately, a weak personality, happier as a follower than as a leader. And that might not have been too dreadful, had it not been for the fact that the person she chose to follow was our youngest sister, Lydia."

Mr. Darcy grimaced.

Elizabeth, alert to his facial expressions, said, "I see you are remembering the infamous bet that Kitty and Lydia made as to whether or not you would return for me. Yes, that is typical behaviour for the pair of them. The sad fact is this: as a result of the entail, my mother would do anything to get her daughters married. She sees Lydia's behaviour as lively and thinks Lydia might attract a husband as a result of it."

"But her behaviour is vulgar, not lively!" Mr. Darcy protested.

Georgiana said, reprovingly, "Brother!"

Elizabeth immediately said, "No, Georgiana, he is quite right. but no one has been able to convince Mama of this. So Lydia carries on as she pleases, and Kitty follows in her footsteps."

"Why does your father not correct the situation?" Mr. Darcy demanded.

"He tried, when Lydia was younger; but his efforts resulted in so much arguing and dissent from my mother that he soon felt that the game was not worth the candle. It was easier for him to sit in his study with his books, and try to block out all the noise. I tell you this in the hopes that you might better understand and, I dare hope, forgive the inevitable breaches of conduct that you will see in my mother and my two younger sisters."

"I recall you had an aunt and uncle from London present at the wedding," Georgiana said. "They appeared very genteel to me."

"My uncle, Mr. Gardiner, is my mother's brother. He has a warehouse in London, and is on his way to becoming quite wealthy; at least as wealthy as Mr. Bingley, I would guess. My aunt, you will recall, is from Lambton. They are well-read, open-minded, and as well-mannered as anyone might wish."

"Do you know, I have just realised – might he be Gardiner of Gardiner Emporium?" Mr. Darcy asked.

"He is, yes."

"I had not made the connection before; I have purchased a good deal from that gentleman over the years."

"I am not surprised. Now, then, William, it is your turn to tell me about your relatives."

"Where do I begin?" he wondered aloud.

Elizabeth eyed him a bit grimly. "You might begin with that aunt of yours who wrote me that dreadful letter."

Georgiana gasped. "You got a letter from Aunt Catherine? Oh, no, Lizzy, I am so sorry. Had I known, I would have torn it up before letting you read it!"

"I wish you had, as its contents have gotten rather lodged in my head," Elizabeth confessed.

"She was our mother's older sister, and they were as unlike as chalk and cheese. While our mother was everything gentle and good, her sister Catherine is opinionated, rude, and as full of pride as if she were the Queen of England!" Georgiana exclaimed.

"Is she married? And has she any children other than the daughter William was supposed to marry?"

"She was married, after several seasons, to Sir Lewis de Bourgh, who has been deceased for ten years now. It was not a love match, by any means; he needed her dowry in order to make necessary repairs to Rosings Park, his estate in Kent. She needed to marry simply because she could not countenance being a spinster. Anne is their only child," Mr. Darcy said.

"And poor Anne! She is confined indoors, as her mother believes her to be ill, and she has no company at all other than a companion," Georgiana added.

"That does sound dreadful," Elizabeth agreed. "Can nothing be done for your cousin?"

Mr. Darcy shrugged. "What can anyone do? Her mother is her guardian."

"Only until she comes of age," Elizabeth argued. "How old is Anne?"

"I think...twenty-three?" Georgiana looked at her brother for confirmation.

"Twenty-four, I believe," Mr. Darcy said.

"She does not require a guardian," Elizabeth observed.

"She is fragile, though no one knows whether because she truly is ill or because she gets no exercise. But as a result, she is unlikely to ever exert her own will over that of her mother."

"And this is the woman you were supposed to marry? But how could she have served as mistress of Pemberley?"

"She could not have, of course; the betrothal, as I explained, existed only in Aunt Catherine's mind."

"And your other aunt?" Elizabeth asked. "What of her?"

"Aunt Elaine is the Countess of Matlock. My mother was the sister of her husband, the Earl of Matlock. Though related by marriage rather than blood, Aunt Elaine and my mother were always the best of friends; Aunt Elaine was devastated when my mother passed."

"And how are the Earl and the Countess as people? Proud, I would guess."

"I would say they are not overly proud; given their rank, of course there is a certain amount of – well, I suppose I could say 'self-satisfaction.' But they are good, charitable, and well-educated. It is no hardship to be in their company."

Elizabeth thought that *self-satisfaction* was likely the new London slang for proud, but she was unlikely to ever be in such exalted company, as her husband did not plan to bring her to London. She asked, "And their children?"

"Two sons; Andrew Fitzwilliam is Viscount Lisle; he is married with two sons. Richard Fitzwilliam, as you know, is their second son. What you might not have known is that he is a co-guardian of Georgiana, along with myself."

"No other relatives?" Elizabeth asked.

"No; we are not a prolific family," Mr. Darcy admitted.

Elizabeth asked, "Forgive me if this is too painful a subject, but might I enquire as to the circumstances of your parents' deaths?"

Georgiana looked down. Mr. Darcy sighed.

"I am sorry," Elizabeth said, quickly.

"No, you have the right to know. My mother died when I was in school; I learned of her death when I came home for the holidays," Mr. Darcy said, his tone expressionless.

Elizabeth gasped. "You were not told when it happened?"

"No; I knew she was not well, of course. She never fully recovered from Georgiana's birth." And here he looked out the window for a moment, recovering himself. "My father passed away eight years ago, after a prolonged illness."

Elizabeth stammered out her regrets as well as her apologies for bringing up so painful a subject. She was stunned at what she had learnt; her husband had come home from school to find his mother gone! And his father had died eight years ago – so William had been in his early twenties when he became the Master of Pemberley, immediately responsible for the well-being of hundreds of tenants and servants, as well as for his young sister. She felt that she understood him far better now. No wonder he was so dour, so morose. Wealthy though he was, his life had been difficult.

The conversation lapsed. Mr. Darcy pulled out a book and Georgiana closed her eyes. Elizabeth looked out the window. Mr. Darcy watched her for a minute; he recalled that she was unable to read in a moving vehicle.

"Shall I read to you?" he asked, impulsively.

She turned to me, her eyes wide in surprise. "Oh! That would be pleasant. I thank you. What are you reading?"

He turned the book so that she might see the title. "Gulliver's Travels," she read aloud. "Oh, I have not yet read that! I would love to hear it read aloud."

And so Mr. Darcy began, "*I lay down on the grass, which was very short and soft, where I slept sounder than ever I remember to have done in my life, and as I reckoned, just above nine hours; for which I awaked, it was just daylight...*"

As he continued the story, he felt all the pleasure of his immediate situation. He was in a luxurious carriage, accompanied by the two females that he most lov – no, that was not right. Accompanied by his beloved sister and by his wife, who had turned out to be rather better than he had originally feared.

Chapter Thirty-Six

Finally, they arrived in Meryton. Elizabeth could not be restrained from gazing happily out her window and waving at passers-by, who merrily waved back. Mr. Darcy felt a little guilty; he had not considered how much she must miss this village, where she had been born and raised. To him, Meryton was a sleepy and insignificant little village; but it had been Elizabeth's her entire world. He had been right, he congratulated himself, to bring her here to attend her sister's wedding.

She had told him that they would stay at Netherfield. He had wondered at that. Why had she not wanted to stay at Longbourn, with her parents and her sisters? And even as he asked himself the question, he knew the answer: she had not wanted to expose him to her ill-behaved family members. He wished he had understood this sooner; he would have at least *considered* insisting that they stay at Longbourn. But it was too late to change it, he thought, as the carriage pulled up to the front door of Netherfield Park.

Bingley came out the front door, beaming from ear to ear. Not waiting for Mr. Darcy's coachman to get down and open the carriage door, Bingley strode to the carriage and opened the door himself.

"Darcy!"

"Bingley!" In the manner of close friends who have not seen each other in some time, the two men pounded one another on the back.

Mr. Darcy turned and offered his hand first to Georgiana and then to Elizabeth. The two ladies shook out their skirts and curtsied; Bingley offered a correct bow. Then he grinned at Elizabeth. "And there is my new sister!"

"Indeed; you must call me Elizabeth!"

"And I am Charles!"

Mrs. Hurst now joined them. Curtsies and bows were exchanged. Bingley informed the Darcy party that Mrs. Hurst was now acting as his hostess.

"And Miss Bingley is gone, is she not?" Elizabeth asked her new brother, quietly. "I had heard that she would be living elsewhere."

"She is still here; I am allowing her to stay for the wedding. But immediately after, she will be taken to our relatives in Scarborough. I could not ask Jane to live with Caroline, as my sister continued to be unpleasant to her. I suggested that she might live with the Hursts in London, but they refused to have her, so to Scarborough she must go."

Elizabeth nodded. "Well done, Charles."

He looked relieved. "I am glad you said so; I thought perhaps I had been too harsh."

"Too harsh? No; if a gentleman must choose between his wife and his sister, he had much better choose his wife. The sister is destined to leave the family and make her home elsewhere, whereas the wife will be beside him for life."

"Exactly my thinking!" he said.

Elizabeth thought it was more likely Jane's thinking, but no matter.

Mr. Darcy had overheard the conversation, and he shook his head. If he had to choose between his wife and his sister, of course he would choose his sister. Of course he would! Wouldn't he?

Mrs. Hurst led her guests inside, and suggested that they might want to refresh themselves before coming to the drawing room for tea. They agreed, and followed her upstairs.

"Mr. and Mrs. Darcy, I have your rooms here. There is a shared sitting room. Georgiana is down the hall."

Mr. Darcy was relieved; he had feared that he and Elizabeth would have to share a room. That would have been awkward in the extreme.

Mrs. Hurst and Georgiana went on down the hall to Georgiana's room.

Elizabeth's sharp eyes had not missed the look of relief in her husband's eyes. Unable to help herself, she held his arm, preventing him from going into his room. "You are relieved that we need not share a room?"

"Relieved? Of course I am. Do you not think that would have been difficult, for you as well as for me?"

"Difficult?" she laughed, but it was not a merry sound. "It must be rather dreadful for you to be married to someone you do not find at all attractive. I am sorry for it, but there is little I can do to change your feelings or my appearance."

"Not find you attractive?" It was ridiculous to have this conversation in the hallway, where anyone might overhear them. He led her through her room, where Carrie was already unpacking Elizabeth's trunk, to the shared sitting room, and closed the door. Was this the first time the two of them had been alone in a room together, with no interruptions? That was a sad commentary on their marriage, indeed!

"Elizabeth, I know not what has caused this confusion, but you cannot believe that anyone with eyes would find you unattractive. Might we not speak frankly, just this once?" He was not pleased that they were having this conversation at Netherfield rather than at Pemberley, but he could not let her continue to believe that he found her lacking.

"You wish a frank conversation? Very well. You clearly do not find me attractive, as you have made no move to share my bed these past months. We both know what must be done in order to produce an heir, but there is nothing I can do to further that aim until you can bring yourself to – to – well, to take appropriate action."

Mr. Darcy's head was pounding. "Elizabeth, I do not understand. Of course I find you attractive."

"Obviously not, or we would, neither of us, be concerned at the thought of having to share a bedroom."

"Allow me the privilege of knowing my own thoughts, please. I do find you attractive; in fact –" and his throat was becoming hoarse –" "I find you *quite* attractive. I simply did not want to frighten you."

"Frighten me? Oh, I am certain to be nervous, that goes without saying, I think, but fear?"

"Elizabeth, I do not know what young ladies are told about the process, and I myself have never – " And he broke off.

She looked at him in surprise. "You have never – what, exactly?"

"I have had some experience in these matters, of course, but never with a young lady who has no knowledge of the marital bed."

"Oh! So you were not quite certain how to proceed?" It would have been humourous, had the subject been less important.

"Yes. I thought it best that we wait until I could be certain that you were well-acquainted with me, until you could trust me to be gentle and kind. And instead you thought that I did not find you attractive." Unbelievable, he thought, shaking his head. "This is what I get for being a gentleman," he added, ruefully.

There was a knock on Mr. Darcy's side of the sitting room. Mr. Darcy sighed; were they never to be allowed time to talk and sort out their mutual misunderstandings? "Yes?" he called out, rather impatiently.

It was Carstairs. "Your trunk is unpacked, sir, if you wish a change of clothing before going downstairs."

"Yes, Carstairs, I will be right there." There was a hesitation, and the door closed again.

"Go on, William; perhaps we can speak again later."

Mr. Darcy was grateful they had finally been able to have this important conversation. How could she think he did not find her attractive? Did he not tell her how pretty she was in her new gowns? No, actually, now that he considered the matter, he had not told her. He had thought it, of course, but he had never said anything. But surely he had told her how the sunlight on her hair…? No, he had not told her that, either. I am an idiot, he thought. Did I expect her to read my mind?

***

Elizabeth was gratified indeed to learn that her husband found her attractive. And the fact that he had been willing to wait until she was certain that – what was it? Oh, yes, that she could trust him to be gentle and kind. What a gentleman he was, in the best sense of the word! A *gentle* man. A man who would take care of his wife, even if he did not love her, even if he had not chosen her. She felt tears starting in her eyes.

Carrie was waiting for her in her room, with a clean gown laid out. When Carrie had deemed her presentable, she went down to the drawing room to await her husband. Bingley, Mrs. Hurst, and Georgiana were already there, and tea and small sandwiches had been brought in.

As soon as Mr. Darcy appeared, Mrs. Hurst began pouring tea according to everyone's preferences. "My wife takes her tea with one sugar and a little cream," Mr. Darcy informed Mrs. Hurst. He smiled to himself upon seeing Elizabeth's surprise; doubtless she had not thought that he had noticed her tea preferences. She knew his, of course, as she prepared it for him every night: one sugar, no cream.

"Well, Bingley, you have gone and done it, have you? About to be leg-shackled?" Mr. Darcy asked his friend.

"Yes, and I could not be happier! She is an angel, Darcy!"

Elizabeth was smiling. "She is, and I am so happy for both of you. But I do not see Miss Bingley; is she not well?"

Bingley and Mrs. Hurst traded a quick glance. "She is not feeling quite the thing, Mrs. Darcy," Mrs. Hurst said, quietly. "She asked to be excused until later."

There was an awkward silence. Then Bingley said, "Elizabeth, I have strict instructions to send you to Longbourn immediately upon your arrival. But I am told that I am not to join you, as it is evidently bad luck for Jane and I to see one another the day before the wedding. I know your horses to need to rest, so my carriage will be brought around directly."

"Of course!" She turned to her husband. "William, you need not come with me if you prefer not to see…" and she trailed off.

MISUNDERSTANDINGS

Not to see her family, he filled in. He recalled that he had seen Elizabeth the day before the wedding; had that been bad luck? Nonsense, he told himself. Just country superstitions!

Georgiana piped up cheerfully, "I would love to come with you, Elizabeth!"

"Let us all go," Mr. Darcy said, trying to sound glad. He could bear the noise and ill-bred remarks for a few hours, he thought. It would mean a lot to Elizabeth.

Soon, Bingley's carriage was ready; Mr. Darcy, Elizabeth and Georgiana climbed in. Elizabeth had the satchel containing the gifts she had purchased in Lambton beside her, as well as Jane's wedding gift.

Soon, the carriage pulled up to Longbourn. Elizabeth was delighted to see her entire family coming out to greet her. "Lizzy!" her mother cried out, arms open wide. Elizabeth climbed out of the carriage with the help of her husband, and was immediately swallowed up by her mother and sisters. Her father stood back a little, beaming.

"Are my Aunt and Uncle Gardiner not here?" Elizabeth asked.

"They will come later tonight," Jane answered.

Mr. Darcy walked to Mr. Bennet; the two shook hands. "And how are you finding married life, Darcy?" his father-in-law inquired.

"Better than I expected," Mr. Darcy told him.

"I am glad to hear it," Mr. Bennet responded.

The clutch of ladies moved into the parlour as Elizabeth was peppered with questions about her home, its furnishings, and her new clothing. What was it like to be so rich? Was the cutlery gold-plated? How many servants did she have?

Laughing, Elizabeth said, "Wait, wait! I will answer no questions until I am allowed to see Jane's dress, and to hear Mama's plans for the wedding breakfast!"

Jane led the way as the ladies hurried upstairs to the bedroom Jane now had to herself. Elizabeth looked around; the room felt small, accustomed as she was to Pemberley's massive proportions.

Smiling happily, Jane took her wedding dress from the closet and held it up for everyone to see; it was Jane's favorite sapphire-blue, trimmed with gold ribbon. "It is absolutely beautiful!" Elizabeth said. "I cannot wait to see you in it! Will Mary stand up with you? Your letters did not say."

An unmarried girl was generally selected to stand with a sister at her wedding, so Elizabeth knew that honour would not be given to her.

"Mary has agreed," Jane said. "Though I wish she were happier about it."

"Mary?" Elizabeth said, turning to her middle sister. "I know you do not like attention; is that the difficulty?"

"I think it rather hard that the plainest Bennet sister is made to stand beside the most beautiful Bennet sister," Mary said, staring at the floor.

"Mary, enough sulking!" her mother said, reprovingly.

"I do not think that will help, Mama," Elizabeth said.

"Let it be, I beg you, Mama," Mary said. "I said I will do it, and I will."

Georgiana stepped to Mary's side and said, "I understand you are musical, Miss Mary; might we try a duet?"

Relieved, Mary immediately agreed; she and Georgiana left the room with alacrity.

Elizabeth watched them go with some concern. "I hope Mary's bashfulness is not impacting your enjoyment of your wedding, Jane."

"It is, rather, but what else could I have done, Lizzy? I could not pass over Mary and select Kitty; how would Mary have felt?" Jane sounded upset.

"It is rather hard that you must navigate Mary's feelings on an occasion when you want to be happy," Elizabeth said. "But it appears there was no way to avoid it. Here, I have brought you a wedding gift."

Jane opened the large, heavy package Elizabeth had so carefully wrapped. She shook out the tablecloth, exclaiming at the quality of the fabric and the beautiful embroidery that adorned the hem of the cloth. "Lizzy! Heavens, when did you become so proficient at embroidery? This is exquisite!"

Laughing, Elizabeth had to confess that it was not her needlework. "I would have done my best, Jane, but it would not have been very pretty. And I know not when I would have found the time!"

***

Mary and Georgiana, sitting side-by-side on the piano bench, were having a conversation on the subject of standing up with a bride. Georgiana began, "I am so shy that I would die of embarrassment if I had to stand up with someone at their wedding. But I have so few relatives that I am unlikely to find myself in such a position."

Mary sighed. "I know Jane had to ask me, as the next oldest sister. But I rather wish she had asked Kitty instead."

"But if Kitty had been asked, Lydia would have felt left out; is that right?"

"It is, I suppose. And if Jane had asked Lydia, Kitty would have felt left out!" Mary had to laugh. "Poor Jane!"

"It really is an honour, though, is it not?"

"It is accounted an honour, I suppose."

"Please do not answer if you feel I am being impertinent, but why do you not want to do it?"

Mary turned so that she and Georgiana were face-to-face. "Because she is so beautiful! I look like – well, I do not know what, but something plain and brown in comparison. A sparrow next to a peacock!"

"Do you think people will be looking at you and comparing you to Jane?"

"I have been compared to my sisters all my life; this will be no different." Mary's voice was subdued.

"I can see how that would be hurtful," Georgiana said. "You look very pretty to me. And are you not the accomplished sister? Surely that is something to be proud of."

"I think I would prefer to be the beautiful sister," Mary said, sullenly.

"And I would like to be far bolder!" Georgiana said. "Instead, I am so often afraid that I do not make friends or enjoy company."

"Let us make a pact!" Mary said, suddenly, turning to face Georgiana.

"A pact?"

"Yes; I will try to be prettier, or at least not to mind being plain, and you will try to be bolder!"

"Yes! And we will write to each other to tell of our successes and failures!"

"And encourage the other!"

Georgiana tentatively extended a hand; Mary seized it. Then the two fell into a hug, laughing.

"I will begin being bold this very minute, Miss Mary," Georgiana said.

"Oh, no, it is just Mary."

"And I am Georgiana. Here is my bold statement: let us go to your room and do something different with your hair. I am not terribly skilled, but I have learnt some things from my own maid."

"We can ask Lucy; she has rather given up on me, I think, but she will help us if we ask."

***

Mr. Darcy had been sitting in the parlour with Mr. Bennet discussing the books they had recently acquired, until Mr. Bennet changed the subject. "I understand that you are giving the newlyweds the use of a house in Brighton for their wedding trip," Mr. Bennet said.

"Sunset House; yes, it is a small holding, but it is close to the sea. My parents went there on their wedding trip, and spent every June there as well, as a sort of anniversary excursion. There is usually only a skeleton staff there, but I have written to the steward to hire more servants and to have the house readied for occupancy."

"Did you take Elizabeth there after the wedding?" Mr. Bennet asked, though he already knew the answer.

"No; we went directly to Pemberley."

There was a brief silence, during which Mr. Darcy began to feel uncomfortable. He spoke again. "You must recall that we scarcely knew one another; we were both pleased to have the distraction of my sister and Pemberley in the early days of our marriage. And, honestly, it is still early days in many ways."

"I do know that your situation was difficult, Darcy," Mr. Bennet said. "But Lizzy would love to visit the sea; she has spoken about it often."

The ladies now rejoined the gentlemen; Mr. Darcy was relieved, as he would not need to hear his marriage dissected any further.

"Where is Georgiana?" Mr. Darcy asked, noticing his sister's absence.

"She went off with Mary; I am sure she will be here directly," Elizabeth responded.

Mrs. Bennet had many questions about Elizabeth's life at Pemberley; seeing that she was looking for items that she might brag about to her friends, Elizabeth told her about the library, the rose garden, the size of her bedroom, the number of drawing rooms, and anything else she could think of that would impress Lady Lucas and Mrs. Goulding.

Mr. Darcy was unhappily surprised to hear his wife boasting, but upon seeing Mrs. Bennet's gleeful countenance, he understood Elizabeth's purpose.

"And the house in London! What is that like?" Mrs. Bennet asked, eagerly.

Elizabeth's face went still. "I do not know, Mama," she said. "I have never seen it and I suspect I am not likely to."

Mr. Darcy intervened, smoothly. "We have been quite busy at Pemberley, and I know Elizabeth prefers to live in the country."

"She does, yes, but I am certain she would enjoy going to balls. And the theatre! Lizzy enjoys the theatre, you know, Mr. Darcy."

Mr. Darcy was saved from the necessity of a reply by the entrance of Miss Mary and Georgiana, arm-in-arm.

"Why, Mary!" her mother exclaimed. "You look – well, I must say, you look quite different!"

Elizabeth said, quickly, "Mama means that you look lovely with your hair arranged so, Mary."

Mr. Darcy saw that Miss Mary did, in fact, look better than usual. Her hair, usually scraped back from her face, was arranged softly, with a few curls escaping to frame her face. Her dress was also different from what she had been wearing before; at least, he thought so. He had, admittedly, not paid much attention to what the girl had been wearing.

"Mary, is that not Kitty's dress?" Mrs. Bennet asked.

"No; it is *my* dress, given to me by Aunt Gardiner, and *stolen* by Kitty, Mama!" Mary exclaimed.

Elizabeth, certain that the theft had been approved by their mother, quickly said, "It looks far better on Mary than it would on Kitty. That is not at all a good colour for Kitty, Mama. I am surprised that you would allow her to wear it."

Elizabeth's opinion carried great weight, now that she was a wealthy woman. Mrs. Bennet insisted that she had never seen the dress on Kitty and that she would never, never permit Kitty to wear such a colour! No, indeed!

Mr. Darcy glanced at Elizabeth; seeing a grin trembling on her lips, he realised what she was about. *She is clever, my Elizabeth,* he thought.

The younger girls began asking if Elizabeth had brought gifts. "For it would be a terrible shame if you came without presents for us, Lizzy!" Lydia huffed.

"Oh, presents! Wait; where is that satchel, Georgiana? Oh, here it is. Mama, Georgiana led me to a store that had the best collection of combs you could possibly imagine, and I got you this." Elizabeth gave her mother a small package; Mrs. Bennet opened it immediately to discover a beautiful tortoiseshell comb, which she squealed over, delightedly. "And this!" Next, Elizabeth gave her mother another package, with proved to be fan with ivory sticks and a painted scene of lords and ladies dancing.

Mrs. Bennet immediately stuck the comb into her hair and began fanning herself vigorously. Mr. Darcy almost laughed at the woman's obvious appreciation of the offerings.

Elizabeth gave her father a book, carefully wrapped in paper. Mr. Bennet opened the book carefully, revealing a seventeenth century edition of *Don Quixote*. "Lizzy, this is wonderful! Wherever did you find it?" He knew such a book must have cost a good deal, but forbore from commenting on that; he knew his daughter could well afford it.

"The bookseller at Lambton was most helpful," Elizabeth replied.

Mr. Bennet passed the book over to Mr. Darcy, who examined it closely before handing it back.

"What about me?" Lydia said, plaintively.

"You will wait your turn or you shall not get your gift," Elizabeth said. "Which would be a shame, as I have brought it all the way from Derbyshire."

Lydia subsided, sitting back on the sofa with arms crossed. It must be hard, Mr. Darcy thought, to always be last. His sudden sympathy for the wayward girl surprised him.

"Mary, I think you do not yet have this music," Elizabeth continued, giving her middle sister several sheets.

"No, I do not! Thank you, Lizzy, this is thoughtful of you."

"Wait – and this!" Another comb was produced; this one was openwork gold filigree, so finely detailed that it looked like lace rather than metal.

"Oh, lovely!" Kitty and Lydia bounded over to Mary to admire her comb.

"And neither of you need steal it from her, as you each will have your own," Elizabeth said, producing two silver combs, each decorated with small paste gems. "Blue for Lydia, red for Kitty," she said.

"Thank you, Lizzy!" the younger girls exclaimed in unison. Lydia added, "I shall look ever so elegant when I next see the officers! Oh, Lizzy, I think I did not tell you that the militia has come to Meryton!"

"Has it? And what has this to do with you?" Elizabeth enquired.

"There are any number of handsome officers to speak with!" Kitty was equally enthused.

"And I am quite their favorite!" Lydia claimed.

"You? No, it is me!" And continuing the argument, both girls hastily excused themselves and ran upstairs to put the new combs in place immediately.

Elizabeth looked at her father. "Are those two girls permitted to visit with officers? I cannot think that a good idea."

"It is no matter, Lizzy, I assure you; they are too poor and silly to be of interest to anyone. But you must come to visit us more often, if you are to come bearing such desirable gifts," Mr. Bennet chuckled, stroking the cover of his new book.

Mr. Darcy was surprised to find that he had enjoyed seeing the distribution of the gifts. How astonishing! His parents had not been in the habit of giving gifts for birthdays or for Christmas, though he now recalled how much Georgiana enjoyed the gifts he always brought her from London. He thought now that he might adopt the custom of gift-giving at Pemberley. He began to think of the gifts he would give Elizabeth... fans... shawls... jewelry. Jewelry! He had never shown her the Darcy jewels! The jewelry collection, like the library, was the work of many generations. She would be very impressed. But hold – the important jewels were in London, where she would not go.

Chapter Thirty-Seven

With many hugs and promises to see one another at the church in the morning, Mr. Darcy, Elizabeth and Georgiana returned to Netherfield. They made a merry party: Elizabeth was delighted to have been in the company of her family; Georgiana was delighted to have found a new friend in Mary; Mr. Darcy was not delighted, but he was feeling less dour than usual, simply because his wife and sister were delighted. He thought that he did not often feel delighted; why was that, he wondered. Did he not have everything a man could possibly want?

Mrs. Hurst greeted them at the front door; Miss Bingley stood beside her. "Dinner will be in two hours," Mrs. Hurst told them. Miss Bingley remained silent.

***

Everyone gathered in the drawing room before dinner. Mrs. Hurst asked them about their time at Longbourn; was everyone ready for the wedding? Elizabeth cheerfully replied that with Mama in charge, there could be no doubt of the preparedness.

Miss Bingley said, "I imagine the breakfast will be superior to what was served at your wedding, Miss Elizabeth, as there was not such a need for *haste*."

There was a minute's silence as everyone digested this comment. It was Mr. Darcy who finally responded. "Miss Bingley, first, I am certain that you meant to refer to my wife as Mrs. Darcy, rather than as Miss Elizabeth. Second, I can assure you that my own wedding breakfast met my expectations in every particular. Finally, we married four weeks after the betrothal, so I do not understand your reference to haste. But if there was to the need for haste, may I remind you of the circumstance that required it?" His tone was acid; Miss Bingley wilted in her seat.

She murmured something; Elizabeth said, "I did not quite hear you, Miss Bingley. What did you say?"

"I *said* that I *apologise* if I said anything inappropriate, *Mrs. Darcy*," was the response. And with that Miss Bingley rose, head held high, and went upstairs without another word.

Mr. Darcy looked at Bingley. "I think I shall remove my family to Longbourn for the duration of our visit, Bingley. I am certain Elizabeth would feel more comfortable there." His displeasure could not be mistaken.

Bingley was shaken. "Darcy, you know how she is. Please – I am about to be married, and I need your support."

Mrs. Hurst added her voice to her brother's. "I am sorry, Mr. Darcy, Mrs. Darcy. It appears that she cannot help herself. But I hope you will not allow her poor manners to deprive us of your company."

Mr. Darcy looked at Elizabeth, who shrugged. "Very well; but you will not force Miss Bennet to live with her, Bingley?"

"No; Caroline will be gone by the time we return from our wedding trip." Mr. Bingley sounded certain.

"You know she will do everything in her power to come back," Mr. Darcy warned.

"But I shall not permit it; I gave Jane my solemn promise."

To everyone's relief, they were called in to dinner. The conversation centered, as one would expect, on tomorrow's event. Bingley expressed, again, his appreciation for the use of Sunset House, while Mr. Darcy silently considered Mr. Bennet's statement that Elizabeth would like to visit the sea. He could not bring her to London, of course, but he could certainly bring her to Sunset House! He would consider doing so, perhaps this summer. By then, he hoped, they would no longer be sleeping separately.

When Mrs. Hurst rose to signal the end of the meal, Elizabeth and Georgiana joined her in the drawing room, leaving Mr. Darcy, Bingley and Mr. Hurst to their cigars and port.

There was a piano in the drawing room, of course, which Georgiana immediately wanted to play, as she had not had the opportunity to try the piano when she had stayed at Netherfield on the occasion of her brother's marriage. "Elizabeth, play with me," she entreated.

Elizabeth looked to Mrs. Hurst for her permission; at her nod, Elizabeth sat beside Georgiana on the piano bench. Georgiana played the opening bars of a duet they had practiced and Elizabeth joined in. The gentlemen soon joined the ladies, and had the pleasure of listening to the music as Mrs. Hurst poured tea for the assembled company.

Mr. Darcy presented his friend with the bottle of brandy he had selected as a wedding gift. Bingley was effusive in his thanks, and begged Mr. Darcy not to tell Jane about how very, very drunk he had gotten when he had last been offered this particular vintage.

Bingley was unable to settle. He first stood beside the piano, teacup in hand. He walked back to his chair and sat down, putting the teacup on the side table. He got up again, and walked to the fireplace. He walked back to the piano. Mr. Darcy watched him in amusement.

"Bingley," he drawled.

"Darcy," his friend returned.

"Are you nervous?"

"Nervous? Of course not."

"Then why are you pacing back and forth?"

"Pacing? Do not be ridiculous, Darcy; I am completely calm." He returned to his chair, sat, and took up his teacup, crossing his legs. He uncrossed his legs and put the teacup back down.

Mr. Darcy leant back to watch, a smile teasing his lips.

Bingley got up and walked to the piano to stand beside Elizabeth and Georgiana. Back he went, then, to his chair and picked up his cup. "My tea is cold, Louisa," he complained.

Mrs. Hurst had also been watching her brother with amusement. "I will pour you another cup, Charles," she said, affectionately. She rose to hand him a refreshed cup. He took it and set it down on the table beside his chair. He rose again and wandered to the fireplace, where he stared for a time at a picture above the mantle.

"Bingley," Mr. Darcy said.

"Yes?"

"Look at me, please."

Bingley obliged. "What is it, Darcy?"

"Tell me; what is the content of the picture above the fireplace mantle?"

"What?"

"You stared at it for five minutes; what is it?"

"It is…well, dash it all, Darcy, I have no idea!"

"So you *are* nervous."

"A little, perhaps!"

"A little?!"

"Just because you have ice water in your veins, Darcy, does not mean that everyone does!"

"Who has ice water in their veins?" Elizabeth asked, turning from the piano.

"Darcy! He did not so much as turn a hair the evening before his wedding!"

There was silence in the room. Elizabeth was not certain what to think about that. She had been terribly nervous the night before the wedding, particularly as that her mother had given her "The Talk" that night, but William had evidently not been nervous at all. What did that say about their marriage? She shook her head, finally deciding not to think about it too hard.

Mr. Darcy watched Elizabeth; what did it mean that she shook her head? Was she unhappy that he had not been nervous? Had *she* been nervous? Likely she had been, and she would be upset that he had been calm. He decided that there was no way to know what she was thinking; he would have to ask her about it when they were alone. Alone! They were almost *never* alone; why was it so difficult for a husband and wife to be able to speak together without someone listening?

The evening drew to a close. With many wishes for a good night's sleep, everyone went upstairs.

Pausing in the hall outside Elizabeth's room, Mr. Darcy said, "Might we speak together in the sitting room?"

Elizabeth nodded her acquiescence. "I will go into the sitting room as soon as Carrie is done with me."

"As will I. But Carstairs, not Carrie." He was aware that he sounded flustered.

Elizabeth's lips twitched. "Very well."

***

Mr. Darcy rushed Carstairs through his tasks, and so was in the sitting room on a small sofa in just fifteen minutes. He had put a robe on over his nightshirt, aware that Elizabeth had never seen him when he was not fully clothed. He did not want to alarm her. But he may as well have taken his time, as it was another fifteen minutes before the door to her bedroom opened, and she hesitantly stepped in.

She, too, was wearing a robe, but her feet were bare, and her hair was in a long plait, hanging all the way down her back. Mr. Darcy's mouth went dry. He had not realised that her hair was so long! What would it be like, he wondered, to unbraid it and let it fall all over him, over his face, his chest, his – and he brought himself up short. This was not the time for such fantasies.

"Will you sit beside me, Elizabeth?"

Without a word, she did so, joining him on the small sofa. He noticed that she sat as far away from him as the dimensions of the furniture permitted. There was a long silence, as they both stared at the floor, the candle, the fireplace, anything, *anything* except the other person on the sofa.

Finally, Mr. Darcy asked, "Are you excited about your sister's wedding? Of course, you must be." That was a stupid question, he thought. Can I not do better?

"I am happy for her."

"Bingley will be an excellent husband."

"Yes; he loves her."

Ah. Love. Right. He did not know how to respond to that. Change the subject, perhaps? Yes. "Everyone was pleased with their gifts; you selected well."

"I know what they like, so it was easy enough. Georgiana was very helpful."

"Elizabeth…"

"Yes?"

"Are you upset that I was not nervous before our wedding?" He looked at her now.

"What?" She was confused.

"The night before our wedding – Bingley commented that I was not nervous. Did that disturb you? I saw you shake your head, but did not know what that might mean."

She was silent.

"Elizabeth?"

"Well, I know that *I* was nervous," she said, finally.

"I have a fairly calm temperament, you know."

She thought about that. Calm was one word; glum might be another. But it was true that she had never seen him lose his temper. "I suppose you do."

"It was not a reflection on you; that is all I mean to say."

She sighed. "William, nothing is served by dishonesty. You did not want to marry me; that is understandable, as I did not want to marry you."

Silence. Then he said, "That is true, I suppose; but I no longer regret my decision to marry you."

"I am glad to hear it," she said, rather shortly. "We should sleep now, William. Tomorrow will be a busy day." With that, she returned to her room.

She had not returned his compliment. She had not said that she no longer regretted marrying him. Did that mean that she still regretted it? Should he ask her? He went back to his own room and stretched out on the bed. It was comfortable, the temperature of the room was perfect, and the house was quiet. Nonetheless, it was some time before he was able to sleep.

Chapter Thirty-Eight

The next morning, when Mr. Darcy finally went downstairs to break his fast, he found the entire household already at the table. It had taken him quite a long time to fall asleep, and he had slept rather late as a consequence.

He made it a point to greet his wife first; Elizabeth looked lovely in her rose gown. Then he wished everyone else a good morning. They had, evidently, been laughing at Bingley, whose hands were shaking so badly that he had spilt his coffee all over his eggs.

"Perhaps you should not try to eat, Bingley," Mr. Darcy advised him.

"I think you are right, Darcy! I do not want to go to my wedding with coffee stains on my cravat. Come now, surely it is time to go to the church!" his friend said, eagerly.

"Hardly," Elizabeth said, her voice quivering with suppressed laughter. "We have yet another hour to wait."

"I do not know how to get through another hour!" Bingley groaned.

"I have an idea; let us play a little game," Elizabeth suggested.

"A game? At breakfast? What a quaint notion!" Miss Bingley interjected, sourly.

"We go around the table, with each person making a suggestion as to how to have a happy marriage; what think you?" Elizabeth continued, ignoring Miss Bingley's comment.

"Excellent idea!" Bingley applauded. "But hold – should the suggestions be made by everyone? Or only those who are already married?"

"Oh, everyone, surely," Georgiana cried.

"Absolutely; everyone," Elizabeth agreed. "Georgiana, you go first."

Georgiana thought for a moment. Then she said, "Compliment your spouse two times a day! At least two times!"

Bingley said, "I shall have no trouble doing that; my Jane is perfection!"

Mr. Hurst surprised everyone by saying, "I shall go next; my suggestion is that you not let the other members of either family interfere with your own happiness!" There was a minute's silence; there could be no doubt that he was speaking of Miss Bingley.

Mrs. Hurst chimed in, "Do not let things fester between you; speak candidly but kindly whenever possible."

Elizabeth said, "I would say that affection must be the bedrock of a successful marriage. Love will come or it will not, but each spouse must do his or her best to try to feel some affection for the other." She did not look at Mr. Darcy, but he was certain the words were intended for him. Did she feel affection for him? Was she at least trying to do so? Was this a hint to him, that he should try to feel affection for her? How would he know if he was feeling affection? It occurred to him that he was not usually aware of what he was feeling.

He felt everyone's eyes on him. It was his turn to speak. He hesitated, and finally said, "Make certain to carve out time for the two of you and only the two of you, despite the responsibilities of family, of estate, of business, all the distractions of life."

Miss Bingley snorted and remarked, "These are old-fashioned views of marriage, in my opinion. You will hardly find members of the first circles behaving in such a manner." She was ignored.

Bingley said, "This is all excellent advice, my friends, and I thank you for it. But surely *now* it is time to go to the church!'

Mr. Darcy shook his head, saying, "He shall know no peace until we are there; shall we?"

And with that, everyone rose to prepare for departure.

***

The church was beautifully decorated with spring flowers and colourful ribbons. It was already full, as both Jane and Bingley were well-liked by their neighbours. Bingley immediately went up to the altar and fell into conversation with the parson, as they waited for the Bennet family to arrive.

The front pews had been reserved for the Bennet and Bingley families. Mr. Darcy was momentarily confused, wondering if they should sit on the Bingley side, given that he was standing up with Bingley, or on the Bennet side, as he was, by marriage, a member of that family. Elizabeth made the decision for him, hurrying to greet her Aunt and Uncle Gardiner, who were already seated in the Bennet pew. Offering his arm to his sister, Mr. Darcy followed his wife.

"I believe I am meant to be standing at the altar beside Bingley," he said, after exchanging the required courtesies with the Gardiners. "Georgiana, shall you stay here or do you want to sit with Miss Bingley and the Hursts?"

His sister's look of disbelief at his question sent them all into fits of laughter. "I imagine that was a silly question," he said, surprised to find that he was almost ready to laugh at himself.

He went to the altar to stand with Bingley, who was practically trembling. "Get a grip on yourself, man!" Mr. Darcy exclaimed.

"I cannot; I am too nervous!"

"About what? Do you think she will change her mind and not come?" Mr. Darcy scoffed.

"Oh Lord, Darcy, do you think that could happen? I had never even thought of that! What would I do?" Bingley was now more worried than ever.

"No, that will not happen, Bingley. I promise you."

"How can you be so sure?"

The entrance of Mrs. Bennet with Kitty and Lydia prevented Mr. Darcy from having to invent a reason for his certainty. "There, Bingley. There is her family. You see? Everything is fine."

The assembled guests turned to watch Mary Bennet walk up the aisle, holding a small bouquet of flowers. Mary looked nice today, Mr. Darcy had to admit. The girl was not unattractive; she was simply reluctant to show herself to advantage.

There was a sudden hush, as Jane entered the church on her father's arm. Mr. Darcy had to admit that the eldest Miss Bennet was a lovely young lady, despite the fact that her hair was blonde, rather than a far more beautiful mahogany, and her eyes were blue, rather than – and he managed to halt this train of thought as Jane stepped to the altar to stand beside her groom.

Mr. Darcy did his best to listen to the parson's words, though his mind kept returning to the astonishing realisation that he found Elizabeth lovelier than her elder sister. When had that happened, he wondered.

***

Elizabeth was happy to be seated between her Aunt Gardiner and Georgiana. Her aunt asked her how she was finding married life; Elizabeth, mindful of Georgiana beside her, tried to think of something positive to say. "It is an honour to be the mistress of Pemberley," she said, finally.

"We shall speak later," her aunt said, narrowing her eyes.

Seeing Jane, absolutely breath-taking in her wedding gown, smiling beatifically as she approached the man she loved,

Elizabeth felt a wave of sadness. She had practically been dragged to her own wedding, understandably reluctant to wed a complete stranger. But, she reminded herself, her own sacrifice on the altar of family reputation had allowed Jane to have this perfect wedding! If she had had to marry a stranger in order for Jane to be so happy, then it had been worth it.

Mr. Bingley – Charles, rather – was a perfect match for Jane. They looked like a golden couple, standing at the altar together. Elizabeth had always thought Charles a good-looking man, though Charles' red-blond hair could not compare to William's thick, dark curls. Charles was downright short compared to Mr. Darcy, who had a good four inches on him. And did Charles have a dimple? No, he certainly did not; he smiled enough that it would have been seen early on. Actually, Elizabeth thought, Charles smiled rather too much. A more sober mien was more to her taste. There could be no question; she thought her husband far more attractive than Jane's. When had that happened, she wondered.

She glanced at her family; her mother had a handkerchief at the ready. Papa was, as usual, uncomfortable in formal clothing and was tugging at his cravat. Kitty and Lydia were whispering together, paying no attention whatsoever to their older sister's wedding.

Mary, standing beside Jane at the altar, looked quite nice. Perhaps Mary would begin to blossom at last.

When it was over, Elizabeth rushed to Jane to hug her. Jane was teary-eyed. "Oh, Lizzy! I am so happy! I only wish you could be as happy as I!"

Mr. Darcy overheard Jane's words. Did everyone know that Elizabeth was not happy in her marriage? It was a most unpleasant thought.

***

At the wedding breakfast, Charlotte made her way through the crush to Lizzy.

"Charlotte! I am so glad to see you!"

"And I you, Eliza! What a happy occasion this is!"

"Yes, it certainly is."

Charlotte looked at her friend closely. They had known each other a very long time now, and Charlotte could see that all was not well with Elizabeth. Of course, this was not the time for a serious talk; instead, Charlotte merely said, "You know I am here if you need to talk."

"I do know, Charlotte, and I thank you. And your letters! I could almost feel that I was home in Meryton while reading them. Though you neglected to tell me that the militia was here; I learnt that bit of news from Lydia."

"I did not want to worry you, Eliza."

"Worry me? What do you – oh."

"Exactly."

"Do Kitty and Lydia spend a good deal of time with the officers?"

"I wish I could tell you that they did not."

"And is it much remarked upon?"

"You know how it is in our small village."

"So everyone's tongues are wagging about my youngest sisters flirting with anything in a uniform, is that it?'

"I am afraid so." Seeing Mrs. Gardiner approach, Charlotte stopped speaking and curtsied to Elizabeth's aunt.

"May I take my niece away for a moment, Miss Lucas?"

"Of course; I shall hope to speak with you again before you depart for Derbyshire, Eliza."

Aunt Gardiner came straight to the point. "Tell me now, truly, how is married life?"

"I hardly know, Aunt; I do not feel married."

"What do you mean?"

"We have not – I mean, he has never – you know what I am trying to say, I think!" Before she could say more, Georgiana came up to them, and the moment passed.

Madeline Gardiner was confused. Elizabeth was a beautiful young woman; for a man, a husband, to not make her his wife in every sense of the word was confounding. No wonder Lizzy did not feel married!

She knew there were men who were not interested in women, but she did not think this was the issue here. She had seen Mr. Darcy look at his wife, and it was clear that he was attracted to her. What could be the difficulty?

She could hardly speak to Mr. Darcy about this, but her husband might be able to. She found Mr. Gardiner speaking with his brother Bennet. "May I borrow you for a moment?" she asked her husband.

"Of course!" Stepping away from the crush and speaking quietly, she told her husband what Elizabeth had intimated.

His eyebrows rose in surprise. "Really? That is rather unlikely."

"I agree; might you not speak with him?"

"What? You want *me* to counsel *Mr. Darcy*? You cannot be serious, Madeline."

"Yes. And without delay, please, as I know not when another opportunity will present itself." She indicated Mr. Darcy sitting on a chair, apart from the celebrants.

"On your head be it if the man takes exception, as he very likely will."

"I will take that risk," she said, pushing her husband toward the man sitting alone.

Scarcely able to believe that he had let his wife talk him into this, Mr. Gardiner approached Mr. Darcy. "May I join you, Mr. Darcy?"

"Of course; please do."

Sitting, Edward Gardiner turned to Mr. Darcy and said, in a low tone, "I will apologise in advance for what will be a most unseemly conversation; but I love my niece dearly and would scorn any number of social norms in order to serve her interest."

Mr. Darcy was immediately wary, but he remained polite. "Yes, Mr. Gardiner?"

"Elizabeth has given my wife to understand that she is not yet a true wife; I think you take my meaning here. I will not enquire as to the particulars, but let me say that this would be a concern for her, as it would be for any woman."

Mr. Darcy was astounded. His silence was evidently enough to curtail Mr. Gardiner's efforts at conversation, as he rose to excuse himself, red-faced and clearly mortified.

"No, wait. Please." The opportunity to get information was too good to refuse, however unorthodox. "Mr. Gardiner, I am certain I have never had a more inappropriate conversation; however, I must appeal to you for assistance. In putting the matter off so as to give Elizabeth time to become accustomed to her new situation, it is as if there is now no easy way to move forward. Does that make sense?"

Reassured, Edward sat back down. "Of course it does; rather than being the normal outcome of a wedding, the event has now assumed enormous proportions in both your minds. What should have been a natural occurrence is now a colossal hurdle."

"What am I to do?" Mr. Darcy's low voice was almost desperate.

"Correct it as soon as possible. Oh, I do not mean at Netherfield; my niece would feel extremely uncomfortable were this to occur for the first time in a strange place. But at your earliest opportunity, you must make this right. Surely you understand that any woman would assume that such a delay indicated that her husband did not find her attractive."

"I will take your advice at my earliest opportunity. I thank you, Mr. Gardiner. I truly did not know where to turn for help." Mr. Darcy's gratitude was evident in his voice.

"We all need help from time to time," Mr. Gardiner assured him.

At that moment, Mr. Darcy heard a young, soprano voice call out, in happy surprise, "George! Oh, I cannot believe it! What are you doing here in Meryton?"

The voice was Georgiana's. And there was only one 'George' in her life – George Wickham.

Chapter Thirty-Nine

Mr. Darcy rose from his chair immediately. He had the presence of mind to bow to Mr. Gardiner before taking advantage of his height to seek out his sister. There! And yes; it was George Wickham standing beside her. Both were laughing with delight at seeing one another so unexpectedly.

Georgiana was turning now to Lizzy, to introduce her to Wickham. This had to be stopped immediately; his wife could not be permitted to have an acquaintance with George Wickham.

In a handful of long strides, Mr. Darcy was beside his sister. "Wickham," he said, coldly, inclining his head a mere inch in acknowledgement.

"Darcy! What a surprise to find you here!" George's tone was mocking, as it always was.

"And imagine my surprise at finding you in a uniform, masquerading as an honourable man." Mr. Darcy felt his lip curling in a sneer.

The two men stared at one another; Wickham looked away first, bowing and disappearing into the crowd without another word.

"Brother? That is George!" Georgiana looked up at her brother in confusion.

"I know all too well who that is, Georgiana." His tone was grim.

"But why were you so unfriendly?"

"He is not a good man, Georgiana. You are to stay away from him."

She began to protest, but Elizabeth took her arm and said, quietly, "We can learn more later, Georgiana; this is not the time or place."

Grateful for his wife's sensible and calm demeanor, Mr. Darcy said, "I will answer all your questions later, Georgiana."

Mr. and Mrs. Bingley were making the rounds, thanking everyone for attending their nuptials. The newlyweds were to depart on their wedding trip almost immediately, stopping for one night on the way before arriving at Sunset House.

"Jane! Oh, Jane, you must write and tell me about the sea!" Elizabeth said, hugging her sister hard. "I envy you this opportunity!"

Bennet was right, Mr. Darcy thought. Elizabeth would love to go to Sunset House.

Mr. Darcy suddenly became aware that Georgiana was no longer beside him. But Bingley was demanding his attention now; Mr. Darcy shook his friend's hand, telling Bingley to let him know if anything was needed for their enjoyment at Sunset House. Finally, he was free to look about for his sister.

There! Georgiana was talking to Wickham! Had he not just told her to stay away from the man?

He strode over to his sister and grasped her arm rather more roughly than he had intended. She cried out in surprise. "Brother! You are hurting me!"

Wickham pulled Georgiana away from her brother. Mr. Darcy was stunned by the temerity of the man. Without thinking, he cocked his fist and planted it in Wickham's face. Wickham fell over backwards with a cry, his hands over his face and blood pouring from his nose. There was a moment of hushed silence, following by a babble of voices.

"Punched him with no provocation!"

"No provocation? Wickham had his hands on the man's sister!"

"No call to punch someone at a wedding breakfast!"

"Bad manners all the way around!"

"It is a wedding breakfast, not Gentleman Jackson's!"

Why did this all feel familiar, Mr. Darcy wondered briefly. He was distracted by Elizabeth saying in his ear, "William, come with me, please." He turned away from Wickham and followed Elizabeth outside to Longbourn's back garden. He saw that Elizabeth had also managed to secure Georgiana, who was sitting on a garden bench and crying.

"Sit, please," Elizabeth said, sternly. Mr. Darcy sat beside his sister. "Now; what just happened at my sister's wedding breakfast?" There was no mistaking the fury in her voice.

Georgiana said, through her tears, "I was saying hello to an old friend of ours! I did nothing wrong!"

Through clenched teeth, Mr. Darcy said, "The man is a menace to polite society; I told you not to speak to him, Georgiana!"

"But we have known him our whole lives!"

Mr. Darcy shook his head. "I will not discuss Wickham."

Georgiana dissolved into fresh tears.

Elizabeth said, "William, I think it is reasonable to tell Georgiana why you are opposed to her speaking with an old friend – from childhood, is it, Georgiana?"

Georgiana could only nod through her tears.

"It is not something I would want my sister to hear."

"William, do you understand that it is truly not beneficial to withhold important information from young women? What would have happened if Georgiana had met up with Mr. Wickham and you were not present? Knowing nothing, because you would tell her nothing, would she not befriend him as a result of their shared history?"

Mr. Darcy was silent.

"No answer? Very well, then; Georgiana, if your brother was not here today and Mr. Wickham wished you to take a walk in the garden with him, would you do so?"

"Yes!" the girl cried.

"And if he suggested perhaps walking a little further on, perhaps to the little copse on the other side of the lane where you could not be seen, would you do so?"

"Of course! George and I have known each other forever, and I trust him!"

"Of course you do; now, William, is there something you wish to tell us?"

Mr. Darcy groaned. He could not help but see the wisdom in Elizabeth's argument. If Georgiana was not permitted to understand Wickham's character, there was no knowing what Wickham would be able to persuade her to do. "Very well; Georgiana is quite right, we have known Wickham since childhood. He is the son of my father's steward."

"Father thought very highly of George, Brother; you cannot deny that!"

"Yes, very highly indeed! So highly that George was sent to school with me; he was given a gentleman's education, despite being the son of a steward. And so highly that he refused to believe me when I told him that George was a gambler and routinely came to me for the blunt to settle his debts. So highly that he would not believe that George ran up debts at school, claiming that he was Fitzwilliam Darcy in order to secure credit. So highly that he would not believe that George was the father of Maggie's baby!" The words were bitter and harsh, sounding as if they had been torn from William's soul.

Georgiana was horrified; her tears had started anew, but this time they were tears of fear and betrayal. "Maggie? The assistant cook's daughter?" she asked. "Her son is George's -?"

"Yes," her brother whispered.

"Is there more?" Elizabeth's voice was calm.

"Wickham inherited one thousand pounds upon Father's death. In addition, on his deathbed, our father asked me to give Wickham the living at Kympton when it became available."

"You gave him the thousand pounds, of course," Elizabeth said.

"Of course. I told him about Father's request regarding the living Kympton and he told me that he had no interest in serving the Church. I certainly was not going to contradict him, knowing his character. He asked for three thousand pounds in lieu of the living, which I gave him. I had him sign a paper, agreeing to the exchange."

"So he had four thousand pounds upon your father's death. That is a generous bequest, indeed," Elizabeth said, surprised. "A man could live for a long time on the interest of that amount."

"Yes, indeed; and so imagine my surprise when he came back, less than two years later, saying that he had no money and asking if he might be given the church living after all."

"Really!" Elizabeth was shocked. "That is – well, of course, he should not be in the church, but how did he run through so much money in so short a time?"

"Gambling, I do not doubt," Mr. Darcy said, angrily. "Georgiana, do you understand now why I do not want you anywhere near him?"

His sister could only nod her head; she was clearly shocked.

"And Elizabeth, you are to stay away from him as well."

"I will, of course. Come; let us go back inside. There will be questions."

The guests stared at them upon their return; doubtless, the sight of a gentleman punching a member of the militia had been fuel for a good many conversations in the twenty minutes that they had been in the garden. Mr. Darcy hung back, not wanting to deal with the opinions of the neighbourhood, but Elizabeth sallied forth into the fray, explaining that the Lieutenant had made an unkind comment to which her husband had rightly taken exception. But no real harm done, Wickham had left, and had this not been a lovely wedding?

Eventually, the mutterings stopped, and everyone went back to their wedding cake and punch.

Mr. Darcy found a seat in one of the back rooms, away from the wedding guests. He was still fuming about Wickham being in the area; was he never to be free of the man? He heard the sound of a throat being cleared and looked up to see his father by marriage standing in the doorway.

"I would like to know what prompted fisticuffs at my eldest daughter's wedding breakfast." Bennet's tone was mild, but Mr.

Darcy recognised Bennet's statement as a command, not a request.

With a sigh, Mr. Darcy again recited his history with George Wickham.

"So, debts and misbehaviour with women, is that it?"

"Yes."

"The townspeople must be told," Bennet said, firmly. "Or did you plan to depart Meryton for your castle up north and leave us to learn about Wickham on our own?"

Mr. Darcy said, "I admit that I had not given it much thought; I am still reeling from my encounter with him. But no, of course, I would not want to leave your neighbours unprotected. What would you like me to do?"

"Why, merely give me your permission to share what you have told me. I do not generally discuss anyone's personal history with my neighbours, but – again, with your permission – I will make an exception in this case. "

"You have it, of course. But I must tell you that my experience of the man is that he puts on an excellent appearance, and thus people are loathe to believe any ill of him. You might find it harder than you expect to convince anyone of his true character."

Bennet said, "I can but try; at the very least, I will keep my daughters away from him."

"Yes, that is essential."

"Come now, Darcy; join the family in the parlour. Do you need something for your knuckles?"

"No; it is nothing," Mr. Darcy said. It was not true; his hand hurt rather a lot, but he did not want any fuss made.

***

Finally, the guests were all gone and the remnants of the wedding breakfast had been cleared away. With the family members all gathered in the parlour, Mrs. Bennet had to be congratulated, again and again, on the success of her arrangements and hear everyone's assurance that such a fine event had never before been seen in Meryton. Mr. Darcy's altercation with Wickham was not mentioned. Mr. Darcy did not know if this was because Bennet had asked everyone not to mention it, or if it was an unusual display of good manners on the part of his wife's family, but he was grateful to not have to discuss it any longer.

The Darcys then excused themselves to return to Netherfield.

Chapter Forty

After dinner, the Darcys were finally alone in their sitting room. Elizabeth began, "William, I am sorry that you had to meet a man you must despise at my sister's wedding. That was most unfortunate. My father spoke with you, I imagine."

"He did; I told him my history with Wickham, and he said he would share the information with your neighbours."

"I hope he does, and that he is able to keep Kitty and Lydia away from him. I know we have many other things to discuss, but I do have a few thoughts about Lieutenant Wickham, if you are willing to hear them."

He nodded, feeling a little annoyed. What could she possibly think about Wickham, other than the fact that everyone should stay far, far away from him?

She hesitated, then said, "Are you familiar with the particulars of Caroline Bingley's education?"

"I believe she was sent to an exclusive and expensive seminary in London."

"I think you are correct; who would her classmates have been?"

"Doubtless young ladies of superior birth and fortune." Mr. Darcy was impatient; he truly did not want to spend his limited private time with his wife discussing Caroline Bingley or George Wickham.

"And do we not agree that association with young ladies from such a different sphere rather harmed her character, as it gave her expectations far above her own social sphere?"

"Yes, indeed; she would have been better served going to a school more in keeping with her true position. She is the daughter of a tradesman, no matter how wealthy. It is absurd to see her flouncing about with her nose in the air as if she were the daughter of an earl."

"So can we not see that Mr. Wickham was in much the same situation?"

Mr. Darcy scowled at her.

She went on. "Mr. Wickham was given a gentleman's education, you said. So his classmates were gentlemen; his friends, everyone he knew was a gentleman, with all the attendant advantages associated with the upper class."

"I suppose so."

"Was there anything else planned for Mr. Wickham? The study of law? Medicine?"

"To my knowledge, it was never discussed; but you will recall that a church living was to be set aside for him."

"Did your father ask Mr. Wickham if he would have liked such a position?"

"I do not believe so. Elizabeth, where are you going with this line of questioning?" He was exasperated.

"Simply this; I think it would be quite difficult for a man to be always in the company of those far better off than he, for no reason other than the vagaries of birth. Might a man in that position not begin to feel resentful?"

"Resentful! Yes, I should say so; Wickham has often said that he was as deserving of inheriting an estate as I was. Worse, Wickham believes he is my father's bastard son, and he thinks he should have inherited Pemberley, rather than me!" No sooner were those words out of his mouth, then he wished he could call them back.

Elizabeth, however, was unperturbed. "Is there any possibility of that?"

Mr. Darcy hesitated. "I do not think so, no."

"Is that based on anything other than your knowledge of your father's character?"

Mr. Darcy was silent.

Elizabeth went on. "I am in no way trying to overturn your edict to Georgiana and myself; certainly we should both stay away from him. I am merely hoping to understand why a man might act in such a manner. Have you never wondered at the motivation for such behaviour? Consider his situation. He has been lifted from what would have been his normal sphere – the local school, where his schoolmates would also have been the children of servants and tradesmen – and is instead placed among gentleman. His fellow students are men with a good deal of ready cash and expectations for a life of ease. He has no funds and no plans have been put in place, apparently, for his future. Resentful, angry, jealous, he is at loose ends. Of course, a man of strong character would have been able to accept the reality of his life, would have been grateful for such an opportunity and would have found himself an occupation. But a weak man would behave exactly as you have described him; indeed, I would almost expect it. Other than the fathering of a child; that I cannot excuse."

"So your argument is that he is weak; is that it?" His voice was flat.

"Please do not misunderstand me. It is clear, from your description, that he has done great wrong, most especially to you. But it seems to me that your father – and I say this with great respect – did not do Mr. Wickham a service in giving him a gentleman's education, without also putting in place any additional plans for a respectable and productive future. A deathbed recommendation of a church living hardly qualifies as such, given that not every man would desire or is suited for such a life. Also, do you not think that the gift of a gentleman's education would serve rather to cement his belief that he is your father's son?"

Mr. Darcy was silent, stewing furiously in his own thoughts. Even his own wife was defending the miscreant! Did she think

Wickham handsome? Is that what was going on here? "You think him good-looking, I suppose!" he burst out.

"What?" Elizabeth was baffled.

"It would not surprise me, madam; please remember that I am your husband, not Mister Wickham."

"William, I have no idea what you are talking about; I scarcely looked at him!"

He opened his mouth to continue his harangue, but she put her hand over his mouth. "William, stop this right now. I have no idea what brought all this on. I have no interest in Mr. Wickham at all. I could not, at this moment, tell you if his hair is light or dark, what colour his eyes are, or how tall he is."

They stared at one another; she took her hand away. They were silent for a long minute.

Mr. Darcy was mortified. He could not believe he had so completely lost his temper. And he had only the day before been boasting about his even temperament! "Elizabeth, I have no idea – I apologise most profoundly!"

"Was there a girl who liked him better? Is that what all this is about?"

"No, not at all. I thought of you and him and suddenly I was…" And he trailed off. He had been overwhelmed with rage and jealousy! He had never felt such things in all his life, always priding himself on his even temper. And he realised that he was obviously far fonder of his wife than he had ever imagined. I am an idiot, he thought. Drawing in a ragged breath, he said, "I cannot speak of this any longer. Let us now think of the pleasant things that happened today."

Elizabeth nodded. "Very well; Jane looked lovely, did she not?"

"She did." He wondered if he might say that Elizabeth was lovelier than her elder sister, but before he could decide, she went on.

"I know she was grateful for the use of Sunset House."

"Bingley said that she was, yes." He wondered if now he might promise her that he would take her to Sunset House, but the words would not come. He wondered, rather desperately, why it was that he had no trouble making business decisions, had no problem speaking clearly with his steward, housekeeper, valet, butler and so on, but could not decide what to say to his wife and actually say it.

"Elizabeth," he began.

"Yes, William?"

"I told you that I do not regret our marriage, but I must know. Do you still regret it?"

She was silent for a moment. "It is not a fair question, William."

"Why is that?"

"Because our situations are not and never were equal."

"I do not take your meaning."

"You did not lose your home and your family; all that happened to you was the addition of a new family member."

"You speak of that as it if were nothing!" He was hurt that she had not simply said that she did not regret it, and so he continued on, angrily and rashly. "I lost the power of choice! You have seen Pemberley; surely you understand that I was expected to marry a young lady of consequence! With a substantial dowry and important connections! And instead –" And here he realised that her face had gone quite pale and a tear had formed in her eye.

"Elizabeth, I am sorry, I –"

She rose, curtsied formally, and disappeared into her room, closing the door behind her.

Mr. Darcy remained where he was, staring at the closed door, and wishing very, very hard that he could start that conversation anew.

Chapter Forty-One

Mr. Darcy had a great deal of difficulty sleeping after his faux pas with Elizabeth; as a result, he awoke late. By the time he was ready to break his fast, his sister and his wife were already in the breakfast room. He wished everyone good morning; he was greeted in return by Georgiana, but Elizabeth refused to look at him.

Georgiana had not spoken to her brother since the incident with George. Wanting to make certain that the air had been fully cleared, she said, cautiously, "Brother?"

"Yes, Georgiana?" He managed to take his eyes off Elizabeth and focus on his sister.

"I know now why you did not want me to speak to George. I did not know anything about him after he left Pemberley."

"That is because I did not want to discuss it, Georgiana."

"I understand, of course. I apologise for not having obeyed you."

"Just – just stay away from him. I know there is some part of you that still thinks of him as your old friend; if I am honest, there is still a small part of me that thinks so as well. I know Father would be upset if he knew how George had turned out."

Georgiana bowed her head. "It is– well, sad, I suppose."

Mr. Darcy replied, "It is, yes."

Georgiana raised her head. "When are we going home?"

"Are you eager to leave?"

"No, indeed; I was hoping I could go back to Longbourn and play duets with Mary. She has not had the benefit of a master, but she is nonetheless quite skilled."

"Elizabeth?"

"I, too, would like to spend a little more time at home." She did not look at him as she spoke.

He nodded. "Let us plan to stay another two days. Does that suit?" He could not help registering the fact that Elizabeth still thought of Longbourn as home, but he forbore to comment on it.

Mrs. Hurst entered the room, smiling. She said, "It was a lovely wedding! You must feel very happy, Mrs. Darcy."

"Oh, of course my entire family is delighted," Elizabeth responded.

"As is mine," Mrs. Hurst agreed. "Jane will be a perfect Mrs. Bingley."

"Where is Miss Bingley?" Georgiana asked.

"Still in her bed; she is not an early riser."

"When is she going north?" Elizabeth asked.

"As soon as she has broken her fast. My brother has made all the arrangements. She will go in our traveling coach, accompanied by a coachman, two footmen and a maid."

"I would hazard a guess that she is not pleased with what she must think of as her exile. Someone may have to rouse her from her bed to get her on that coach," Mr. Darcy said.

"She is certainly not pleased, not at all; but she has no one but herself to blame." Mrs. Hurst hesitated, and spoke again. "It has been impressed upon me that I did not do enough to correct her."

No one spoke.

Finally, she added, "Caroline has always been stubborn. I think we all got into the habit of giving in to her; it was easier that way."

There was nothing to say. After a minute, Mr. Darcy cleared his throat and told Mrs. Hurst that they would spend the afternoon at Longbourn. Mrs. Hurst nodded, and said she would remain at Netherfield, as Caroline would doubtless require some assistance before her departure.

Privately, Mr. Darcy thought it unlikely that Caroline would get into the carriage at all; he would have been willing to bet that she would still be here at Netherfield that night. He thought grimly that he should find Wickham and place that bet; the man had never been able to resist a gamble.

He thought now about Elizabeth's words about Miss Bingley and Wickham. In watching her interact with servants, tenants and Georgiana, he had discovered that his wife was unusually insightful. She was able to understand people in a ways that he could not.

Mr. Darcy was under no illusions about his own abilities; he knew himself to be a kind master, a conscientious man, and a careful investor. He was liberal-minded, rational, generous and honorable. But he also knew that he did not understand other people.

Elizabeth, on the other hand, had an intuition about what motivated people to behave as they did, as well as an ability to smooth over difficult situations. Look at how well she had bonded with Georgiana! It was almost impossible to recall that Georgiana had once been shy, nervous and unable to speak in company; now she was confident and poised. He had feared that Georgiana might never be able to be brought out in society, but now he knew she would have no difficulty, as long as Elizabeth was with her.

But wait – that was not going to work. He had no plans to bring Elizabeth to London. It would be impossible for her to know how to behave amongst the haughty, mean-tempered gossips of London's high society. Elizabeth would not be an asset to Georgiana in society, as Elizabeth would be struggling herself. Well, he need not solve that problem now; Elizabeth would not even look at him, let alone want to accompany him anywhere.

***

They were soon at Longbourn. Georgiana and Mary immediately disappeared into the music room. Mr. and Mrs. Bennet and Mr. and Mrs. Gardiner were in the parlour, as were Kitty and Lydia.

Bennet had a letter in his hand, which he had been reading aloud to his family. Judging by everyone's expressions, it had been most amusing.

"Start it again, Papa; Lizzy must hear it!" Kitty insisted.

Bennet said, "Darcy, Lizzy, the two of you will doubtless enjoy this. I have a letter here from my heir apparent, Mr. Collins."

Mr. Darcy immediately said, "No; he is your heir presumptive, is he not?"

Bennet studied his son by marriage over his spectacles. "I suppose he is, now that you bring it up."

Mrs. Bennet said, "Oh, I have never understood anything about this entail! Heir apparent, heir presumptive – what is it all about?"

Mr. Darcy answered promptly. "The heir apparent is a person whose right to inherit is fixed as long as he outlives the property holder. The heir presumptive is a person who may lose the right to inherit if a nearer heir is born. If you were to bear a son, this Mr. Collins would have no rights with respect to Longbourn; thus he is an heir presumptive, not an heir apparent."

Mrs. Bennet argued, "What is the difference? He will come and throw us all out into the street, in any case!"

Mr. Darcy, recalling Elizabeth's words, now leaned forward, saying earnestly, "Mrs. Bennet, you will never live in the street. You will be under my protection in the event that Mr. Bennet predeceases you. I do not think you would enjoy living at

Pemberley, as we are rather isolated from any society, but I do not doubt that we could find an acceptable house for you right here in Meryton."

Mrs. Bennet looked at him, her mouth open. "A – a house? Here?" she managed.

"Of course. I swear to you, most solemnly, that you need not fear. It may be that Bingley purchases Netherfield, which would be all the more reason for you to remain in Meryton. You could live at Netherfield, of course, but I suspect you would prefer to be mistress of your own home."

Mrs. Bennet stared at him for a long minute. Then she took out a handkerchief and blew her nose. In a weak, trembling voice, she said, "I thank you, Mr. Darcy. That is most kind of you."

Elizabeth could see that William was now quite uncomfortable. She was still hurt from their conversation last night, and could not imagine how they could move forward at this point; but she could not deny that his words had meant a great deal to her mother.

"Go on, Papa," Kitty said. "Read the letter!"

"Very well; as I said, this letter is from Mr. Collins."

> Dear Sir,
>
> *The disagreement subsisting between yourself and my late honoured father always gave me much uneasiness, and since I have had the misfortune to lose him, I have frequently wished to heal the breach; but for some time I was kept back by my own*

doubts, fearing lest it might seem disrespectful to his memory for me to be on good terms with anyone with whom it had always pleased him to be at variance.

I received ordination at Easter, and was so fortunate as to be distinguished by the patroness of the Right Honourable Lady Catherine de Bourgh, widow of Sir Lewis de Bourgh, whose bounty and beneficence has preferred me to the valuable rectory of this parish, where it shall be my earnest endeavor to demean myself with grateful respect towards her ladyship, and be ever ready to perform those rites and ceremonies which are instituted by the Church of England.

I have long been concerned at being the means of injuring your amiable daughters, through the circumstance of being next in the entail of Longbourn estate, and it has long been my object to make what amends I could to them, as I am now in the fortunate position of being able to afford the support of a wife.

However, Lady Catherine has lately leant that your daughter, one Elizabeth Bennet, has been the means of harming her own daughter, Miss Anne de Bourgh, the fairest flower of Kent, by utilising various arts and allurements to lure away the man who ought by all rights to have been Miss de Bourgh's husband. As a result of your daughter's behaviour in this regard, Lady Catherine de Bourgh has forbidden me to have any intercourse whatsoever with your family until such time as I inherit the estate.

William   *Collins*

Elizabeth was dumbstruck. "Lady Catherine, is that – is that –"

Mr. Darcy replied, "My aunt, yes, Elizabeth, the one who wrote you that dreadful letter earlier this year. Longbourn's heir presumptive is my aunt's rector? Astonishing!" He turned to Bennet. "I can only apologise, sir, for the inanity of my aunt's behaviour. She is not the most reasonable of women."

Elizabeth gasped. "Not the most reasonable! Heavens, I begin to think her quite mad!"

"You would not be alone in thinking so, Elizabeth."

She was not done. "This is absurd; my family is looked down upon for having relatives in trade, but because this woman has a title, she is allowed to indulge in the worst behaviour imaginable."

The Gardiners looked embarrassed. Mr. Darcy recalled his conversation with Mr. Gardiner, and how the man had eased his mind by showing him a way forward with Elizabeth; he quickly said, "You are absolutely right. Mr. and Mrs. Gardiner, I would far prefer to claim you as relatives than my Aunt Catherine."

The Gardiners laughed and thanked him.

Kitty said, "Did I understand that Mr. Collins had thought of marrying one of us? Is that not what he meant?"

Her father replied, "Yes, that was certainly the implication. But I think he cannot be sensible; I would not have consented to any of you marrying him."

Mrs. Bennet said, half-heartedly, "But it would have kept Longbourn in the family, were he to marry one of the girls."

Her husband shook his head, firmly. "We will not marry the girls off to anyone for whom they do not have an inclination." He realised then what he had said, for he looked at Elizabeth and winced. In an apologetic voice, he began "Lizzy…"

"It is all right, Papa. I understand." Her words were reasonable, but her tone was bleak.

The ensuing awkward silence was broken by Georgiana and Mary entering the room, arm-in-arm.

Mr. Bennet asked Mary to sit, saying that he has something he wished to discuss with all of his younger daughters. "You have all met Lieutenant Wickham, I think."

"Oh! He is the handsomest man I have ever seen!" Lydia said, predictably enough.

Kitty added, "And so well-mannered!"

Mary frowned. "It is not seemly for us to be interested in a man like that; we know nothing about him."

Kitty and Lydia rolled their eyes, but Mr. Bennet said, "Exactly right, Mary; that is the point I am about to make. I have become privy to some things about this man's history that make me extremely uncomfortable at the idea of any of you being in his company. You are to avoid him entirely."

Lydia said, "This is unbelievably unfair! We heard that Mr. Darcy punched him right in the nose; how is that Lieutenant Wickham's fault?"

Mr. Darcy was embarrassed at having his lack of control brought up in front of everyone, but he had to support Bennet in this matter. He said, "Miss Lydia, Wickham has been known to me since childhood. He is a gambler and a liar; and he is not to be trusted around young ladies."

"Might he not have changed, though?" Kitty enquired.

"I cannot say that it is impossible for someone to change, of course; but I find it quite unlikely."

Mr. Bennet cleared his throat and said, "Any discussion as to whether or not he has changed is not relevant. You are not to be in his company. If I hear that either of you – I think I can count on Mary to stay away from him – have disobeyed me in this regard, I will confine you to the nursery. Is that clear to both of you?"

There was silence.

"Kitty, Lydia, I am waiting."

"I understand, Papa," Kitty said, unhappily.

"I understand, but I do not agree!" exclaimed Lydia.

"I am not interested in your agreement, as it happens, Lydia." Mr. Bennet said, calmly. "I am only interested in your obedience."

The two young girls crossed their arms and flopped back on the sofa, in unison. Elizabeth managed not to laugh at their expressions.

Mr. Darcy had watched Elizabeth all morning; she had not once looked at him directly. He did not know how they were to move forward from here. His words to her last night might have destroyed their already fragile relationship. But it occurred to him now that Mr. Gardiner might have some advice for him. How could he get the man alone?

Finally, he said, "Mr. Gardiner, I wondered if I might ask you some questions regarding certain investments I am considering."

Mr. Gardiner's eyebrows rose; a look of amusement crossed his face. "I am at your service, Mr. Darcy," he said. "Thomas, might we borrow your study?"

"Of course," Mr. Bennet replied.

Once in the study, Mr. Gardiner said, "Unless I miss my guess, you have more questions for me about marriage, not investments."

"You are right," Mr. Darcy admitted.

"I am happy to assist in any way I can."

Mr. Darcy sighed, and put his head in his hands. "I am a fool."

"That is a good start," Gardiner said, agreeably.

"Last night, I said terrible things to Elizabeth." And he recounted the entire conversation.

"You wanted her to tell you that she no longer regretted marrying you; when she did not do so, then you listed all the reasons that she was not your ideal wife. Is that an accurate summation of the situation?" Gardiner's voice was cold.

Mr. Darcy flinched at hearing that description. "It is, yes."

"I am tempted to write you off completely, as I begin to believe that you are not good husband material. But it would be Elizabeth who would suffer from my decision, so I must reconsider."

"So do you have advice for me?"

"Never speak to Elizabeth again, was the first thought that crossed my mind! Very well. I believe I will bring Mrs. Gardiner in to help you."

"Must you?" Mr. Darcy asked, unhappily.

"I think I must."

Mr. Darcy groaned as Mr. Gardiner left the room. A few minutes later, Mr. Gardiner returned with his wife.

"Go on, Mr. Darcy. Tell my wife what you said to her favorite niece."

Mr. Darcy looked at Mr. Gardiner in disbelief. "Is it your intention to humiliate me, sir?"

"Oh, it is, indeed. Did you not humiliate Elizabeth?" Turning to his wife, he briefly recounted what Mr. Darcy had told him.

Mrs. Gardiner listened in silence. She nodded at her husband and then left the room.

Mr. Darcy was now confounded. What was going on? He was even more dumbfounded – or, he supposed, befuddled – when Mrs. Gardiner returned with Elizabeth.

Elizabeth saw her husband sitting in the study and immediately turned to leave.

"No, Lizzy, wait," her aunt said.

"I will not speak with him."

"I know. But we must get the two of you past this. Elizabeth, what did your husband say to you last night that was so upsetting?"

Elizabeth's temper flared. "He was pleased to present me with a list of the things that I did not bring to the marriage. Dowry, connections, consequence – did I miss anything, William? Perhaps the ideal bride would have had golden hair, blue eyes? And play the harp as well as the piano? And speak Italian as well as French?" She was sobbing now.

Mr. Darcy said, helplessly, "Elizabeth, that is not what I meant!"

Leaning forward, Mrs. Gardiner said, "What *did* you mean, Mr. Darcy?"

"I was trying to impress upon her that she should be grateful that I married her!"

"And listing all the attributes that you thought she was missing was how you intended to accomplish that?"

"No! She is not missing any attributes! And she is absolutely lovely!"

"Good; Elizabeth, what did you hear?"

"He thinks I look tolerable, but of course I am still missing the dowry, the connections, and everything else!"

"Mr. Darcy, is that an accurate restatement of what you said?"

"Of course not! I said that she is lovely and is not missing any attributes!" Mr. Darcy was utterly confused.

"Let us try again; Elizabeth, what did your husband say just now?"

There was silence. "Elizabeth?" her aunt prompted.

Hesitantly, she said, "That I am lovely and not missing any attributes." Her voice was low.

"Mr. Darcy? Is that what you said?"

"Yes, it is."

"Good; tell me, Mr. Darcy, why did you recite all that about the dowry, the connections, and so on to Elizabeth last night?"

There was silence. "Mr. Darcy?" Mrs. Gardiner prompted him.

"I was hurt that she still regrets marrying me." His voice was flat and bleak.

"Elizabeth, did you say that you regret marrying him?"

"No, I did not!"

"What did you say, then?" Mrs. Gardiner asked, quietly.

"Well, he said that he no longer regretted marrying me; I knew he wanted me to say the same thing, but I was trying to make him understand that what had happened to me as a result of our marriage was not what had happened to him."

"In what way?"

"I told him that I had lost my home and my family, and I did! It is true!"

"And how did that make you feel, Mr. Darcy?"

"I felt sad, I believe. No; I felt angry."

"Why did you feel angry?"

"Because I believe I have given her a lovely home, far better than Longbourn! And why is it that Georgiana and I cannot be her family?" He was angry again.

"Do you think Elizabeth would marry someone in order to gain a large house?"

He recalled seeing her with her head buried in her hands. He remembered how infrequently he had seen genuine joy on her face. He had to reply honestly. "I suppose not."

"And do you think that after a mere few months, she can think of you and Miss Darcy as a replacement for her birth family? And even if she did, would that mean that her parents and her sisters should no longer have a place in her heart? That she would no longer miss being with them?"

He could only shake his head.

Mrs. Gardiner went on, relentlessly. "Mr. Darcy, when Elizabeth said that she missed her family and home, what did you think she was saying?"

"I thought she was saying that she still regretted marrying me."

"Elizabeth, is that what you said?"

"Of course not."

"Well, then, let us get down to Mr. Darcy's question. Do you regret marrying him?"

She considered the question carefully. She did not wish to hurt William, but she did not want to be dishonest. She thought about his kindness to his servants and tenants, and the way he had taken on enormous responsibility at such a young age. Then she looked at William directly. "Generally I do not, no."

"Why did you bring up missing your family and home?" Mrs. Gardiner asked.

"I do not know; I suppose I wanted him to acknowledge that it had been easier for him than for me."

"And he responded by telling you why it was not easier for him."

"I suppose so, yes."

"Would it be reasonable to say that each of you have given up something that you felt was important to you when you were forced to marry?"

They both nodded, hesitantly.

"Do you both understand that Elizabeth will always love and miss her family, but that this does not mean that she will not, in time, come to love and appreciate her new family?"

They both nodded.

"And with that in mind, is it true that neither of you regrets the marriage?"

They both nodded.

"Can you each say that to one another?"

Mr. Darcy immediately looked at Elizabeth. "Elizabeth, I do not regret marrying you."

Elizabeth looked at Mr. Darcy. "And I do not regret marrying you."

Mrs. Gardiner smiled at both of them. "There! That is what should have been said last night."

Elizabeth looked at her aunt in wonder. "How did you learn to do this?"

"My mother; she taught all of us how to resolve our differences. Generally a problem arises because we do not accurately hear what the other person said, or because what was said was not what was truly meant."

"No wonder you and Uncle Gardiner get on so well. I wish you could teach this to my parents."

Mrs. Gardiner did not respond to that. Instead, she said, "May I ask the two of you to promise that if you get angry with the other, you will always – always! – talk it out. Misunderstandings can escalate quickly if they are not dealt with promptly."

Mr. and Mrs. Gardiner left the room, leaving Elizabeth and Mr. Darcy alone.

After a minute's silence, Mr. Darcy spoke. "Elizabeth, I find it difficult to tell you how I feel about – well, anything. I am not accustomed to discussing such things, I suppose."

Elizabeth said, "I think that is common for men, is it not?"

Mr. Darcy said, "It might be; there are things I feel that I want to say and I cannot seem to do so."

"Like what?" she asked. She looked at him so earnestly, so hopefully, that the words burst from his lips.

"I think you are far lovelier than Jane," he burst out.

"Me? Really?" She looked shocked.

"Yes. Oh, yes. There are so many different colours in your hair, and it shines beautifully in sunlight. I think your eyes, the way they light up when you are happy, are the most beautiful eyes I have ever seen."

"William, I – I thank you. I did not know –"

He growled, deep in his throat. "Exactly; you did not know because I find it so difficult to speak such things!"

"Yet you just did."

He stood up, never talking his eyes off Elizabeth, and opened his arms. Elizabeth rose, and walked into them. They held each other for a long minute. Mr. Darcy pulled away, just a bit, and slowly, very slowly, bent his head down. He touched his lips to hers, very gently, very softly, and for only a moment.

Then, conscious of the fact that someone could walk in at any time, they separated. Silently, arm in arm, they made their way back to the parlour.

Chapter Forty-Two

Mrs. Bennet invited everyone to stay for dinner. Elizabeth felt that William had likely had enough of the Bennets for one day and declined with thanks. "I believe Mrs. Hurst expects us for dinner, Mama."

On the carriage ride home, Elizabeth asked Mr. Darcy, "Do you think Mrs. Hurst was able to get Miss Bingley out of her room and into the carriage?"

"I do not," he replied promptly. "Have you ever, even once, seen Miss Bingley abide by her brother's strictures?"

"I have not, no. So are we to believe that Miss Bingley is still at Netherfield!"

"I suspect that she is; we shall see." His tone was cheerful.

He was soon proven right. No sooner were the Darcys inside the house, than they heard Mrs. Hurst arguing with Miss Bingley.

Georgiana's eyes were wide. "But her brother told her to go!" she whispered.

"He did, but Miss Bingley is not in the habit of doing what he tells her to," her brother replied.

The Netherfield housekeeper came out to tell them that dinner would be ready in an hour, if that would suit. Upon assuring her that an hour was fine, they went upstairs to change.

***

The Hursts joined them for dinner, but Miss Bingley was absent. The Darcys politely did not comment on the fact that Miss Bingley was still in the house, but the tension between the two Hursts was palpable. Tea was served in the drawing room after dinner, but Elizabeth said she was tired, so the Darcys did not linger.

Elizabeth and Mr. Darcy met, by unspoken agreement, in their shared sitting room. They were a little shy with one another, so they began by speaking of Miss Bingley's stubborn refusal to leave Netherfield.

"Should we not assist Mrs. Hurst?" Elizabeth wondered.

"Do you want to?"

"No, not at all. If I am honest, I hope to never set eyes on Miss Bingley again. But nor do I want Jane to come back to Netherfield and find her still here."

"Elizabeth, I know you want everything to go well for Jane, but you must understand that this is now Bingley's responsibility, not yours."

She paused, struck by that thought, and threw her head back and laughed merrily, her eyes alight with humour. "You are right, William! Honestly, I feel like I have spent a good part of my life guarding my gentle sister from hurt and harm. It was a labour of love, of course, but it was nonetheless a labour."

"And now you are labouring to guard Georgiana, are you not?"

She sobered. "Yes, of course; is that not my responsibility as her sister?"

"It is, but it is one that we share. Elizabeth, you no longer need to bear *any* responsibilities alone. I am here to share all of that with you. A burden shared is a burden halved, is it not?"

"It is. But, William, that has to go both ways."

"What do you mean?"

"Simply this: I am here to share your burdens as well. I cannot allow you to share my burdens if I am not also permitted to share yours."

"Do you know, I did not think of that," Mr. Darcy admitted. "I am accustomed to carrying my burdens alone."

"Yes, in stoic silence. But I shall insist on it, you know."

He laughed, unexpectedly. "I know you will."

Elizabeth smiled at him, warmly. His dimple had popped out when he laughed. Whereas that dimple had once caused her pain, it now gave her happiness to see it.

Mr. Darcy admitted, "But I feel rather uncomfortable being here at Netherfield with Bingley gone and only the Hursts here, particularly when they are struggling to deal with Miss Bingley."

"We will we leave tomorrow, then?"

"I would prefer that; however, I do not wish to cut short your time with your family. I do understand that you miss them."

"But we will come back, will we not? William?"

"Of course; or they will visit us. We should certainly have the Gardiners stay for a time at Pemberley. I think your aunt would like to visit her childhood home."

"I am certain that she would. But, William, I must warn you that they have three small children. You have not met them, as they have been leaving the children with their nursemaid, but they would not want to be separated from their children for a long period of time."

"Of course not; the children must come to Pemberley as well," he answered, promptly.

"That would be wonderful! Oh, I must not forget to tell you how very much I appreciated what you said to my mother. She has been afraid for years and years; you promising to buy her a house meant the world to her."

She could see that he was embarrassed. William would always do what was right, but he could not bear to be praised for it. The more she learned about him, the more she lov- liked him.

Chapter Forty-Three

Early summer 1812

The Darcys were on their way home. They had stopped at Longbourn to say their farewells, with many promises of return visits and letters. Mr. Darcy was glad that they had made this journey, as Elizabeth was now much more content. She was smiling as she looked out the window, enjoying the passing scenery.

He had recalled that she could not read in the carriage, so he had made it a point to bring along some books that he thought she would enjoy hearing read aloud. They had finished *Gulliver's Travels* on the way to Meryton, but he knew *Much Ado About Nothing* was her favorite comedy; he had borrowed it from Bennet so that he might read it to her.

He opened the book and began. "*Act 1, Scene 1 Messina - before Leonato's house. Leonato: I learn in this letter that Don Pedro comes this night to Messina. Messenger: He was not three leagues off when I left him. Leonato: How many gentlemen have you lost in this battle?*"

Elizabeth smiled broadly upon hearing William reading her favorite comedy aloud. She understood that he had brought the play deliberately for her enjoyment. Their relationship had improved dramatically, despite the unpleasantness with George Wickham.

***

The journey home was, Mr. Darcy thought, a very long three days. Georgiana and Elizabeth continued to share a room at the inns, and he continued to sleep alone. This had not disturbed him on the way to Meryton; indeed, he had been grateful for Georgiana's presence. But now he wished he could speak to Elizabeth in private, as he knew there was still much that needed to be said. Moreover, he was very much looking forward to taking Mr. Gardiner's advice.

***

They finally arrived home, tired and dusty. Elizabeth was immediately whisked upstairs by Carrie, who had arrived at Pemberley a few hours earlier. She had already unpacked Elizabeth's trunk, and had fresh clothing laid out for her.

"A bath first, Mrs. Darcy," Carrie said, firmly.

Elizabeth was grateful for the warm, rose-scented bath. How spoiled I have become, she thought. Growing up at Longbourn, the sisters were lucky to get one bath a week; here at Pemberley, she bathed every day, and Carrie was waiting to wrap her up in an enormous towel when she emerged.

More and more, she understood and appreciated what her aunt had told her. She could miss her family and still appreciate what she had now. The two were not incompatible. And while she would never have married for material gain, there was no denying that she loved living at Pemberley. The house was magnificent, filled with endless treasures and delights; Georgiana was everything charming; Mrs. Reynolds was wonderful, the tenants appreciative of her support.

And then there was William...

***

At dinner that night, Mr. Darcy and Elizabeth were a little shy with one another. Traveling in the coach with Georgiana, they had both known that things between them would change once they were home. And now here they were, and it was evening, and soon it would be time to go to sleep. Or, at least, to bed.

***

When Elizabeth heard a tap on her bedroom door, her breath caught in her throat. The tap came from the door into the sitting room, not the door into the hallway, so there was only one person who could be tapping.

"Come in," she whispered. Realising that he could not possibly have heard that, she said, a little louder, "Come in!" The door opened. William stood there, clad only in a dressing gown. She had never seen a man in such a state of undress; she stared for a moment and looked away, embarrassed.

He approached her. "Do not look away, Elizabeth," he whispered. "Please. Look at me. And let me look at you."

He stood still and silent, inviting her inspection.

Elizabeth knew – indeed, it could not be denied! – that her husband was a handsome man. The dressing gown could not disguise his broad shoulders and well-muscled calves. His hair was dark and thick, much darker than hers; it was almost black. She longed to run her hands through it. His arms were thick with muscle and sinew; she wondered what it would feel like to be held by them.

And while she was looking at him, blushing hard, he was devouring her with his eyes. She was exquisite, he thought. She was dressed in a nightgown that reached the floor, but by the candlelight he could easily see her body, small but firm. Her waist was narrow; he could span it with his two hands, he thought, dizzyingly. Her hips flared out delightfully from that narrow waist. Her breasts were perfectly sized for her small frame.

He could not wait to touch her and to be touched, but he knew that he dared not rush her. Everything, his happiness and hers, rested on how he proceeded tonight. He was almost afraid to approach her! But desire overwhelmed scruples, and finally Mr. Darcy whispered, "Elizabeth." And he moved closer to her. Then he stopped, watching her. Would she move away? He waited, not wanting to do anything that would make her uncomfortable. She was motionless, still watching him.

Elizabeth's breath caught in her throat; was he about to – about to – and his lips touched hers, and all thoughts flew out of her head.

Tentatively, she kissed him back, not at all certain if she was doing this right, but that thought flew away as well, and there was only him, her, his mouth, hers…

Was there return pressure? Was she truly kissing him back? She was! His heart pounded. Slowly, Mr. Darcy, slowly, he reminded himself. He gently deepened the kiss. Then he pulled away.

"Elizabeth?"

"Yes?" Her voice was soft.

"Is this all right?"

"Yes," she whispered.

He had been holding himself under tight control, all too aware of the consequences of failure, but her whispered "yes" broke his control. He swept her up into his arms, carried her to her bed, placed her down as gently as his inflamed senses would allow, and began to love her, with his body, his mind, and his heart.

Chapter Forty-Four

Mr. Darcy awoke before Elizabeth; it took him a moment to understand why he was in a strange bed. The events of the prior night swam into his recollection, and he caught his breath.

She lay beside him, still sleeping. He watched her, marveling that he had ever thought her only tolerable. What long lashes she had! They lay like tiny dark fans on her white cheeks. At that moment, she took a deep breath and opened her eyes. It took a moment before her eyes focused; seeing Mr. Darcy staring at her, she stared back. Neither wanted to break the spell that held them both in thrall.

He stayed motionless for a time, watching her, waiting for the rather obvious signs of his renewed interest in her to subside before rising from the bed. While he would have been more than happy to be intimate with her this morning, he suspected that her body, unaccustomed to such exertions, needed time to recover.

Remembering their activities from the previous night, Elizabeth began to feel embarrassed. What was one to say to someone who – who – well, someone with whom one had done *that*? If there was a protocol here, she was ignorant of it.

William saw her begin to blush. Was she embarrassed by what they had done? He hoped not; for him, it had been the most magical night of his life. "Elizabeth," he whispered. Reaching a hand out, he touched her hair. "So beautiful!" he said.

She smiled at him; relieved, he smiled back. "Are you well, Elizabeth? Not in pain, I hope?"

"A little," she confessed. "But I think it is to be expected."

"Is there anything I might do to ease your discomfort?"

"No, I will be fine."

"Very well; I will leave you to Carrie's ministrations. Will I see you at breakfast?"

"You will."

Mr. Darcy went back through the sitting room to his own room and rang for Carstairs. His valet appeared, and they began the process of getting Mr. Darcy ready for the day. Mr. Darcy was still in a bit of a daze from the prior night, but he eventually became aware that Carstairs was smiling indulgently.

Mr. Darcy stared at his valet. "Why are you smiling like that, Carstairs?"

"Why, you appear to be happy this morning, Mr. Darcy, so I was smiling to see it!"

Mr. Darcy found it surprising that his mood was so obvious.

Seeing his master's confusion, Carstairs supplied, "You were whistling, sir."

Whistling? He never whistled; did he? "I was whistling?"

"Yes, sir; I had not heard you whistle before."

Mr. Darcy realised that his bed had obviously not been slept in. Servants knew everything, of course. Mr. Darcy did not know whether to be embarrassed or pleased, so he simply did not reply.

***

Elizabeth was having a similar discussion with Carrie. Carrie had taken one look at Elizabeth's rumpled bed and had immediately come to the correct conclusion as to what had happened (finally!) the previous night. Without a word, she prepared a bath for Elizabeth.

"I thought I would go down to breakfast first, Carrie," Elizabeth said.

"With respect, Mrs. Darcy, you will feel better it you have a quick bath first."

Servants knew everything, she thought.

***

When she finally entered the breakfast room, her husband and sister were already there. Mr. Darcy rose. "Did you sleep well, Elizabeth?" he enquired, eyes twinkling.

"Exceptionally well," she replied, smiling.

"May I fix you a plate?"

"Yes, thank you," she replied.

Georgiana watched them, glee written all over her face. She did not understand any of the details, but she could see that a change, a big and important change had occurred between them. At last, she thought.

"What are your plans today, Elizabeth?" Mr. Darcy asked.

"I must speak with Mrs. Reynolds, of course, to see what needs to be done around the house, and I must give attention to the household accounts."

Had he truly doubted her ability to be the mistress of Pemberley? Mr. Darcy wondered. His musings were interrupted by his sister.

"Will you go to Kent this year?" Georgiana asked.

He frowned, as Elizabeth turned an enquiring eye on him.

"Kent?"

"Brother usually goes to Rosings Park to help our Aunt Catherine with her estate, but I think this year…" And she trailed off.

"No, I will not go to Kent," he said, firmly.

"But if you usually go," Elizabeth began.

"Elizabeth, after that astonishingly bad-mannered letter she wrote to you, and the letter your father received from her parson, I feel no obligation to her whatsoever. I will write to her and tell her so." He turned to Georgiana. "I imagine you will spend the day practicing your piano."

She groaned, "Yes, I must! Mr. Galiani will be so angry that I have not practiced for over a week!"

Going to her office, Elizabeth was pleased to find a letter from Jane on her desk.

Dearest Lizzy,

I am the happiest woman alive. Charles is so kind, so good, there are no words for it! And Sunset House is lovely; you must make Mr. Darcy take you here!

I think of you often, dearest sister. I know that you did not marry for love, but I pray that you are able to find some affection in your marriage. The way Charles speaks of your husband, he is practically a god, so there must be good in him. And, as you and I agreed, he is very handsome, which a man should be if he can possibly help it!

We will return to Netherfield in another week. Charles thinks of buying it, but I have said that we should wait and see how we like living so close to Mama. I know that you understand me.

I am a bit concerned; Charles had a letter from Mr. Hurst, saying that they have been unable to get Miss Bingley to get into the carriage to travel north. I had understood that she would be gone when I returned from my wedding trip, but now it looks as if this will not be the case. I know Charles would like me to say that his sister may stay, and quite honestly, it is taking all my strength not to agree! I will keep you apprised.

Your fondest and happiest sister,

Jane Bingley

P.S. Does my new name not look lovely?

MISUNDERSTANDINGS

Going to his office, Dary was puzzled to see a letter from Aunt Elaine on his desk. She rarely wrote to him, so his first thought was concern for Richard. Praying silently that his cousin was not injured – or worse! – he opened the letter and skimmed it quickly. No, thank God, it was not about Richard. He read it again, slowly, and frowned.

> *Dear Nephew,*
>
> *Henry has been coughing a little, which I attribute to London's terrible air. He agrees that a little time in the country is what is required. It has been ages since we have visited you at Pemberley, and I long to see Georgiana.*
>
> *You may expect us in two weeks.*
>
> *With Love,*
>
> *Elaine Fitzwilliam, Countess of Matlock*

The Matlocks were coming to Pemberley? Whatever for? He did not believe for a minute that Uncle had a cough. And even as he asked himself the question, he knew the answer: to meet Elizabeth.

What was he to do? He cared about Elizabeth, that he knew. He could enumerate the reasons with no difficulty. She was a far better mistress for the estate than he could have imagined; she was a perfect sister for shy Georgiana; she was beautiful to look at. He realised he could spend an hour cataloguing her virtues.

But none of these were the reasons for his feelings; there was something, something about her, something undefinable that made him care about her. He supposed there was no logic behind such things.

But the fact remained that she was not the woman everyone had expected him to marry. She would be judged by the Matlocks and found wanting, and he could not let that happen to her.

He considered some options. He could have Elizabeth go back to Longbourn when the Matlocks arrived. This would work, he thought. Bingley and Jane would be back at Netherfield; surely Elizabeth would want to see them. Or he could suggest that she visit the Gardiners. They would love to see her, he was sure, and though they lived in London, the Gardiners did not move in the social circles that he did. No one would associate her with Mr. Darcy of Pemberley.

But he knew he was putting off the inevitable. Sooner or later, the Matlocks would meet his wife, so it might as well be now. At least now Elizabeth would be on home ground, a place where she was comfortable and supported by everyone around her. She would not have the added discomfort of being in an unfamiliar place.

Sighing, he put his aunt's letter in a separate pile and sorted through the rest of his correspondence. He lost track of time, and was surprised when a knock on his study door alerted him to the fact that it was teatime; a tray was being brought to him.

"No; I thank you, but I will take tea in the drawing room," he told the maid.

"Very good, sir; Mrs. Darcy and Georgiana are there."

He put his correspondence aside and went to join them.

Chapter Forty-Five

Once Elizabeth had handed out teacups for Mr. Darcy and Georgiana, Mr. Darcy thought it time to begin.

"I had a letter from the Matlocks," he said, hoping he sounded casual.

"Oh! I hope all is well?" Georgiana said, immediately concerned. Of course, she would think of Colonel Fitzwilliam immediately, as had he.

He hastened to reassure her. "Everyone is fine, though Aunt Elaine says that Uncle has a bit of a cough. She hopes that some country air will do him good."

"They are coming here?" Elizabeth said. She sounded calm.

"They are, in two weeks."

Georgiana looked at him, then at Elizabeth, then back at him. He nodded at his sister.

Elizabeth saw the gestures and said, "Yes? What are you not telling me?"

"They are doubtless coming to meet *you*, Lizzy!" Georgiana said. "I cannot remember the last time they visited us at Pemberley, so there is no other explanation."

"Are they? Good; I look forward to meeting them."

Why was she so composed? "Elizabeth, you are not nervous?" Mr. Darcy asked.

"Is there a reason I should be?" She sounded surprised.

"Well – no, I suppose not," he said, taken aback.

She looked at him for a long minute. "I see; you assume they will disapprove of me." Her tone was flat.

"No! Not at all. I am simply concerned that they might say something that will hurt your feelings."

"If that is truly your concern, I beg you to think on it no longer. As long as *you* are not distressed, certainly I shall not be. It is only the opinion of my family that matters to me – in this instance, you and Georgiana. But perhaps you would tell me something about them."

"I believe I told you that the Earl was my mother's brother. He married the daughter of a baronet. Her father was Sir Grenville."

Elizabeth nodded. "So she was Miss...what is her name?"

"Elaine. Yes, she was Miss Elaine; now she is Lady Matlock."

"So she married well."

"She did, indeed, but she has done exceptionally well in her new role. She is a credit to the family."

Elizabeth nodded. "I hope to be considered so as well. What can you tell me about their culinary preferences?"

Mr. Darcy looked puzzled. "I have no idea; I suspect Mrs. Reynolds will be able to tell you."

"They have been to Pemberley before, have they not? So there are likely rooms that they prefer. Yes, very well, William, I will direct such questions to Mrs. Reynolds!" Elizabeth laughed.

"You are calm about this, Elizabeth; one would think that you entertained an earl and a countess every day of your life." Mr. Darcy could not account for the fact that he was very nervous about this visit, while she was not.

She shook her head. "William, I am not overawed by the aristocracy. I will treat your relatives with every respect, of course, but if they are expecting me to crawl on the ground in their presence, they will be deeply disappointed. But oh! Let me tell you about the letter I received from Jane. Jane and Charles are now returning to Netherfield, and Miss Bingley is still there!"

Georgiana sat bolt upright. "Oh, no! What will your sister do?"

"She wrote that she knows Charles wants her to let Miss Bingley live with them, but she is trying to be strong in saying that Miss Bingley must go."

Mr. Darcy wondered if Elizabeth would blame him for not helping the Hursts with this situation; but he thought that no, that sort of pettiness was not part of her character.

And his opinion was borne out not a moment later, when she said, "I suggested to William that we should help Mrs. Hurst get Miss Bingley into the carriage, but he quite rightly said that she was Charles' problem to deal with, not ours. I am glad we did not get involved in that thankless situation."

That night, Mr. Darcy went to Elizabeth's room again, clad in his dressing gown. She welcomed him rather shyly. Doubtless it would take some time for them to become accustomed to their new intimacy.

But he should ask her, he thought. "Elizabeth, is it all right for me to be here?"

"What do you mean?"

"I do not want you to ever feel that I am forcing myself on you."

She shook her head. "You are not forcing yourself on me. But I will tell you if, for any reason, I do not want us to – to – to do *that*. Is that reasonable?"

"Absolutely. But is it not good for us to speak together when we are alone, even if we are not doing *that*?" He found himself smiling. Had he smiled so much before Elizabeth?

"I would like it very much, William," she said, smiling in return.

"Good; as would I. Are you truly not angry with me for not staying at Netherfield to help the Hursts force Caroline Bingley into a carriage?"

"I am not, no. I would like for Jane to not have this difficulty immediately after returning home, but she and her husband must learn to sort such things out for themselves."

"I agree, and I am glad that you see that. But I must tell you that my experience with Charles tells me that he will always take the path of least resistance."

"So Jane must stir up enough of a fuss that taking Miss Bingley away is the path of least resistance? That will be difficult for my mild-tempered sister."

"It is a dilemma," he agreed.

"But not ours to solve."

"No."

"Well then, William, was there anything else on your mind tonight?" As she spoke, she reached up and stroked his chest. He promptly rolled onto his back, pulling her on top of him.

She gasped in surprise, but took advantage of her position to open his dressing gown and run her hands down his chest. Immediately aroused, he flipped their position so that she was beneath him.

"Are you in discomfort from last night?" he remembered to ask, though his heart was pounding.

"No; you were gentle with me," she said, her eyes raised trustingly to his.

Gentle, he thought, rather desperately. I must remember to still be gentle; it is only her second time. He reined himself in, teasing her lips, her throat, her breasts, until she was squirming beneath him, wanting more.

There was no more discussion of Jane and Charles that night. Elizabeth's last coherent thought was that her Aunt Gardiner had been very, very right: marital activities were *not* to be dreaded.

Chapter Forty-Six

Elizabeth was not concerned about the Matlock's visit, but as it was obvious that William was, she would do everything she could to make the visit a success. Of course, if they were determined to dislike her, all the perfect meals in the world would not change their minds.

She and Mrs. Reynolds spent several hours together searching Lady Anne's journals, looking for information about their past visits.

"Here," Mrs. Reynolds said. "This, I think, is the most recent visit from the Matlocks."

Elizabeth looked over her housekeeper's shoulder. "So…three courses each night, and the Earl prefers rich sauces. His favorite dessert is lemon custard. How do these people not gain a stone every week? And they prefer to use the Blue Suite. Might it need updating, or perhaps new sheets?"

The two went upstairs to inspect the rooms in question. Elizabeth had not seen these rooms before. She had learnt her way around the rooms that she must know, as the mistress of the estate, but she had not yet seen all the guest rooms. The Blue Suite was a lovely set of rooms, connected by a sitting room, much like her room and William's. These rooms were every bit as large and possibly larger, and they were beautifully decorated in various shades of blue with yellow accents. The colours served to make the room feel both cheerful and restful.

"When was it last cleaned?" she asked Mrs. Reynolds. "It looks as if someone has attended it recently."

"The guest rooms in this part of the house are cleaned monthly; if I recall correctly, the maids were here two weeks ago."

"Well, let us have them give this room their full attention as soon as possible; I certainly do not want to give the Earl and Countess any excuse to dislike me straight away."

Mrs. Reynolds immediately spoke against anyone disliking Elizabeth. Elizabeth was unconvinced, well aware that this was the older woman's affection for her speaking, but she allowed herself to be soothed.

Chapter Forty-Seven

A few days later, both Elizabeth and Mr. Darcy received letters from the Bingleys. Elizabeth's was from Jane, of course.

Dearest Sister,

We are back at Netherfield and Caroline is still here. She says she does not know why I am so upset, she is certain her behaviour is impeccable, and so on. Charles says he wonders if perhaps we both overreacted and Caroline should not have to leave.

I do not know what to do, Lizzy! Please advise me!

Your Loving but Unhappy Sister,

Jane Bingley

She rushed to William's study to show it to him, and found him reading his own letter. As best they could decipher Charles' handwriting, it said:

Darcy,

I told Caroline she had to move up to Scarborough because she is so very rude to Jane, but she will not go! She says she does *not know what Jane is talking **** [undecipherable handwriting] and I do not know what to do!*

I cannot make Jane unhappy, but Caroline is my sister! Can you **** [more undecipherable writing}.

Please advise me!

Charles Bingley

"I know you said we should not get involved, William."

"And you agreed that I was right," he reminded her.

"But they have both appealed to us for help; does that not change the situation?"

He considered that. "I do not think that is necessarily true."

"You do not?! Do you recall the Gardiners helping us?"

"I do, of course, but I think it a good practice in general to not get involved in someone else's relationship."

"But – but this is Jane and Charles!"

"I do not see how that changes the situation."

She stared at him, frustration building. "But Charles promised Jane that Miss Bingley would not live with them! And now he is going back on his promise!"

"I understand that, Elizabeth; I simply do not see that it is my responsibility to point it out to him."

"Even though he has asked for your advice?!"

"Yes."

She huffed in frustration, turned on her heel, and left the room. Mr. Darcy stared after her, wondering what, precisely, he had done wrong.

***

At dinner that night, Georgiana could feel the tension between them. "Lizzy, is everything all right?" she said, tentatively.

"Yes, Georgiana," Elizabeth replied.

"Brother?"

"Everything is fine, Georgiana," he said, not looking at her.

It occurred to Elizabeth that Georgiana could be of some assistance. "Georgiana, what would you do if you had to live with Miss Bingley?"

Mr. Darcy immediately looked up and scowled at Elizabeth.

Undaunted by her husband's expression, Elizabeth looked at Georgiana for an answer.

"Do you mean what would I do if she were to live at Pemberley? I cannot imagine that Brother would allow that to happen, but if he did, I went write to my Aunt Elaine and beg her to come and get me."

Mr. Darcy growled under his breath.

"Did you say something, William?" Elizabeth asked him. Her eyes were narrowed.

"I do not like you dragging my sister into this, Elizabeth."

"Into what?" Georgiana wanted to know.

Elizabeth chose this moment to become interested in her plate, leaving Mr. Darcy to answer. "Jane and Charles Bingley returned to Netherfield and Miss Bingley was still there," he said, tersely.

"What?!" Georgiana gasped. Her shock was everything Elizabeth could have hoped for. "But he promised her when she agreed to marry him!"

"Yes, and Jane has asked me for advice and Charles has asked William for advice," Elizabeth explained.

"But of course the advice must be for him to abide by his promise. Surely there cannot be two opinions on the matter."

"As it happens, I agree with you," Elizabeth said, sounding satisfied.

Georgiana realised then that Brother did not agree. "Brother?" she asked.

"Georgiana, I do not think this should have been discussed in front of you."

"How am I to learn about anything if all the interesting discussions are *not* in front of me?"

He exhaled, loudly. "Very well; Georgiana, the relationship between a husband and a wife is fragile. No one outside that relationship should interfere in any way."

"Even if those outside people have been asked for advice?"

Elizabeth felt like cheering Georgiana on, but she remained still, focused on her dinner.

Mr. Darcy said, "I do not wish to speak about this again."

And with that, the room became silent except for the clinking of the silverware and crystal. When Elizabeth rose at the end of the meal, Mr. Darcy remained in his seat, not looking at his wife and sister as they left the room.

In the drawing room, Elizabeth sat beside Georgiana. "He was right," she said, taking the girl's hand. "I should not have involved you in the discussion. I knew you would agree with me and so I used you to make my point. I am so sorry, Georgiana."

"No, Elizabeth, do not apologise." Georgiana sounded unusually determined. "He is wrong and we are right."

"Being right is not the most important thing in a relationship, Georgiana. It does me no good to be right if my husband is unhappy with me."

"But Jane needs you!"

"It feels that way to me, of course; but someone once suggested that in order to be happy in marriage, one must never let other family members get in the way. Also, Georgiana, I tell you this: once you are married, your relationship with your husband must become the most important relationship in your life."

Mr. Darcy walked into the room in time to hear Elizabeth's last few sentences. She had quoted – was it Hurst? – who had said that you should not let other family members get in the way. He had been referring to Miss Bingley, of course. And then she had said that her relationship with her husband was the most important relationship in her life. Theirs was her most important relationship! Coming from a woman who was devoted to her family, that was a remarkable declaration.

He paused for a moment, reconsidering his own priorities. Sighing, he sat down across from Elizabeth and Georgiana. "Very well; what is it you want to tell them to do?"

Elizabeth beamed at him. That smile, directed at him, was all he needed to convince him that he had done the right thing in agreeing with her position.

"Of course, Charles must honor his promise. It is not well done for a man to promise something to a woman when she agrees to be his wife, and then go back on his word."

"Of course," he said, agreeably. "I shall write to Charles directly and tell him he must certainly send Miss Bingley to Scarborough."

"And I shall tell Jane that she must hold firm!"

Georgiana sat back, satisfied that all was now well.

Chapter Forty-Eight

Mr. Darcy wrote his letter, Elizabeth wrote hers, and both settled back into the various demands of the estate, satisfied that they had done their best for the Bingleys.

A week later, however, a carriage pulled up in front of the house. Elizabeth was informed by Mr. Baldwin that she had a visitor. Up to her metaphoric elbows in balancing the household budget, she sighed and asked, "Who is it, Mr. Baldwin?"

"It is Mrs. Bingley."

Elizabeth leapt from her chair; both the journal and the chair went crashing to the floor. She brushed past the butler with a mumbled apology and ran down the stairs, through the enormous entry way, into the formal drawing room.

"Jane!" She and her sister ran into each other's arms. And then Jane burst into tears.

"Jane? Oh, Jane! Whatever is the matter?"

"It is Charles! Charles..." and her sobs rendered her unable to speak.

"Come, Jane, sit down. Let me get you refreshments." Elizabeth pulled the bell and a maid came immediately.

Elizabeth said, "Betsy, tea and whatever cook has on hand, please." And she added, quietly, "And ask Mr. Darcy to join us."

She held Jane as she wept, handing her a handkerchief, as Jane's was sodden. The tea tray arrived, complete with small sandwiches and tiny cakes. Elizabeth quickly poured for Jane – sugar, no milk – and prepared a plate for her sister as well.

"Oh, Lizzy, I did not know where else to go! I did not know exactly where Pemberley was, but our coachman said he had been here before, and I took a maid – I do not know where she is, I suppose still in the carriage – and – and –" And here she broke down again.

Mr. Darcy walked into the drawing room in time to see a weeping Jane. He immediately understood the situation. "Mrs. Bingley, you are welcome here at Pemberley. I will see to your maid and your coachman; you need not be concerned." He bowed and left.

"There, Jane, you see, everything will be taken care of."

"Lizzy, I have to tell you what happened."

"I would guess that Charles refused to have Miss Bingley leave Netherfield."

"Yes! That is exactly what happened! How did you know?"

Elizabeth sighed. There was no way to say that Jane's husband would always take the easy way out. She felt again how superior a man William was; he would do what was right, no matter how difficult. She said, cautiously, "Well, Charles is a kind man, and so he would not want to upset his sister."

"But he is willing to upset his wife?!"

Mr. Darcy now came back into the room. "Mrs. Bingley, I had your trunk brought to the Green Room; the maid you brought with you is there as well."

"Come, Jane. Let me show you to your room. Everything will feel better once you have rested."

Jane nodded, bleakly, and let Elizabeth lead her upstairs. Jane's maid was waiting. As soon as Jane entered, she rose, curtsied and asked, "Shall I unpack, Mrs. Bingley?"

"Yes, please do," Elizabeth replied, in Jane's stead. "Jane, there are footmen all over the house; as soon as you feel ready, ask one of them to find me."

"The house is huge, Elizabeth,!" Jane remarked, with the first beginnings of a smile on her face.

"I am still finding my way around, I assure you!" With that, Elizabeth left her sister and went to find her husband.

***

"William, what shall we do?"

"There is nothing *to* do, Elizabeth; we must wait."

"Wait for what?"

"Well, either Bingley will come to retrieve his wife, or she will decide to return to Netherfield. They are both so accustomed to pleasing other people that it is impossible to say which will happen first."

She thought about it. "I suppose you are right. In the meantime, I will try to console her."

"I am certain she will be grateful for your concern."

At that moment, Mr. Baldwin walked into the drawing room. "The Earl and Countess of Matlock!"

Now? Really? But they were not supposed to come yet! Elizabeth and Mr. Darcy shared looks of stunned disbelief, but they both rose, automatically. An elegant, middle-aged lady in a stylish costume swept into the room, closely followed by an older gentleman wearing a tall black hat and carrying a walking stick.

Mr. Darcy performed introductions. Elizabeth curtsied respectfully, reminding herself that they were just people, no matter how well-dressed. "Lord and Lady Matlock, may I offer refreshments? Or would you prefer to go to your rooms first?"

They elected to go upstairs. Elizabeth led them to the Blue Suite, saying, "I understand that this is your preferred suite; I hope you will let me know immediately if there is anything that you need to ensure your comfort. Are your servants coming?"

Lady Matlock replied, "Their coach was delayed by a broken wheel; they should be here in another hour or so. I thank you, Mrs. Darcy, for your hospitality."

"I hope you will be willing to call me Elizabeth or Lizzy," she said, cordially.

"Thank you, Elizabeth; I am Aunt Matlock and this is Uncle Matlock."

"That is kind, I thank you!" Elizabeth was surprised at this mark of cordiality. With that, she curtsied again and left them.

Going back downstairs, she found Mr. Darcy still in the drawing room. "The Matlocks *and* Jane?" she asked, shaking her head. "I must let Mrs. Reynolds know immediately. And Cook must be informed." And with that, she scurried off.

***

About thirty minutes later, the Earl and Countess were led back into the drawing room by a footman. "Handy that you have these fellows all about, Darcy," the Earl remarked. "Pemberley is still devilish easy to get lost in!"

Elizabeth, who had returned from her hurried conversation with Mrs. Reynolds and Cook, chuckled. The Countess looked at her and smiled. "Elizabeth, are you able to find your way around?"

"I believe I am finally able to find my way to most of the principal rooms, but I do not think I have yet seen all of the guest rooms, nor have I yet been on the fourth or fifth floors."

Georgiana had been informed by Mrs. Reynolds that her Aunt and Uncle Matlock had arrived. She had quickly run upstairs to change into nicer clothing, and then joined the family in the formal drawing room.

"Georgiana! How lovely to see you!" Lady Matlock opened her arms to give her niece a hug. "I have not seen you in – I believe it has been about a year, has it not?"

"I think so, yes; was it not a year ago at Easter? Brother dropped me off at Matlock House when he went to visit Aunt Catherine."

"Oh, and speaking of Aunt Catherine, would I be correct in believing that you did not go to Kent this year, Darcy?" Lord Matlock asked.

"You would be correct, yes," Mr. Darcy replied.

"Because you did not want to leave your lovely new bride, no doubt?" Lord Matlock said.

"I would have been pleased to bring my lovely new bride with me to Rosings Park, had Aunt Catherine not found it necessary to write her a vitriolic letter when we first married."

"Did she, really?!" Lady Matlock sounded horrified.

"Are you truly surprised, Aunt Elaine?"

"Well, I suppose I am not truly surprised," Lady Matlock admitted, with a huff. "As I consider it, I would have been surprised had she *not* done so. I am sorry you had to read such a missive, Elizabeth."

"I was upset at first, if I am honest," Elizabeth confessed. "But I realised that there were doubtless any number of ladies who were upset that William had married someone who was not their daughter."

"You are certainly right about that," Lord Matlock said. "One of the *ton's* most sought-after bachelors!"

Mr. Darcy was turning red. "And I think we have now said enough about that."

Elizabeth said, "I should mention that my sister, Jane Bingley, is also in residence. You will doubtless meet her soon."

"She is married to Mr. Bingley, then?"

"She is."

"How nice for you that she is able to visit."

Georgiana had first looked confused, as she had not known Jane had arrived, but now her face cleared and comprehension filled her eyes. "Oh! So he did not force Miss Bingley to move out!"

The Matlocks looked at her with enquiring faces; Georgiana blushed and said, "Oh! I should not have said anything. I am so sorry, Lizzy."

Elizabeth sighed. "It is best if we do not discuss it; I hope you will understand that she is not at her liveliest right now."

Lady Matlock felt that she understood everything quite well. Mrs. Bingley had found herself unable to live with the terrible younger sister and had left home as a result. Mrs. Bingley evidently had some sense, as well as some pluck, to have left the marital home! She would look forward to meeting her.

***

Jane had not yet come downstairs, so Elizabeth went up to tell her what time dinner would be served, as well as to warn her that the Matlocks were in residence. Jane thought that she should leave immediately, as she did not feel in any way ready to be in such august company.

Elizabeth shook her head firmly. "They are kind, Jane. If you wish to return to Netherfield, I understand, but even so, you should not leave until the morning."

Jane was finally convinced to remain, though she now began to worry if she had adequate clothing for dinner with an earl and countess.

***

Everyone gathered in the family drawing room before dinner. Jane was introduced to Lord and Lady Matlock, and was greeted kindly.

"I have heard very nice things about your husband, Mrs. Bingley," Lady Matlock said.

"Thank you, Lady Matlock," Jane said, embarrassed.

"But you must miss your sister, Elizabeth, quite a bit. It is good of you to pay her a visit."

"Oh, indeed, for I miss her terribly!" Jane said, fervently.

"How long have you been married, Mrs. Bingley?"

"Only – only a month, Lady Matlock."

Elizabeth, concerned that Jane's distress would be revealed, quickly turned the conversation to London. Had the Matlocks attended any events? Theatre? Opera? Lady Matlock understood her hostess' purpose, and obediently spoke of their doings in the City.

Dinner was elegant and formal, in keeping with Lady Anne's notes about the Matlocks' preferences. When lemon custard arrived for the sweet course, Lady Matlock glanced at Elizabeth. The new Mrs. Darcy had obviously consulted Lady Anne's notes prior to their arrival. This confirmed what Richard had said and what she had observed for herself: Elizabeth Darcy was an intelligent young lady, likely to be a worthy mistress of Pemberley.

Jane was quiet throughout the meal, though the others kept a lively conversation going. Mr. Darcy contributed to the conversation, as he knew he must, but he was rather concerned about Jane Bingley. Was he supposed to mediate between Jane and Bingley? Should he send a messenger to Bingley asking what he should do? Come to think of it, did Bingley even know where his wife was?! Had Jane left a note of some sort, or was Bingley even now combing the countryside, looking for her? And to have the Matlocks descend upon them as well. He shook his head in disbelief.

He caught Elizabeth's eye. She had seen him shake his head and with a quirk of her eyebrow, she was asking if he was all right.

He gave her a quick nod, knowing that she would understand from that gesture that they would speak later. It was a great comfort, he realised, to have a companion who was so attuned to his gestures.

When Elizabeth rose to lead the ladies into the drawing room, he and his uncle stayed in the dining room. Brandy was poured, and Lord Matlock leaned back in his chair, snifter in hand.

His uncle wasted no time. "How is married life, Darcy?"

"Better than I expected," he said.

"She is a pretty little thing."

For Elizabeth to be summed up in such a way struck Mr. Darcy as wrong. "That is the least of her attributes, Uncle."

"Indeed? Clever as well, is she?"

"She is extremely intelligent, well-read, sensible, and hard-working."

"You were lucky, then."

For the hundredth time, Mr. Darcy considered what his fate would have been had he fallen upon Miss Bingley, or upon any of the other young ladies who were at that assembly! "Lucky does not even begin to describe it!" he replied, with deep feeling.

His uncle chuckled. "I am glad to hear it, Darcy. When I heard you were being forced into a marriage, I feared the worst. How does she do with Georgiana?"

"I could not have imagined a better sister for her."

"You are besotted, then!"

Besotted? He chuckled. Lord Matlock looked at him, questioningly. He explained; "When we were preparing to marry, I was told that she would have me befuddled. Now you have added besotted to the mix. No, Uncle, I do not think I am besotted, though I do admit to being occasionally befuddled, as predicted. I am simply aware of my good fortune and I believe we have come to feel some affection for one another."

His uncle shook his head. "No shame in being besotted. I was besotted with your aunt, you know. Still am, come to that."

***

Upon entering the drawing room, Jane and Elizabeth sat together on a small sofa; Lady Matlock took the largest chair, and Georgiana went to the piano and began playing softly.

Lady Matlock wasted no time. "Elizabeth, I was told of the situation that resulted in your marriage to my nephew. That must have been difficult for you."

"Oh, it was! I was prepared to run off to Canada, rather than marry against my inclination."

"What changed your mind?"

"I did not have a ticket to get to Canada, nor the funds to effect the purchase!" Elizabeth laughed merrily.

"And then?"

"Well, I suppose Georgiana helped change my mind."

"Did she? How?"

"She obviously adored William and since I knew her to be a sensible and sensitive young lady, I had to give her opinion some credence."

"And then?"

"Well, Lady Matlock –"

"Aunt Matlock," came the correction.

"Yes, thank you. Aunt Matlock, it is not some sort of deathless romance, but we work well together, and I believe we have even come to feel some affection for one another. I am quite content."

Quite content! Lady Matlock knew a woman in love when she saw one, and she was looking at one now; but she knew Elizabeth must come to understand that in her own time. She had also seen a marked change in Georgiana's demeanor, entirely to the good. "Will you come to London?" she asked.

At that, Elizabeth's expressive face closed up. "Evidently not."

"What can you mean? Darcy always comes to London for two or three months a year."

"He does not want me to go to London," Elizabeth explained.

"Whyever not?"

"He does not think I would do well in high society."

"Really! Well, we shall see about that!"

"No, Lady – Aunt Matlock, I beg you, do not say anything to him. I do not want him to think I have been complaining to you," Elizabeth said, urgently.

"Credit me with a little more finesses than *that*, please," the Countess returned. She turned to Jane, who had been listening intently.

"Now then, Mrs. Bingley. I take it that Miss Bingley has made your life unpleasant, and thus you have sought refuge at Pemberley; is that not right?"

Jane's mouth opened and closed again. Tears filled her eyes. "She is so – and he promised – and then she –"

Elizabeth immediately put her arms around her sister. "Jane, Jane, please do not cry! All will be well, you will see. William will make Charles see reason."

Lady Matlock's lips quirked at Elizabeth's surety that Mr. Darcy could fix this. She was clearly besotted with her husband. Quite content, ha!

"You did the right thing to leave, Mrs. Bingley. My mother taught me that men will treat you exactly as you allow them to, and this is a perfect example of that. A wife must stand her ground."

"But I miss him!" Jane whispered, sounding desperate.

"And I warrant he misses you even more. I have met this Miss Bingley; your husband will never choose her over you. Give it time."

The gentlemen now joined the ladies and Elizabeth rang for tea. Once the tea tray had been brought in and the door closed, Lady Matlock immediately addressed Mr. Darcy. "I look forward to introducing Elizabeth to my friends. When will you come to Town?"

Mr. Darcy's face froze. "I have no such plans, Aunt."

"I must insist, nephew. How will Georgiana fare when it is time for her come-out, if Elizabeth is not already known and respected?"

Georgiana! Mr. Darcy had not considered the effect Elizabeth's absence from society might have on his sister. But how could Elizabeth, a country girl lacking a dowry and connections, possibly do well with London's Upper Ten Thousand? She would be ostracized! Her feelings would be hurt! How could he allow this?

His Aunt was continuing. "I myself will sponsor Elizabeth, Fitzwilliam. She will have no difficulties."

He knew his aunt would get her way eventually. She would wear him down the way water wore down a stone. Mr. Darcy looked at Elizabeth and saw that she was watching him, with wide eyes. He bowed his head and accepted the inevitable, though with fear in his heart.

***

That night, when Elizabeth and Mr. Darcy met in their sitting room, Mr. Darcy took her hand and said, "Elizabeth, did my aunt say anything to make you uncomfortable?"

"Not at all; she was graciousness itself. But, William, I am sorry that she raised the question of me going to London. I did not bring the subject up, I assure you."

Mr. Darcy sighed. "I suspected as much. Once she gets an idea in her head, there is no changing it."

"Stubborn?" Elizabeth supplied. "Certain that her way is the right way?" She was laughing.

"Yes, all of those things. Why is it funny?"

"Well, you could easily be described that way as well, William."

"Me? Stubborn?" His voice was disbelieving.

Elizabeth shook her head at him, still laughing. Then she became sober. "What will we do about Jane?"

"Does her husband know where she is?"

"I do not know; I did not think to ask."

"I think we have a duty to at least inform him as to her whereabouts. I shall send a messenger informing him of her safe arrival. And then I will –"

And Elizabeth never did learn what else he would do, as she pulled him toward her and met his lips with her own.

Chapter Forty-Nine

The next morning, Elizabeth and William went down to breakfast early, but found Jane already seated. After greetings were exchanged, William asked, "Mrs. Bingley, may I ask if your husband knows where you are?"

"I left a note," she whispered, head down.

"Telling him that you were coming to Pemberley?"

"Yes." And she looked up at him, blue eyes wide with worry.

"I beg you to not misunderstand me; you are welcome here for as long as you wish. I do feel, however, that I should let Bingley know that you arrived here safely."

"I suppose so," she said, eyes down again.

Mr. Darcy and Elizabeth exchanged concerned looks.

"Jane, once he knows you are here, he will doubtless come for you. Will you go back with him?" Elizabeth asked her.

"I cannot live with Caroline, Lizzy. I have done my best, but you have no idea – everything I do, everything I say, she picks and picks and – and – I cannot bear it any longer! Charles promised me, most solemnly, that she would go to Scarborough, to her relatives there, but she convinced him that he had a duty of care to her, until she got married. What am I to do?"

Elizabeth reached across the table and took Jane's hand. "You are to do exactly what you did; come to Pemberley! William will sort all this out." Four eyes, two blue and two chocolate, turned trustingly to Mr. Darcy. He winced.

The Matlocks joined them soon after. Mr. Darcy eyed his aunt knowingly, and said, "Uncle's cough appears to have improved already."

Aunt Elaine looked embarrassed. "I did not think I could fool you, Fitzwilliam, but I had to come up with something."

"You could have said that you wanted to meet Elizabeth," he remarked.

"And where would be the fun in that?"

He shook his head at her.

Lady Matlock turned her attention to Elizabeth and began speaking of the gowns she would need, the events they would attend, the balls, the dances, and oh! And vouchers for Almacks! And Elizabeth could be presented to the Queen! Elizabeth did her best to appear enthusiastic, but Mr. Darcy could tell that her heart was not in it. She truly was a country girl, as she had said.

He, too, was not entranced with Town life or Town society. What would he have done if he had married a woman who preferred city life to country life? He might have chosen a *ton* miss with a dowry and connections, and have her complain endlessly about living at Pemberley. He shuddered to think of it.

***

Immediately after breakfast, Mr. Darcy sent a messenger to Netherfield.

Bingley,

Your wife is here at Pemberley. What in the world are you thinking, letting your sister chase her off?

Darcy

There, he thought. I can do no more at this point.

***

Lady Matlock insisted on examining Elizabeth's wardrobe, to assess what she would need for London. "For the Season is already underway, Elizabeth!"

"Perhaps we could delay my entrance into society until next year, Aunt Matlock," Elizabeth said. "I am only now finding my way about the estate, and I truly would prefer not to leave it now."

Lady Matlock was firm. "And next year, you might very well be in the family way. No, no, it must be soon."

"And my sister is here now; I cannot leave if she is here."

That gave Lady Matlock pause. "No, I suppose you cannot. But you could bring her with you! It would cheer her spirits immensely, would it not?"

"And Georgiana? Are we to leave her here on her own?" Elizabeth asked, concerned.

"Of course not. She is not out, of course, but there is no reason that she cannot go to the theatre, to museums, and to private family dinners. I will speak with Fitzwilliam about it immediately. Now then, that pink dress is becoming; it will do for a private dinner…"

Elizabeth sighed. Lady Matlock had an answer for everything. It was exactly as William had said. Once she got an idea in her head, there was no changing it.

***

Later that day, Lady Matlock had a moment alone with her nephew. "William, I shall speak frankly."

Mr. Darcy cocked his head, indicating that he was listening.

"There is already talk in Town about what might be wrong with Elizabeth."

"What! There is nothing whatsoever wrong with her!" he said, immediately furious.

"But there must be something wrong, or else Mr. Darcy would have brought her to London," his aunt concluded. "That is what is being said about Town; surely you knew this is what would happen. I warned you about it before you married her, you will recall."

Mr. Darcy was fuming. "Of all the nonsensical, irritating –"

His aunt cut him off. "Tell me the truth now. Have you not brought her to Town because you are concerned for her well-being, or because you fear that she will do something to embarrass you?"

He avoided his aunt's sharp gaze. "Perhaps some of both," he admitted.

"I hope you do not plan to tell her that you fear that she will shame you," the Countess said, coldly.

"Of course not. But I truly do fear that she will be hurt. You know that she is completely unaccustomed to society."

"I do know, of course," Lady Matlock said. "But there is nothing for it. You must bring her to London. If you do not, it could be Georgiana who will pay the price when she comes to London for her come-out, as she certainly must."

The threat to Georgiana did the trick, as Lady Matlock had known it would. Mr. Darcy finally agreed to bring Elizabeth to London for four weeks. Lady Matlock had hoped to have Elizabeth in London longer, but she accepted Mr. Darcy's decision; she was wise enough to know when to stop. She directed Mr. Darcy to send her a messenger the minute – the very minute! – that they arrived in London.

Having gotten most of what she had wanted, she and Lord Matlock left the next morning, with fulsome compliments to Elizabeth. Mr. Darcy admitted to himself that he had been surprised. He had feared that these relatives would look down on his new wife; instead, they had been kind and supportive. He was grateful and glad, but he nonetheless dreaded the upcoming journey to London.

Chapter Fifty

Georgiana was delighted beyond words at the prospect of going to Town with her brother and her new sister, but Jane, upon hearing that she was to be taken to London, had simply nodded and gone back to her room.

Elizabeth decided to take their upcoming absence as an opportunity to update their sitting room. She gave instructions to Mrs. Reynolds to use the same colour scheme as her own bedroom, as William had complemented her on the new décor. Confident that this was well in hand, she focused now on more important concerns.

For Elizabeth was very, very worried about Jane. Her sister was normally of a placid disposition; her current air of resigned sorrow was something Elizabeth had rarely seen. After a few days of watching Jane move about the house in silence, not speaking unless it was to answer a direct question, Elizabeth decided it was time to address the issue.

"Jane, I know you do not wish to go to London. Would you prefer to return to Netherfield? It is a short enough journey from London; I know William would be happy to have the carriage bring you home."

"No."

"No? Just – no?"

"I will not go back to Netherfield as long as Caroline Bingley is there."

"Jane, I admire your determination, and you know that I will support you in whatever you decide. If London holds no appeal, and you do not want to go to Netherfield, would you like to go back to Longbourn?"

Jane lifted her eyes to Elizabeth's in amazement. "Can you imagine what Mama would say, were I to return home, after having left my husband?"

Elizabeth had to admit that her sister had a good point. "What, then?"

Jane shook her head.

Frustrated, Elizabeth left the room. But that afternoon, Mr. Baldwin found Elizabeth in her office. "Mrs. Darcy, there are visitors," Mr. Baldwin said, somberly.

At last, Elizabeth thought. "I will see Mr. Bingley immediately, Mr. Baldwin."

"Very good, Mrs. Darcy. But it is two people; Mr. Bingley, as you surmised, and Miss Bingley."

Bingley had brought his sister?? If he was on a mission to fetch his wife home, bringing the cause of all the trouble along with him was the worst possible course of action. As she stomped down the stairs, seething, Elizabeth wondered if her brother by marriage might be just a bit...simple.

She entered the drawing room with her face tight. "Charles," she said, curtseying ever so slightly. "Miss Bingley," and here she just nodded.

Charles said, "I have come to collect my wife, Elizabeth."

"May I ask what took you so long, Charles?"

"What do you mean?"

"I mean that Jane left a note, saying where she was going, and William sent a messenger as soon as she arrived, to let you know that she was well. I had thought you would have come before now."

"My loving sister here tore up Jane's note and threw Darcy's message into the fireplace. I learned where my wife was only a few days ago, when Caroline finally confessed."

Elizabeth looked at Caroline Bingley. Miss Bingley showed no remorse whatsoever. "Whatever could you have meant by such actions, Miss Bingley,?" she asked, coldly.

"I do not answer to you, Elizabeth Bennet!" Miss Bingley said, furiously.

A deep voice from the doorway said, "That is Mrs. Darcy to you, Miss Bingley." Elizabeth spun around to find her husband striding into the drawing room, a frown on his face.

"Darcy!" Bingley exclaimed. "I heard that you sent a message, and I am grateful for it. But Caroline here decided to destroy it. I found out where Jane was only two days ago, and we have been on the road ever since."

"But why is Miss Bingley with you?" Elizabeth asked. "You cannot expect Jane to accompany you if your sister is still living at Netherfield."

"We are on our way to Scarborough," Bingley said, with an air of determination that Elizabeth had not seen in him before. "I have come to ask for a room for the night, as Pemberley is directly on the way there. We will be gone immediately after breakfast tomorrow, and we will reach Scarborough by dinnertime. Caroline will stay with our aunt and uncle until – well, until she marries. I will return here for Jane the following day and return with her to Netherfield."

"I will not stay there!" Miss Bingley said through gritted teeth.

She was ignored.

"If you prefer not to house us for the night, we can go to the inn in Lambton," Bingley said, sensing the disapproval in the room.

"Of course you can stay here," Mr. Darcy said. "But allow me to offer you an alternative. If you will but give me the direction, I will have your sister escorted to Scarborough by two of my men and a maid. That will enable you and Mrs. Bingley to leave tomorrow for Meryton." And that way, Mr. Darcy thought, there is no chance that your sister will convince you to let her come back to Meryton, as my people will be immune to her blandishments.

Bingley was effusive in his expressions of gratitude. While he was speaking, Elizabeth slipped upstairs to get Jane.

"He is here, Jane."

Jane startled violently, dropping the handkerchief she was embroidering. "Where??"

"Downstairs; but listen, dearest, Caroline is with him."

"What? But why?" Her voice was despairing.

"He is escorting her to Scarborough; he has stopped at Pemberley for the night. He said they would continue on tomorrow morning. He will escort her to her relatives and return for you here at Pemberley the next day."

"But she will convince him –"

"I know; wait. My husband offered to send his own coach and servants to bring Caroline the rest of the way so that you and Charles can leave to go back to Netherfield tomorrow."

Tears started from Jane's eyes. "Oh, Lizzy! What a wonderful idea! But did Charles agree to it?"

"He did."

Jane flew downstairs and was in her husband's arms a moment later. "Charles!"

"Jane! I was so worried!"

"I did not want you to worry; that is why I left the note!"

"I know, but –"

"But?"

"I did not get it." He glanced at his sister, his meaning unmistakable.

"But – " And here Jane looked at Miss Bingley. "You destroyed my note?" Her voice reflected her astonishment.

Miss Bingley looked away, nose in the air.

Jane said, softly, "What did I do to make you hate me so, Caroline?"

Miss Bingley gasped in shock at such plain speech. "Why, this is most untoward –"

"No. For once, for *once*, let us speak our minds. What did I do, Caroline?"

Caroline looked at Jane with loathing in her face. "Very well; you want me to speak my mind? You – you! Charles was supposed to marry well, very well, so that I would have a chance to do the same! And instead, he falls for a pretty, dull-witted little country girl, with no dowry! How does that help *me*? Does no one think about *my* needs?" Her tone was furious, filled with rage.

Elizabeth shivered. There could be no doubt that this woman hated Jane with every fiber of her being. She thought there was a possibility that Miss Bingley might actually hurt Jane! "But what about your brother?" Elizabeth asked. "Does he not deserve happiness? Is he to sacrifice himself on the altar of your ambition?"

"Happiness! That is exactly the sort of thing I would expect from you, Elizabeth Bennet. All this blathering on about *love* and *happiness* – such things are the consolation prizes, given to those who cannot rise in society!"

"Who taught you such things, Miss Bingley?" Elizabeth asked. "For I know that your brother and older sister do not think as you do."

She scoffed. "What do they know? I learned what was important at my seminary. The girls there were – were high society, the daughters of peers! They knew what mattered!"

Charles murmured, "I had no idea she had learned such dreadful things there."

Elizabeth said, firmly, "Very well. I do not think you are feeling well enough to join us for dinner; a tray will be sent up for you, Miss Bingley."

"I would just as soon take a tray," Miss Bingley spat. "All this *love* and *happiness* would spoil my meal in any case."

"Miss Bingley, allow me to show you to your room." Leading the way up the stairs, Elizabeth signaled to a footman who was stationed in the corridor. The footman followed Elizabeth and Miss Bingley to a guest room. Elizabeth said, "I will send a maid up to attend you, Miss Bingley," and with that, she closed the door.

"She is not to leave her room, Bentley," Elizabeth said in a low voice to the footman. "Have someone relieve you as soon as you are weary; I do not want the door left unguarded at any time."

"I understand, Mrs. Darcy," he replied.

***

That night, William lay awake, thinking about what Miss Bingley had said about the girls she had been at school with. Is this what had happened to Wickham? Would he have turned out differently if he had not been sent to school with men in such superior social classes? It was impossible to say, of course, but Elizabeth's words about Wickham had given him much to think on.

Chapter Fifty-One

Summer 1812

The next day, Miss Bingley was taken to Scarborough in the company of a coachman, a footman, and a maid, all employed by Mr. Darcy. They had been given strict instructions from the master; Miss Bingley was to be watched every minute, as she would likely attempt to escape. She was to be left with her relatives in Scarborough, no matter what she said.

Once Miss Bingley's carriage had disappeared from sight, Jane and Charles set off to return to Netherfield, with heartfelt expressions of gratitude to the Darcys.

Elizabeth watched Jane's carriage disappear with mixed feelings. She would miss Jane, of course, but she was happy that Miss Bingley would no longer present an obstacle to Jane's happiness. She also knew that she would need to focus all her attention and energy on her behaviour in London; having Jane back at Meryton would allow her to do so. Elizabeth was well aware that her husband was excessively concerned about their upcoming visit to Town, and she was determined to show him that this particular country girl was well able to manage London society.

The household was thrown into disarray as the Darcys prepared to depart for Town. Elizabeth had been advised by Aunt Matlock to not bring too many clothes, as Elizabeth would need to have more fashionable clothing crafted by a London modiste. Nonetheless, Elizabeth knew she would need at least a week's worth of clothing, as it would take that long for new gowns to be made. She wrote to Jane and Charlotte, letting them know to direct their letters to Darcy House for the next month.

Georgiana was in a frenzy of packing, running into Elizabeth's room every few minutes to get Elizabeth's opinion as to what she should bring to London. She and Mary had exchanged several letters regarding their mutual pact, so a letter giving Mary the direction of Darcy House had to be sent immediately.

Mr. Darcy, of course, simply left the packing to Carstairs, spending his time ascertaining that correspondence would be sent to Darcy House, consulting with his steward about matters that would not wait until their return, and sending a message to Mrs. Holmes, alerting her to the fact that they would be arriving soon.

***

Finally, they were ready to depart on the three-day journey to Town. Georgiana took a few novels to read; Mr. Darcy brought along some books to read to Elizabeth.

Elizabeth realised that she would have to tell Georgiana that she would not be sharing a room with her during the journey. She grimaced, anticipating an awkward discussion, but to her surprise, when she stammered out that she and William would be sharing a room, rather than she and Georgiana, the girl simply smiled at her and said, "I know, Elizabeth."

***

Three days later, the weary travelers arrived at Darcy House in Grosvenor Square. Elizabeth stared up at the townhouse, appreciating the elegance of the three-story dwelling with its columns and ornate mouldings. William helped her out of the carriage; she straightened her spine and stretched her arms above her head, grateful for the opportunity to move about.

The door opened and several servants rushed out to stand on the steps, waiting to greet the master and mistress. Mr. Darcy offered his arm to Elizabeth, and he escorted her up the steps, Georgiana trailing behind them. He introduced the butler, Mr. Alfred, and the housekeeper, Mrs. Holmes, and then the other servants.

Mr. Darcy asked if the Pemberley servants had already arrived, and he was assured that they had. He escorted Elizabeth into the townhouse.

Accustomed now to beautiful surroundings, Elizabeth was not overwhelmed by Darcy House. Nonetheless, she found much to admire in the elegance of its appointments, the floor-to-ceiling windows, the paneled walls, thick carpets, and painted ceilings. The furniture was light and delicate, almost feminine in appearance, quite different from the heavy pieces she had found at Pemberley.

William took her arm and escorted her up to the suite that they would share, with Georgiana leading the way. Recalling Mrs.

Holmes words some months ago, he said, "The mistress' room has not been redecorated in many years. You will doubtless want to update it."

"We are only here for four weeks, William," she reminded him. "I hardly think it worth the expense."

He smiled to himself. There was not a *ton* miss alive who would have considered the expense of redecoration; this was yet another way in which Elizabeth was superior to them. He could only hope that she would not be badly hurt by society.

Whereas her room at Pemberley had been decorated in rose and gold, this bedroom was blue and gold. Again, she found gold a little pretentious, but she certainly could accustom herself to it for four weeks.

She walked into the sitting room. This room was easier on the eyes, with the gold trim supplanted by cream. William had evidently heard her open the sitting room door, as he now opened his.

"Your room does need redecorating, does it not? Mrs. Holmes thought that it did."

She shrugged. "It is of no matter." She hesitated.

He knew by now when she wanted to speak of something but was reluctant to do so.

"Tell me, Elizabeth," he said.

She sighed. "I wish you had more faith in me, that is all."

"Faith in you? I have all the faith in the world in you!"

"That is patently untrue, as you had to be forced by your aunt to bring me to London."

He sighed. "Elizabeth, I simply do not want you to be hurt. The ladies of the *ton* can be vicious."

"I think I can manage viciousness; I am acquainted with Caroline Bingley, after all."

"Now imagine ten Caroline Bingleys sitting in your drawing room, each hoping to be the first to draw blood."

"I shall not invite them."

"You will not have to invite them; they will come on the pretext of getting to know you better, but what they really want is to rip you to shreds."

"I am more than able to defend myself against such ladies."

He thought now the best thing he could do was to drop the subject. He could hardly tell her that he was also afraid that she would disgrace the family name!

She continued, "I must send a message to the Gardiners, as they will want to know we are in London."

"And I must send a message to the Matlocks," Mr. Darcy agreed. "But first..." And he bent his head down to kiss his lovely wife.

Chapter Fifty-Two

The Countess arrived the next morning, prepared to take Elizabeth shopping in her sleek black coach, sporting the Matlock crest. "What you wear is crucial; you cannot be seen in anything that is not in the first stare of fashion," she informed her new niece.

"They will have to work quickly, as my husband has allotted us only four weeks in Town," Elizabeth reminded her.

But a surprise was in store for her. They stopped at a Madame Boisse's establishment on Bond Street. The door was opened wide for the Countess, Elizabeth trailing after her. A middle-aged woman, beautifully dressed, hastened to curtsey low before Elizabeth and the Countess.

"Is everything ready?" the Countess asked.

"Mais bien sûr!"

Madame Boisse led them to a back room, where an entire wardrobe was hanging on racks: morning dresses, promenade dresses, evening gowns, ball gowns, in hues varying from cream to deep garnet. Elizabeth's mouth fell open – she had never seen so many beautiful gowns! A young girl, clad in a black dress and cap, rushed up to Elizabeth, curtsied, and motioned for her to turn around. A little bewildered, Elizabeth obeyed, and soon found herself stepping out of her pink striped walking dress. Clad only in her chemise, corset and stockings, she felt a little nervous, until Madame presented her with an emerald morning gown.

"Belle, oui?"

"Très belle," Elizabeth replied, automatically. Obeying the modiste's direction, she stepped into the dress and it was fastened behind her by the girl in black. The dress fit perfectly.

"But how?" she asked the Countess, stunned.

The Countess said, with an elegant shrug, "We had no time to wait for clothes to be made, so I had my maid get your measurements from your maid. Madame Boisse was more than happy to have the wardrobe prepared in time for your arrival. There will be a few adjustments to be made, but that is all."

"Do you mean to say –" And here Elizabeth gestured to the array of gowns before her.

"Yes, these are all yours." The Countess wore a smug smile.

"But the cost!" Elizabeth gasped.

Another shrug. "It is no matter. Fitzwilliam knows the cost of a wardrobe and will pay for it with no fuss. And you must have him show you the Darcy jewels; you will need those as well."

Elizabeth could only shake her head at such largesse. Evidently, every single garment had to be tried on, examined, notes made as to what had to be altered and what was now ready to wear. After three hours of stepping in and out of gowns, and being poked, prodded and pinned, Elizabeth was exhausted.

The Countess saw Elizabeth's countenance and judged that she required a rest. She pulled the modiste aside and whispered to her; Madame Boisse nodded vigorously. Five minutes later, Elizabeth found herself back in her pink striped gown.

"Come, Elizabeth," the Countess said, kindly. "Just up the street there is a lovely coffee house."

A grateful Elizabeth soon found herself sitting at the back of an attractive, brightly lit establishment with a pot of hot chocolate and a delicious scone. "Thank you, Aunt Matlock," she murmured.

"I could see that you were tiring," the Countess said, compassionately.

"I was, indeed, and I am grateful for the opportunity to rest. But I am also thanking you for everything you have done to ease my way in Town. I would never have imagined needing so many gowns! It seems a little..." Elizabeth trailed off, not wanting to offend the Countess.

"Absurd? Ridiculous? Wasteful?"

"Well, if I am honest, *yes* to all those descriptives."

"And I would agree with you. Sometimes being in Town for the season has the feeling of being stuck on a carousel, unable to get off."

"Unable? Or unwilling?" Elizabeth enquired sharply, and quickly began to apologise.

The Countess waved away her apologies and said, "Perhaps some of both. But I have found in my many years of dealing with the *ton* that there are two sorts of people – those who sincerely believe that their positions in life have made them superior to others; and humbler sorts who understand that an accident of birth is responsible for the life they enjoy."

Elizabeth leaned forward, now deeply interested, the scone forgotten.

Her aunt by marriage continued. "The former take themselves quite seriously. These are the ladies who will resent you for having so effortlessly moved into a high sphere. Your manner and your manners, both, will be scrutinized and criticised, and rumours of a forced marriage due to compromise will be doggedly repeated by them. You will want to avoid them whenever possible."

"And the latter?" Elizabeth asked.

"At the very least, they will not gossip about you. But if they believe you to be like-minded, they are likely to assist you and may help to quell the gossip."

"And how do I recognise the two sorts of people?"

The Countess chuckled. "I wish I could tell you that there was some sort of secret sign, or some such thing! But no, it is not that easy."

A lady of the Countess' age stopped by their table. "Elaine! I have not seen you in an age!"

"Hermione, it is lovely to see you. May I present my niece to you?"

"Please do," was the polite response.

Elizabeth rose, curtseying deeply, and was introduced to Lady Hermione, the Viscountess Bolingbroke.

"Your niece, you said?" The lady enquired of Aunt Matlock.

"Indeed; she is married to my nephew, Fitzwilliam Darcy."

"I had heard that he was lately married! But I also heard that the marriage was the result of –" And here the lady stopped.

Elizabeth understood immediately. The Viscountess was unwilling to mention the word 'compromise' in front of the Countess, as the Countess obviously approved of the match, as here she was in a coffeehouse with Mrs. Darcy.

Curtseying again, Elizabeth said, "My Lady, there was a most unfortunate misunderstanding upon the occasion of my marriage to Mr. Darcy. It has resulted in a good deal of false gossip, exacerbated by the fact that I am an unknown in London, though my father is a gentleman. I am newly married as well as new to Town, and my Aunt Matlock and I would be appreciative of any efforts to quell that gossip, particularly efforts made by ladies of high rank, such as yourself." And here she did her best to look like a demure new bride, overwhelmed by the exalted company in which she found herself.

Charmed, the Viscountess vowed that she would quash the gossip whenever she heard it.

When the woman had departed, eager to tell her friends that she had met the newly minted Mrs. Darcy, the Countess eyed Elizabeth with new respect. "Well done, Elizabeth," she said.

Elizabeth had resumed her seat. "Which sort is the Viscountess?" she asked. "Superior or not?"

"Superior," the Countess replied immediately. "And your shy, demure persona worked well with Hermione. However, others of that type may simply take it as a sign that you are weak, and they will begin sharpening their claws."

"I begin to see why my husband did not want to take me to Town," Elizabeth said, thoughtfully.

"There is no help for it, Elizabeth." And the Countess repeated what she had told her nephew, that judgements were already being made about Elizabeth because she had been immediately hidden away in the country.

"So we should have come to London directly?" Elizabeth asked. "But we scarcely knew one another!"

"There were good reasons for going to Pemberley, of course. But that does not mean that there will not be repercussions for your failure to appear in Town immediately after your marriage."

Once Elizabeth had rested and her face had regained its colour, the Countess insisted on going out again for shoes, fans, hats, gloves and stockings.

***

The afternoon finally ended. The Countess returned a weary Elizabeth to Darcy House, reminding her that she would come for tea the next day to outline Elizabeth's social calendar for the next four weeks.

Mr. Alfred greeted her at the door. "Is Mr. Darcy at home?" she asked the butler.

"No, Madam. I believe he is at his club."

Thanking him, she went upstairs to her room, where she found Carrie surrounded by boxes. She was unpacking them, one by one, and storing their contents in the large wardrobe. "Such beautiful gowns!" Carrie exclaimed.

"There are more; these are the gowns that did not require adjustments. For which, by the by, I must thank you. I understand that you gave my measurements to the Countess, enabling her to have an entire wardrobe crafted before I even set foot in London."

Carrie nodded. "There was no other way that your clothes could have been ready in time."

There was a knock at the door; Carrie ran to open it. "It is Miss Darcy," she told Elizabeth over her shoulder.

"Oh! Come in, Georgiana. You will not want to miss out on the fun."

Georgiana certainly did *not* want to miss out on the fun, and she joined Carrie in exclaiming over the yards and yards of fabric covering the bed and floor.

***

Later that night, in Elizabeth's room, she recounted the events of the day to her husband. "I believe I have spent the equivalent of Longbourn's yearly income on four weeks' worth of clothing," she said in disgust.

He reassured her that he had expected that her clothing would be costly. "My aunt was civil, I hope? I know she can be rather autocratic."

"Oh! She was kindness itself," Elizabeth reassured him. "But she did direct me to ask you about jewelry. She says jewels are necessary."

"Have you any of your own? I have not seen you wear anything except your amber cross," he said. *I should have given her jewelry before now,* he berated himself.

"No, only the cross. I have not felt the lack, however."

"You have quite a bit at your disposal. I keep the Darcy jewelry in the safe here in Town; I will bring it all out tomorrow."

"Tomorrow your aunt will come with what she calls my social calendar." There was laughter in Elizabeth's voice.

"I do not want you to have to do anything that makes you uncomfortable, Elizabeth," Mr. Darcy said.

"I beg you not to concern yourself; I am capable of saying 'no' if I must."

"In general, I do not doubt your ability to do so, but Aunt Elaine is capable of talking anyone into anything. If Whitehall would allow her to speak with Napoleon, he would immediately stop his programme of conquest and instead turn his hand to farming."

"Perhaps you should write to Whitehall and suggest it!"

"Perhaps I will, but first –" And here he tumbled his laughing wife into bed, ending the conversation.

Chapter Fifty-Three

The following day saw the Countess returning with her schedule, carefully written out in an elegant, feminine hand. William joined the ladies in the drawing room, knowing that his participation would be required for a good many of the events on the Countess' list.

"Aunt, thank you for taking such good care of my wife," he said immediately, bowing to his relative.

He was assured that spending time with Elizabeth was entirely a pleasure. Then the Countess got down to business. "I have made a list of events that Elizabeth shall attend," she said, regally.

Elizabeth and William shared an amused look, which the Countess saw but ignored.

She presented Elizabeth with a list of balls, musicales, dinners, theatre performances, operas, concerts, and more. Elizabeth's eyes grew wider and wider as she read through the list. She looked up at William in dismay.

Mr. Darcy took the list from her, glanced over it, and then returned it to his aunt saying, "It is far, far too much. One-third of these must be crossed out."

His aunt shook her head, firmly. "No, Fitzwilliam; the girl must be seen!"

"I do not disagree, but Elizabeth is not accustomed to Town hours. In addition, she has relatives of her own in London, with whom she will wish to visit. If you will not scratch out one-third of those, I will."

The two locked eyes. The Countess finally sighed and said, "Very well."

"Thank you," her nephew said, stiffly.

"Have you taken the jewels out of the safe yet?"

"I have." And here Mr. Darcy walked to the table near the fireplace and returned with a large mahogany jewelry chest. He placed it on the table beside his wife.

"Open it," he told Elizabeth.

She did so, revealing a wonderland of diamonds, sapphires, emeralds and rubies. She looked up at him, helplessly. "What in the world am I meant to do with all this?"

The Countess shook her head, laughing. "Only you, Elizabeth."

"I would be afraid to wear these! What if something happened? What if a clasp came loose?"

"The pieces are checked regularly for loose clasps and the like," Mr. Darcy reassured her.

The Countess ordered, "Look through it, Elizabeth, so that you will know what pieces will complement your ballgowns. No one expects you to wear such pieces during the day, but to the theater, the opera, balls – any evening event will require jewels."

Elizabeth complied, laying the pieces out on the little table. Necklaces, earrings, bracelets, brooches – it was a king's ransom worth of jewelry! She shook her head in bewilderment.

"Elizabeth?" William said, softly.

She looked up, seeing her husband and aunt-by-marriage watching her.

"It is just so strange," she replied, her confusion evident in her voice.

"What is strange?" he asked.

"Sometimes I am not sure of who I am," she confessed. "In my heart, I am plain Elizabeth Bennet, second daughter of an insignificant gentleman in an insignificant little town. Yet here I sit, with a fortune in jewelry at my fingertips, wife to one of the wealthiest men in the kingdom. But I am still me. Do you understand that it is sometimes a little confusing?"

He did understand, then, that it would be *very* confusing – not because she was unintelligent or unwilling to learn a new role, but simply because at the core of her being, she was still Elizabeth Bennet. And it was Elizabeth Bennet that he had come to admire, to appreciate. "I do understand, Elizabeth," he said, softly. "And I am grateful that you have been willing to learn to be part of my life, despite the confusion."

He glanced at the Countess, willing her not to say anything hurtful. He was surprised to see that her eyes were moist.

***

Shortly after the Countess' departure, the Gardiners came to visit. There was a good deal of excitement and happiness from Elizabeth as well as from her relatives. Mr. Darcy was surprised to find himself glad to see them as well. He had, he realised, been quite sincere when he had said that he would prefer the Gardiners as relatives to his Aunt Catherine. The Gardiners were everything kind, warm and loving, as well as sensible, intelligent and well-informed. In short, they were everything that his Aunt Catherine was not.

***

It was not until late in the day that Elizabeth had the leisure to look through her mail. She was happy to see a letter from Jane, reporting her joy at having Miss Bingley absent from Netherfield. There was also a letter from Charlotte.

Dear Eliza,

All is quiet here in Meryton; in fact, quieter than usual, as the militia has finally left us in favor of Brighton. While there have been some tears shed at the loss of so many handsome men, I find myself grateful to have the streets less crowded and the young girls less silly.

You wrote me about the perfidy of one Lieutenant Wickham, for which I remain grateful. Maria was well on her way to having her head turned by him until I had a word in Papa's ear, at *which point the man (I hesitate to write <u>gentleman</u>!) in question was no longer welcome at Lucas Lodge. I tremble to think what might have occurred had your Mr. Darcy not made his character known.*

On that score, however, I think it wise to alert you to the fact that Lydia has gone to Brighton as well. She and Harriet Forster, who you will remember as a rather silly seventeen-year-old, became quite friendly. When the militia left, so did the Colonel and Harriet Forster, and evidently Mrs. Forster could not be easy if Lydia Bennet was not with her. I hope that the Colonel is a sensible man and will watch over your sister.

Please write and tell me all about your visit to London!

Your dear friend,

Charlotte Lucas

Lucky Lydia at the seaside! Elizabeth made a little moue of displeasure at the knowledge that even Lydia had managed to visit the sea before she did; then she silently chastised herself for her pettiness.

Chapter Fifty-Four

The next weeks were to remain forever in Elizabeth's mind as a frenetic whirl of dances, dinners and diversions of every description. Much to her own amazement, she wore every single one of the dresses that the Countess had ordered for her, and had worn a good many – though not all! – of the pieces of jewelry in her husband's safe.

Georgiana had attended those events that were considered appropriate for a girl who had not yet had her come-out. She, too, had been treated to some new dresses.

But Georgiana had more important things to think about. Now that her brother and Elizabeth had managed to sort out their differences, she was at liberty to focus on her music. Brother had persuaded Signore Bianchi, a well-known master, to give her piano lessons while she was in town. Georgiana was one moment in alt at the prospect, and the next moment terrified that she was not good enough to please the maestro.

But she recalled the pact she had made with Mary Bennet, and so she wrote to Mary, telling her that she was going to be bold when auditioning for the Signore, and play her most difficult piece to showcase her abilities. Mary wrote back, telling her that she had been living up to her own part of the pact, convincing her mother that she needed new gowns in dusty pink, soft blue, and similar colours to replace the greys and browns that now populated her wardrobe.

Georgiana's worries were groundless, as it turned out, as the Signore informed Elizabeth that Georgiana was "un prodigio!" Elizabeth did not speak Italian, but the meaning was clear enough.

The Countess had been correct in saying that judgement had already been passed on Elizabeth. Her detractors delightedly spread the rumour that her marriage to Mr. Darcy had been the result of a compromise; her supporters argued that any rumours of a compromise were the result of jealousy.

There was even a snippet of gossip in *The Morning Post*. '*Mr. FD of Derbyshire has been seen out and about Town, squiring his lovely new wife. How did he come to meet this unknown country miss? And where has she been hiding? Rumours abound!*'

The Countess had told Elizabeth to take no notice of it, but Elizabeth could not feel at ease. She was not at all accustomed to being in the spotlight, particularly in such a manner. Ladies began to call on her in the afternoons, hoping Elizabeth would let slip some tidbit of information that would either confirm or quash the rumours.

One afternoon, she found herself hosting a number of such ladies, keeping the kitchen busy supplying trays of tea and various delicacies.

Lady Penelope began, "Oh, Mrs. Darcy, I did not see you at the Daggerton's ball last night! Is it possible that you were not invited?"

Elizabeth replied, swiftly, "We were indeed invited, but chose to go to the theatre instead."

"The theatre is preferred to a ball? How droll!" And there was a titter from certain of the ladies in the room.

"Droll? I think not," Elizabeth replied, calmly. "Edmund Kean was playing in *Othello*; Mr. Darcy and I were delighted to have the privilege of watching one of the finest actors of our generation in one of his most famous roles."

"Quite the bluestocking, are you not, Mrs. Darcy?" Lady Edgeware chimed in, voice sharp.

"Oh, I am indeed, but I have no cause to repine. My husband tells me that an intelligent man need not fear an intelligent woman," Elizabeth replied.

"And did he have to go to the country to find one?" Lady Adams asked, looking down her nose.

"I could not say, Lady Adams," Elizabeth replied, demurely. "Though he did say that he could not find what he wanted in Town, which is why he had remained unattached for so long."

"Do you mean to say that there are more intelligent ladies in the country? That hardly seems likely," Lady Penelope sniffed.

"It is more than likely, Lady Penelope; it is fact. You must remember that in the country we have not the diversions that you have here in Town. As a result, we are forced to improve our minds so as not to expire from boredom."

Lady Harriet, the Countess of Clarendon, began to laugh. "Well done, Mrs. Darcy."

Lady Edgeware scowled. "I will not agree that country chits are more intelligent than Town ladies; it is simply impossible!"

The resulting gaggle of voices, arguing the point, allowed Elizabeth to sit back and simply listen. Such nonsense, she thought, but kept her features calm.

Her husband walked into the drawing room. The voices paused, but quickly rose again.

"Oh, Mr. Darcy!"

"How nice it has been to meet your charming wife!"

"I looked for you at the Coventry Ball last week, but did not see you!"

"Are you to go to the Cumberland's house party next month?"

He held up his hands, successfully quelling the noise. "Ladies," he said, in his deep voice, bowing to the room. "I must beg your indulgence for intruding upon your time with my wife. In truth, I missed her dreadfully, as I have not seen her these past two hours, and so had to find her."

Elizabeth blushed rosily, and the voices began again.

"And you tell me he was compromised! I shall never believe it!"

"But my cousin said –"

"Your cousin is clearly wrong!"

"But Miss Bingley –"

Hearing that name, Elizabeth sat up straight. Unable to identify who it was who had mentioned the woman, she asked, "Did someone mention Miss Bingley?"

Lady Matthews, the wife of a baronet, said, "I did; she and I were at school together. We correspond on occasion, and I can tell you that she was not at all complimentary towards yourself, Mrs. Darcy." Her tone was one of triumph; she would be happy to put this unknown country chit in her place!

"My sister is married to her brother. May I enquire, Lady Matthews, as to your opinion of Miss Bingley, based on your school experience?"

Lady Matthews replied, "She was the worst gossip in school, forever spreading nasty rumours that had no basis in fact."

"So not someone we would want to emulate, would you not agree?"

There was a moment's silence in the room while everyone digested Elizabeth's remark. Lady Harriet was the first to laugh at Lady Matthew's discomfort, but others soon chimed in.

Elizabeth decided to take pity on her. "Lady Matthews, I know Miss Bingley can be very persuasive. But I hope you will bear in mind that she has taken a dislike to my family because of her brother's marriage, and she has not a kind word for any of us."

"Why would she dislike her brother marrying your sister?" One of the ladies asked. "A connection to Mr. Darcy is not insignificant. And your sister is a gentleman's daughter!"

"Indeed, and my sister is everything lovely and gentle. But Miss Bingley felt that her brother could do better, and that as a result, she herself would have been able to marry a titled gentleman."

The ladies were now focused on Miss Bingley's hubris.

"To think that a tradesman's daughter –"

" – would aspire so high –"

" – and attempt to tarnish the reputation of a gentlewoman!"

"Very bad *ton*!"

"Very bad indeed!"

Lady Harriet, the Countess of Clarendon, said quietly for Elizabeth's ears only, "That explains the rumours, then."

"At least in part," Elizabeth replied, softly.

"I will do what I can for you."

"I thank you, Lady Harriet!"

The ladies finally departed, leaving Elizabeth with a pounding headache.

Chapter Fifty-Five

The combined efforts of the Countess of Matlock, the Countess of Clarendon, and Mr. Darcy himself finally quashed the rumours surrounding Elizabeth's marriage. Mr. Darcy remembered to speak in glowing terms about his wife whenever possible, a task which he had found to be not difficult at all. The Countess of Matlock made it her business to be seen with Elizabeth in public as often as possible. The Countess of Clarendon spoke sternly to members of her own circle, forbidding them to spread any rumours that cast Elizabeth in a bad light. She told them, "If you must say something, then say that Mrs. Darcy is a lively, lovely, literate young lady!"

Once the cloud of rumours had abated, Elizabeth had found that London could be a very agreeable place to visit, despite the summer heat. While she could not find most of the society ladies to be agreeable company – with the notable exception of the Countess of Clarendon, who had become a friend – the theatre, the opera, the museums, the public lectures, all served to keep her entertained and informed. She was, in short, having a delightful time, especially as she was able to find opportunities to visit with the Gardiners.

MISUNDERSTANDINGS

At the end of the third week in London, the Countess of Matlock came to call. Elizabeth was upstairs writing letters when she was informed of Aunt Matlock's arrival. As she made her way downstairs, she heard the Countess say, "Well, Fitzwilliam, I would say that your fears of Elizabeth disgracing the family name have proven groundless."

And then she heard her husband reply, "Yes; I have been most pleased with her performance."

Elizabeth stopped cold, stunned. William had told her that he did not wish to bring her to Town because he feared that she would be hurt by gossip. But in truth, he had been afraid that she would disgrace the family name? She considered running back up to her room and claiming that she had a headache; but no, she would not take asylum in such subterfuge.

Schooling her features to hide her hurt, she went into the drawing room, welcomed the Countess and called for tea. She spoke calmly about the ball that the Darcys would attend that night, and the garden party they would attend the following day.

Mr. Darcy knew immediately that something was wrong. He knew Elizabeth well enough by now to know when she was keeping herself under rigid control, as she was doing now. She had been fine this morning, laughing over something Georgiana had said. So what could have – oh, of course. She must have heard what the Countess had said immediately before she had entered the drawing room. He closed his eyes briefly and drew in a deep breath.

His first instinct was to leave the house. She would get over it, as hers was not a resentful disposition, but Mrs. Gardiner's words flashed into his mind. *Misunderstandings can escalate quickly if they are not dealt with promptly.*

The moment the Countess left, Elizabeth was up out of her chair and headed upstairs.

"Elizabeth!"

She ignored him, continuing her climb.

"Elizabeth, wait."

She paused, but did not turn to look at him.

"You heard what the Countess said about not disgracing the family name."

She remained motionless.

"Will you not talk to me about it?"

She resumed her climb up the stairs, head held high.

"Do you recall what your aunt said?" And he repeated Mrs. Gardiners' words. "Misunderstandings can escalate quickly if they are not dealt with promptly."

She turned now and looked at him. "I suppose I have no choice." Her tone was flat.

He caught up with her and offered his arm, which she ignored. Elizabeth continued up the stairs and went into her room; he followed close behind her. She went into their sitting room and sat on a chair, so he was unable to sit beside her. Instead, he sat on the sofa across from her.

He cleared his throat. "Very well; it is true that I was afraid that you would not be able to make your way in London society."

She flared, "You are ashamed of me!"

Wait; that was not what he meant at all. Recalling Mrs. Gardiner's teachings, he shook his head. "That is not what I said, Elizabeth. I said that I was afraid that you would not be able to make your way in London society. Remember what your aunt taught us to do? Tell me what you just heard."

Sullenly, Elizabeth said, "You were afraid that I would not be able to make my way in London society."

"And is that the same thing, do you think, as being ashamed of you?"

There was a long silence. Then – "No," she said, softly. And her temper flared again. "But Aunt Matlock said you were afraid that I would disgrace the family name!"

He winced. "Yes, and I am not proud of the way in which that was phrased. I was concerned for Georgiana's prospects, which will be affected by anything that you or I do."

"And what you told me was that you were concerned that I would be hurt by society ladies! That was a lie, was it not?"

"Can they not both be true?" he asked, spreading his hands wide.

She thought about it. "I suppose they can, yes." Her response was guarded.

"Elizabeth, the truth is that yes, I was afraid of what would be said about us. I know I do not need to remind you that we were not wed under the most fortunate circumstances. It was inevitable that rumours would abound, and that those rumours could affect Georgiana's come-out. And – and! – I did not want to see you hurt! Of course I was concerned about you! I lov –" And here he stopped.

She raised her head to look at him, eyes wide. "You what?"

"It does not matter," he whispered, and he rose and went into his own bedroom.

It was true, he realised. He loved her! When had that happened? How could he have been so blind? The truth of it had him gasping for breath, his heart pounding in his chest. Could he tell her? Was he ready? Was *she* ready?

He went back to the sitting room, but she had already left. Very well; he was glad they had managed to sort out their misunderstanding. The advice the Gardiners had given him had proven excellent.

Hadn't there been some sort of game they had played around the breakfast table when Bingley got married, where everyone contributed their suggestions for a good marriage? He recalled that one of them had been to pay your spouse compliments at least twice a day. That had been Georgiana's contribution, in fact. Perhaps he should take that one to heart. Surely it would be no hardship to compliment his wife!

***

Beginning the next day, Mr. Darcy made it a point to tell Elizabeth how lovely she looked when they were about to go out for an event. It was easy enough, as she looked very lovely every day and every night. He noticed her hairstyles, and complimented them as well, but then told her frankly that he loved her hair best when it was down at night. She laughed at him and told him that she would not tell that to Carrie, who worked hard to put up her hair in the elaborate styles required of the *ton*.

***

Elizabeth had heard what William had almost – almost! – said at the end of their argument. His slip had brought to her attention something that had lurked in a corner of her heart for some time now.

She loved William.

Of course she did. How could she ever have imagined that all she felt for this tall, generous, responsible, intelligent, well-read – oh, the adjectives could go on and on! And how she delighted in his touch, his kiss, even the warm glances he bestowed upon her. And when they were together in bed – she felt her face growing warm at the thought of it.

How could she have imagined that what she felt for him was something as timid, as frail, as cool, as mere affection?

Yes; she loved him. And she knew now that he loved her as well. If he was not yet ready to speak, then she would wait.

***

Mr. Darcy found himself more attuned than ever to Elizabeth's moods. She was tired, he realised. Tired of the balls, the parties, the dinners. Enough, he thought. Enough! At the start of their final week in London, Mr. Darcy told Elizabeth that he was throwing the Countess' schedule into the trash. "You have worked very hard these past few weeks, Elizabeth, and I want you to know how much I appreciate those efforts. Let us spend this last week exactly as we wish," he told her.

They spent an entire afternoon at Hatchard's, where Mr. Darcy selected a full dozen books to be sent to Elizabeth's father. In an unaccustomed burst of whimsey, he had written, "From an admirer" on a card, and then instructed John Hatchard to deliver the books and the card to Longbourn by messenger. He chuckled to himself, imagining Bennet's face upon opening the package.

They pried Georgiana away from her instrument for a full day, treating her to ices, then shopping on Bond Street for whatever she wished, and finishing with a trip to Vauxhall Gardens.

Mr. Darcy took Elizabeth to Rundell, Bridge and Rundell, a jewelry store holding a Royal Warrant. He gave her carte blanche to purchase anything she wished, but she simply shook her head. "How can you even think of buying more jewelry?" she asked.

"I want you to have something that was purchased for you, not just heirlooms."

She laughed at him. "*Just* heirlooms?"

"Very well, then. I shall have to surprise you." He went over to one of the shopkeepers and spoke softly. They then shook hands.

When Mr. Darcy returned to Elizabeth, she narrowed her eyes at him.

"What?" he asked, innocence personified.

"You bought something!" She accused him.

"Perhaps," he admitted. "Wait and see."

***

That night, in Elizabeth's bed, he said, "Perhaps rather than returning to Pemberley, you might like to go to Sunset House."

She stared at him in surprise, and then her face lit up. "Really?! Oh, William, I would love to! Has Georgiana ever been to the sea?"

"She has, but it has been many years. I know she would like to come."

"I hope there is a pianoforte there for her."

"There is, and I will send a message to let them know we are coming and to have the instrument tuned."

Georgiana was elated to learn that they were to go to Brighton. "We will need more new clothes, Lizzy!" she said.

"How can we possibly need more?" Elizabeth protested, weakly.

"Oh, what is worn in Town is completely different from what is worn at the seaside," Georgiana assured her.

***

Elizabeth and Mr. Darcy called on the Matlocks before leaving. Elizabeth was effusive in expressing her appreciation for the Countess' help. "I could never have managed on my own," she admitted freely. "Do you think we have successfully laid the gossip to rest?"

"There will always be talk about influential families, but I think we have allayed the worst of it. However, I do expect you two to be here for at least two months every year."

"Two months?" Elizabeth asked, weakly.

"Yes, indeed; and in two years, Georgiana will have her come-out, and you will have to be here for the entire season."

Both Darcys grimaced, causing the Matlocks no end of amusement. How had Fitzwilliam managed to find the one woman in all of England who shared his distaste for the social whirl of London?

Chapter Fifty-Six

The journey to Brighton took two days. One evening, in their room at the inn, Elizabeth recollected that Lydia was there as well, staying with Harriet Forster. She could not like the idea of Lydia being so poorly chaperoned; perhaps Lydia should come and stay with them at Sunset House.

Mr. Darcy watched the expressions on his wife's face with amusement. He could see her remembering something, then realising that the 'something' was less than pleasant, and then coming to a decision.

Elizabeth saw him smiling at her. "What is it?" she asked.

"What were you thinking of?"

"Lydia."

"Lydia!" Well, that was unexpected. "What about her?"

"I think I must have told you that she is at Brighton."

"Did you? I do not recall."

"Oh! I received a letter from Charlotte, telling me that the militia had gone to Brighton, and Lydia had gone as well, as the Colonel's wife's friend." She realised, only then, that this meant that George Wickham was at Brighton as well. "Oh, William, Lieutenant Wickham will be there; perhaps we ought not to go."

He considered it, briefly, but then thought he would be damned if he would let Wickham ruin his wife's seaside holiday. "No, I am certain we need not see Wickham. It is not a small town, after all, and we have no business socializing with the militia."

"I had thought to have Lydia stay with us, rather than with the Forsters."

He did not like the idea at all; having that wild girl in the same house as Georgiana was not to his taste.

Elizabeth observed him closely; the small movement of his mouth told her that he did not like the idea. "It is concern for Georgiana, is it not?"

"It is," he confessed. "I do not think Lydia likely to be a good influence on her."

"But perhaps Georgiana might be a good influence on Lydia," she returned.

Mr. Darcy considered it. Lydia was now his sister, after all, and if harm befell the girl, it would likely fall to him to amend it. But – "Is Lydia likely to prefer Sunset House to the excitement of the militia camp?"

"Possibly not," Elizabeth allowed. "But the offer should be made, should it not?"

"It should, yes."

***

When they arrived at Brighton, Elizabeth had her head out the window, sniffing the air. The look on her face, her utter delight, had both Mr. Darcy and Georgiana laughing out loud.

"I cannot believe you have never seen the sea, Lizzy," Georgiana said.

"My father hates to travel, and my mother would have only come to Brighton if there had been the prospect of suitors for her girls."

Mr. Darcy was glad Elizabeth had not been to the sea before; it mean that he would have the pleasure of giving her the experience.

Sunset House was a charming house, close to a sandy beach. Elizabeth insisted on walking to the beach as soon as possible. She had quickly changed out of her traveling dress and into a light summer walking dress, had tied a straw bonnet onto her head, and was ready to set out. She waited impatiently for her husband and sister to be ready. What could be taking them so long?

Finally, they were ready. "Take a parasol, Lizzy," Georgiana warned. "The sun is hotter than you think!"

"I bow to your superior knowledge," Elizabeth replied, and just then Carrie ran down the stairs with a parasol in hand.

"Mrs. Darcy, you should take –"

"I thank you, Carrie!" Elizabeth laughed. "Now, then, let us be off!"

Mr. Darcy thought he had never before truly appreciated the ocean. Seeing it now, through Elizabeth's eyes, was a completely different experience. How had he not noticed that there were a hundred different shades of blue? How had he not noticed the striking contrast between the white of the sand and the jewel tones of the sea? How had he not noticed the graceful arc of the gulls and starlings, as they sailed over the water? In truth, the entire experience seemed new to him. Why was that?

He was aware that he had been, by necessity, focused on the estate, the investments, the care of his sister, the vast myriad of responsibilities that being the Master of Pemberley entailed, for the entirety of his adult life. The idea of enjoying life was foreign. It was not that he had dismissed such a concept; it was that there never seemed to be time for it. And yet – why not? He had a steward, had he not? There was, in fact, a steward for each and every property that he owned. And a housekeeper, and a butler, and a valet, and a hundred different servants for a hundred different tasks. Did he really have to work as hard as he did, as he had for the past decade?

It came to him, quite suddenly, that he had been working as hard as he had in reaction to his parents' deaths. When he was focused on the crops, the investment returns, the servants, on and on, then he did not have to think about how much he missed them, how hard it had been to carry on alone. Work had kept the black demon of grief, a grief so enormous that it threatened to swallow him whole, at bay.

The idea was so unexpected, so striking, that he stopped in his path, unable to move.

"William?" Elizabeth asked, concerned.

"I am well," he said, hoarsely. "But I must sit down."

The three of them quickly made their way back to the pier, where benches and tables were available for pedestrians.

Worried, Elizabeth sat beside him and took his hand. "What is wrong, William?"

"I – I am not certain."

Georgiana, on Mr. Darcy's other side, said, "Should we go back to the house?"

"No. No, Georgiana, do you recall how you always say that I work a good deal?"

She nodded, puzzled.

"Would you say that I enjoy my life?"

She replied, "Well, I think you do now, more than you did previously. Because of Elizabeth, I suspect."

He just nodded. His realisation was too new to share; he could not speak of it. But for now, he could sit here by the beach, with the two females he loved more than life, and perhaps...just be content.

***

That afternoon, sun-warmed and happy, the Darcys returned to Sunset House. Mail had been forwarded from Darcy House, which had already been forwarded from Pemberley. Mr. Darcy's habit of attending to duty made him reluctant to simply ignore the correspondence, particularly as it had traveled all over England to find him.

Most of it was from his solicitor, requesting decisions about investments. These he put aside. But one envelope – why did that writing look so familiar? Frowning, he opened it.

> *Darcy,*
>
> *Before you throw this letter into the fireplace, read it! I know you are related to Lydia Bennet by marriage. I write to alert you to the fact that I have reason to believe that she is contemplating an elopement with Captain Denny.*
>
> *You and I are not friends, but I do not want to see the Darcy name tarnished by such an event. I suggest you make your way to Brighton with all possible haste.*
>
> *George Wickham*

Scarcely able to believe his eyes, he read it again and then a third time. Lydia Bennet about to elope with a soldier! The letter was not dated, but it had been sent first to Pemberley, then to Darcy House, now here to Brighton –

"Elizabeth!" He rushed out of the study to find her.

"William?"

"It is Lydia, she – here, read for yourself." He thrust the letter at her.

She paled as she read it. "Can it possibly be true?"

"What reason would he have to make up such a thing?" he asked.

She shook her head. "I do not know."

"I will find the militia encampment immediately."

"Wait – I will accompany you."

"To a camp full of soldiers? I think not!"

"She is my sister!"

"And mine as well," he said. "I beg you, Elizabeth, to stay here with Georgiana." With that, he took her hand, kissed it, and ran out the door.

***

It was a full twenty minutes before Mr. Darcy was able to learn where the militia were headquartered, and another twenty minutes before he was able to get there. His concern had, by now, given way to fury. Upon arriving at the Colonel's small house, he banged on the door. It was opened by a manservant. Mr. Darcy pushed his way past the man, who was sputtering out objections, calling out, "Forster? Forster! Where the devil are you?"

The Colonel appeared before him, drawing himself up tall in his uniform, prepared to oust the intruder. But Mr. Darcy, Master of Pemberley, was not about to be intimidated by anyone, not now and not ever.

"What have you to say to this?" Glowering, he thrust the letter at the Colonel.

The Colonel read it, colour draining from his face. Then he looked up at Mr. Darcy. "You are Mr. Darcy?"

"I am. Lydia Bennet is my sister by marriage. Where is she? I demand to see her at once!"

The Colonel spoke quickly to one of the servants, who scurried off. Five minutes later, that same servant returned and whispered to the Colonel.

"Well?" Mr. Darcy growled.

"It appears she is not in her room and some of her clothing is missing as well," the Colonel wiped sweat from his brow.

"Where is your wife? I must question her. Now, man! What are you waiting for?"

The Colonel himself rushed upstairs, returning with a very young woman who was trying her best to put on a brave front.

"Mrs. Forster?" Mr. Darcy asked in surprise. He wondered how it was that this – this *child* had been permitted to marry a Colonel and live in a military encampment. What had her parents been thinking?

"Yes?" she replied, chin thrust forward.

"Did you know that Miss Lydia was gone from her room?"

She looked at her husband, helplessly. "Answer the man, Harriet," the Colonel ordered.

"Yes," she said, looking at the floor.

"And when did she leave?"

"About an hour ago." She looked up at Mr. Darcy, a challenge in her eyes. "They are in love! They are going to Gretna Green."

"In love? So why did he not go to her father and ask for her hand, as a gentleman would?" Darcy swiveled to the Colonel. "I need not remind you that you were responsible for her well-being, Colonel. We will need your fastest horses and riders." His tone was harsh and unforgiving.

Forster nodded, brusquely. He looked at his wife and said, "We will speak of this later, Harriet."

***

At the encampment, the Colonel selected three men who he believed to be trustworthy, including – to Mr. Darcy's surprise – Wickham. The Colonel issued instructions to the men, stating that Denny must have found means to hire a carriage to convey his intended bride. With only an hour's lead, it would be easy enough for men on horseback to catch up.

Mr. Darcy could not stand by idly; he had been traveling by carriage since leaving Pemberley, so he did not have a readily available saddle horse. At his request, the Colonel lent Mr. Darcy a horse. "Tis my own mount, Mr. Darcy," he said. "Thunder will not let you down."

Thunder was a spirited creature, but Mr. Darcy had been in the saddle since he could walk. With a nod of thanks to the Colonel, Mr. Darcy and the three men selected by the Colonel galloped away.

As he rode, Mr. Darcy was running numbers in his head. The carriage was likely traveling about five miles per hour. They had left about an hour before Mr. Darcy had barreled into the Colonel's house, but it had been another half hour or so before the rescue had been arranged. Denny could be as much as seven or eight miles away by now. He knew he and Thunder could travel at least twice that fast and likely more; he expected to come upon the runaways' carriage with the hour.

He was not disappointed. After about three-quarters of an hour of fast riding, Wickham called out, "Carriage ahead!"

Evidently this Denny was not going to give up easily. Instructions must have been given to the coachman, for hearing riders behind him, he whipped his horses up into a full gallop. Nonetheless, a carriage and four cannot outrun men on horseback; eventually, the carriage horses tired; the carriage slowed and then stopped.

The coachman climbed down, claiming ignorance of any wrongdoing, but he was ignored.

Lydia Bennet poked her head out the window and yelled out, "What are you doing? Leave us alone!"

Mr. Darcy rode up to the carriage, dismounted, yanked the carriage door open and dragged the young woman out. Ignoring her squawks of outrage, he yelled out, "Wickham!"

George Wickham was at his side in a moment.

"Hold onto her," Mr. Darcy ordered.

"There's Denny!" one of the men called out.

Indeed, a young man in uniform was climbing out the other side of the coach, doubtless hoping to hide in the shrubbery. One of the men collared him and marched him to face Mr. Darcy.

"Put him on a horse and get him back to the encampment. The Colonel will know what to do with a deserter," Mr. Darcy snarled. It was unlikely that the absence of a few hours would garner much of a punishment, but that was not Mr. Darcy's concern.

Without a word, Mr. Darcy tossed an outraged Lydia Bennet onto Thunder's back and leapt up behind her. "Wickham, will you accompany me?" he asked.

"I will," was the immediate reply.

Thanking the soldiers who had accompanied them, Mr. Darcy, Lydia and Wickham returned to Sunset House, while the other men returned to the encampment.

Chapter Fifty-Seven

Back at Sunset House, Elizabeth had been pacing the floor, torn between wanting to find the soldier's camp herself but knowing that she should do as William had asked. How could Lydia be so – and she caught herself. Why would anyone be surprised at Lydia doing something as outré as eloping with a soldier? The girl had been ungovernable for as long as Elizabeth could recall.

Georgiana watching Elizabeth walk about, wringing her hands; she wished there was something she could do to help her. Suggesting that she play a duet was impossible; Lizzy could not possibly focus on that. Perhaps a cup of tea, the never-yet-failed panacea for all ills? No. Inspired, then, Georgiana tugged Lizzy down to sit beside her on a sofa.

"Tell me about her," Georgiana invited.

"Her? Who?"

"Lydia. Tell me about her."

Elizabeth took a deep breath. "She is the youngest, as I believe you know. She was Mama's last chance to produce a boy, so there was that disappointment, but Lydia was such a beautiful baby! I know babies are all supposed to be beautiful, but many of them are not."

"I recall seeing tenants' babies; some of them are very red and squashed-looking," Georgiana contributed.

"Doubtless Lydia was also red and squashed-looking, but she outgrew that very quickly and became this golden-haired, blue-eyed, pink-cheeked little cherub. Everyone came to coo at her and try to make her smile. Maybe that's how she got so spoiled," Elizabeth said.

"And when she got older?" Georgiana was glad to see that Lizzy was now engrossed in her tale and no longer pacing.

"She was always strong-willed," Elizabeth remembered. "She had very strong likes and dislikes. Where someone else might have simply disapproved of something, Lydia would hate it; where someone else might have liked something, Lydia would love it. She lives in extremes."

"Was she difficult as a sister?"

"Difficult! Oh, heavens! Indeed she was! If your hair ribbon was missing, you would soon see it in Lydia's curls. If the lace you had saved up for and finally purchased had vanished, you would find it in her room. If Cook baked gingerbread cookies, you had better get downstairs quickly, for Lydia would snatch them right up!" Elizabeth shook her head.

"But no one corrected her, you said, so it was not to be wondered at."

"No, I suppose it was not. I fear –" And now Elizabeth's voice broke. "I fear for her, Georgiana, I truly do," she finished in a whisper.

"Brother will find her," Georgiana said, her voice ringing with certainty.

"I do not doubt it," Elizabeth said.

The two sisters then sat together in silence, hands intertwined.

***

It seemed an eternity before Elizabeth heard footsteps in the entry way. She shot out of her chair and ran to the front door. There was William, George Wickham, and Lydia. She threw her arms around her sister, and then pulled back, scolding her. "Lydia, of all the foolhardy, bird-brained ideas! Whatever were you thinking?"

Lydia scowled at her older sister. "You need not chastise me, Lizzy, as I have had quite enough of it from your husband. He has no right to do so, though, as he is not my father!"

"But I am your brother," the man in question said, steel in his voice. "And as your brother, I am confining you to this house. You are not to go outside for any reason whatsoever without my express permission."

Furious, Lydia stomped into the drawing room and threw herself face down onto the sofa. "Nothing exciting ever happens," she mumbled into the pillow.

Elizabeth's eyes told her husband that she would thank him properly later, when they were alone. Guessing that George Wickham had somehow aided in the rescue, she curtsied to him, asking if he would like refreshment. Wickham looked to Mr. Darcy for guidance.

"Yes, thank you, Elizabeth," Mr. Darcy said. "I think Wickham and I could both use something."

Elizabeth rang for a tea tray and asked the housekeeper to prepare a room for Miss Lydia. "She will be staying with us for a few days," she said simply, though she was certain the story of Lydia's rescue would be known to the entire household by sundown.

Mr. Darcy and Wickham recounted how they had caught up with the coach and brought Lydia to Sunset House. Lydia was now sitting up on the sofa, staring at the floor. Georgiana listened with mouth agape; she had never heard of such goings-on!

"Lydia, what shall we do with you?" Mr. Darcy asked her. His tone was almost conversational, but Elizabeth knew he was furious.

"Where is Denny?" she demanded.

"I do not doubt he is being disciplined by Colonel Forster for his actions," Wickham told her.

"And I think Lydia should be disciplined for hers," Elizabeth said.

Lydia looked at her sister in alarm. "How?" she asked.

Elizabeth looked at her husband. "It is up to our father, I suppose; he is her guardian."

William thought the girl likely needed a rather stricter guardian, but he held his tongue. "Could she not be sent to a school of some sort?" he asked. "The Countess will doubtless know of someplace suitable."

"My mother will never agree!" Lydia proclaimed.

"Oh, she may, once she hears that you tried to elope with a soldier," Elizabeth assured her. "You have finished your tea? Very well; come with me."

"Where are you taking me?"

"To your room."

Protesting loudly, Lydia was helped to her feet by Mr. Darcy, and she trailed after her sister, looking surly. The room that had been prepared for her was on the second floor. It was large and beautifully decorated. Lydia nodded approvingly; this was what she deserved in life!

"I presume your clothing was left in the carriage?" Elizabeth asked.

"Your husband gave me no time to retrieve it!"

"I will have clothing brought from the Forster's home; meantime, I suggest you get some rest. You have had a stressful day and are doubtless weary. I will call you when dinner is ready." Elizabeth stepped out of the room and closed the door behind her.

She went quickly to her own room and said to Carrie, "My sister is two doors down; find a manservant as quickly as you can and have that door guarded. She must not be permitted to leave."

Nodding her understanding, Carrie ran to comply.

Elizabeth went back downstairs; the conversation in the drawing room stopped when she walked in. "She is in a guest room; the door is being guarded."

Mr. Darcy nodded. "Good; she must stay in the house until we can decide on our next step." Turning to Wickham, he said, "It appears that we owe you a debt of gratitude." By an effort of will, his tone was neutral.

Wickham shrugged. "I have caused you enough trouble, Mr. Darcy, that even now the scales cannot be considered balanced."

Elizabeth leaned forward. "Lieutenant Wickham, given what I know of your history with the Darcy family, whyever would you now chose to aid us?"

The man looked uncomfortable. "I have been thinking about that history, as you put it, Mrs. Darcy, and I recently came to realise that I have, for many years, labored under a misapprehension."

"And what might that be?" Mr. Darcy asked.

"I thought I might be your father's son, Darcy. I was sure of it, in fact."

"And you have recently come to the conclusion that you are not?"

"Precisely."

"What convinced you?"

"Because I was born in March." Seeing the confusion on Darcy's and Elizabeth's faces, he continued. "If I was born in March, then I would have been conceived in June."

Mr. Darcy's face cleared. "And you know that my parents were always here at Sunset House in June."

"Yes, and in London for the two months prior. I did not consider that until I came here to Brighton and recalled that June was their 'honeymoon month,' as they called it."

Mr. Darcy could not speak, overwhelmed by memories, but Elizabeth continued. "How does that make you feel, then, Lieutenant?"

Wickham looked uncomfortable. "Feel?"

"Yes; you have hated my husband for years, have you not? What about Georgiana?"

"Georgiana is like my baby sister; I would never do anything to hurt her!"

"I am glad to hear it; but you have certainly hurt William."

"I know." The simple acknowledgment was said softly.

Mr. Darcy spoke now. "Wickham, it has been pointed out to me that my father may not have done you a good turn by sending you to school with me."

Wickham said, ruefully, "I do not think I learned much."

Mr. Darcy suspected that Wickham had learned very little, busy as he had been with unsavory activities, but he did not say so. "It has been suggested to me that you might have felt resentment that your classmates were men of higher social standing."

Wickham's lip curled; it was an expression with which Mr. Darcy was all too familiar. "Oh, you mean that I was the only man in our class who had no expectations? That my father was a steward, while my classmates' fathers *hired* stewards? Is that what you mean?"

Mr. Darcy was silent, so it was Elizabeth who replied. She said, softly, "Exactly."

"I was furious, of course. Who would not be?"

Mr. Darcy sighed. "Wickham, I am sorry; it never occurred to me."

"Of course it did not! Why would it?" Wickham's voice was almost savage.

"Should you have preferred to go to the village school, though?" Mr. Darcy asked.

Wickham considered that. "I suppose I would have felt more at home, though…"

"Yes?"

"I would have felt angry that the legitimate son went to Eton and the illegitimate son did not."

"So there was no right thing for my father to do; you would have been angry no matter what," Mr. Darcy summarized.

"I suppose that is correct." Wickham sounded surprised. Then he laughed. "But I would have been less of a nuisance to you, Darcy, had I gone to the local school!"

Elizabeth asked, "Might you have instead simply decided to get the best education you could? After all, it is not every steward's son who goes to Eton and then Cambridge."

"Someone else very likely could have. But I could not have, no, at least not as I was then," Wickham spoke quietly. "By the way…" he trailed off.

"Yes?"

"I send money to Maggie every month. It is not much, as I am paid very little, but I am trying to take responsibility for her – her situation."

"I did not know that," Mr. Darcy admitted. "I have been supporting her and her son – *your* son – for years." Mr. Darcy then found himself posing a question he had never expected to ask. "How can I help you, Wickham?"

"You want to help me?" The surprise in Wickham's voice was almost humorous.

Mr. Darcy hesitated. "We have a shared history; might we not have a shared future?"

Georgiana gasped; there were suddenly tears in her eyes. "Oh, Brother! That would be wonderful, would it not?"

Wickham slowly extended a hand. "Darcy, I would like us simply to not be at odds with one another."

"As would I," Mr. Darcy said, and he grasped the proffered hand. "Perhaps you could visit Pemberley when you next have leave."

***

Later that day, Elizabeth motioned to Mr. Darcy to follow her, with a finger to her lips. Understanding, he followed her upstairs, moving quietly and not speaking. She paused outside Lydia's door; the manservant stationed there stepped aside. They heard Georgiana say, "Was it very exciting, running off in the carriage?"

"Oh! The most exciting thing ever!"

Mr. Darcy frowned; he extended his hand to open the door and pull his baby sister away from this bad influence called Lydia Bennet, but his wife stayed his hand. Then he heard Georgiana say, "What were you going to do once you reached Scotland?"

"Be married by a blacksmith, of course. It is legal, you know."

Elizabeth could picture Lydia tossing her hair, proud to have this tidbit of knowledge at her fingertips.

"But then what?" Georgiana enquired.

"What do you mean?"

"Well – I do not understand where you were to live." She sounded puzzled.

"The Colonel and his wife have a nice house! We would have one like that."

"But the Colonel is – well, a Colonel. I am certain that the lesser ranks do not have houses. I have a cousin who is a Colonel, and I know that you either have to be promoted because you have done well in battle, or you have to buy the office. It costs, I do not know exactly, but something like four hundred pounds, I believe."

"Four hundred – Denny does not have that sort of money!" Lydia gasped.

"But this is why I am so confused. Oh! I suppose you had planned to live in the barracks with him. I would find that dreadfully uncomfortable. I think you must be very brave indeed!"

"Barracks?" Lydia's voice was faint.

"Yes, and sharing the mess with the men. Or you could have cooked for the two of you; that would have likely been his preference. You must have learnt to cook at home; I would not have the faintest idea how to even begin. How clever you are!"

Lydia was silent.

Elizabeth was convulsing with restrained laughter, and she hurried herself downstairs where she could safely burst out with merriment. William was right behind her.

"How did you know what would happen?" he asked, utterly befuddled.

"I did not, not entirely. I know Georgiana; she is a sensible girl and could not possibly be influenced by Lydia. But this was far, far better than I could have ever hoped for."

"Lydia would not have listened to you, of course," he began.

"Of course; but a girl her own age, telling her how brave and clever she is? Lydia could not possibly resist such a conversation."

***

That night, when Lydia was summoned downstairs for dinner, her demeanor was remarkably different. She could not admit that she had been in error, of course, but her earlier truculence was gone.

"I think I should like to go home, Lizzy," she said.

"Even though nothing exciting ever happens?"

"Well, it does not, you know. But I find that I am rather weary from all the excitement that I have just had."

"Very well; we will bring you back to Longbourn on our way north," her sister promised.

After the meal, Elizabeth found a moment to pull Georgiana aside. "I overheard your conversation with Lydia. That was very clever," she said, admiringly.

"I do not think Lydia is stupid," Georgiana said. "She just does not think things through."

"Which some might say is the very definition of stupid," Elizabeth returned.

"I think stupid means someone is *unable* to think things through; Lydia is simply *unwilling*. So I would say she is headstrong and spirited, rather than stupid."

"Either way, she almost got herself into terrible trouble. Thank you for explaining her foolishness to her. I know she would not have listened to me."

Chapter Fifty-Eight

Mr. Darcy sent an express to Longbourn, explaining only that Lydia was now staying with them at Sunset House, and would be returned to Longbourn in a fortnight.

The next two weeks were delightful for everyone at Sunset House. Elizabeth was on the beach every single day, gazing out onto the horizon, with her husband beside her. The two girls were not as bewitched by the view as she, but they waited as patiently as possible until she had gazed her full, and then begged to be taken into town. There, they ate ices, tried on bonnets, twirled parasols and generally had as agreeable a time as anyone could have wished for.

Lydia persuaded them all to try sea bathing. Georgiana refused at first but, unable to resist Lydia's pleas, she soon found herself enjoying the experience of being "dipped" into the sea.

Elizabeth and William could not help but notice Georgiana's enjoyment of Lydia's company. It made sense, when they discussed it, that she might sometimes feel alone, with just a married couple for company.

"I am certain we do not want Lydia living with us, but perhaps Mary? I know they have been corresponding," Elizabeth suggested.

"Would you like to have Mary at Pemberley?"

"She is the quietest of the Bennet sisters; is that not a point in her favour?" Elizabeth teased her husband.

"I have discovered that I enjoy a certain amount of liveliness," he told her. "But I believe Georgiana and Mary would both benefit from the experience. They can share lessons and practice duets together. And in a few years, when Georgiana makes her come-out, perhaps Mary can have a Season as well."

Elizabeth was reluctant to mention the plan in front of Lydia, but of course the girl would find out sooner or later in any case. So it was with some trepidation that she quietly asked Georgiana how she would feel about having Miss Mary – who by now should properly be called Miss Bennet – accompany them to Pemberley. Georgiana gasped in delight and exclaimed that she would like that above all things!

"But what of Lydia?" Georgiana asked.

Elizabeth shook her head. "She is not a suitable companion for you; not now, at any rate."

Georgiana said, "I understand, but – well, let me tell her. Is that all right?"

"Of course."

***

MISUNDERSTANDINGS

All good things must come to an end, and so it was with the Darcys' holiday at Brighton. All too soon, the four of them were in the Darcy carriage, traveling north. Georgiana and Lydia shared rooms at the inns, to Georgiana's delight.

On the final day of the journey, Georgiana began complaining loudly about their return to Pemberley. "You cannot begin to imagine how dull it is there, Lydia," she confided.

William looked at Elizabeth in concern. He began, "Georgiana, what can you –"

Elizabeth cut him off. "I understand, Georgiana, but you have had your share of excitement. First London, then Brighton! I know Pemberley is tedious, so far as it is from any sort of shopping or society, but it is time that you paid attention to your studies."

What in the world? Willian opened his mouth to object, but a sharp poke in his ribs had him closing his mouth.

Lydia preened and said, "How glad I am that I am not going to Pemberley with you! For there is bound to be an assembly at Meryton soon, and the Lucases have their card parties every week!"

Georgiana moaned, "That sounds heavenly!"

William then caught on. How clever Georgiana was!

By the time they reached Longbourn, Lydia was convinced that Pemberley was the dullest place on earth, and Longbourn downright lively in comparison.

Then Georgiana said, "Brother, I was thinking of inviting Mary Bennet to come to Pemberley; do you not think that a good plan?"

Lydia immediately said, "Oh, indeed, for Mary loves nothing more than to sit in a corner and read. A dull life would suit her very well."

Chapter Fifty-Nine

Upon arriving at Longbourn, Lydia was made to recount the events of her failed elopement to her parents. It was clear to Wiliam that Mrs. Bennet was torn between relief that the elopement had been prevented and dismay that Lydia had returned from Brighton unmarried.

He felt that he might provide some clarification on the matter. "Mrs. Bennet," he began.

"Yes, Mr. Darcy?" she asked, fanning herself with the fan Elizabeth had gifted her. Her tone was deferential; the matron had treated him with the greatest respect since learning that he would take responsibility for her in the event that she became a widow.

"You do understand that an elopement is considered disgraceful, do you not? Had it succeeded, Miss Lydia would have been on the road with Mr. Denny, unmarried, for at least four days before reaching Scotland. Such a thing would have caused the reputations of her remaining unmarried sisters, Kitty and Mary, to be ruined."

"I understand, yes, I do," she assured him.

Not at *all* convinced that she understood, Mr. Darcy plowed on. "Which means that Kitty and Mary would likely never have wed. In addition, Lydia would have had to live in a camp with other soldiers, as Denny was only a lieutenant. She would have had to cook for him." He cocked at eyebrow at her.

"Cook? Cook! None of my daughters have anything to do in the kitchen!" She was horrified at the idea of it. So reputations meant very little to her, but the idea of a daughter in the kitchen was abhorrent. He sighed. Very well, as long as she now understood the danger Lydia had been in.

However, Mr. Bennet had understood the situation very well. He thanked Mr. Darcy repeatedly, shaking his head at his youngest daughter's idiocy.

"What will you do with her?" Mr. Darcy asked.

"I know not; her foolishness is beyond my understanding," her father confessed.

"What think you of sending her to a school?"

"Do you know of an institution that would accept such a girl?"

"I can find one," Mr. Darcy assured him. Silently, he thought that he would be pleased to pay the fees himself, if it would keep the girl out of trouble. Despite himself, he had learned to feel some liking for the silly child.

"Please do, Darcy. I am at my wit's end."

"I shall," he promised. "And I was hoping to take Miss Mary with us to Pemberley, as she and Georgiana have formed a friendship. Would you have any objection to that?"

He was promptly assured that Mary's father had no objection at all, though – "Will Lydia not object to Mary being given such preference?"

Schooling his features so as not to laugh out loud, Mr. Darcy assured his father-in-law that he felt certain that no such objection would be made.

And he was right; Lydia made no protest at all upon learning that Mary was invited to accompany the Darcys north. Instead, Lydia just laughed, saying she was glad it was not she who would have to live in such a dull place. Kitty also made no objection; if Lydia thought it would be dull to live at Pemberley, then she could only agree.

Chapter Sixty

Elizabeth asked William to have the carriage stop at the same vista point that had given her the first view of Pemberley; she wanted Mary to appreciate the beauty of her new home.

She chuckled when Mary's mouth fell open. "That is how I felt as well, Mary," she assured her sister.

"This is where you live?" Mary's voice rose to a squeak.

"This is home," Elizabeth said. Mr. Darcy heard her and smiled to himself. At last, she considered Pemberley home!

***

During the long journey north, Mr. Darcy had had ample opportunity consider what he had learned about himself over the past weeks. He had known himself to be a sober gentleman, but he now thought that morose was likely a more accurate description. He thought again of the realisation he had experienced at the seaside, how he had used work to keep his grief from consuming him.

His responsibilities required a good deal from him, of course, but he knew he could easily delegate some portion of it. Which would allow him, perhaps to focus on his marriage.

He was now certain that fate had selected better for him than he would have selected for himself. Doubtless, given the criteria he had given himself for a wife – dowry, connections – he would have ended up with a society miss all too eager to spend his coin and parade herself in London. Instead, he had Elizabeth. Elizabeth, who had set herself to becoming the mistress that Pemberley needed...Elizabeth, who would have read every book in his library before she was done...Elizabeth, who had treated Georgiana as a beloved sister before they had even been wed...Elizabeth.

***

Much of their first day home was spent speaking with the steward and housekeeper to see if anything untoward had occurred during their time away, and helping Mary settle into her new home. Mrs. Reynolds, notified that Mrs. Darcy's sister was coming to stay, had already selected a maid for Mary. The room originally chosen for her was immediately vetoed by Georgiana, who insisted that Mary be given the room next to hers. They would share a sitting room, which suited both girls admirably. Georgiana already planned to take Mary to visit Mrs. Morris, for, as she explained to Elizabeth, "Mary's clothing is a vast improvement over what she once wore, but I would like to see her in new gowns." Elizabeth, who had not even begun to spend her pin money, told Georgiana that she would be delighted to pay for her sister's clothing.

***

That evening, when dinner was over and William and Elizabeth finally – finally! – had some time to themselves, William watched his lovely wife sit on the sofa that they often shared. She patted the seat beside her, inviting him to sit. Instead, he sank to his knees in front of her.

"William?" her voice was confused.

"I must tell you – I can hide it no longer! I love you, Elizabeth. I know not when or how it started, but it feels to me now that I have loved you for months!"

Tears began making their way down her cheeks.

"Elizabeth?" he whispered. She was crying?

She slid off the sofa, sinking to the floor before him. "I love you, too, William," she said, tenderly. "I know not when or how –"

And he interrupted her here, wrapping his arms around her, pulling her close, so close that he could feel her heartbeat as well as his, and he kissed her, hard, as if that kiss could turn two beings into one, two hearts into one, two souls into one. He picked her up and carried her into her bedroom. There, they fell into a cocoon of love, passion and tenderness, and finally slept in one another's arms.

Chapter Sixty-One

After the Darcys had been home a week, Elizabeth and Mr. Darcy were amazed at the transformation in Mary.

Mary had never been a worldly young lady. While her retreat into religion might very well have been the result of her feelings of isolation in the Bennet family, she truly did believe that wealth, over and above what was required to keep body and soul together, was unimportant. So while she did not scorn the luxuries of her new life, she found the absence of criticism and the affection freely offered her to be of far more significance.

It was clear to her elder sister and brother by marriage that she was blooming in this new soil, and not just in her hairstyle and dresses, as supervised by her personal maid, but in her reading preferences, her manner of speaking, and her very countenance.

And it was equally obvious that Mary was already Georgiana's dearest friend. Georgiana generously offered to share her piano lessons with Mary, and the two were often heard laughing together as they worked on duets.

Elizabeth was vastly content with her decision to have Mary live at Pemberley. But the question of what to do with Lydia still remained.

"Have you had a moment to write to Aunt Matlock about a school for Lydia?" she asked her husband.

Mr. Darcy was forced to confess that the matter had slipped his mind entirely, but promised to write directly.

Just four days later, a reply came.

> *Dear Nephew,*
>
> *You were right to enquire of me about a school for lively young misses, as I have just the place: Mrs. Balder's School for Young Ladies in Brunswick Square. I have already penned a note to Mrs. Balder, telling her to expect the young lady.*
>
> *Please do give your lovely wife my fondest regards.*
>
> *With Love,*
>
> *Elaine Fitzwilliam, Countess of Matlock*

"London! That is convenient indeed, as the Gardiners can keep watch on her," Mr. Darcy remarked.

Mr. Darcy sent a message to Mrs. Balder, informing her of the particulars of Lydia's situation, as these were not known to the Countess, and stating that he would be responsible for the school fees. He did not want the question of finance to prevent Bennet from sending his wayward daughter to school.

His letter to Mr. Bennet told him of the school and that a "scholarship" had been arranged for Lydia. (Bennet was not deceived for a moment, but gratefully and gracefully accepted his son-in-law's subterfuge.)

Mr. Darcy also sent a letter to the Gardiners, telling them in some detail about Lydia's failed elopement, and the Countess' suggestion of Mrs. Balder's School. The dilemma, he told them, was how to make Lydia willing to go? He hoped that Mrs. Gardiner would visit the school and write to Lydia, telling her how wonderful and – most of all – exciting this new opportunity was. That, he confided to them, would be the key to ensuring Lydia's cooperation.

His plan was successful in every respect. Mrs. Gardiner, grateful that something was being done for Lydia, immediately visited the school and wrote of her visit to Lydia in glowing terms.

To cap it off, Georgiana, who had been told of the plan, wrote to Lydia herself, saying how very much she herself wished she had been allowed to attend such a school. "How lucky you are!" she wrote.

Mary refused to participate in the deception, as it seemed wrong to her, but she allowed herself to be persuaded to simply remain silent on the matter.

***

Thus it was that Lydia Bennet, aged sixteen, found herself sharing a room with a stranger and expected to attend classes in French, deportment, geography, arithmetic and history. There were optional classes available in music, art and dancing.

Her initial reaction, of course, was rebellion, as she was immediately aware that a deception had been practiced upon her. However, Miss Dalton, her roommate, made the mistake of sneering at Lydia for having no knowledge whatsoever of history and geography. Unable to resist a competition, Lydia promptly engaged her previously unused intelligence and rose to the challenge, earning top marks in all her classes. The dancing classes met her need for physical activity, as did the daily walks around the square.

Lydia's letters, at first full of complaints and resentment at having been ill-used, soon showed that she was happy in her new situation. "Miss Dalton is now the dunce of the class, while I am the top student!" her letter crowed. "That will teach her!"

Elizabeth could only shake her head. Lydia would always be Lydia, but she was now as safe as Mrs. Balder's costly tuition could make her.

But what, she wondered, would become of Kitty? She wrote to her sister.

Dearest Jane,

With Lydia safely ensconced in London, and Mary here with us at Pemberley, I am now thinking of what may be done for Kitty. I do not worry for her as I did for Lydia, as whatever trouble Kitty got into was only a result of Lydia's leadership, but now I am concerned that she has no company at all.

Neither of our parents are good correspondents, so I have been unable to learn anything about Kitty. Is she lonely? Has she friends?

Your loving sister,

MISUNDERSTANDINGS

Elizabeth Darcy

A week later, Elizabeth received a reply.

> *Dearest Lizzy,*
>
> *I am surprised that no one has written to tell you of Kitty, but it is good news indeed!*
>
> *First, I must tell you that Meryton has a new rector, Mr. Braithwaite, who is all of twenty-five years old, unmarried, and is so handsome that the church is crowded to overflowing every Sunday with eager young ladies and their parents.*
>
> *Next, you must understand that with the rest of us out of the way, all of Mama's efforts have been focused her one remaining daughter; as a result, Kitty has the best clothing Meryton can offer and Lucy's undivided attention.*
>
> *So when Mr. Braithwaite cast a critical eye over the young ladies in the parish, his eye landed on our sister! They are not yet engaged, but if I am not much mistaken, that happy day is not far off. Yes, you might be required to attend yet another wedding in Meryton, which does not displease me at all!*
>
> *Still Your Favorite Sister,*
>
> *Jane Bingley*

Elizabeth laughed out loud upon finishing the letter and ran to show it to William.

Chapter Sixty-Two

Fall 1812

A few months after the Darcys returned from Brighton, William had two surprises ready for his beloved wife. Immediately after breakfast one day, he enquired what her plans were for the morning. She had a list, of course, that included conferring with Mrs. Reynolds about reinstituting the once-famed Darcy Christmas balls, as well as a visit to a tenant family who had just had a new baby.

"Might you spare an hour for your husband?" he asked.

Upon being assured that nothing would delight her more, he suggested that she put on half boots, as he wanted to take a walk with her.

Elizabeth nodded; they often walked together, and it was always a pleasure for her.

They met at the back door twenty minutes later, and he tucked her arm into his as they set off.

"This is not our usual route," she said.

"I am aware," he responded. His voice was playful.

He stopped before a lovely old chestnut tree that Elizabeth had admired. "Do you notice anything different?" he asked her.

She shook her head, puzzled.

"Walk around it," he suggested.

She did so and discovered, to her amazement, a set of wooden steps! Peeking back around the enormous trunk, she looked at him. "Is it safe?"

"Very safe," he assured her. He followed her as she climbed the steps, up, up, up, until she reached – was it a treehouse? Truly? She stood up on the small platform, turning around and around, and then found herself in William's arms! "You built me a treehouse!" she cried.

"You said you missed climbing trees, so…"

"This is wonderful!" Her delight was unmistakable.

"I selected a tree close to the house so that you can reach it easily. All I ask is that you let someone know when you come here."

Elizabeth nodded, her heart too full to speak.

But there was one more surprise in store for her. William reached into his pocket and took out a small box, handing it to Elizabeth.

"I was right; you ordered something from that jeweler in London. Oh, William, we have so much already!"

"Open it," he said.

She did; it was a beautiful gold brooch, fashioned in the shape of – a feather! She laughed in delight. "A feather! That is perfect!"

"Yes, for it was a feather that brought us together, dearest Elizabeth!" And he encircled his wife in his strong arms, gazing out over Pemberley, his heart filled with joy.

Epilogue

Kitty's engagement was announced right after the new year, necessitating another journey to Meryton. Lydia had been permitted to come to the wedding as well, so the Darcys stopped in London on their journey south to collect her.

This time Mr. Darcy insisted that they stay at Longbourn rather than Netherfield, as he knew that was what Elizabeth would want. He and Mr. Bennet spent a good deal of time together sipping brandy and discussing books, and he came to feel a good deal of affection for the older man who had done so much to shape his beloved Elizabeth.

Mrs. Bennet was astonished at the change wrought in Mary's appearance and could not stop commenting on it, to Mary's immense embarrassment.

Lydia's alteration was in her behaviour, rather than her appearance. Lydia's conversation was now intelligent; if she was still occasionally loud, it was usually in service of expressing a strongly held opinion on a book she had read.

Elizabeth and William went to London the following year, in accordance with the Countess' instructions. This time, she was able to find friends with whom she felt at ease. This experience allowed her to be of assistance to Georgiana and Mary.

Georgiana and Mary did indeed come out together. They had Elizabeth to rely on, of course, but they also supported each other through what might otherwise have been a frightening experience. Mary's strong grip prevented Georgiana from fleeing their first ball; Georgiana's encouragement kept Mary from sitting on the sideline at that same event. Their stellar performances on the pianoforte garnered them many invitations, more than they would have desired.

Both refused offers of marriage in their first season, feeling that they were too young to make good decisions. In their second season, Georgiana fell hard for the very musical second son of an earl, while Mary realised that Richard Fitzwilliam, who had visited often once he had resigned from the army, was the man of her dreams. The Matlocks gifted the couple a small estate, where the two lived contentedly, eventually producing five children, all boys.

Lydia did indeed eventually marry a man in a red coat, though this time she held out for a Colonel who could afford a house and servants. The idea of living in a barracks and having to cook was, of course, insupportable.

Chalotte Lucas visited Darcy House during the Season, and Elizabeth introduced her to a number of gentlemen. One of them was struck immediately by Charlotte's calm and rational manner, and made her an offer one week to the day after their introduction. Thus, plain Charlotte Lucas became Lady Granfield.

Wickham did indeed pay a brief visit to Pemberley when he next had leave. While Mr. Darcy could not entirely forgive and forget Wickham's past offenses, he could see that his childhood playmate was making an effort to improve his character. In service of that effort, he enlisted in the regulars. Sadly, he met his end in the Battle of Waterloo on June 18, 1815. The Darcys mourned his passing.

Caroline Bingley eventually married a wealthy merchant in Scarborough. She occasionally visited her brother Charles, who had purchased Netherfield, but she was not permitted to stay more than a week.

The Gardiners and their children were invited to visit Pemberley every year. Mr. Gardiner's business prospered to such an extent that the couple eventually purchased a small estate in Derbyshire, much to the delight of the Darcys.

Regrettably, Mrs. Bennet passed away soon after seeing her last daughter married. Mr. Bennet, finding himself alone in a large house, accepted the Darcys' immediate offer of a permanent home at Pemberley. Finally free of estate responsibilities, Thomas Bennet was able to – at last! – devote himself entirely to his studies, claiming one of the library tables as his very own. He took it upon himself to teach all four of Elizabeth's children, two boys and two girls, to read. The eldest boy was named Bennet, much to his delight, and the youngest girl, Rose Anne Darcy, was so much like Elizabeth that he felt as if he was reliving what had once just been fond memories. He lived to be ninety years old, and died as he would have wished, sitting in the Pemberley Library, surrounded by its thirty thousand volumes.

William and Elizabeth squabbled, as couples inevitably will, but they never forgot Mrs. Gardiner's advice: *Misunderstandings can escalate quickly if they are not dealt with promptly.* With this as their marriage motto, their love grew ever deeper and ever stronger over the passing years.

THE END

About the Author: AnnaMarie Wallace is the pen name of a retired tax preparer living in the Arizona desert with two cats and her very own Mr. Darcy. She is a very serious Anglophile and cannot understand how she ended up in Arizona when, by all rights, she should be living at Pemberley.

Other books by this author:

Saving Jane

The Life and Times of Charlotte Lucas

A Familiar Face

ANNAMARIE WALLACE

Printed in Great Britain
by Amazon

45567264R10253